HAVEN

CHRONICLES OF WARSHARD BOOK ONE

KATHERINE BOGLE

HAVEN

CHRONICLES OF WARSHARD
BOOK ONE

KATHERINE BOGLE

MAP OF
WARSHARD

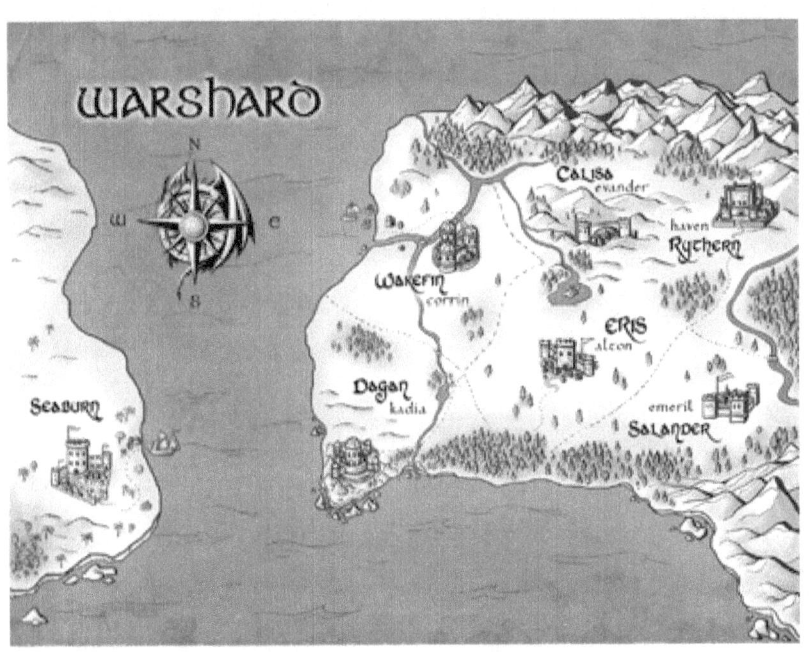

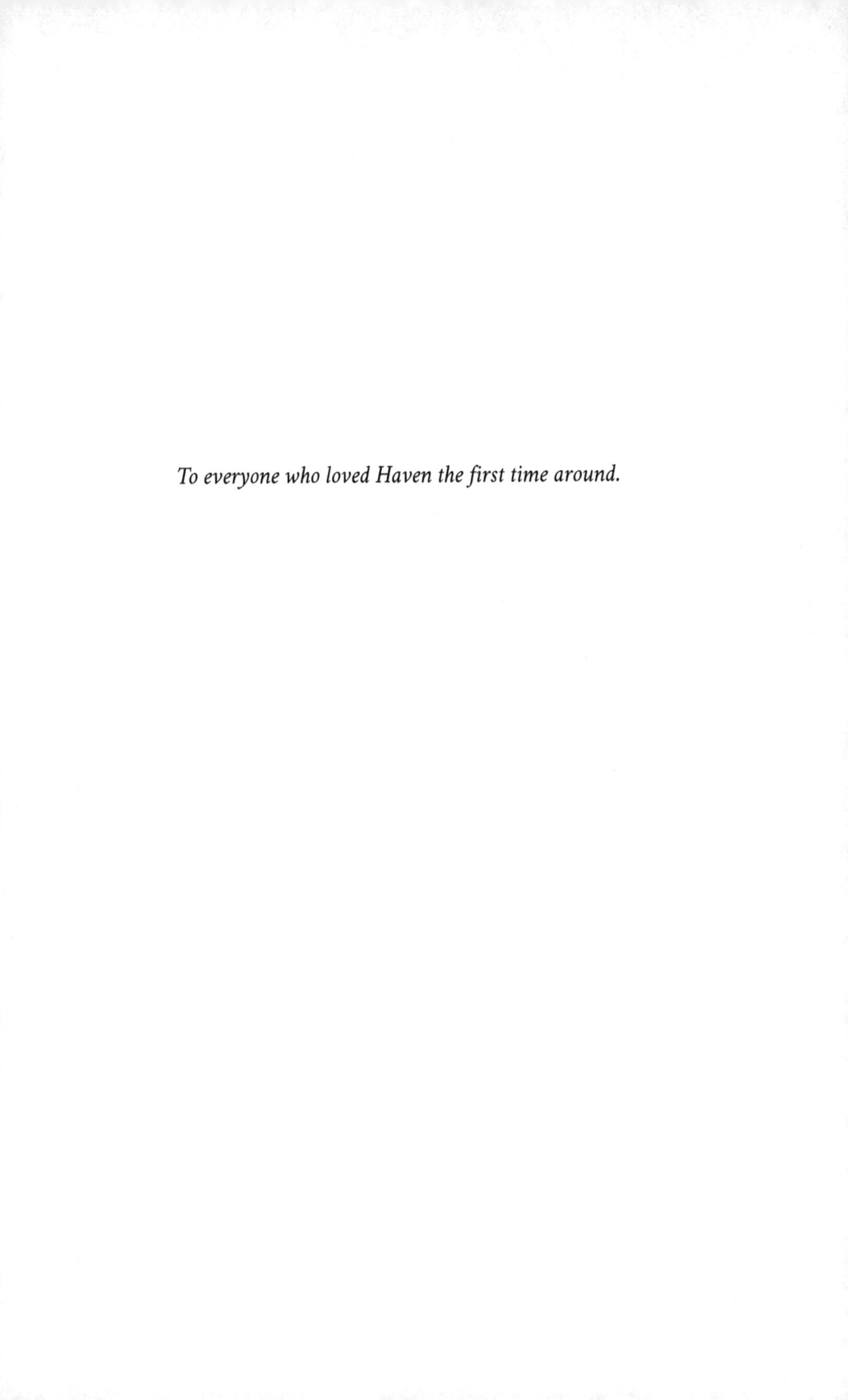

To everyone who loved Haven the first time around.

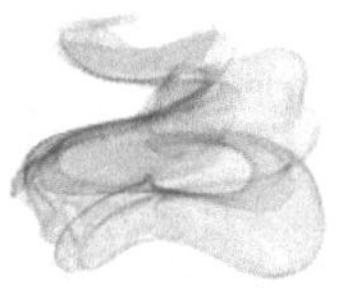

ONE

"You will be perfect. You will be great. You will be a just queen." Haven paced the length of the hall, trying to calm her rattled nerves. "You will lead them fairly. You *will* save them. By the grace of the gods, you will."

The distant boom of drums startled her. Her heart leapt for her throat and she stopped abruptly. Her gaze lingered on the large oak doors leading to the throne room.

"All rise," a muffled voice said behind the closed doors.

The time had come.

Clearing her throat, Haven smoothed her regal skirts and stepped up to the ornately carved entry. Warm afternoon light spilled across the floor, bathing her dark-red dress in fire. Sparkles from her jewel-covered throat cast a dazzling pattern across her olive skin.

Haven never thought she'd live long enough to take the throne. In a family of two older brothers and a healthy father, the eldest daughter would never be expected to ascend. But it was her misfortune to be blessed with longevity. Haven had outlived much of her family, and as the idea of becoming Queen grew nearer, that blessing only became a curse.

Her fists clenched around her dress, her palms sweaty.

She had thought of perhaps ending her life just to spare her people her inadequacy. She could try hanging herself, but the moment she was released from the noose, even if her neck broke, air would return to her lungs and her neck would mend itself. She could slit her wrists, or even her throat, but the wounds would heal in minutes, the scars in hours. There were many ways Haven had contemplated death—until she realized something. The only thing worse than living forever without her family was to leave her people without a Queen, especially in times like these.

With war at their doorstep, Rythern needed a queen, one who would not die like the rest of her family. They needed Queen Haven Fyre, one of the last remaining members of her royal lineage. Only she could lead the kingdom past this time of turmoil, or so she hoped.

"You can do this," she told herself, her amber eyes drawn forward as two Queen's Guard parted the doors. She smoothed her skirts and took a deep breath.

Her coronation was held in the main throne room, as per the custom. With high vaulted ceilings, large stained-glass windows, and a red carpet leading up the center aisle, it was just how she'd imagined. The red-and-gold banners of her family hung from the walls to her left and right. Candles dappled the walls and the ends of the aisles, dusting the room in a golden glow.

A flash of concern sent her heart racing. Were the guards too close to the open flame? She paused. Not a piece of fabric stuck between the metal folds of their uniforms. She sighed in relief. They were dressed in full Queen's Guard armor.

Turning her gaze from the décor, Haven basked in the warm glow of candles. Tears sprang to her eyes. This was a glorious room, filled nearly to the brim with people.

Her people. The ones she would lay her life down for. Even if, for Haven, there could be no such reality.

She wished her mother were there, standing beside her most

trusted adviser, once the adviser to the king. She'd known Toma since birth. There had never been a time when the aged man hadn't been at her father's side. But Toma wasn't her mother.

Toma stood in front of the throne at the end of the never-ending aisle, a golden scepter in one hand and a great silver sword with a hilt of gold and rubies in the other. These things would dub her Queen of Rythern, along with the crown that she assumed was hidden until the right moment.

Blinking away the tears that threatened to fall, Haven steeled herself. She had to be strong for her people. For her parents. For her kingdom.

Her cheeks warmed as she stopped at the end of the red carpet. All eyes rested on her, lighting her skin aflame with nerves. She wouldn't trip. She wouldn't mess up.

Haven held Toma's gaze for a moment before kneeling. Her long brown hair tipped from her chest, its red ends blending with the fire of her dress.

"Princess Haven Fyre of Rythern, we are gathered here today for your coronation." Toma's voice echoed over the crowd and through the great hall. All were silent as they bowed with her. "My Lady, in our greatest hour of need, do you consent to be made Queen of the kingdom, in sickness and in health, until your final hour?" A smile pricked at her lips, as she was sure it pulled at Toma's. She knew as well as he that no sickness or injury could ever take her. She would be Queen of Rythern until old age took her last breath.

"I do." She kept her gaze on the floor as she had been instructed.

"Will you treat your people fairly and with justice, so long as you live?"

"I will."

"Will you put down your own life for the people of Rythern if the day should ever come? And will you, My Lady Princess, lead us into the glory of battle should war ever return to the Warshard realm?"

"I will."

"Rise, Princess."

Haven stood. Her eyes found Toma's, which blazed like the sunrise at dawn. Pride swelled within them, glossing them in tears. She smiled.

"By the grace given to me by all the realm and the people of Rythern, by your mother and father, Queen Denica and King Keane Fyre, I now pronounce you, Princess Haven Delyth Fyre, Queen of Rythern. Long may you reign."

"Long may she reign," the people echoed back.

Haven couldn't help the smile lighting her face. This was it. She was about to be queen for the rest of her days.

Taking her skirts in hand, she climbed the stairs to join Toma, who gently turned her to face the crowd. He placed the scepter in her left hand and the sword in her right. Both were cool to the touch. She bowed again, hours of rehearsal leading her movements. Heavy metal sat atop her hair—the royal crown of a thousand rubies. Her heart fluttered. This crown had sat on the heads of many kings and queens throughout Rythern history. Now, she was one of them.

Straightening, Haven looked to the crowd.

Every person present echoed again, "Long may she reign."

Haven turned to her queen's throne: a high-backed dark wood chair with gold patterns weaved through the wood. Sitting there would complete her marriage to the kingdom. In a very real sense she'd said her vows and married her husband. Though her husband was not a man, but a great country. One that she never imagined would be entrusted to her.

Turning to face her people, Haven's gaze roamed the still crowd. Her knees bent to sit. This was it.

A shadow flashed through the rafters. Her eyebrows furrowed, and her lips parted. But it was too late. As she opened her mouth to shout for her guards, an arrow pierced her chest. Blackness swallowed her.

Haven awoke with a gasp. Frantic screams rang all around. Toma kneeled at her side, along with two others. She blinked slowly, her mind struggling through the haze to get to the surface. What had happened? Why was she on the floor?

She leaned on her elbows and wiped her eyes. Haven had three women as her personal guards, and these beautiful ladies were two of them. Deep-blue eyes met hers. Soothing words floated through the fog clouding her brain. Lareina, a warrior and a healer, must have been the one to pull the bloody arrow from her chest.

The weapon lay on the step beside her, still clasped in Lareina's right hand. Dark red dripped from the metal point.

"Thank you." Haven shifted to stand.

The second girl held her down. "Just a moment, My Lady Queen." Blythe cautiously glanced around in a stance blocking Haven from further attack.

"Blythe, come now," Haven chastised. She sighed. "If my assailant were still in the rafters you could be dead. I should be the one shielding all of you."

That earned her a smile from the strong-headed Blythe. Dark-brown eyes met hers. She nodded and stood, taking Haven's hand and helping her majesty to her feet.

"Thank you." Haven smoothed her dress.

"Of course." Blythe nodded before joining the protective formation that Haven hadn't realized encircled her.

"Are you all right, My Queen?" Toma asked, inspecting her for further injury.

"Honestly"—Haven rolled her eyes—"this is far too much of a fuss." Her cheeks burned with embarrassment.

She turned past her Queen's Guard. Some had fled the throne room, while others were frozen in place. A few candles had been knocked asunder, but no one was hurt.

She thanked the blue skies that whoever had made an attempt on her life seemed to be long gone. "Toma, how do we get these people to remember their heads and quit running about like a pack of startled hens?"

Toma, who still seemed concerned over her person, finally met her gaze and understood. They needed order in the throne room so her guards could pursue the would-be assassin. "Raise your voice and they will listen, My Queen."

"All right." Ignoring the sweat collecting in her palms, she cleared her throat. "Ladies and gentlemen, I will have silence in my court."

For a moment, the noise continued. Had she not spoken loud enough? She prepared to repeat herself, but once the moment had passed, a hush passed through the crowd. Their panic lulled now that the Queen, who'd clearly been shot straight in the heart, seemed to have made a full recovery.

"Thank you." She hesitated, unsure of what to do next.

"We should remove the people from the throne room, My Queen," Toma whispered.

Haven smiled and gave him a grateful look. "As you can see, I am all right. Now if we are to find my assailant, we must clear the hall." She tried to give a grave look to the crowd before continuing. "We will continue with this evening's festivities as planned in the ballroom where you will find plenty of wine to soothe your souls. Could I please have everyone evacuate the room in a civilized fashion?" Haven took this moment to motion to a few guards to escort the lot outside. "I will join you soon."

Once the crowd seemed assured no one else was going to be targeted by flying arrows, they fled the room in a relatively organized manner. As the buzz of conversation left, Haven turned back to her guard and adviser.

"Well done." Toma nodded before moving on to a tall, broad man, the head of the Queen's Guard. Toma spat orders for a full-scale investigation and to have the castle put under lockdown until the archer was caught.

Haven turned back to her personal guard and friends. Lareina waited patiently with her third guard, Malka, a gifted archer in her own right with emerald-green eyes and short brown hair. Blythe had yet to rejoin them, and as second-in-command of the Queen's Guard, she also barked orders about securing the throne room. Haven smiled at all of them. She'd known these three since she was a child, and she trusted them more than words could say. They were likely blaming themselves for her temporary injury, and she wouldn't have it.

"My ladies, it appears we still have a party to throw and I am covered in blood." Haven held her dress out to demonstrate her point.

"We will have to get you to your rooms, then, My Queen." Lareina smiled, gently placing her hand on Haven's forearm.

Having overheard their intent, Blythe rejoined them. "I will gather a few guards to bring with us," she said before calling out to several of her trusted Queen's Guard nearby.

Haven didn't say a word, didn't bother to argue. Though having a dozen men and women surrounding her seemed like too much, she hoped it'd put her guards' minds at rest. One look at Blythe and Haven knew there would be no arguing anyway.

Once the guards had been gathered, they formed a loose circle around her, Lareina always staying by her side. They ushered her through the back entrance to the throne room, slowly making their way to her chambers.

Her heels clacked on the smooth stone as Blythe paused, seeming intent on investigating every dark corner they passed, which made their usually short journey quite long and tiresome.

By the time they reached her rooms, she feared the banquet would already be over.

"Blythe," she said, pausing as per instructed.

"Yes, My Lady Queen?"

"I don't mean to rush you, but I don't think my assailant is going to jump out at me when I'm surrounded by guards."

Blythe considered this, and with a quick nod she sheathed her sword. "You're quite right, My Lady."

Haven sighed, pleased to find their pace quickened through the dark stone hall. Soon she was safe in her rooms. Lareina nearly danced over to her dressing room, always eager to pick a dress for her Queen. Blythe stood guard at the door, and Malka disappeared into her bathing room, leaving Haven to herself.

Blood was smeared across her chest, drowning the reds and golds of her dress in darkness. Her heart clenched. With the amount of blood soaking her bosom, she should have been dead. She knew that, and so did her guard. They would always be overprotective of her for fear of her death, and she would always be protective of them for they could die.

Raising her gaze from the sight of her own blood, she caught her own amber gaze in the vanity mirror.

"Is this what it's like to be Queen?"

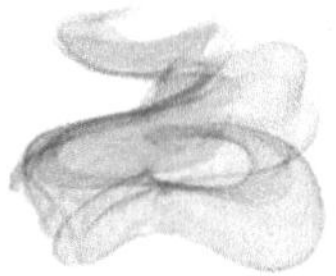

TWO

The ballroom doors swung inward at her approach. Two guards stood on either side of the doors while more soldiers meandered within.

Haven smiled and nodded to the men as she stepped through onto the ballroom floor. Her hands clasped tightly together and her palms sweat. This was her first royal gathering as queen. Her first ball and banquet without her family.

She gulped the lump in her throat, proceeding as slowly as possible —anything to keep from joining the partygoers.

Noblemen and noblewomen drank wine from goblets while a string quartet lit the grand space with music. She wished she'd paid more attention in her lessons or during introductions at the last few gatherings. She'd always been quick to run off with her brother Marcel or slip off to the edge of the room where she could speak with her guard ladies in private. With so many unfamiliar faces gazing at her with expectant eyes, her heart fell to her heels.

This was far too much, too soon. What on earth had she been thinking?

"Queen Haven Fyre of Rythern."

She froze. The voice of the squire announcing her arrival nearly sent her lunging for the doors.

"Take a breath, My Lady." Lareina's gloved fingers brushed her elbow.

Haven dipped her chin slightly. Breathe. Yes. That's all she needed to do. Inhaling deeply, Haven counted to three before exhaling. Her shoulders relaxed, and she unclenched her fingers.

"You may want to step out of the doorway now." Lareina chuckled quietly.

Haven narrowed her eyes at the woman. This was not the time to laugh at her expense. Lareina smiled and motioned inside, where golden light bathed the ballroom and Rythern colors were displayed at every chance.

From the silk wrapping the pillars to the banners hanging from the second-story ceiling and the tablecloths protecting the dark wood from harm, red and gold lit the space. She took another deep breath.

This was a gathering like any other. She could do this.

Haven stepped from the doorway and between the nobles and the emissaries from the six kingdoms. They smiled, offered congratulations, and bowed at her every glance. She nodded in return, her cheeks twitching from grinning so much.

A long banquet table lining the edge of the dance floor peeked from between the dancers. Goblets waited, silver pitchers at their sides, ready to be filled with wine.

Maybe she should indulge. Maybe wine would soothe her nerves.

Haven turned for the table, but beyond the thick, velvet curtains lining the walls between the pillars on the back edge of the ballroom, silver caught her eye.

Blythe and Malka stood between the cracks. What were they doing out there?

She glanced over her shoulder at Lareina, who was mingling with two noblemen around her age. Her pale skin shimmered with blush.

Good timing. She could slip away and see what her other guard ladies were up to. Haven hiked her skirts up and slipped between nobles until she reached the edge of the ballroom. Pressing her back to the cold stone pillar, she folded her hands and tilted her head.

"Blythe, you cannot hide these things from the Queen," Malka whispered furiously.

Haven had never heard Malka so angry in all of her life.

"She doesn't need to know the assassin got away!" Blythe barked back.

The assassin? Her heart lurched. So he had fled without capture. Then why had Blythe informed her that the chase had just begun before she'd entered the ballroom? Why lie?

"I know you don't want to worry her, but she isn't a little girl anymore." Malka's voice shook.

"Of course not, but she has enough on her plate. The war could start up again at any moment, and that will take precedence."

"It will. But she should know her assassin has fled Palmyra." Malka paused. "It's her choice what to do next."

Blythe sighed. "I'm sorry, Malka, but this isn't your decision."

Silence filled the space behind the curtains.

Haven stepped away from the pillar. She wasn't meant to hear this conversation, even if it pertained to her. Yet she couldn't begrudge Blythe for not speaking up. Her stomach turned. With war not far off and an unknown assassin seeking her head, she would have liked to go on not knowing.

* * *

"Toma really knows how to dance when he's had a few glasses of wine." Lareina laughed.

When the four women entered Haven's chambers at the end of the night, the mood was high among her ladies and low with the new Queen. The festivities had been grand, amusing, intriguing, and most certainly fit for a coronation. But Haven's mind was elsewhere. Through all the luxury, something had been missing. She hadn't realized what until she returned to her bedroom, kicked her heels off, and lay in bed.

Silk embraced her limbs, cool to the touch.

She stared at the ceiling, tracing the intricate carvings over and over. Through the dark wood, her mind conjured images of her deceased family. Her brothers. Her mother. Her father. All of them gone.

Part of her blamed them for having left her with this burden. She couldn't fathom taking care of an entire kingdom herself. Haven was never meant to be Queen, but the moment her mother had fallen in a pool of blood in the main courtyard, she had known it was her only option.

"Queen Haven, are you all right?"

Haven glanced up. How long had she been staring at the ceiling? "I'm fine. Just tired." She sat up.

"We'll take our leave, then." Lareina's brow furrowed as she turned to take her leave. The concerned whispers of her lady guards drifted from her sitting room and into the hall before disappearing altogether.

Once the doors had closed softly, Haven stripped off her heavy gown and her opulent jewels before diving into the safety of her sheets.

Every time she closed her eyes, she saw blood.

Haven sighed and turned over. She closed her eyes to brown curls and dazzling blue eyes tainted red. It had been two weeks since the news of her family's demise had come—and it had come from the bloody lips of her mother.

That day, Haven had sat in the beautiful summer sunshine with Lareina, braiding her hair and laughing about something she couldn't quite recall. It was one of her many days of leisure in the great castle. She loved watching the people of Rythern go about their days. There was such intricacy in how everything came together so seamlessly.

Her bliss was soon shattered by a shout from the castle steps. Before Haven knew what had happened, Lareina leapt in front of her, her sword drawn. The entire courtyard froze in anticipation.

Up the castle steps limped her mother, Queen Denica Fyre.

Blood soaked her riding clothes. Her left leg was twisted at an awkward angle and a large cut ran diagonally across her face.

"Mother?" Haven whispered. Her voice cut through the surrounding silence like shattered glass.

She pushed Lareina aside and ran, her heart pounding in her ears. Before Haven could reach her mother, Denica collapsed. Blood quickly pooled around her still body. Shouts echoed through the courtyard, but Haven hardly heard them. She fell to her knees beside her mother, soaking her skirts in red. Two daggers protruded from her mother's back.

Two pieces of obsidian had sealed two fates.

"Mom?" Tears filled her eyes.

Denica shifted slightly, tears trailing down her cheeks. "My love. My Haven," she murmured.

Haven bent to hear her, gingerly touching her shoulder and brushing her hair from her face. Her heart raced so fast she feared it might rip from her chest.

"Mom, what happened? Where is Father? Why are you—" Her voice broke.

Denica's lips curved in a ghost of a smile. Her fingers twitched beside her face. She frowned when she couldn't move but an inch.

"They killed everyone," Denica whispered. "Your father, your brothers...all those soldiers. They're all gone." Her eyes widened at the recollection. Fear stole her gentle gaze.

Haven tried to soothe her, but Denica only shook her head and continued.

"You'll be Queen now, my love. But you have to run. Haven, promise me you'll run." A cough racked her mother's body. She shook, and crimson dripped from between her lips. "You have to run," she repeated. "Promise me."

Haven slowly nodded. She couldn't find the words any more than she could escape the blaze of blue fire in her mother's eyes.

"Run," her mother repeated. The light faded from her eyes. "You have to run. Promise me you'll run."

"I promise."

Haven held her mother for the last time.

Starting from the memory, Haven sat up in bed. She pushed back the tears threatening to fall. Queens didn't cry. She had to be strong. She had to be strong for her—for her mother.

But when would being queen no longer be a death sentence?

Settling back into bed, Haven found sleep. In her dreams, she found hope. In the morning, she prayed that hope would remain.

"My Lady Queen."

Haven groaned, refusing to open her eyes. Surely it could not be morning already. Her head still swam with sleep.

"My Queen, please rouse yourself at once."

Sighing, she opened her eyes and found Toma at her bedside. "Toma? What is it?"

"There is to be a meeting." He bowed before retreating to the door of her bedchamber. "We are expected at once."

"You know that you may call me Haven when we are alone, Toma." As she slipped from her sheets, the silk fabric called for her return. Cold brushed her bare skin, lending goose flesh to her arms.

She had told Toma time and time again to call her Haven, and still, he spoke as if she were a stranger.

"Yes My—Haven." He cleared his throat.

Haven paused midstride to her dressing room. "Did you say there is to be a meeting?" She peered out her window into the darkness of night. Hardly a single lamp lit the city below. "At this hour?"

"It is a secret meeting, My Lady."

She turned. "What sort of secret meeting?"

"A meeting of royals. We must make haste. We have a bit of a journey ahead of us," he said. His brow creased with worry, and the corners of his eyes twitched. Nervous.

She had never heard of secret royal meetings in the middle of night, but she supposed royals had to meet somehow.

Dressing quickly, Haven donned a simple navy-blue dress and a dark-gray cloak. She joined her adviser at the doorway to her chambers. "Toma, how are we to slip past my guards? Or the dozens of emissaries from the six kingdoms? If I am seen, surely they will wonder where the new Queen slips off to in the middle of the night."

A small smile flashed across Toma's normally stoic face. "Secret tunnels for a secret meeting, My Queen."

Haven didn't miss the glint of mischief in his eyes. "Secret tunnels?"

Toma nodded. "We must hurry, My Queen. I'm sure the others have long since arrived." Haven agreed, and Toma stepped forward. "You may need this." He handed her a long black sheath.

"A sword?"

"Just in case."

Haven met his gaze. She'd never been good with a sword and had abandoned her lessons long ago. He knew she could barely wield one, yet he'd handed her a dangerous weapon. However, as she was unsure of their destination, she nodded in agreement. "Just in case."

Making haste, the two slipped quietly through the castle. Hidden passages behind paintings, statues, and thin walls made their escape almost effortless. Haven did her best to remember the route, repeating the directions over and over in her head as they went. She hoped for a future when she needn't use the secret tunnels ever again.

They emerged on the outskirts of her capital city, just beyond its high stone walls. Not far through the trees, two horses awaited.

"Wren!" she gasped. Her heart leapt.

Her beautiful white-snouted, brown-haired stallion raised his head at their approach. He pawed the ground and bowed his head, causing Toma's black mare to stir.

Haven closed the space between them and wrapped her arms around his thick neck. "I missed you," she whispered into his mane.

Wren snorted quietly in response.

It had been a while since she'd seen her handsome horse. He wasn't needed as much as when she was always trotting off to cause mischief with her brothers.

Her heart ached. She'd raced through the city streets side by side with her brothers so many times. The pounding of hooves on cobblestone still made her grin from ear to ear.

Cold licked the back of her neck. She shivered and pushed the memories to the back of her mind. Toma was right. They needed to move quickly. She mounted her steed. The familiar leather squeaked beneath her as she settled in.

Moments later, they were off, riding through a forest of tall pine trees smelling of sap and into the windswept grasslands. In the distance rose hills, and beyond those, the snow-topped mountains of Calisa, the valley kingdom to the west.

Toma pushed them onward, steering toward the distant peaks. Calisa was the kingdom closest to hers, with its capital built into the mountains itself. Haven had never seen it, but it was said to shine in the morning light, its smooth stone reflecting the sunrise, turning the city to fire. She couldn't imagine a sight more beautiful than that, and she hoped one day to see it for herself.

The journey sent them tearing across hills, skirting villages, tree groves and rivers. Wren lent her his strength as her worry only grew. Now that she was wide awake, her mind sharpened in the cold night air.

Why had a secret meeting of royals been called? Why now?

There was always strife in the kingdoms, from civil war to spats over land, but since the war had taken a pause after the death of her loved ones, all had been quiet. That peace couldn't last long.

It seemed sudden when the mountains appeared before them. Barely visible through the distant haze of Rythern, they loomed like sentinels up close. The horses slowed their pace when they began climbing the narrow mountain path, sending rocks careening loudly over the ledge to the drop below. Her heart lurched as she glanced over the edge. The fall might not kill her, but it'd definitely hurt.

Toma led the way, his mare, Reyn, moving with ease over the rough terrain. A small plateau crested halfway up the mountainside. The soft sounds of horses grazing filled the night.

"Halt."

Toma stopped. Haven squinted in the dim light. Who had spoken in the darkness?

"At ease, Nikolai." Toma swung down from his horse and handed his reins to a man-shaped shadow.

"Apologies, Toma. Everyone is already inside."

"Thank you." He turned to help his Queen dismount her own horse before handing her reins off as well.

"Have we arrived?" Her stomach fluttered with nerves. She felt silly asking, but she hadn't imagined their meeting would take place on a cliff.

"We have." Toma guided her to the side of the mountain, where Nikolai appeared again.

Her eyes slowly adjusted to the shadows, which revealed a large man with shaggy hair. The stars moved with him, dancing off his sleek metal armor. The crest at his breast glinted beneath the moonlight, revealing twin pikes. Nikolai was a Calisan soldier.

"This way, Lady Queen, Toma." The large man motioned them to the mountainside, disappearing into a dark hollow.

"What is this place?" Haven wondered aloud, following Toma into the tunnel. She ran her fingers along the wall to her right, its edges rough but not jagged. This had to be a natural formation of sorts or she'd have cut herself already.

"The Calisan meeting place. It's a rare occasion that we meet elsewhere," Toma replied.

They turned a corner, a soft glow emanating from the stone ahead.

Haven followed in silence. The warm torchlight grew brighter as they went. Whispers echoed off the walls, hollow to her ears. There had to be at least half a dozen men up ahead.

Her gut clenched. What could possibly lie ahead? What if this was some sort of trap? Though she trusted Toma implicitly, that could very well lead her to her death.

She hadn't the strategic mind of her brothers or the fighting prowess of her father. If she got herself into trouble, she wouldn't be ready. Before she could contemplate a plan of action, they emerged in a large cavern with torches lining the walls. A long table sat at the center of the room. Several men stood around it, and almost a dozen guards lined the cavern walls. Crests of four of the six kingdoms were represented by the guards' uniforms.

Silence fell and all gazes shifted to Haven and her companion. She froze, all too aware of her new status as queen. Though she'd been a princess since birth, she shrank under the gazes of these kings. All had much more experience than she and had led their kingdoms through war, famine, and crises.

She only hoped she could one day measure up to them.

"Lady Queen," they greeted almost entirely in unison. Each gave a slight bow before the most familiar of the group stepped forward.

"Emeril." Haven heaved a sigh of relief and smiled.

Though he wasn't a king yet, she had to assume he came on behalf of his sick father, the King of Salander. The southern kingdom had always been close to Rythern. She and Emeril had been childhood friends, and she still had fond memories of the handsome prince. He was the only heir to the throne of Salander, and she couldn't help her slight surprise at seeing him there.

He was supposed to be staying in her castle tonight.

"Lady Haven." He grinned before bending to kiss her hand. His blue-green eyes held the same smile as his lips when he stood. "Or should I say Queen Haven?"

"You should," Toma chastised, though she could hear the lightness in his voice. Like Haven, Toma had a soft spot for the dying King's son.

"Always a pleasure, Toma." The young prince winked.

The others introduced themselves in turn. King Alton of Eris, the plains nation, well known for its vast farmlands. It was just to the south of Calisa and west of Salander. The tall man nearly beat Emeril for height. Broad and a bit overweight but well-tanned and very blond. He put on a serious demeanor, but she caught the smirk beneath his bushy mustache when Toma glowered at Emeril.

"Well met, Lady Queen." He shook her hand and gave her a quick nod.

"Well met, Lord King." Haven returned the nod.

Her other neighbor, King Evander of Calisa, stepped forward. She'd met him a few times throughout her princess days, and the King had sent his daughters to her coronation in his stead. He wasn't quite as tall as the others, but he always held his chin high, which gave him a regal appearance.

"Congratulations on your coronation, Lady Queen."

She had yet to see a frown grace the face of the Calisan King.

"My deepest regrets for the loss of your family."

Her heart clenched. She nodded stiffly. "Thank you."

She couldn't think about them. Not now. She had to keep her mind on the present.

The last of the royals, King Corrin of Wakefin, stepped forward, shaking her hand.

He greeted her with the mischievous smile he was known for. She'd heard stories of his womanizing even in Rythern. Haven had never understood why so many women fell for his tricks until now. He was quite possibly the most handsome man she had ever seen. Not quite a decade older than she, he stood tall with sandy-blond hair and tan skin so rich with freckles that he had to be from the port city.

"What a lovely new Queen." He flashed his teeth before he bent to kiss her hand. It was a gesture of familiarity and respect. Though she respected the man, they were certainly not familiar enough for this kiss. "I can already tell I will enjoy your company far more than Toma's."

Revulsion widened her eyes. Though he was pretty to look at, she sensed a snake beneath his freckled skin. Never had anyone been so forward with her.

Haven yanked her hand back. "You will enjoy my company far less if you do not address my adviser and me with some respect." Her face flushed red as she turned away.

King Alton burst into laughter, and she caught an amused look from Evander. For a moment, she wasn't sure where her internal storm should take her. It was then she remembered the scene she had come upon. Stepping around the obnoxious King, she let her torrent lead her to a wide table with a map of the six kingdoms of Warshard and beyond. It was a very detailed map, with carved figurines representing each of the kingdoms and a few representing the movements of war.

She glanced at each king who joined her around the table, disbelieving she hadn't realized it before. Only one kingdom was not represented there.

Dagan.

The port city was the closest to the open sea. It wasn't known for anything in particular until recent years, when a new queen had taken control of the city. Not long after her reign began, terror and death littered her kingdom. She started wars, attempted to take over her neighbors, halted all trade on her shores, and began to strip her forests bare. She was said to be completely mad, though her people still worshipped her.

They called her insane Queen Kadia.

Haven's stomach twisted. Her parents had done their best to keep her in the dark when it came to the Evil Queen. She wished they hadn't. Kadia was the reason her parents and her brothers were dead. When the battle had begun, they'd chosen to fight in the wars she'd started, aiding Eris and Wakefin both on the warfront.

It had cost them their lives. Though Kadia's madness only seemed to grow, all had been quiet in recent weeks—until her mother had shown up beaten and bloody on the palace steps.

"Would someone please explain?" Haven motioned to the figurines.

Black soldiers stood at the edges of Dagan, facing inland just south of its closest neighbor. Gray soldiers, presumably of Wakefin, blocked their path.

Torchlights flickered. Silence descended. She glanced at the kings.

"I'm sorry, Lady Queen. I hadn't the time to tell you why this meeting was called." Toma appeared at her shoulder, his expression grave.

"Tell me."

"Queen Kadia has taken war to Wakefin once more. This time, it appears she is trying to take the capital city of Dessa."

Haven faced her adviser. "Only five years into her reign and she is trying to take another nation?" Her breath escaped her lungs. Her whole body cooled. The damp air lay heavily on her shoulders. Nothing good would come of this.

"It seems so, My Lady."

Haven turned to Corrin. The handsome man stared with a furrowed brow at the map of his kingdom. His fists shook, and his smirk disappeared. Though he had seemed obnoxious only a moment ago, his crestfallen face made her regret her presumption of his nature.

After a long moment of silence, Haven spoke. "I'm sorry, Corrin," she began, forgetting to say his title. She steeled herself under his troubled gaze. "What can we do?"

Corrin's eyebrows pulled together, and he looked back at the map. "I need swords, men. Soldiers." He shook his head. "I need to get my people to safety."

"Prepare for the worst," Alton agreed in his deep, gruff voice. His graying beard trembled as he nodded.

"I'm sure we can take in some of your people." Haven glanced at Toma for reassurance. This would be her first real act as Queen, and she needed to make sure it was a good one. With a nod of affirmation from her adviser, Haven held Corrin's gaze.

"Thank you." The storm swirling in his blue gaze settled. He truly meant it.

"I will lend you my aid as well," Evander agreed. "We can begin at first light. I will send my soldiers from the western tower to help with the transition. We will escort them to you, Queen Haven. We will keep as many as we can here in Calisa."

"And I will lend you my soldiers," Alton piped in, holding his fist to his chest.

Emeril shifted on his heels, leaning his hands on the table. He stared intently at the map. His gaze did not leave the row of shadow soldiers threatening Corrin's kingdom. "I will confer with my father and send word. I'm sure we can spare a few resources."

"I am grateful to all of you." Corrin's shoulders lowered, and he sighed in relief. A bit of weight lifted from his back.

The kings, the prince, and the queen took their seats around the table. Plans were discussed, as well as things the Kings had heard.

Because Eris and Wakefin bordered Dagan, they were the most privy to rumors of the dark country.

Corrin confessed to the bizarre nature of the attacks on his kingdom. The soldiers who had attacked seemed to appear from nowhere, and they'd disappeared just as quickly. They'd amassed in shadow and disappeared in the same way. They'd left hundreds dead and few alive to tell the tale of what had actually gone on. Those who did survive spoke of shadow soldiers with armor and masks as black as night. When one fell to the blade of another, the body quickly disappeared. When the fighting was over, only the bodies of their own soldiers remained, as if they'd only ever been fighting themselves.

It was strange, to say the least. Though such magical occurrences weren't completely unheard of, they were most certainly rare.

Alton admitted to having seen similar things on their borders. Though they hadn't been attacked yet, his spies kept a close eye on Queen Kadia's army—an army that hadn't moved from the city in weeks. With the attacks on Wakefin mere days ago, there was a piece of the puzzle the royals weren't quite getting.

Haven shivered. It was disturbing in a way she couldn't quite describe—an enemy who attacked suddenly without warning and simply disappeared in the aftermath. It had to be some sort of trick. But, if Alton's spies were correct, it meant there was something far more sinister at work.

"My spies have returned similar information," Corrin agreed.

No one at the table had seen these things with their own eyes, which made them skeptical of the situation. The guards along the walls shifted, growing increasingly restless as their conversation continued.

"If this is true," Toma began, "we may not have merely a mad Queen on our hands anymore."

All eyes turned to her aged adviser.

"We may very well have an Evil Queen with very strange abilities in her grasp," he continued, "and with powers such as these, beyond our understanding..." He paused, obviously troubled by something deeper.

Haven took his hand. This man was like a father to her, and she hated seeing him in such distress. She had a feeling that these meetings were why he'd been distant many days in the castle. Dark circles under his eyes always accompanied those days, along with a large amount of tea.

"It will be okay, Toma. We will figure this out together." She squeezed his hand.

Toma smiled slightly. Though the gravity of the situation was thick in the air, it was only made worse by his next words.

"I fear this is only the beginning."

THREE

"I am beginning to see why my brothers were so keen on heading into war." Haven sighed.

A day had passed since the secret meeting in the Calisan Mountains with no word from King Evander. Her place in this war was uncertain. Though she looked forward to aiding the people of Wakefin, Rythern didn't have the military force it once had. Not since Kadia had decimated the warfront.

Haven was certain the Eris-Wakefin attack had already begun, but still she received no letter on how things were going. Their plan was simple. When Kadia's army attacked the capital city of Dessa, Alton's soldiers would lie in wait, blindsiding Kadia's from the rear. While the attack took place, King Evander would usher refugees from Wakefin into his own kingdom of Calisa and through to Rythern.

While all of this took place miles from Palmyra, Haven was stuck with her advisers, doing paperwork. Much to her dismay, this seemed to be at least eighty percent of a queen's duties.

She impatiently tapped her fingers against the thick, wooden desk. She was to read and sign papers, decreeing this and disallowing that.

All while war raged in Wakefin. Though it was all rather boring, it kept her guards happy and her out of danger. There in the castle, she was safe. With the assassin gone and her coronation over, she could set her sights on the future of Rythern.

Once she was done signing, of course.

"Your brothers were only keen on going into battle because they were reckless boys, My Queen." Toma's eyebrows pulled together like a disapproving caterpillar.

"At this moment, battle sounds much more interesting, Toma."

"You mustn't say such a thing, Lady Queen. War is never a pleasant thing to wish upon the kingdoms."

Haven paused, staring blankly at the page before her. Stacks of parchment lay on her desk while many men were sitting around her at desks of their own. They mostly ignored her conversations with Toma, scribbling decrees as quickly as their fingers would allow. What were they always writing about so furiously?

"I don't wish war upon the kingdoms." She worked her jaw back and forth. Truly, she didn't. War was the last thing she wanted. "I suppose paperwork does still help Rythern, does it not?"

"Of course, Lady Queen." Toma smiled to assure her.

He paused a few more moments while she finished her current work. Her skin crawled beneath his gaze. The only reason Toma ever held his tongue was when he was about to ask something she might not approve of.

"Have you said your goodbyes to Prince Emeril, My Lady?"

Haven froze. Not this again.

Her parents had always pushed a Prince of Salander–Princess of Rythern match upon her. It would have been a great pairing, bringing both of their families great honor while keeping them both in a royal line. The match would mark a great union of countries, an alliance that could have bolstered the economies of both kingdoms.

But it was not meant to be.

As they'd drifted apart and the kingdoms had grown, her parents and her brothers had perished at war, leaving her to be Queen. Haven's fist clenched around her quill. Images of blood flashed before her. She squeezed her eyes shut, pushing them away with all of her might.

Emeril. The images faded. The young prince was the only heir to the Salander throne. Toma could not think it a responsible idea to push such a marriage on her after her coronation. Where would that leave her kingdom? Or Emeril's, for that matter? His father surely had only a few years left and was well past the age of siring more children. He hadn't even taken a new wife after Emeril's mother passed.

"Of course. We said our farewells this morning." Haven didn't look up from her paper, relaxing her hands and pretending to read on. "I'm sure the Prince has long since departed court."

"Perhaps," was all Toma added. He returned to his own work.

A loud rush of footsteps from the hall froze her to her chair. What now? Haven exchanged a glance with Toma, who slowly rose. Lareina, her guard today, pushed away from the wall behind her desk, her hand on the hilt of her sword. She positioned herself between Haven and the door, an act Haven was all too familiar with.

Nikolai burst through the office doors, his chest heaving and his face wild. With muddied boots and brown, wind-whipped hair, he had to have been riding in a hurry. He searched the room with bright blue eyes before finally settling on Haven.

"Lady Queen," he croaked, his voice hoarse.

"Nikolai." Toma stepped forward and motioned for Lareina to sheathe her sword. "What has happened?"

It took Haven a minute to realize why Nikolai had burst into her study. She glanced between Toma and the Calisan soldier until Nikolai thrust a piece of parchment forward. A letter about Wakefin at last.

"Word from King Evander!" Haven stood to greet the messenger. Her heart pounded in her ears. *Please let it be good news.*

"Yes, Lady Queen." Nikolai stepped forward with his note. "There is terrible news."

Her heart plummeted into her stomach, and her breath seized in her throat. What now? Through the wild look in his bright gaze, she finally saw it. Fear.

"Let me see it." She lowered her voice in an attempt to sound gentle and understanding, but her voice trembled. What had happened to make such a large man so afraid?

Nikolai handed her the letter before bowing and stepping aside. Her hands shook as she parted the seal across the single page. The scratchy writing had been done in a hurry. Haven read on.

Queen Haven,

The battle for Dessa has gone horribly awry. Kadia's soldiers have passed the great river and attacked the main city. Wakefin soldiers have been called back—those who were in the castle at the time are feared dead. Alton's army was wiped out, and Kadia has hold of the Wakefin capital. Corrin is safe and being taken into hiding. We have worked through the night to aid as many refugees as possible, but there are many more than we can handle.

Following Nikolai will be the injured. We kept as many as possible, but our resources are limited. I urge you to seek aid from Salander. I know your kingdoms have always been close, and we will need any healer they can spare.

A meeting will be held soon.

Stay safe,
King Evander of Calisa

Haven slowly rose. Her limbs chilled, which sent a shiver down her spine. Never had she imagined that Dessa would fall so quickly. Wakefin's army was grand enough on its own, but the soldiers of Eris should have overwhelmed even the largest of battalions.

"How can this be?" Her voice barely rose above the flipping of papers at her back.

"What is it, Lady Queen?" Toma came to her side.

She handed him the letter. "Dessa has been taken. Alton and

Corrin's armies were obliterated." Haven sat down hard, the legs of her chair scraping along the floor.

The rustling of pages and the scratch of quills hushed. Whispers filled the room. It was the first time she'd seen her advisers distracted from their work.

She froze. Her breath seized. Wait. She could do something about this. "Emeril." Haven stood, her eyes wide.

"Emeril?" Lareina looked at her queen.

"He may not have left court yet. I must find him."

If Emeril had yet to depart, she could ask him for medics. They might very well be able to secure reinforcements in a few days' time.

Haven fled the room as fast as Nikolai had entered. She hiked up her skirts, which whipped against her ankles in her haste. Lareina's boots thumped behind her as she jogged to catch up with the young queen.

"Haven, you should send someone in your stead. Toma needs you to form a plan." Lareina met Haven's pace, glancing at her with widened eyes and a furrowed brow.

"I must tell him myself." If she didn't, Emeril might not understand the severity—the urgency—of the situation.

Dark stone walls and lavish tapestries flashed by as she ran the length of the hall. Her heels clacked loudly on the steps as she flew from the third floor to the first. Her breath heaved with every step, and her heart beat in time with her footsteps. Lareina followed her all the while.

The Salander envoy would depart from the main courtyard, only paces away from the main entry. *Be there,* she urged. *Please be there.*

Stone steps gave way to the smooth main floor, lush with red carpet. She raced past maids, soldiers, and noblemen, out the front doors.

Sunlight spilled over the courtyard, sending white spots flying over her vision. She paused by the palace steps for only a moment before descending the curved staircase. She held a hand up to block the sun, only as she reached the cobblestone, a shadow blocked the harsh rays from her face. She lowered her hand.

Emeril's back was outlined in the afternoon sunlight. But it wasn't Emeril who blocked the sun.

A long shadow stretched from the center of the courtyard through to the main entrance, its arms spread and its head tilted to the sky.

"Haven," Lareina said.

Haven was already crossing the length of the yard. The shadow passed, leaving the sun to pour over a young man stuck through with a wooden pike.

She froze. Her heart hammered against her ribs.

His blue eyes were glassy and bloodshot, staring sightless at the sky. From his open mouth, the end of the pointed pike emerged, dark red. His jaw was unhinged, hanging as if by a single thread. A single red rose peeked out from behind his teeth. Blood poured down his body, sullying his leather tunic and his white shirt before pooling at the base of the pike, which sat between a pile of rocks. At his feet leaned a bow and a quiver.

Could this be her assassin?

A gasp passed through her lips, and she stepped back, tripping over her skirts and crashing onto her behind. Cold leeched the sun's warmth from her limbs. Her gaze locked on those sightless eyes, wide and filled with terror.

"Haven?" a familiar voice called. Emeril trotted over and kneeled to block her line of sight. "Haven, don't look."

She couldn't help but peer past him at the man on the pike.

"We need to remove the queen." Lareina took her arm and pulled her to her feet.

Emeril held up her other side. His blue-green blocked her from the dead archer. "Haven, close your eyes," he murmured gently.

Haven didn't listen. She couldn't.

How could someone have done this to another human being? And what did it mean? The pike. The rose. The bow and arrows. It was a message.

Lareina and Emeril turned her back toward the castle and led her away. Several soldiers stood watch, their eyes wide and vacant as they stared at the sight before them. Haven let them lead her, trying to find the energy inside herself to walk on her own instead of being carried.

Her gut soured, twisting and writhing up into her throat. She pushed Emeril and Lareina away, ducking her head into the bushes that lined the courtyard cobblestone and retched.

Blood, blood, and more blood. Why did this war demand so much *blood*?

Lareina brushed Haven's temples with her fingers as she gently pulled her hair back from her face and shoulders. She rubbed small circles on her upper back as Haven rid her body of breakfast.

Once Haven was finished and could breathe again, Emeril and Lareina led her back inside the castle. Shadows descended upon her shoulders, cooling the built-up heat from her vomiting. Being careful to avoid any windows facing the courtyard, they returned to the study once again. Nikolai was nowhere to be found.

"Lady Queen!" Toma gasped as he stood from his desk. "What on earth happened?"

Lareina silenced him with a glare and deposited Haven behind her desk. Haven sat down hard, feeling returning to her numb limbs. She took a few deep breaths and met her guard's eyes.

"Thank you," Haven whispered.

Lareina simply nodded and fetched Haven a glass of water from a nearby jug before standing at her back, much closer than she normally would. While Haven composed herself and sipped on cold water, Emeril updated Toma on the situation in the courtyard.

Toma cursed before covering his mouth. He dispatched another guard to take care of the courtyard display and returned to his own desk. He sat down just as heavily as Haven had, rubbing his hands over his face before his gaze met hers.

"What was that?" Haven gulped the lump in her throat.

Toma glanced at Emeril and Lareina before answering, "I don't know, Lady Queen."

"Who could have done such a thing?" Her voice rose an octave.

No one answered the queen.

Haven stared at her adviser until something tickled at the back of her mind. "Could it be Kadia?"

"We have no way of knowing that." Emeril rounded her desk and lay a hand on her shoulder.

Haven took a deep breath before she reached up and squeezed his fingers in thanks. He stepped away.

"We will launch an investigation, Lady Queen." Toma nodded.

"I don't want to hear of it, Toma." Her own words surprised her, but her weakness betrayed her. She wasn't ready for all of this blood. She wasn't ready for any of this. "Investigate, but please do not mention it until the killer is caught." Her fingers found her lips. Her stomach recoiled at the thought of the man on the pike. She clenched her muscles. She would not vomit. Not again.

"Of course, Lady Queen." He cleared his throat.

"Please, Toma. Distract me. What are we to do with the news Nikolai has brought?" Haven smoothed her dress and made herself comfortable. She needed something else to think about, something important. Something she could put her heart into.

"Oh, yes." He paused, shuffling through his desk full of papers. "The attack on Wakefin. We must make decisions, provisions, and preparations."

"Attack?" Emeril perked up.

Haven hadn't given him the news yet. "Dessa has been taken. Evander sent word." She handed Emeril the letter.

He read it quickly, fear and disbelief slowly creeping into the grooves of his face. "This can't be." Her wide eyes scanned the study for answers.

"But it has, and we must act quickly." This she knew. Without a plan her people would fall. She couldn't let that happen. "Preparations must be made. Injured refugees will pour in at any moment. We must be ready." Haven blindly sorted through papers while she tried to think.

There was no telling how many refugees they were about to take on, but from Evander's warning, there had to be hundreds, if not more. What was the population of Wakefin? What percentage could she expect? For the life of her, she couldn't remember anything. "Toma?"

"Yes, Lady Queen?"

"How many healers do we have in the castle?" She should have already known this, like the population of Wakefin. But she didn't.

As queen, she would need to take a greater interest in not only the workings of her castle, but of her city and her kingdom. How many hospitals were in the city? How many nurses could they conjure? Should students of medicine be brought in to help?

"About half a dozen, My Lady," Toma said, starting to sound a bit more like himself.

Like Haven, he needed a problem to solve, something to focus on. Together, they would resolve this predicament, and she would hopefully forget about the man on the pike.

"That won't do," she said. "We need an area big enough to house these refugees, with as many doctors and nurses as possible."

"We can bring in physicians from nearby towns if we need to, My Lady." Toma moved about the room, pulling documents from the shelves lining the far wall and barking orders at the other advisers.

"Where can we find a large enough space for so many people? Surely the hospitals will be overwhelmed."

"The ballroom, My Queen." Lareina smiled down at her. Her blue eyes danced with something akin to pride. "The ballroom could easily fit a hundred bunks for refugees. We could have the less injured brought here and the most grave cases sent to the hospitals. The doctors would be of better use in their own environment."

Yes. That was it! She couldn't believe she'd almost forgotten that Lareina was trained in medicine. She could have been a doctor if her heart hadn't belonged to her kingdom.

"You're absolutely brilliant, Lareina." Haven stood to hug her lady guard.

Lareina had always been a great friend, but she very well could have been Haven's first female adviser too, if she'd had the inclination.

"Thank you, My Queen." Lareina stepped out of her embrace. "I will help you in any way I can. I shall send another guard to keep the towers on lookout. We should be ready to open the gates when the refugees arrive."

"Yes. That would be perfect. Thank you."

Lareina bowed slightly and removed herself from the room.

"Emeril." Haven turned to the prince. With all the happenings in the courtyard, she'd nearly forgotten why she'd run to catch him. "We need you, Emeril. Rythern can't do this without aid. Hundreds of refugees are about to pour into my city. I can't very well care for them all on my own. We simply do not have enough healers."

Emeril's gaze widened in understanding. His jaw set, and he nodded. "I will help you in any way I can, Haven. Just tell me what you need." He assured her with the full intensity of his blue-green gaze.

Haven smiled, grateful to have a friend like him. "We need your resources. Any healers you can spare. Medicine." She paused to think but found her imagination lacking under Emeril's fierce gaze. "And your knowledge. Help me set up centers for these refugees. You know much more about being a King than I do."

"Of course." Emeril grinned. "Let's begin."

* * *

Can't wait to find out what happens next? Read *Haven* for free with Kindle Unlimited or **buy now!**

FOUR

hree days had passed since the fall of Wakefin, and Haven was growing restless. She had taken to the hospitals and the clinics to soothe the people of Wakefin as well as the growing concerns of her own.

After the man on the pike was removed, she used anything she could find to distract herself. As per her request Toma was hell-bent on keeping her out of the investigation, but rumors of the castle guards who'd been found vacant-eyed and entranced flew. None had any recollection of how they had gotten that way or what had even happened in the last few days.

Something strange was at work in her castle. But what exactly was going on?

With the help of her ladies, Haven swallowed her troubles while out in town, but paperwork was piling up, and Toma's reprieve wouldn't last any longer.

On the third day, Haven remained in the castle. Emeril was expected to return with healers, and she wanted to be there to greet him. It also gave her a chance to check on the makeshift hospital in her ballroom.

She had heard good things from her guards, who often checked on the people for her. Some of the injured had already recovered enough to leave, but they stayed because they had nowhere else to go. Haven was surprised at the amount of volunteers who had come to her aid in this matter, taking refugees into their homes and their inns as well as volunteering in the hospitals. It warmed her heart to see her people so giving. Throughout her nineteen years of life, she had never known her people as well as she'd wished. As much as she regretted that, it did present a valuable opportunity to make their acquaintance in her new role.

Sweeping into the grand hall, Haven took in the high vaulted ceilings, large crystal chandeliers, and huge stained-glass windows lining the upper half of the ballroom walls. Pillars lined the marble floored room, leaving the center of the space wide open with burgundy-and-gold-trimmed walls.

It was the perfect size to suit this purpose, and she was glad Lareina thought of it.

Several rows of bunks and cots were full of people, from the healed to the recovering. Doctors and nurses moved up and down aisles, assisting as many as they could. Volunteers distributed bread and water while children ran around the pillars, screeching with laughter.

The hundred there had been well taken care of. She sighed with relief. As her little party stepped inside, many eyes turned to her.

Haven smiled in greeting, her cheeks flushed. "Good day." She held her skirts up as she glided through the crowd, greeting the people and hearing their concerns.

Lareina stayed by her side, assisting the patients she sat with. After Haven had spoken with nearly every conscious person, she joined the children at the edge of the crowd. Even in such trying times, their simple joy and laughter warmed her heart.

"Children, what would you like of me?" Haven asked.

"Games!"

"Chocolate!"

"Dance!"

Each child shouted something different. A laugh escaped her chest. Their high spirits were infectious. With much sorrow plaguing the city, it was a welcome change to see their smiling faces.

Haven bent to brush the bangs from a young girl's face. She had been one of the few children not to shout.

"How about you, my dear?" Haven took her hand when she offered it. The child's tiny fingers barely wrapped around hers. She was so young that she still sucked on her thumb. "What can I do for you?"

"My mummy used to sing," she whispered, her eyes big and lost.

Haven's smile faltered. *Used to.* How unfair to have lost her mother at such a young age.

Haven squeezed her fingers. "Did you lose your mother?" Her chest tightened, and images of the bloody courtyard assaulted her mind. Why did this war insist on taking all of their mothers?

When the little girl finally nodded, blond curls bounced around her soft baby-doll face.

"I lost my mother too. She used to sing to me as well."

The girl met her eyes. "What did she sing?" she mumbled around her thumb.

"Many things. Of the kingdoms, Rythern, the sea, and the great cities beyond."

"What was your favorite?" She removed her thumb from her mouth, peering at Haven with newfound wonder.

Haven gazed off into the ballroom. A painting of a long trail through the forest, leading to a wishing well, caught her eye.

"I'd have to say my favorite was 'The Path to Seaburn,'" Haven told her. "The Republic always fascinated me as a girl."

"I haven't heard that one." Her fingers tightening around Haven's. "Will you sing it for me?"

Haven blinked at her, somewhat startled. She'd sung many times with her mother, but never to a crowd. Her stomach turned and nerves prickled in her chest, but how could she refuse such an adorable child?

Gulping the lump in her throat, Haven nodded. "I will sing for you, but I would like to know your name first." She glanced at Lareina, who nodded in turn.

Lareina was a beautiful singer, and she hoped her friend knew the song as well.

"Mirabel." She flushed. "But my mum called me Mira."

"Mira." Haven grinned. "What a beautiful name."

Mirabel's smile grew, and it was startlingly lovely. Haven would sing for this girl, these people, and hope their spirits would be lifted by her words. Mirabel released her fingers.

Haven turned to Lareina, who nodded at her cue and began to hum. Her cheeks and her chest flushed. Heat coursed through her limbs. She might have been embarrassed, but she could do this. Haven joined in with the humming before the words returned to her.

She could picture her mother so clearly, the morning light catching her brown curls as she twirled Haven in a flurry of giggles. Haven was young in this memory, but she still felt as if it were yesterday.

With the late Queen Denica in her mind, she sang. Haven's voice rose through the air, and a bubble of happiness and loss filled her chest. Lareina joined in, and a hush fell through the room. Their voices, high and delicate, echoed off the vaulted ceiling. The sound reverberated back to them, low and soft. Once to the chorus, several women of Rythern joined in. "The Path to Seaburn" was a common song throughout Warshard. Many would know it, and she hoped more would join.

By the fourth verse, the room became awash in dozens of voices, high and low, deep and soft, practiced and not.

Haven glanced at her little friend to make sure she was enjoying herself. Mirabel's eyes filled with tears even though a smile so big and bright spread across her face. Haven's eyes stung. She couldn't help it. They were both trapped in memories of their mothers for the rest of the song.

When it finished, Lareina met her gaze. A pleasant hush fell over the room. Echoes bounced back until slowly fading with the final lyrics. When the ballroom held not a single sound, Mirabel pushed forward, tightly hugging Haven's legs. Claps echoed through the great hall.

"Thank you," Haven whispered to her friend.

Lareina only nodded.

"I never knew you were such a lovely singer, Lady Haven."

Haven turned and found beautiful blue-green eyes on her. "Emeril!" She barely held her gasp back. Embarrassment flooded her all over again. It was one thing to sing for her people and those of Wakefin, but to sing in front of royalty was another matter. "You're back."

"I am." He smiled. The dazzling look in his eyes brought heat to her face. "I have what you requested."

Behind the prince stood at least a dozen men, all carrying packages. Behind *them*, another dozen waited, dressed in Salander guard armor.

"You have brought many!"

Mirabel unclasped herself from Haven's legs enough to let Haven move toward the great ballroom doors where Emeril awaited.

"We are forever grateful," Haven said.

"Salander is happy to help, Lady Queen." Emeril held his hand over his heart and bowed to her in greeting. "I see you have a new friend."

Haven looked down at her small leech. Mirabel clasped her hand, her thumb returning to her mouth.

"Yes, this is Mirabel. She is a lovely girl, is she not?"

Mira blushed and hid behind the young queen's skirts while still peeking out at Emeril.

"That she is," Emeril agreed. "May I borrow you for a moment?"

"Of course." Haven turned to bid farewell to Mira. She crouched and embraced the girl. Mirabel was warm in her arms. "I will return to sing to you soon, young Mira. Be well."

"Thank you, Lady Queen," Mira murmured against Haven's hair.

Haven released Mirabel and waved before joining Lareina at the hall doors. Emeril dismissed his guards and his healers, whom Haven directed to Toma. Her adviser would know the best place for their aid.

Once free of the ballroom, Haven led Emeril to her personal

sitting rooms. Only there would she find somewhere quiet to speak in private. When they arrived, her chambers were clear of maids and servants. Some peace at last. She ushered her guest inside before taking a seat on a long, red sofa, urging Emeril to join her. He sat, keeping a respectable distance.

"Is there news?" she asked.

Emeril shook his head. "Not much. But I wanted to convey a message to you from King Alton. A meeting will be held tonight. I'm sure Toma will receive word soon, but I thought it best to prepare you."

"Prepare me for what?" Her eyebrows furrowed.

"I'm not sure, but Alton urged me to warn you in advance. I'm sure it's something to do with the war."

Goose bumps rose on her arms. Surely a warning could not mean good news. Her stomach flipped. Fear for her kingdom rolled inside her gut. What could the news possibly be? Another kingdom taken? Salander to be next? Eris under siege? Calisa in ruin?

Her imagination took hold until Emeril finally stopped her.

She took a deep breath.

"It doesn't seem to be terrible news, My Lady."

Her fingers brushed the velvet beside her dress.

"But I think Wakefin may need our help again. You should spend some time thinking about your decision. Speak with Toma. He seems wise in the ways of the kingdoms."

Haven nodded. "He is." She was sure her concern showed on her face. After all, things couldn't be as bad as she thought. She voiced her worries anyway. "King Corrin is going to battle again, isn't he?"

"I imagine that is what the meeting is about, yes."

"I don't know if I can put my people in so much danger, Emeril."

"I don't think I can, either."

They looked long and hard at each other. In this regard, they were on the same page.

"Come to my chambers again when you're heading out. We shall travel together tonight," Haven said.

Emeril stood. "I shall." He bowed.

Haven stood to see him off.

He paused halfway out the door. "You really do have a beautiful voice, Haven."

Blush crept onto her cheeks. "Thank you." She wasn't sure whether to be shocked, flattered, or both.

"You have a very positive effect on your people." He paused, avoiding her gaze. "I hope to have the same effect on mine someday."

It was the first time Haven had heard him question his ability to lead.

She'd gone to him for aid with the refugees, instinctively knowing he could help. From the look on his face, she recognized her own doubt. Being the leader of so many was difficult, especially without much experience. Emeril had grown up knowing he would one day be king, but to follow in his father's footsteps would be the challenge.

"You are your father's son, Emeril." Haven smiled. "You will be a great king one day. Your people will love you."

Emeril's lips curved slightly. He thanked her before he left.

"You know, Prince Emeril is a very handsome man." Lareina stepped away from the wall, giving her queen a meaningful look and a sly smile.

"Yes, I am aware, Lareina." Her cheeks remained hot.

"You two have always been close, and now, he even looks up to you."

"Your point?"

"Nothing." Lareina grinned. "Nothing at all." She laughed as she left her quarters.

Haven stared after her.

The match had always been pushed on her from many fronts, but this was a new one. If even her friends thought she should consider Emeril, did it mean she was a fool not to? Though she'd put some thought into it as a girl, the idea hadn't crossed her mind in years. Would Emeril be a good match for her in the end? Could she handle running between two kingdoms just to have a husband?

She knew it would be expected of her to eventually marry and produce heirs, but she couldn't help recoiling at the thought. She couldn't bear to pass her curse on to her children, and ever since her power had become known, she'd sworn never to marry.

It could save her unborn a life full of misery and loss in the case they were born like her.

She couldn't—no, she *wouldn't*—do that to her children.

Haven would never marry or bear children. She would never bestow the misery of long life upon them.

THAT NIGHT, Toma and Emeril met in her chambers.

"Good evening, My Queen." Toma passed her the black sheath once again.

She'd only held it once or twice since the last secret meeting, and she found it awkward in her hands. The sword would be useless to Haven without proper training, but she took it on principle. If anyone needed protecting, she should be the one to do it.

"Good evening, Toma, Emeril." She attached the sheath to her belt.

Blythe had insisted that, if she were to sneak from the castle at night, she should be in trousers. Dresses were inappropriate for riding and would only hinder her if it ever did come to a fight. Haven had to agree, happy to wear something much less formal and much more comfortable.

"Shall we be off?"

"Yes, My Lady." Toma led them through halls and secret passages until they were outside the castle walls.

With their horses tethered nearby, it wasn't long before Haven mounted her trusted steed and raced across the dark terrain.

The journey seemed much quicker this time. With the wind whipping through her hair and the cold pressing against her body, she was wide awake. Nerves crept into her stomach, as she was fearful of what Corrin might ask of her. She had to trust herself and her adviser.

They had decided that evening where they would stand if Corrin should ask them for soldiers. Haven would stand her ground, no matter how much it bothered her to hold back.

Climbing the mountainside, they soon found themselves in the presence of Nikolai, who greeted them each in turn. He helped them dismount their horses before tying them with the others.

"Well met, Nikolai," Haven said.

"Well met, Lady Queen," he responded. "You are the last to arrive. We must go inside."

"Of course."

Nikolai led them through the dark tunnels and into the meeting place. Torchlight cast the large room in a warm glow. The center table was yet again surrounded by Kings. Guards stood watch at the walls, and the table held its usual map and figurines, though their placement had changed.

"Lady Queen," Evander greeted warmly.

"Lord King." Haven bowed slightly.

"It is good to see you well," he said. "Well met, Lord Prince."

"Well met, Lord King." Emeril bowed.

"We should begin immediately," Evander said.

They all agreed.

Around the table, the queen, the kings, and the prince took their seats. Toma stood at her shoulder, a comforting presence against the turmoil swirling inside her. Haven was surprised to see Corrin there, even though the meeting had to do with him. She wouldn't have wanted to leave her people in a time like this. It suddenly occurred to her that she had no idea where he had gone into hiding. It had to be have been in another kingdom. From the look on his face, things were not going well.

"King Corrin, why don't you begin?" Evander urged gently.

"Yes, of course." The king sighed, turning from his daze to look upon the other royals. A stark contrast from the first time Haven met the young King, his eyes were sullen, his mouth set in a deep frown. No glint of the obnoxious king she knew remained. "As you all know by now, Dessa has fallen. Kadia has taken most of Wakefin."

They all nodded, and Haven, who was sitting beside him, patted his arm for reassurance.

"Evander has been kind enough to shelter me while we come up with a plan for retaliation." He looked at each of them in turn.

Haven could see the question in his eyes. Corrin was going to ask more of them than she had originally expected.

"It is my desire to take the war to Queen Kadia," Corrin said. "We need to attack Dagan's capital."

Haven couldn't help the gasp that escaped her, and apparently, neither could the other Kings.

"Attack Cidra?" Alton nearly growled. "Are you mad, boy?"

Corrin stared coldly back at Alton. "I believe it to be the best course of action. Instead of combating one small problem at a time, we can take the fight right to the source."

"I wouldn't call retaking Dessa a small problem, Corrin!" Evander's voice rose.

"In comparison to ending this war, it is small." Corrin looked around the table. "I wouldn't say this if I didn't believe it to be the best course of action. I have thought this through for some time, and I can't see an end to this unless we fight that evil witch ourselves."

Haven stared at Corrin with wide eyes. She'd only known him for a brief time, but she didn't believe him so passionate. He clearly cared for his people and thought this was the best way. It was unfortunate that she didn't agree.

"I won't risk my soldiers for your gain, Corrin!" Alton shouted.

"Then who *will*?"

A hush fell over the royals before the arguing started. Haven and Emeril sat in stunned silence while Alton, Corrin, and Evander debated. While Corrin had some good points about ending the war, it was true that, if they stood up and lost, they could put everyone at risk. Alton made his case, unwilling to bring Kadia's wrath upon Eris. Corrin argued that he would be next if they didn't fight back. Alton wouldn't hear of it, and soon, Evander called a halt to the entire thing.

"Corrin, you cannot expect us to risk our kingdoms for yours. I'm sorry, but I will not attack Cidra under these circumstances." Evander calmly sat back in his chair and crossed his arms.

"Under *what* circumstances, then?" Corrin hissed. "Will you wait until Calisa is under attack? Until Eris is taken? Until they've set fire to Salander? *What* will it take, Evander?"

Alton scoffed. "The ambitions of young kings. You should respect your elders, boy!"

Corrin turned his glare to the blond man. "Seeing as kings and princes are dropping left and right, maybe more stock should be taken of the opinions of *young kings*."

His words sent a knife through Haven's heart. She stared at Corrin in horror, her fists clenched. His kingdom might have been close to ruin, but *her* family was dead.

Her mother had died at her feet, and *her* brothers had died for this war.

"That is enough!" Evander slammed his fist on the table.

Everyone froze. Evander positioned himself between Alton and Corrin before things came to blows.

Evander met Corrin's glare with the most serious expression she'd ever seen from the gentle man. Haven concentrated on the exchange, using the kings as a distraction to tame the angry beast inside.

Taking a breath, Evander motioned for Corrin to take a seat. After several long moments, he obliged. The storm had passed, at least for the moment.

"I'm sorry, Corrin. Truly, I am. As a sign of good will toward you and your people, I will offer you my soldiers. *Not* to attack Cidra, but to retake Dessa." Evander paused.

Corrin didn't object.

"We will retake Wakefin," Evander said, "and then decide on the next course of action."

Corrin stayed silent. His eyes darkened with defeat, but he had to see that this was better than nothing. It was certainly the more reasonable of options.

"All right. I accept your offer. Thank you, Evander."

"It is nothing." Evander nodded.

"Will anyone else offer their aid in these matters?" The young king turned his hopeful gaze on Haven and Emeril.

They had both remained completely silent until this moment. For good reason.

"I'm sorry, Corrin, but I cannot offer soldiers to this cause." Emeril paused, glancing away. "Not without my father's permission, at least."

Corrin nodded solemnly.

"I would, however, like to offer my assistance with your people. I know Rythern has reached its capacity and Calisa can't be faring much better."

Evander nodded in agreement.

"I thank you," Corrin said, his fist to his chest.

"I cannot offer my soldiers, Corrin. I'm sorry." Haven couldn't bear to see anyone else die, especially her own people.

Corrin nodded. "I understand, Lady Queen."

A short pause fell in which the royals relaxed. All fight seemed to have left the young King Corrin.

"I will offer my resources, as I cannot expend my soldiers," Alton said, his voice gruff. His mustache twitched back and forth. Did he regret his earlier outburst?

"Thank you, Alton."

After a consensus was reached, there wasn't much else to speak of. The royals dispersed, leaving Haven alone with Toma, Emeril, and Nikolai. They were ushered out by the large Calisan man, who helped them along their way. The trio was nearly down the mountain when Toma spoke up.

"You did well, Lady Queen," he said.

Haven smiled and looked back at her adviser. "Thank you, Toma. I did as we'd discussed. I fear for Wakefin and the other kingdoms, but we don't have the resources in our present state to handle an attack."

"Certainly," Toma agreed.

"I was surprised to hear of Corrin's plans for Cidra," Emeril spoke.

They reached the forest floor and continued at a leisurely pace, staying close as they wove through the trees and found the path.

"I was as well," Toma said. "He always seemed like a confident boy, but I didn't think him suicidal."

Haven glanced at Toma, surprised by his brash words. He'd never been one to speak out of turn. She had to agree with her adviser all the same. Corrin's plan did seem like suicide if he were to try it himself. She hoped he had only come up with this scheme in case another kingdom were willing to join forces. Even so, with Wakefin's depleted army, they would hardly stand a chance against whatever Queen Kadia had in store.

"I don't believe he is suicidal." Why was she standing up for him? Haven swallowed the lump in her throat. "I think he's just like the rest of us. He wants to protect his people. The way he's going about it is just rash and slightly insane."

Both men paused and nodded.

"Maybe not insane, but he's certainly not thinking straight," Emeril agreed.

"I can't imagine what the loss of so many soldiers would be like." Haven gazed into the darkness. The sky was clouded over, and she feared rain would find them before they reached home.

What would it be like to be Corrin right now? A splinter of fear shot through her chest. One day, would her kingdom be like Wakefin? Would war come to her doorstep? Would Queen Kadia bring her dark soldiers through the other kingdoms and ravage her own?

She shivered in the cold night air. "If I were him, it would break my heart."

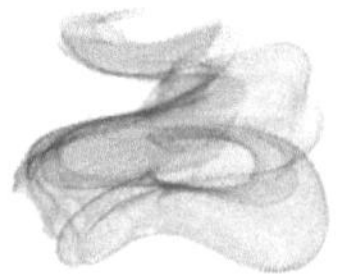

FIVE

"Word has arrived, Lady Queen." Toma handed her a letter.

The red Calisan seal was unbroken.

"Thank you, Toma," Haven said.

The young queen sat in her study with her many advisers. Several days after the secret meeting, it was back to paperwork for her. The hospitals needed less and less of her help. While she appreciated it, she wished to return all the same. Unfortunately, there was no injury she could feign to take her there.

Breaking the seal, Haven opened the note and read on. Her heart swelled with every word. Though the letter was brief, it held only good news.

"Dessa was retaken." Haven exhaled loudly.

Several sets of eyes rose from their work, and smiles were evident on their faces.

"That is wonderful news, Lady Queen." Toma stood behind his desk. "Does Evander mention the casualties?"

Haven nodded. "Next to none."

"Brilliant! I'm sure a great celebration will be held in Wakefin tonight."

"I'm sure it will," Haven agreed.

It had been too long since she'd heard good news in this war. Person after person had been taken from her. Her parents. Her brothers. Her kingdom's soldiers. Having such low casualties was a great blessing.

It seemed almost difficult to believe.

Haven sat back, her brow furrowed. With Wakefin back in the hands of Corrin, maybe the King's scheme to take on Kadia directly could work. Though she could hardly imagine sending her own soldiers, this might be the push for Eris or Calisa to lend their aid.

Perhaps this war would be over sooner than she had hoped. If only things had gone quite so well when her family was still alive. Her heart clenched.

Haven reread the message. Only about a dozen casualties had been reported, even though hundreds of soldiers had invaded Dessa to retake it. Surely there should have been more deaths. Worry creased her brow. It didn't make sense.

If Kadia had wanted to take Dessa so badly, surely she would have guarded it better than this. There had been fifty to a hundred men guarding the capital city. No more. Though this was good news, Haven found it difficult to accept. In the past, her worrisome nature had always bothered her, but trusting her instincts had always been advantageous.

Her stomach continued to twist. She had no way to explain this to Toma, but maybe her guard friends would understand.

"What is it, My Queen?" Toma asked. "You look troubled."

"It is nothing, Toma." She shook her head.

"You don't seem quite as pleased by this news as a moment ago."

Haven said nothing, only stared at the letter. She knew what she had to do. Turning to Malka, who was guarding the door today, she locked eyes. The girls had known each other for so long that it was obvious when something was amiss. With one simple look, Malka understood and nodded.

Haven needed out of this room *now*.

"I'm going to take a walk, Toma." Haven rose from her seat.

Her advisers stood out of respect. She quickly motioned them back to work.

"Can I help, Lady Queen?" Always the empathetic one, Toma sensed her unease.

He would be good to speak with in most cases, but in this, she feared he would find her paranoid. She needed reassurance from her friends before she brought such matters to her most trusted adviser.

"Don't worry, Toma. It is nothing." She smiled to reassure him. "I will speak with you later."

"All right."

Haven took her leave. Malka led the way down the quiet hall. It took a moment for Haven to realize she didn't know where she was going or where to find her other guard girls.

She stopped. "Malka, where do you suppose Blythe and Lareina are at the moment?"

The spiky-haired brunette took a moment to think about it. "Blythe is most likely organizing the guard in the rear courtyard," she began, "while Lareina is likely in the infirmary or aiding those in the ballroom."

Haven nodded. "We will fetch Lareina first, then."

SOMETIME LATER, Haven gathered with her three guards in the gardens behind the castle. She assumed they were far enough from prying eyes and attentive ears, but just to be safe, Haven sat them near a fountain. It wouldn't drown their voices out if someone was nearby, but they would go unnoticed if someone approached.

Settling alongside her ladies on a set of delicately carved stone benches, Haven folded her hands in her lap. She met the three girls with a concerned gaze. Brown, blue, and green eyes stared back at her, all equally curious.

"My apologies for the intrusion into your day," Haven said.

Lareina laughed, and Blythe scoffed.

"My Queen, you never need to apologize to us." Malka smiled.

"And none of you need ever speak to me so formally," Haven countered.

"That's fair," Lareina said.

After a long moment of pause, Haven took a deep breath. "Dessa has been retaken," she said before launching into a brief story of her thoughts and findings. Then she explained her suspicions at the lack of casualties and fear of what could be next. She included her encounters with the royals, detailing Corrin's plan to attack Cidra and their lack of willingness to comply. "I fear for my people," she continued, "but most of all, I'm afraid that, if I cannot protect myself, how can I protect anyone else? My curse saves me, but it helps no one else." Her shoulders slumped.

Blythe and Malka exchanged a look.

"You mean your grace, Haven." Lareina took her hand, but Haven shook her head.

"It is your grace, My Lady, and it does help your people." Blythe's fists clenched. "*You* help your people. Your grace keeps you alive so you may live another day and keep helping them."

Haven had never thought about it like that.

Her immortality had been her curse long before her coronation, when the first inklings of hope for something more had sprung within her. As a queen who couldn't die, she would live a long time and help her people for many decades. If she were a good queen, this would be a gift to Rythern. If she weren't, surely it was a curse. She had to hope the curse she saw truly was the grace these girls accepted.

"Grace or not, if you want to protect yourself, we can help," Malka said.

Blythe shot her a look. "Malka."

Clearly these two had shared this conversation before.

"She is queen. She should know how to use a sword," Malka snapped.

Haven had never seen such a look of shock on Blythe's face, nor such a fierce bite to Malka's tone. A smile plucked at the corners of her lips. She'd always suspected they were more than friends, and as she witnessed their lovers' quarrel, it became much more obvious.

"I agree with Malka," Lareina said.

"I do too."

Each of them looked to their queen.

"If I am to save even one life…" She stopped. "If this war comes to my capital, I need to be able to protect those I love. I will not have any of your deaths on my hands." She had never been so glad that her sister was at their vacation home in the mountains. Though Astrid hadn't been happy to go, at least she would be safe from all of this nonsense.

Her guards and her adviser, on the other hand, were not.

"If I know how to fight, I can fight alongside you, my warriors," Haven continued. Warmth filled her. She hadn't realized how much she'd meant her words until now. "Teach me. Train me. Make me strong. I will fight with you if Kadia comes to our door. You need not protect me." Haven raised a hand to their objections. "A queen who cannot die does not need protection. Though I cannot expect you three not to fight, you should not expect me not to join you."

Lareina, Malka, and Blythe sat in stunned silence. Smiles pulled at their lips. It had been a long time since they had seen this side of their queen. As a girl, Haven had readily given up on everything she was not good at. Swordplay had been one of them. After her grievous failures, she had sworn never to pick up a sword again, yet there she was, pledging to her guards that she would be a survivor.

"Of course we will train you after a speech like that." Lareina leaned forward and hugged her friend and queen.

"I suppose there's no stopping it now," Blythe agreed, a smile as wide as the sun lighting her features.

"Once you learn how to use a sword, I can even teach you the art of the bow." Malka grinned.

Haven laughed. "Let's take this one step at a time, ladies."

* * *

THE VERY NEXT DAY, Haven met her guard girls in one of the inner courtyards. Wooden and metal swords alike decorated the walls. Shields lined up beside them, sporting a range of shapes and colors. Haven couldn't help but notice that Malka had slipped a bow and a quiver full of arrows among them.

She took a deep breath and shook her limbs out to rid herself of nerves. Though anxiety prickled her skin, excitement filled her belly. With her hair tied back and trousers on, she was ready.

"You look more like a warrior already!" Lareina called to the queen as she entered.

Blythe laid the last of the shields into place along the wall. How much time had she spent setting up? Too much, she suspected. Malka balanced on her heels nearby. Now that they had all arrived, it was time to get down to business.

"Take stance," Blythe instructed.

With a wooden sword in one hand and a shield in the other, Haven dropped back into what she could remember of a defensive stance. "How is this?"

"Not bad, but your footing is wrong." Blythe approached Haven and switched the positions of her sword and her shield before nudging her feet farther apart with her boot. "Better."

Lareina took up her sword and her shield, standing opposite Haven. "Now, strike like this." She demonstrated a simple maneuver.

Haven gave it a try. She slipped halfway through the arc. It'd take some training to emulate the natural movement these girls had, but she was determined.

"Tell me what I'm doing wrong."

"Watch Lareina," Blythe said.

Lareina demonstrated again.

"Mimic her movements." Blythe paused. "And hold your blade like this." She fixed Haven's hold. "Try it again. You needn't hold the sword as if your life depends on it. Use it as an extension of yourself. If you don't, you'll keep fumbling like that."

Haven sighed and watched Lareina demonstrate several times before attempting to mimic her movements.

"You're getting there. Try this."

They continued: move after move, offensive, defensive, Lareina attacking first, Haven attacking first. They were at it for hours before Blythe called it quits. It was getting late and Haven's whole body ached. She hadn't used her muscles for anything but the occasional swim through the nearby lake since she was a girl. Though her guards seemed as determined as she, Haven was weary and happy for the day to end.

"You'll need to improve your strength before we let you try a real sword." Blythe joined them in a ring on the floor.

Haven caught her breath while the others cleaned their swords. She had known that this would happen and simply nodded. She was not a strong girl and never had been. She'd need to develop a lot of muscle to swing a real sword with any accuracy.

"You should start lifting weights when you have the time, My Lady," Blythe suggested.

They all agreed.

IN THE DAYS THAT FOLLOWED, the four girls began to gather a crowd. The lessons took place in a public courtyard on the main level of the castle, where many passersby stopped to see what the queen was up to. Haven improved as the days went on, even if it was a painfully slow process. She went to bed sore every night, quickly did her paperwork in the morning, and then adjourned to her courtyard for her lessons. Many came to know this as her afternoon ritual, sometimes gathering before she had even arrived. She was embarrassed by her failures, but she tried to remind herself that this was for them. It was for the people watching as well as the girls teaching her.

Almost a week after they'd begun, Haven failed to learn a simple move. Her chest burned, and her fingers were sweaty. She watched Lareina, Malka, and Blythe perform the move dozens of times and then tried her best to mimic their movements. She could never quite get it.

"Enough," she called several hours into practice.

Haven collapsed near a pile of wooden swords, her head in her hands. She pressed her back to the stone wall. It cooled her sweat-covered back through her shirt. If she couldn't get this simple move, how could she ever protect anyone, let alone herself?

"My Lady, are you all right?" Lareina swiftly came to her side.

Blythe hurried after her, and Malka went to disperse the crowd. Malka had always been good like that. She knew things even Haven herself didn't know she needed. She couldn't have her subjects seeing her so wrapped in defeat.

It was humiliating.

"I'm fine. Just tired." Haven sighed, burying her face from her friends. Tears burned at the backs of her eyes, but she refused to look so weak in front of everyone.

"What's wrong?" Blythe kneeled beside her.

"I can't even achieve these simple moves," she mumbled into her hands. "How can I protect anyone?"

"You will improve, Haven." Lareina put her arm around the queen's shoulders.

"I will *not*. I've had enough of this failure, Lareina." Haven glanced sharply at her friend.

Lareina didn't recoil from her gaze, only squeezed her shoulder harder.

"I can't do this anymore. I will never improve."

Both girls stared at her silently. A moment later, Malka joined them.

"Enough of these lessons. I should go." Haven began to rise, but she stopped when Blythe's scowl stood in her way.

"We will not allow you to give up." Blythe crossed her arms.

Haven narrowed her eyes. "You cannot tell your *queen* what to do."

"Haven," Lareina gasped.

She had never spoken to them before as subjects, only as friends. She'd regretted the statement the moment it left had her lips.

Blythe leaned closer to Haven, her breath hot on Haven's cheeks. "What will your people think if you give up on such a simple task?"

Haven winced.

"Will you leave them to die too if Kadia comes to our door? Will you give up on the people in the hospitals because you don't think you can do it?"

Her eyes burned. All fight fled from her body.

"No, you would not, *My Queen*."

Haven shook her head and set her face back in her hands. Shame consumed her.

"We will help you get through this," Lareina said.

"We are your friends, Haven," Malka added. "We know you can do this."

"Don't just do it for yourself, Haven." Blythe sighed. "Do it for us. Do it for your people. Do it for Rythern. You are a strong queen. Everyone knows that. Be that woman for your kingdom. Do not give up on yourself before you've even begun."

"I'm sorry," Haven whispered. "I'm awful and selfish." Tears leaked down her face. She looked at her guards. "Please forgive me. I will not give up on myself if you won't."

They all hugged her as one—something they hadn't done since they were girls. Haven let herself cry and clutched the warm bodies around her. Her heart clenched. She loved these ladies more than words could properly say. If they weren't going to give up on her when she had so shamefully given up on herself, then how could she? Her brilliant guards let her get it all out of her system before they parted and helped her to her feet.

"I am not worthy of your affection." Haven wiped her eyes on her sleeve.

"You are worthy of the whole realm's affection, My Lady." Lareina squeezed her hand.

"I don't know what I'd do without you girls." Haven smiled like a fool, her gaze falling on each of them in turn. "Please continue to train me. I can do this with your help."

"It will be our pleasure, My Lady."

* * *

"A LETTER HAS ARRIVED, LADY QUEEN." Toma appeared in the archway of the courtyard. He gently pushed through the crowd until he reached the queen.

Several days had passed since her weakness, and as promised, she'd continued to try. Haven had eventually passed her slump and improved every day. The more people showed up to cheer her on, the stronger she felt.

"Thank you, Toma." She handed her sword and her shield to Blythe.

Toma passed her the letter. The seal was once again unbroken.

"I hope this is more good news."

"We all do, Lady Queen." He bowed and stepped back while she read.

A frown worked its way onto her face as she read. The words were written urgently, not from Evander, but from King Alton of Eris. It had been nearly two weeks since the successful retaking of Dessa.

Things could only keep going well for so long, it seemed.

"What is it, Lady Queen?" her adviser implored.

Upon finishing the letter, Haven met Toma's gaze. "Eris is under attack."

Lareina gasped. Blythe and Malka froze.

Toma grew rigid, his eyes widening. "This cannot be. Dessa was just retaken. Another attack couldn't have come."

"It has. King Alton himself sent this letter. He's asking for reinforcements from every kingdom. Salander has already offered its aid, but Kadia's army has almost reached the Eris capital."

"Ryulung? How could they not have sent word sooner?" Toma paced the smooth stone floor.

"I don't know, Toma. It seems they are in a lot of trouble." Haven swallowed the lump in her throat. "I fear we must prepare for battle."

Toma stopped in his tracks and spun to face her.

"We will not send our soldiers into battle for Eris," she corrected quickly. "But, in case Kadia gets through Eris and into Salander, we need to be prepared."

Toma nodded, relief clear on his face. "A good decision, Lady Queen."

"Thank you." She nodded.

It took her a moment to realize that this exchange had been made in front of her people as well as a few Wakefin refugees who typically watched her train. Haven turned with wide eyes. They returned her somewhat surprised expression. Toma followed her gaze and froze upon making the same realization. This news would eventually reach the entirety of her kingdom, but making it known so early could be cause for panic.

Clearing her throat, Haven stepped forward. "Please do not fear. We are well protected here in Rythern. Eris and Salander will fend off the attack. I'm sure we have nothing to worry about." There was no ring of truth to her words. She hoped, at the very least, that her fear wasn't so obvious.

A small girl of maybe twelve, with brown hair and soft eyes, leapt forward. "Train me too!" she said. "I want to protect myself like you, Lady Queen!"

Haven gaped. Never had it occurred to her that other women would feel the same. Her army readily employed both men and women, but the common folk would have no experience with a sword at all.

"Look at what you've started." Lareina grinned from ear to ear.

"I want to learn as well." A woman stepped forward. Her blond hair and her blue eyes marked her as a Wakefin refuge.

"Me too." A petite brunette came forward.

Then girl after girl followed.

"Well. We can't very well train them all ourselves," Blythe huffed.

"Then we will need more guards." Haven turned to her ladies and her adviser.

"You mean..." Malka began.

"These ladies deserve to defend themselves as much as any soldier," Haven said.

Determination was clear on the faces of the spectators. They would learn to fight alongside their queen.

"I believe we have preparations to make." Haven raised an eyebrow at Toma, who nodded and scurried off. "Ladies." She turned to her personal guards. "Please fetch any guard we can spare. Class begins in one hour."

SIX

"Hold your sword like this," Lareina instructed.

A week had passed since the news of the attacks on Eris. The news had spread through the city like wildfire, which had brought more and more women to Haven's lessons every day. She couldn't have seen herself coming this far, let alone her people.

A few days ago, Blythe had dubbed her strong enough to wield a real sword, which made her lessons more interesting—and much more dangerous. The few other skilled women graduated along with her, rising to a secondary class at the far side of the courtyard. While Lareina taught the basics on one side of the long room hedged in topiaries and stone arches, Blythe led the other, teaching Haven and her strongest pupils more advanced attacks.

Swinging her blade in an arc, Haven smiled. Only two weeks ago, she had been ready to give up, and now, she was having practice matches with real guards. Though she hadn't won yet, she felt victory close at hand.

"What's next, Blythe?" she called.

Brown eyes met hers, pride glowing from within. It had been slow going to get to where she was today, but Haven had her stances down and her defense positions memorized. Offense would be the trick.

"Let's do something a little more complicated." Blythe stepped away from her students and plucked her sword from against the wall. She stood strong, moving into the offensive stance Haven had come to recognize.

The small class fell in line, mimicking her pose. Blythe spun and thrust her sword out in one fluid motion, but then she turned and sliced the air. Two opponents.

Haven flexed her fingers around her blade, ready to give it a shot.

"Now, let's try it one at a time." Blythe motioned to the end of the line.

The women backed into a circle, each trying the move one by one. Blythe gave pointers to each, fixing their stance, their aim, and the way they held the sword. When Haven's turn finally arrived, her skin crawled with anticipation. Haven pictured Blythe's movements in her mind, and then executed the routine.

"Well done!" Malka joined them.

Blythe eased Haven's feet apart with the tip of her blade, showing her a new way to move during her lunge. Haven tried again.

"Much better," Blythe said. "You'll keep your balance much easier this way."

Haven agreed. The sword hadn't pushed her too much to one side. Instead, she'd stayed grounded.

"Now, let's try—"

"Lady Queen!" Toma raced inside, his eyes wide and sweat dripping down his forehead.

Haven lowered her sword. "Toma, what is it?"

"Come with me at once."

Her eyebrows furrowed. Haven exchanged a glance with Blythe, whose expression hardened. "Go on without me," Haven said.

Malka broke away from the group and joined her in following Toma from the courtyard.

Haven's heart beat faster with each step. "What's going on?"

Toma's pace was brisk, his urgency palpable. "Word has come."

No matter how much she pried, Toma wouldn't speak another word until they reached the safety of her empty study. He produced a letter from his robes.

The seal of Salander was broken.

"Toma, you must tell me what has happened this instant." Haven eyes widened. "Is Emeril all right? What of the king?"

"Emeril is fine, My Queen." He handed her the letter.

"Then what is so important that—" Haven stopped, staring at the letter.

Several words jumped out at her. *Fallen. Refugees. Fleeing.* She returned to the beginning and read.

Lady Haven,

The worst has come to pass. Ryulung has fallen. The people of Eris are fleeing every which way. Refugees pile into Salander faster than we can make preparations. With the farmlands of Eris gone, I fear for the coming winter. How will we feed our people in such a time as this? My father grows increasingly ill. His uselessness is a plague. I fear he may soon die and leave me to rule. I'm afraid, Haven. I don't want to let my people down. I've tried to calm their unrest, but people have been fleeing into the mountains all day. I fear the civil problems this could cause with the native mountain folk. We've lived in peace for years and I don't want to disturb them with our troubles.

Salander will soon be in a panic. Alton is missing, and I fear this is only the first of what is to come. Fear is catching worse than fire in the grasslands. I must ask your advice, Haven. What should I do? Will Salander be next? I fear choosing between fight or flight. What if I choose wrong? Please, Haven, send word when you can. A meeting will be held soon and I must be ready to ask for aid if it comes to that.

With regards,
Prince Emeril of Salander

"This is madness." Haven collapsed into the chair behind her desk. "Bring me quill and ink. I must write to Emeril immediately."

Toma nodded and fetched her supplies. Haven pulled parchment from between her files. Her fingers shook as she set quill to paper.

The eyes of Toma and Malka burned into her skin as she wrote.

Dearest Emeril,

I am so sorry for the state of things. It is an awful time to be a monarch, it seems. I am distressed to hear of Ryulung, but do not lose heart. There is still time to salvage the situation. If Dessa can be retaken, so can Eris. I will discuss with my advisers a plan for food shortage. We will come up with a something before the meeting. As for advice, I am afraid that someone more experienced may be able to help you more than I. Please stay strong, Emeril. Things will improve. If you need anything, send word immediately. I'm sure we will be dealing with refugees of our own soon, but we will see what we can manage. I will return your healers to you at once. My only advice to you will be to contact Evander or Alton if you can find him. Their wisdom is much greater than my own, and certainly they will help.

With deepest regrets,
Queen Haven of Rythern

Haven folded the letter before her adviser could read it. She sealed it and passed the note to Malka. "Send this to Salander at once. Prince Emeril must read it before the day is done."

Malka gave a swift nod, worry creasing her brow.

Haven turned to Toma. "We must make preparations."

"Of course, Lady Queen," Toma said. "Malka, would you please send in the other advisers?"

Malka passed the letter to a guard outside the door, giving quick instructions before motioning to the advisers hovering outside the door

Five advisers piled inside, returning to work at their desks. Malka returned to her side, hovering closer than usual.

Haven met Toma's widened gaze. "You read the letter?"

"Yes, My Lady."

"Good." For the benefit of the others, she added, "Ryulung has fallen. Refugees are fleeing between Salander and Rythern. The farmlands of Eris have been decimated. We must prepare in the case of a food shortage."

Malka gasped, her fingers flying to her lips, too late to stop the sound. The others ceased their scribbling.

"If anyone has any ideas," Haven said, "please come forward immediately. I fear this loss could take effect at any time."

Haven didn't know much about the distribution of food throughout her kingdom, let alone the others. Shipments constantly flowed through Wakefin and Eris, bringing food to all of their nations. More than that, she did not know. It suddenly seemed paramount. How could she never have learned these things?

"Let me explain, My Lady." Toma cleared his throat.

In the six kingdoms, famine had never been common. Eris provided much of the grain, wheat, vegetables, and meat to the kingdoms, while Wakefin supplied large amounts of fish. Once upon a time, Dagan had assisted in such matters. In exchange for these services, Salander always provided ample wood throughout the kingdoms. Most of their land was covered in forest, which made this a lucrative trade for them.

For these goods, Rythern always exchanged stones, from rubies to diamonds. Many sorts of metals could be found throughout their mines, nestled into the mountains bordering the kingdoms to the north and east.

This she knew, but she never realized that most of their income came from these mines. The cold of Rythern made it difficult to harvest many crops, but cow farms were common in the flatlands. Those lands could very well be their saving grace. Calisa was the only kingdom with no ample supply of any goods. They dabbled in mines, wheat farms, fishing, raising cattle, and deforestation, but they had none of these in abundance, only enough to support their own people.

After a long explanation, Haven couldn't help but sigh. Surely there would be more options than this.

"If I am to understand this correctly…" She paused. "The end of summer is upon us, and come the winter, we will only be able to supply what cattle we have to the people."

"We do have large rice stores, My Lady," one of her advisers interjected.

"And wheat stores as well," another added.

Her eyebrows rose hopefully. "Will it be enough?"

No one answered.

Her heart fell. "Will this be enough to feed our people and the refugees flooding my city?"

A deep silence settled in the study. Haven met Toma's gaze. The creases of his aged face sank, especially around his eyes.

"It will not, My Queen," he said.

Haven sat back, gripping her desk for support. If she couldn't even feed her own people, how could she expect them to fight for her if the time came? How could she expect them to go to war if Salander needed them? How could she expect any more of them than she did herself?

"What can be done?" she asked.

"We can ration." Toma's usual certainty didn't back his words.

"How?"

"We could create a team to see to it." Toma ran his fingers along the sides of his face as he thought. "They could investigate what can be gathered from the fields, the cattle, the stores. We'd have to estimate a number as well, which they could assist with."

"A number of what?"

"The number of people, My Queen. We have refugees on their way from Eris, and many still remain from Wakefin. We need to know how many people we will be feeding this winter."

Haven nodded. "See to it. I want a full report two days from now." Then she took her leave, fleeing the stifling uncertainty of her study. She didn't know where she was going, but she needed to think.

Malka trailed a few steps behind her.

Where do I to go from here? Haven wondered. *If Salander is attacked, should I interfere? If we cannot afford to keep all of these refugees, can I really turn them away? If my people starve this winter, will it be my fault? How am I expected to rule a kingdom I'm only beginning to understand?*

Her pace quickened as frustration licked her heels. Haven was lost in a whirlwind of her own thoughts when voices broke through her reverie.

"Eris has fallen? I can't believe it!"

Haven stopped in her tracks. Young girls whispered down the adjacent hall, huddled by a window streaming golden afternoon light.

"Who will be next? Would Kadia come for Salander?"

"But that means—"

"Rythern would be next."

"Blue skies, I can't believe that. This war is nonsense."

"But it is still war, Anna."

"I heard that people are fleeing into the mountains. Maybe it's not such a bad idea."

"We'd freeze to death!"

"Not west of Salander. They have hot springs in the caves. We could survive."

"But what of the natives?"

"What of the castle?"

"What of our lives? Will we risk ourselves staying here? Our families?"

Her chest burned with anger. Haven had had enough. She walked swiftly toward the three gossiping maids, and they finally noticed their queen. Wide eyes met hers as she halted before them.

"What do you speak of?"

"Apologies, My Queen." They bowed.

"I will not have you gossiping like hens in my halls. Escaping into the mountains would be suicide with winter on its way. Rythern will survive as it always has. Away with you. Back to your duties."

The three apologized and scuttled away, leaving only the faint scent of perfume in their wake.

"Madness, Malka. This is utter madness."

"It is, My Lady." Malka's brow furrowed. She twisted her lip between her teeth. "I fear this will become a common string of thought if things get much worse."

"It mustn't. I will not allow it. They will be dead before Kadia's army even arrives." Frustration boiled inside her. "They are right though. War is upon us, and I don't know how long we will be able to protect them." She continued down the hallway. "I must learn to fight, Malka, and I must learn *now.*"

Haven swept through the crowd and entered the courtyard-turned-sword-academy. The beginners continued the basics of defense with Lareina, while Blythe moved the advanced students on to single combat with the guards. They practiced without shields.

Blythe met her gaze as she entered. "My Lady." Her concern was obvious in the firm line of her lips and the flicker of her gaze. She glanced between Malka and the young queen.

"Blythe, what did I miss?"

"Are you sure now is the best time—"

"Of course. There is no time for pause. I must learn to fight properly before the war comes." Haven unsheathed her sword.

Blythe hesitated. "Very well." She motioned to a guard leaning against the wall.

The young man's cocky smile disappeared the moment Blythe motioned him to Haven.

"Eli, unsheathe your sword. You will be dueling the queen."

All color drained from his olive skin. "You cannot be serious, Blythe!" he nearly shouted, staring wide-eyed at Haven.

"She is quite serious," Haven cut in. She circled to an empty area of the floor before dropping into her defensive stance. "Get ready."

The young man obeyed.

Blythe and Malka exchanged a look and then backed away from the two.

"Ready?" Blythe asked.

"Ready," they answered.

"Fight!"

Eli dropped into a familiar offensive stance, holding his sword with the ease of a well-trained soldier. Haven paused. She needed to recall her training. In the case of no shield, her best advantage was her speed. Being small had its advantages. She might have lacked strength, but if she was quick enough, she could easily subdue an opponent.

Trying to keep that in mind, Haven dodged Eli's first blow. His sword sailed past her shoulder before she swung her counter strike. Eli's blade slammed against hers.

He pushed her back with ease. Haven flew off her feet and onto her behind. She blinked in surprise. He was strong. She needed to keep up. Haven leapt to her feet.

"Continue." She swung at her opponent.

"Remember your footing, My Queen," Blythe called to her.

Haven nodded and adjusted her footing. *Remember your training.*

Eli swung again. Haven stepped aside and dove for his torso. The young soldier blocked again. Their swords *shing*ed against one another. Again, he pushed back. Haven dug her heels in. She wouldn't be sent to the floor again. Not this time.

She spun, her blade slicing for his chest as she'd been taught. Eli leapt from reach—faster than she expected. The tip of her blade swung clear. She spun again. His sword slammed against hers once more.

Their routine continued for quite some time—blow after blow, dodge after dodge. Haven was only knocked off her feet a few times when Eli surprised her with his strength. Each time, she made note of her mistake and continued. She wouldn't be swayed so easily. As their fight continued, Eli grew more confident in his swings, maybe aware that his opponent wasn't completely useless.

His blade shot out faster and harder, his speed and accuracy surprising the breath from her lungs. Sweat dripped down her temples as she struggled to keep up while still trying to keep her lessons in mind.

Eli thrust his blade at her belly. She jumped back. He brought his sword down upon her. Haven raised her arm as if she had her shield. Eli must have pulled back at the last second, because she was surprised to find she still had her arm.

"Haven!" Blythe gasped.

Pain exploded through her arm, through her muscles, and down to her bones. She cried out, collapsing to her knees, cradling her arm in her opposite hand. Her sword clanged against the stone floor. Blood poured down her arm and into her lap. It seeped across the floor. Her sharp breaths filled the sudden silence in the courtyard. All she could see was blood. All she could feel was pain. Haven cried out again, and this seemed to return people to their senses.

Footsteps flew across the floor in a rush of boots. Malka and Lareina kneeled by her side. How the blond healer had darted across the courtyard so fast, she couldn't be sure.

"Haven, let me see it." Lareina pried at Haven's fingers, but Haven just shook her head. "You're bleeding a lot. Please let me see."

The clang of another sword hitting stone brought her out of her daze. She blinked away the haze lying heavily on her brain. Past Lareina's shoulder, Blythe held Eli up against the wall by his neck. Her fingers squeezed around the young man's throat.

"How dare you harm the queen!" Blythe shouted. Her voice echoed in the hollow space.

Eli spluttered, wide-eyed. He didn't struggle for release, only stared at the queen's bloody arm. "I-I—" the boy tried to speak, but Blythe's hold cut him off.

"Blythe!" Haven gasped. She stood quickly. Pain coursed through her arm once more. "What are you doing? He didn't mean to strike me!" Panic seared her throat. Would Blythe hurt this boy just because he'd accidentally wounded her? She would heal any minute and be fine by tomorrow. "Blythe, unhand him *this minute!*"

Blythe didn't release him.

Haven held her bloody arm up. Her heart pounded in her ears. "It's already healing, see? I'm fine!" Tears stung her eyes.

Blythe didn't move.

"Release him *now*! That's an order!"

Blythe froze. Her shoulders stiffened, but her grip loosened. Eli slid to the floor, gasping for breath.

"I-I'm sorry," Blythe stammered. Her eyes widened as she glanced from Eli to the queen. "I don't know what came over me."

"It's okay," Haven motioned her over.

Blythe came to her.

Haven enfolded her in her arms. "It's okay, Blythe. You didn't mean it. You were just worried for me, but I'm fine. It's okay. I promise." She stroked the woman's hair with her clean hand. The pain dulled. Her flesh ached, but other than her sudden lightheadedness, she was fine.

After a few moments, Blythe pulled herself together, thanking her queen and stepping from her embrace. Her brown eyes darkened with the deed she'd nearly done. Blythe checked on Eli before leaving the courtyard.

Haven stared after her, sadness piercing her heart more painfully than the sword. Lareina brushed her elbow. She glanced at her friend. The blonde motioned to her arm. Haven simply nodded and extended her injured forearm, which was bathed in red.

Lareina used a cloth to wipe away the blood. She gasped. Her wound had already sealed.

"Your ability to heal always astonishes me still, My Queen."

Haven was too distracted to answer. Her mind swirled with uncertainty as she stared at the archway to the courtyard. Malka shifted from foot to foot on her other side. Haven glanced back and found Malka staring longingly at the arch.

"Go to her, Malka."

The archer turned to Haven. Malka's eyes watered under raised eyebrows. She nodded, giving the queen a look that said more than words. She was grateful to Haven for understanding—and for much more than that.

Nodding, Malka took off.

"You're okay, My Lady?"

Haven turned to Eli, who had finally risen to his feet. He didn't look so confident anymore. His once cocky smile had twisted into a terrible frown, washing his handsome face in shame.

Haven smiled and extended her arm. A bright-red gash extended across the olive skin of her forearm. But the once deep wound had closed.

"I'm fine, Eli. Please do not trouble yourself. It was my mistake. I was caught in the moment and forgot I had no shield to stop your blade. No harm done."

Eli smiled a little. "I'm glad you're okay." After bowing, he took his leave.

"We should get you to your chambers, My Lady," Lareina said.

"That sounds wonderful, Lareina."

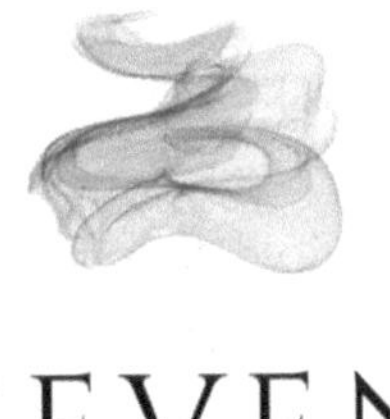

SEVEN

$\mathcal{A}$top her favorite horse, Haven climbed the narrow path behind Toma to the Calisan meeting place. After the taking of Ryulung, Toma had received word to meet the other royals. As the situation grew more and more bleak, her dread only burned hotter. What would come of this meeting? Had Alton been found? Was Dessa still in the safe hands of its King?

"I believe we are the first to arrive," Toma called back.

"You're right." Haven pulled up on Wren's reins.

He huffed softly in the cool night air, his hot breath fogging beneath the starlight. The familiar sounds of horses grazing didn't occupy the dark space. Nikolai was nowhere to be found.

"We must be earlier than I thought." Haven dismounted, her glove-less fingers tightening around the leather reins.

Though stars lit the sky and bathed the earth in cold light, shadows reigned on the mountainside. Where was the post Nikolai always tied their horses to?

A post shadowed by the mountain dug into the earth beside the steep incline near the edge of the cliff. She made her way toward it before tying Wren to the post beside Toma's mare. They grazed quietly while Toma found the tunnel entrance.

"This way, Lady Queen."

"Haven," she corrected.

"Lady Haven." Toma cleared his throat, bringing a smile to her face.

She followed Toma into the darkness, stretching her fingers out to trail along the smooth walls. Cold rock met her fingertips and guided her around the first corner. The soft glow of torchlight ahead promised a greater cavern.

She quirked an eyebrow. Someone must have arrived already if the torches had been lit. Ominous shadows climbed the walls of the tunnel, dispersing by the cave entrance. Torchlight flickered throughout the hollow room, illuminating the council table and the surrounding chairs.

Haven stepped inside. Toma froze. The soft *shing* of Toma's sword broke the silence.

"Get back, Haven!"

"Toma?" she gasped as he pushed her back into the tunnel. "What is it?"

She looked over his shoulder. Blood. Her stomach clenched, and her eyes widened.

Red ran across the floor and soaked the walls. Blood poured from the meeting table, atop which lay a severed head.

"Nikolai!" she cried. Her breath fled her lungs.

Though his eyes had been gouged from his head and his jaw broken, his tan skin and his short stubble were easily recognized. Inside his open mouth was a red rose. Her heart leapt. She had hoped she'd never see one again.

Haven backed into the corridor until her heels met rock. The metallic bite in the air assaulted her nostrils, squirming its way down into her stomach. Nausea rose inside her. A halo of roses surrounded Nikolai's head. Their petals mingled with the spray of blood across the floor.

Toma spun, grabbing Haven's arm and yanking her back down the tunnel. Her feet moved mechanically, her heart pounding loudly in her ears.

Nikolai. Who could have done something so horrible to such a sweet man?

The tunnel disappeared to open sky. She gasped in air. Copper fled her nostrils, giving her room for fresh air. She doubled over, one hand on her knee, the other on the mountainside. Her whole body trembled.

"Lady Queen?"

Haven glanced up. King Evander dismounted his white stallion.

"Do not go inside!" she cried. "Do not enter that place!"

"What are you talking about, Lady Queen? What has happened?" Evander approached, glancing from her to Toma, who leaned against his mare for support.

Evander offered his hand, which Haven gladly took. He helped her across the flatland to her own horse. She embraced Wren's thick neck, clasping his course hair between her fingers.

"Tell me what's happened," Evander said.

"Nikolai." Haven shook her head. Though she'd been trying to push the image from her mind, blood still flashed behind her closed lids. She took another breath. She would not vomit. Not in front of a king. "He's dead."

"*What?*" Evander gasped. "How can that be?"

Haven shivered. "The roses."

"Roses?"

"The man on the pike. He had a rose in his mouth too."

Evander stilled. His eyes widened as he gazed at the entrance to the cavern. "This must be Kadia's doing."

"We can't be sure of that," Toma said. His voice rose higher, but he no longer slouched against his mare.

"Who else would kill Nikolai?"

Haven pretended not to notice the catch in the elderly king's voice.

"I don't know," Toma admitted.

They lapsed into silence, taking a few moments to grieve their fallen comrade. Emeril soon arrived, the clop of his horse warning of his arrival.

Toma quickly explained the situation. Before they could recover from the incident once again, Evander led them down the mountainside. Her heart fell with each step. A heavy lump settled in her gut, weighing her down.

No one spoke a word until they met the Wakefin envoy at the base of the path. Once again, they explained quickly, all too aware that, if Kadia was behind this, the evil queen could still be nearby.

Toma offered to move the meeting—as if a change of scenery would help Haven forget Nikolai's mangled head. She simply shrugged her agreement.

The party set off for Rythern.

In a small, abandoned mill near the Calisan border, the royals found a safe place to meet. The mill was quiet. The air was stale and damp, but it would do. Emeril and one of his guards pulled a table to the center of the dust-laden floor while Evander's guards set up enough seats for the royals. Their group seemed much smaller than usual, even though they were absent only one.

King Alton of Eris was still missing, Evander confirmed once they had all settled. The loss was like the shadows on the wall, speaking of dark things to come. King Corrin had sent an adviser in his stead. The retaking of Wakefin was far too recent, leaving two large personalities absent this night.

"I think we ought to start this night anew. Well met, Lord Prince, Lady Queen," King Evander began. His gaze settled on Alton's empty seat before moving to the newcomer. "And you, adviser. What can we call you?"

"Well met, Lord King," said the man, a short fellow with graying orange hair. "You may call me Del."

They greeted each other appropriately before silence took over. It was hard to know where to begin when so much had gone wrong.

"If it is all right, I would like to begin."

All gazes fell on the newcomer, Del. Evander nodded and motioned for him to proceed.

Del took a deep breath. "King Corrin wishes that I explain to you what his spies have seen." He swallowed audibly. "These things I tell you only because my king demands it. During the taking of Eris, there were finally reliable eyes to tell the tale of the battle." Del launched into a long story of shadows turning into soldiers.

These creatures slew soldier after soldier, effortlessly taking each small village. They pillaged and ransacked their way to the capital of Ryulung before decimating Alton's castle, led all the while by Queen Kadia.

This truly was the most disturbing news. Often, monarchs stood back in their castles and waited for their armies to conquer. In this case, the insane queen was leading her army of darkness through the lands, watching as each village was taken. It was a brash move, and surely it could only mean the worst. Del went on to describe the size of these armies, which fluctuated anywhere between hundreds for a small village to thousands at the castle. It seemed Kadia could somehow manipulate them, creating more or less as she pleased.

"This has to be some sort of trick," Emeril said.

"Or black magic," Evander agreed.

Haven stayed quiet. If she were a normal girl, she'd have had to agree with them. It had to be a ludicrous trick, well planned and executed on Kadia's part. But Haven wasn't a normal girl. Her fight with Eli had proved it once again. Though she had been gravely injured, her wounds had healed in minutes. If she could heal at such an insane rate, who was to say someone else couldn't manipulate shadows. She had to at least consider the possibility.

"We don't know how she does it," Del continued. "But it's nearly impossible to get to her through those armies. Many of Alton's warriors tried."

Her heart ached. They all observed a moment of silence for the fallen soldiers, for Alton's loss, and for Nikolai. Even though the Eris king was not present, it was the respectful thing to do.

After the moment had passed, Haven exchanged a look with her adviser. This was good intelligence on Corrin's part, but it did nothing to help their cause. It was finally time to voice her opinion to the others.

"I think it is nearly time to make a decision, Lord King, Lord Prince." Haven gulped.

Emeril gave her a curious look, and the others rested their attention on her.

"I do not wish to put my people at risk, as I'm sure neither of you do."

They nodded.

"Then we have to decide. Fight or flight. With Eris under siege so soon after Wakefin, we can only assume Kadia's mission is to take all of our kingdoms. It's only a matter of time before one of us is next." Haven paused. *Let it not be Salander.*

If Salander fell, Rythern would be next.

"Where could we run?" Del asked. "With that many people? We'd be mad to try to flee into the mountains."

"I will not have my people live in those mountains," Haven snapped.

"Then where?"

Evander interrupted. "The only place we can go."

All eyes fell on the elderly king. He was the oldest of the group, even with Toma present. She hoped he was also the wisest.

"Seaburn."

"You cannot be serious!" Del gasped.

Evander turned his harsh gaze to the young adviser. "It is the only place we can escape to. We could go across the sea or under it. We could regroup and take our people to Seaburn. They would be safe there."

"The Seaburn armies," Emeril gasped. "We could ask for the council's help. Maybe they will lend their armies to us. I've heard incredible things of their prowess. Surely we could take on Kadia with their aid."

Her lips twitched into a small smile. Though getting their people to Seaburn could prove quite dangerous, she was glad they were at least considering it an option.

"Surely we could," she agreed.

"Then a decision must be made by our entire council. We must decide to stay or go." Evander paused, most likely to let the weight of his words sink in. He knew as well as they this was not an easy decision to make.

The journey to Seaburn would be difficult, but it would be worth it if they could save even a portion of their people. If they stayed and fought, the outcome was uncertain. Either they would fight and win or, if the stories about Kadia were true, they would lose and their people would fall under Kadia's reign. Haven shivered.

She could never let that happen.

"We will decide in a week's time." Evander sat back in his chair. "Please take your time to think through your decision." He took a deep breath, pausing before his next question. "Now, what news is there of King Alton?"

Haven glanced at Del. Seemingly the master of spies, he was the only one who could have this information.

"I don't know." He avoided their gazes. "The spies have searched and searched, but he is nowhere to be found."

"What of his children? His wife?" Haven asked.

Del met her gaze. His eyes widened, and the inner corners of his eyebrows rose. Dismay. Her heart plummeted.

"No. You can't mean..." Her fingers covered her mouth.

Del shook his head.

"They were so young," she said.

Alton had three sons and a beautiful wife. His boys ranged in age from eight to sixteen. She couldn't imagine what monsters would take their lives.

"Blue skies embrace them," Evander murmured.

"Blue skies embrace them," the others echoed.

"Keep searching for King Alton," Evander said. "If he is alive, there could still be hope for Eris."

Del nodded.

"In the meantime," Evander continued, "I assume you both have shared my concerns for food among the kingdoms."

Haven and Emeril exchanged a look.

"Of course you have. With Eris's farmlands up in flames, we need a plan for the winter."

"Yes we do," Haven began. If the kingdoms didn't work together in this, they'd all starve. "I've been working on a plan with my advisers."

"Please, speak."

Haven motioned for Toma to join her in the explanation. "We don't have much, but if Wakefin stays in the hands of Corrin, surely fishing will resume shortly." She glanced at Del for confirmation.

"If things keep going well, then yes," he agreed.

"The fields will be cultivated soon in Rythern, as I imagine they will be in Calisa and Salander."

Both kings nodded.

"Then we must ration what we have for now," she said, "use our cattle as needed, keep our stores full, and hope for the best."

"We'd also like each kingdom to set up teams to fish in the rivers as much as possible," Toma added. "Especially during the migration."

"Yes," Haven agreed. "And, Emeril, if you can send boats off the southern coast, I'm sure they could fish in those waters."

Emeril agreed.

"Then that's really all we have to go on, unfortunately. My advisers have been working out a plan for rationing in our own city," Haven said, "but we wouldn't want to impose upon your own decisions."

"That is plenty, Lady Queen." Evander smiled. "My advisers have been working on a similar plan."

"As have mine," Emeril said.

"Then we are all like-minded," Haven said. She bit the inside of her cheek. She had been hoping for more from Evander. If all they could think of were the same things, she hoped to come up with more before the cold set in.

With nothing more to discuss, the group broke up and vanished into the darkness of night. Haven had hoped for better news, but it all seemed pointless in the end. They had gone around in circles over what she knew very well herself, and with Kadia deep in Eris territory, Salander had to be next.

Haven and Toma rode in silence through the trees. Her breath fogged the chilly air. Her kingdom would soon be at risk, yet she had no idea how to stop this war.

The river roared ahead, drowning out the night crickets and owl hoots. They had reached the bend in the river, where the flowing water turned west, when someone shouted behind them.

Haven glanced over her shoulder, pulling up on Wren's reins. He snorted and halted alongside Toma's mare.

Emeril trotted up to join them. "Haven, may I have a moment of your time?" He anxiously glanced at the surrounding shadows.

Haven nodded. Her gut still twisted from the memory of Nikolai's missing head. The shadows seemed more ominous than ever.

"Of course, Emeril." Haven sent Toma ahead. She dismounted Wren and tied him to a tree.

Emeril did the same with his stallion. Then he led the way between the trees. Only the river broke the silence between them. After several long minutes, a small stream broke the lush forest floor. A fallen tree lay beside it. Haven sat on the fallen log, twisting her a ring around her finger. The moon reflected in the still surface. The stream hardly moved on the flat land.

"I fear my father will die soon."

Haven glanced at Emeril. Her heart fell. "Don't say such things."

"He will if his condition does not improve." Emeril sighed. "He was once such a powerful man. I've looked up to him since I was small. I hoped that, one day, I would be like him, a great king." He shook his head. "But not like this. It is far too soon. I'm not ready to rule a kingdom and be in charge of so many people."

Her lips twisted into a rueful smile. She knew his feeling exactly. Her parents and her brothers had died not long ago, which had left her in charge of a kingdom she barely knew. She was a queen at nineteen, hardly capable of doing anything right. But she continued on, worked hard, and did what she thought was best. She could only hope to be half the queen her mother was. If she could be anything like her father, she would have the love of her people one day.

"Emeril, you will be a great king." Haven gently patted his knee. "Do you think I knew what I was doing when I became queen?"

Emeril smiled.

She laughed. "No, I didn't. I knew nothing of being a queen because I never thought I'd be one. But you, Emeril—you've always known. You've been governing your people for months, and I don't see anyone complaining. You are your father's son."

"Thank you, Haven."

"You don't need to thank me." She smiled. "Thank your father for raising such a wonderful heir. And, if the worst comes to pass, I'm sure you have many advisers."

They both laughed.

"You are a marvel, Haven." Emeril grinned. "If only I had taken my father more seriously when he wished that I marry you."

Heat rose to her cheeks, and her eyes widened. Her laughter ceased.

Emeril glanced at her, a glint of mischief in his eyes. "You didn't know our parents wanted to arrange our marriage?"

She shook her head. "No one told me such a thing!"

"You never wondered why we had so many play dates as children? It's not a quick journey from Salander to Rythern, you know." Emeril's grin continued to grow, as did her shock.

Her heart raced. "I never thought anything of it." She'd been foolish. *So foolish.*

Haven had never met any of the other royal children unless it was at a gathering. She'd never played with them, spent time in their castles, or traveled for days to their capital city. She'd spent half of her childhood with Prince Emeril, certain that they were simply meant to be friends.

"I'm a fool. An utter fool."

"I wouldn't say that, My Lady." Emeril laughed. "But your observation skills leave a little to be desired."

Haven swatted him before she realized what she was doing. It was something she had done as a child, but it was inappropriate at her age. Emeril caught her hand and held it, grinning from ear to ear.

"I'll have you know my observation skills are brilliant," she huffed. Her heart lightened, as if a weight had lifted from her chest.

"If that is so, what was King Evander wearing?"

Haven blanked. "Calisan colors, I'm sure."

"Are you sure?" Emeril doubtfully raised his eyebrows.

Haven sighed. "No."

"He was wearing Calisan colors, but I knew you wouldn't be sure."

Haven hit him again. Inappropriate or not, she couldn't help it. It felt like they were young again, sitting outside, under the moon, sharing a teasing conversation.

"Emeril, you are a fiend." She could no longer tame her smile.

"You've always known that, Lady Haven."

Haven sighed as their laughter came to an end. Relaxing against the tree trunk behind her, she glanced at Emeril from beneath her lashes. "So, why did you not want to marry me?" She couldn't restrain her curiosity a moment longer.

They had always been friends, and they would have made a good match if she weren't queen. Long ago, he never would have known she would one day take the throne. There had to be another reason.

Emeril froze. The joy of their earlier conversation fled him like the tide had washed it all away.

"I'm sorry if I have misspoken, Emeril." Her heart clenched. She wanted her happy, smiling friend back. "Please forgive me, I did not mean to offend or upset you."

Emeril shook his head, avoiding her eyes. "It's not your fault, Haven. It has been some time since I've spoken of her."

Understanding dawned on Haven. There was a *her* involved. A woman had broken his heart.

Haven took his hand. "Will it make you feel better to talk about it?"

Emeril stared at their hands for a long moment, her olive skin against his lightly tanned hand.

She flushed under his intense gaze. "I've never loved someone more than as a friend, but if she makes your face fall like that, something bad must have happened."

Emeril squeezed her hand. "Yes." He paused. "I was with her for a long time. She was *so* beautiful. Everyone wanted her. The way she moved, her hair, those green eyes. She was absolutely hypnotic."

A pang of jealousy struck her heart. Her eyebrows furrowed. Why would she have been jealous of this woman? She twisted her lip between her teeth. She had never known of this woman in the many years she'd been Emeril's friend. It wasn't her jealousy of his feelings for the woman, which so clearly remained, but envy because she could only hope someone would feel like that about her one day. But, even if they did, she wasn't sure she could ever be with him, for if she were, he might expect children of her.

That was something she could not give.

"Keep going." Haven took a deep breath, trying to calm her swirling thoughts.

"She was exotic—from across the sea, she told me. She was so caring in the beginning, so attentive." He sighed. "I loved her for years, but I'm not sure if she returned my feelings for even a moment. I gave her everything she wanted: jewels, money, dresses. None of it satisfied her. As time passed, I wondered how much I really knew about this strange, beautiful woman. But, when I tried to ask, she always turned me away. She became distant, and once, I caught her with another man." His grip on her fingers tightened. "She denied her involvement with him, but I know now that she lied. She fled Salander soon after, and I never saw her again." Emeril hung his head.

Her breath caught in her throat. What was she supposed to say to that? She had never been in a relationship, had never loved a man, and had certainly never thought of what it would be like to feel this hurt. She could only imagine the pain he was in.

"I don't know much about this woman, but it seems to me she is not worthy of you," Haven said. "If she could be with you and even think of betraying you, I'm glad she's gone."

Emeril smiled.

What was he thinking? Was she out of place with her feelings?

"You're probably right. Nakta isn't worth the sorrow I feel anymore." He sat up straight. His smile was clearly faked. Understandably so.

"And she never was."

Emeril nodded. Her gaze returned to the pool of water before them. The moon shone brightly.

What time was it?

Haven stood, releasing his hand. "How long have we been here? I must find Toma. Surely he is worried."

"I'm sure he hasn't gone far."

"I must go." Haven turned to her friend, who stood. "If you need anything, send word."

"Same to you, Lady Queen." Emeril enfolded her in his arms.

Warmth wrapped her like fire, stealing the breath from her lungs. She froze.

"I'm glad you are all right," he said. "When I came up the mountain, I feared something had happened to you."

Heat flooded her cheeks. "I'm fine."

"That's good." He released her. "Goodnight, Haven."

Haven nodded, stepping away in the direction of her horse. "Goodnight, Emeril." She fled through the trees, thoughts of marriage and the future swirling through her head.

THE NEXT DAY, Haven called a meeting of her own. Her advisers and three friends gathered in her study, speaking quietly to one another as she stood behind her desk. She needed to explain the events of the previous night, and she needed help deciding which way to go. Flee or fight. It was a tough decision, but one she had to make.

Haven addressed the group. "I'm glad you all could come."

Recounting the events of last night, Haven and Toma relayed the news of Alton's absence, the decision to be made, and the lack of thoughts on the coming food shortage. Worry creased every face in the room. Such looks sent her heart racing. Nonetheless, she needed to look to them for advice.

"If we fight, many people would die," Lareina said. She twisted her hands at her side, wiping sweat on her trousers.

"They would," Toma said. "But we could remove a tyrant from power and gain peace in the kingdoms."

"If the war goes well," Blythe interjected.

"If the war goes well," Toma agreed.

"If it doesn't, we would use up all of our resources in this war. The people would suffer," a young adviser spoke quietly.

"And, if we try to flee, they could suffer just as much," another adviser said.

"But, if we are to flee to Seaburn, we could take ships, get people to safety quickly and in vast numbers," the first adviser argued.

"It is a long journey to the sea. We have many sick and injured to care for along the way." The second crossed his arms.

"Better they suffer a long journey than death at Kadia's hands."

"Enough," Haven snapped. "I brought you here for advice, not to argue."

"Apologies," they both said.

"I'm swaying heavily toward fleeing to Seaburn. King Evander believes it's the best option as well. I believe we'd have his vote when the council meets next," Haven said. "It would be a hard journey, but a necessary one. If we go to war, hundreds and thousands could die. But, if we use the resources we still have to flee, we may return to fight another day." She paused. Hope welled in her chest. "With the Seaburn armies at our backs."

One of the advisers gasped.

"The armies of Seaburn?" another asked. "I've heard stories of their warriors. They're savages taken from the Southern Lands. How could they be better than our soldiers?"

"They are better trained than our soldiers," Toma said. "They are taken and sent through an academy for years before they join the military. Seaburn has the greatest army in any realm we yet know of. If they were to lend their aid, we would outnumber Kadia by the thousands."

"*If* they were to lend their aid." Blythe was again the voice of reason.

This plan relied heavily on possibilities, but what choice did they really have? Stay and fight only to be slaughtered? Or flee while the coast is clear and come back stronger than ever?

There was really only one option. Even if Seaburn wouldn't lend them warriors, perhaps they could barter or pay for them. The one thing she was certain of? If these were her only options, they would flee to Seaburn.

She would not lead her sheep into the land of wolves.

EIGHT

"I never knew Seaburn used savages in their armies," Haven said.

All eyes fell on the young queen. After the meeting, Haven had returned to her chambers, adjourning to her sitting room along with her guards and her most trusted adviser. Toma sat heavily on a burgundy armchair. He slouched against the velvet, sighing loudly.

"They are hardly savages by the time they join the military," Toma said.

Her eyebrows furrowed. The creases of Toma's face turned downward. His normally olive skin was nearly gray.

"Tell me about this process," Haven urged.

Her guards exchanged looks with each other. Lareina took a seat beside her, while Malka sat at the window and Blythe stood guard at the door.

None seemed keen to answer.

"Well, My Lady." Toma cleared his throat. "From what our sources have told us, Seaburn takes people from the lands south of the Republic and puts them into an academy." He paused. "For all of their great marvels in science, they still abduct young men and women and break them. After they're taken through a cleansing period, they're trained to be superb warriors. The process takes from three to five years or more. Their armies are known far and wide and quite feared across the sea." Toma's face wrinkled in disgust. "They may call those people savages, but the practices of Seaburn are what is savage."

"That's horrible," Haven gasped.

Lareina took her hand to comfort her, but there would be no suppressing the souring of her stomach.

"They take them from their homes and *break* them?"

"Yes, Lady Queen." Toma didn't meet her eyes. He slumped in his chair.

"How do they get away with such a thing?" Haven glanced between her guards, her eyes wide and filled with desperation. "How do they break them?"

Toma froze.

"You don't need to hear such things, Lady Queen." Blythe crossed her arms.

"I will hear of them this moment."

"Haven, really you must not insist on this." Lareina squeezed her hand.

Haven met Lareina's wide gaze. The blue depths of her eyes sparked with sadness and pity. She bit her lip. Lareina knew that whatever this was would break her heart.

If Seaburn and its people were committing such atrocities, she wouldn't want to work with them, let alone use them to fight her battles. Her stomach twisted. Haven clamped her lips shut. If she listened to what these ladies had to say, she would be once again sheltering herself from the world. But, if she didn't, would what they had to say ruin her plans and possibly risk the lives of her people? Or, worse, would it keep them from returning to the kingdoms and taking Rythern back if that day should come?

Haven swallowed the lump forming in her throat. "Fine. Don't tell me, but please distract me with other tales of Seaburn. I wish to hear the good they do instead of the bad. Make me believe I can ask for their aid and not hate myself for it."

Her guards breathed a collective sigh of relief. While her ladies might be relieved, shame bubbled within her. She was choosing the lives of her own people over the lives of others. Even though it wasn't her duty to care for anyone but her own people, the impact of her choice was like a weight against her chest.

Was this the type of queen she would be? One who would save the lives of her own just to let others bear the burden? It wasn't right. But her weakness stopped her from changing her mind. She was queen of Rythern and nowhere else. She had to remember that.

"The Seaburn Council came together to depose the monarchy," Lareina began. "The king at the time was cruel, gorging himself with food and wine while his people suffered and starved. The treasuries remained full, yet he didn't share a penny. Such large sums would have saved the people from starvation, aided in trades, in schools. But he hoarded it for himself." She paused. "As time went on, the people began to riot. One uprising after another turned into a full rebellion. They would have been much more successful earlier on if they had the council backing them. Unfortunately, the council didn't agree with their violent ways and left the rebels to wear themselves out. The king always kept his soldiers happy and at his side for matters such as these. He wasn't a stupid king, only a very greedy one.

"It didn't take long before the rebels ran with tails between their legs into the Southern Lands or across the sea. With the rebels gone, the king grew soft and fat again, content in his position. It was, of course, the perfect time to depose him. It happened swiftly, and none but the nobles could complain. Even they hushed up once the council was ushered in and food returned to the villages. They restructured and changed everything the monarchy had stood for. They held elections in the towns, called them representatives of the council. The king would rot in jail while his city thrived. The only practice the Council kept the same was how the armies were formed." Lareina turned her wary gaze on Haven.

"Traditions die hard," Malka muttered. Her gaze didn't leave the gardens outside.

"Especially in Seaburn," Lareina agreed.

Haven leaned against the backrest of the sofa. The deposition of a monarch didn't seem like such a bad idea if it brought peace to a kingdom. Having a Republic or a democracy would keep out the majority of crazy monarchs like Kadia. Maybe, if the six kingdoms had had their kings deposed long ago, they wouldn't have been facing war at present.

"Tell me of the path to Seaburn." She wanted away from thought of death and turmoil, of deposing kings and queens. She let her mind drift and found that it became stuck in the ballroom with Mirabel. How was Mira doing?

"There are two paths, My Lady," Toma said.

"I know the way across the sea. Tell me of the other." Haven had grown up singing "The Path to Seaburn" but had never fully grasped the words or what they meant. Until now, she had assumed it was a fairy tale drummed up by her mother. Maybe she was wrong.

"The other path"—Lareina shifted uneasily—"isn't a desirable one."

Haven met her blue eyes. Worry filled them.

"I don't wish to take this path, Lareina," Haven said. "I just want to know of it. 'The Path to Seaburn' will not leave my mind."

Lareina sighed in relief and smiled. "Of course, My Lady."

Just like the song, Lareina began by telling how the path went through the trees, across the lands of Salander and Eris. The path was long and dangerous. It curved through forests and across rivers, ending at a strange little building on the very edge of Dagan.

Though the path to Seaburn began in the six kingdoms, which each held a beauty all their own, this path was different. It was quite often described as magical in nature. Not many lived to tell of the crossing. The ones who did went on and on in their ravings. They claimed to have seen great beasts and jungles in the tunnel. Cats twice the size of a person, orange and striped, with huge claws and teeth. In other ravings, they mentioned rooms of glass and mirrors reflecting and refracting light to confuse anyone who entered. It all sounded beautiful though quite mad.

How could such places exist in tunnels under the sea?

"Perhaps the lack of air drove them mad," Haven suggested.

"No one knows for sure, My Lady."

"Hopefully we will never find out." Blythe returned to her post by the door.

Once the tales of the great Republic across the sea had ceased, Haven's thoughts returned to her song. The song quickly led her back to the ballroom and Mirabel. She had promised to visit the young girl. Maybe now was the time.

Haven stood and smoothed her skirts. The others stood with her out of respect.

"I'm going to visit Mirabel," she said.

Toma nodded and took his leave. The rest of her ladies fell into their usual positions, leading her out of her chambers and down the halls to the great ballroom.

The large, wooden doors were ajar. The hum of voices and excited cries of children echoed in the wide chamber. Haven stepped inside. She craned her neck and saw the painted ceiling, with large stained-glass windows in the upper half. It brought her back to a time before war, before famine, long before she was queen.

In those days, they'd had huge gatherings, dances, and costume parties. They had bored her endlessly as a girl, but luckily, she often snuck away with her older brother Marcel. Her heart clenched.

With all the happenings in the kingdoms, she'd hardly thought of her brother in days.

She blinked the images of great gatherings and feasts from her mind, turning back to reality and the refugees before her. If it were possible, they had fit even more into the room. A few Eris-born mingled with the others, their dusty-brown hair and green eyes obvious among all the blond Wakefin refugees.

"Lady Queen!"

Haven turned to the high-pitched voice, a smile pulling at her lips and her thoughts of the past drifting away.

"Mira," Haven cooed as the young girl collided with her skirts and wrapped her arms around her hips. "Have you grown? I swear you were not this tall when last we met."

"I grew an inch!" Mira released the queen and stepped back. Her blue eyes beamed with excitement. "You kept your promise."

"What kind of queen would I be if I didn't?" Haven took Mira's hand.

They walked and talked as they moved through the aisles. All eyes seemed to be on them. Haven stopped every now and then to help an attending physician or lend a cheerful smile. Though Mirabel had been shy when last they'd met, it seemed the young girl could not get enough of the queen or the people of Eris. She ran from cot to cot, telling jokes and recounting the story of when she first met the queen. She even egged Haven on to sing more than a few times, but Haven respectfully declined. The spirits of the recently arrived people of Eris slowly rose with those of the others, and before she knew it, Haven was basking in smiles.

Riding on the happiness of others, she was only more dismayed when a messenger burst through the ballroom doors. The young man was ragged from travel, his hair wind-whipped and his eyes wild. He scanned the crowd until his gaze met Haven's.

"Lady Queen!" He tripped over a few of her people on his way to her.

"Calm yourself," she urged. "What is it?"

The messenger held a letter out. Haven sighed and reached for it. Her fingers stopped inches from the page.

The black seal of Dagan glared back at her.

Haven recoiled. "Who has sent you?"

"This message has been passed through several messengers, My Lady Queen. It has taken several days to reach you," he said. "I don't know the original sender, but it has been passed on with the utmost urgency."

Haven stared at the black seal. Her heart rammed against her ribs. The messenger paused, seeming unsure why she hadn't already taken it already. His hand shook.

"Thank you," she finally said. She held her breath as she took the letter. "You may leave."

The man nodded and bowed before rushing back the way he'd come.

"Are you all right, Lady Queen?" Mirabel tugged on her dress.

Haven took a deep breath to steady herself. "I am, little Mira."

"Are we safe?"

She froze. Her heart plummeted. "Of course." She didn't believe her words for a moment, and it was clear—neither did Mira.

"What is going to happen to us?"

"I don't know," she admitted. "But I will protect you, Mira." She bent to hug the little girl. Her heart swelled. "I will protect all of you."

AFTER BURSTING through the ballroom doors as the messenger had, Haven fled down the hall, tearing the letter open. Her hands shook, and sickness crawled inside her stomach. Anything from Queen Kadia couldn't be good. Would she gloat over her victories? Threaten the fall of Rythern?

Her guard girls swiftly followed her, their steps heavy on the smooth stone floor. Haven read the letter.

Little queen,

It is almost time for us to meet. For weeks, I have been working my way through the kingdoms, and though the time has not yet arrived, it soon will. I can barely contain myself anymore at the thought. You've passed my little test wondrously, and you will be mine. My collection is so stark and barren without you. I'm sure a pretty girl like you will fit in perfectly. I do hope to see you soon.

Now, I feel it is my duty to warn you, little queen, so that you may save your young lover and his father. Salander will burn. Run while you can, or come to their aid. I will set fire to Ithrendel City.

With deepest affection,
Queen Kadia of Dagan

Haven collapsed to her knees. Her tears stained the page.

"Lady Queen!" Lareina gasped and hurried to Haven's side. "Are you feeling all right? What's wrong?"

Haven shook her head and crumpled the page between her hands. Her heart raced. Warmth fled her limbs, leaving a chill in her bones. "I need to send word," she mumbled through her tears.

"Haven." Blythe wrapped an arm around her. "We will do anything you wish. Please, just tell us you're all right." She squeezed Haven's shoulder.

"I need to send word," Haven repeated as she tried to stand.

"Send word to whom?"

"To Salander, to Calisa, to Wakefin—"

"What is happening?" Malka hissed.

They blocked the queen in on all sides to shield her from prying eyes. Though rumors would surely fly over the scene, their only care was for their friend.

"*Kadia,*" Haven said. "This letter is from Kadia." She stood, holding on to her guards for support. She dried her tears on her sleeve before meeting Malka's emerald gaze. "Send word to Salander. An attack comes at once."

The three stared with wide eyes.

"Then Calisa. We may need their aid." Haven paused. "Let Corrin know as well, but he is not the priority. We need to ready the troops. Kadia means to attack Ithrendel City. I pray we aren't too late."

Malka nodded and flew down the hall faster than the winds on the plain.

"The troops, My Lady?" Blythe asked.

"Yes." Haven cleared her throat. She had to get ahold of herself. "We will stand with Emeril and his father. She has gone too far this time." The strangeness of her words seeped back to Haven. They crawled across her skin like a bug, turning her stomach. There was something wrong with those words, something deeper she didn't understand.

Kadia wanted to add Haven to her collection, but her collection of what? And what test did she speak of? Could Kadia have been watching her all along and no one had known?

Haven shivered.

"We will ready your soldiers, Lady Queen," Blythe said.

"Ready only a hundred. I will not leave my city unguarded," Haven added. "We leave at dawn."

NINE

The hooves of one hundred horses beat the cobblestone road leading out of Rythern's capital, Palmyra. Haven set out at dawn with her guards at her sides and a small army at her back. Her thighs ached as she pushed them long and hard, urging them across rivers, through valleys, and over the Salander border. Tall pine trees lined the dirt road, and soon, their thunder emerged in the open. They had hardly crossed the Salander border when a scout spotted smoke up ahead. Haven dug her heels into her stallion's sides, urging Wren forward and increasing their pace as much as possible.

It was nearly evening when the smoke came into full view. Darkness billowed into the cloudy sky. The journey to Ithrendel City typically took several days with regular rest and housing for the night. At the speed with which Haven pushed them, she more than halved that time, arriving at a nearby village before dusk.

"Lady Queen, we must rest the horses," Lareina called from her right, patting her beautiful white mare.

"We cannot rest when Ithrendel is up in flames," Haven snapped, wide-eyed and worried. It was difficult to tear her gaze from the billowing smoke in the distance.

"Look." Malka pointed down the hill.

Haven tore her gaze from the sky. Over the ridge on the other side of the village came the Royal Guard of Salander. Her heart leapt. Haven nudged Wren forward, riding with her guard to meet them. Only about fifty accompanied their prince and their king.

"Emeril!" she shouted.

Emeril's brown hair whipped toward her. He dispersed from the crowd with a soldier by his side. "Haven!"

Haven yanked on her reins, bringing Wren to a halt. She dismounted quickly, as did the prince. He pulled her into an embrace, his warm cheek pressing against her ear. Her breath fled her lungs as he squeezed. After a long moment, he let go. Sad blue-green eyes met hers. The color was striking against his soot-covered face and hair.

"We're too late." Her eyes widened.

Emeril grimaced. "It came so quickly. There wasn't any time." He shook his head, defeated.

Her heart clenched. She glanced back at her guards. "We will proceed."

"What?" Emeril gasped. "The city has already fallen, Haven. There's no saving Ithrendel."

He was right. Smoke and flames rose from the city in the distance. From high on the hill, the entire city was visible, even if it was still far away in the valley. She understood why Emeril thought his city was lost and why his guards would pull him from its ruins. They needed to save the only heir to the throne.

"But there is saving your people." Haven turned back to the prince. "Continue to Rythern. We will send any of your people we can find in the same direction."

"Haven, this is madness. The city is on fire. There's nothing you can do!"

"We will see." She set her jaw and pressed her lips into a firm line. She couldn't be sure if it was cowardice or good sense that drove him from Ithrendel, but her determination would not be squashed. "I must insist you make haste. I will return to Palmyra soon." Haven swung up into her saddle and joined the rest of her soldiers.

Emeril called after her, "Be careful, Haven!"

Haven waved back.

LATE INTO THE NIGHT, Haven and her soldiers arrived at the city. Smoke rose into the dark night sky, and flames licked the edges of the castle walls. As they approached the city, they urged anyone they found toward Rythern. Some listened, while others headed toward the mountains. They hadn't the time to stop all of them.

Haven steered them toward the outer villages. Most had already evacuated, but some clung to the hope that it would rain and the fire would be smothered.

After organizing her soldiers into teams, Haven set them to work. Two larger groups would work their way along the outer villages, helping anyone left to escape the blaze. While these groups worked, another would head into the country and yet another would keep watch for Kadia's soldiers. The last team, which Haven commanded, would head into the city.

"Lady Queen, you really should stay with the outer groups," Blythe said.

"I will stay where I am needed, Blythe." Haven led them over a well-worn bridge and into the large town just outside the main city walls.

Fire fell from the burning debris, setting the nearby homes ablaze. Heat warmed her the closer they got to the city walls. Her men dispersed throughout the homes, checking each structure for anyone left behind.

The crackling of flames rose above the pounding of boots and the clop of hooves on cobblestone. She paused. Her eyebrows furrowed. Over the crackling was something else. Something higher.

Screams.

Her eyes widened, and her fingers tightened around her reins. She whipped the leather and dug her heels into Wren's sides. Her stallion took off running.

There were still people left inside the main city. Inside the walls. She had to help them. Had to free them from their fate. She wouldn't let them all burn alive.

Blythe stopped in front of her, cutting off her path to the city. Wren reared and whinnied. Haven pulled back on her reins and patted Wren's mane to settle him. She glared at her guard.

"I will not allow you into that city, Lady Queen," Blythe snapped. Her brown eyes reflected the fire around them—as well as the determination in her heart.

"I can help them, Blythe."

"At the risk of your own life."

"I cannot die!" Haven shouted. Frustration burned her chest worse than the smoke in her lungs.

"But you *will* suffer if you go in there. You will burn alive!"

"Just like they do!"

"You don't need to save every life, Haven!"

"No, but I will save everyone I can!" Haven pulled back hard on her reins.

Wren reared, kicking his hooves in the air, but Blythe didn't budge. She growled. After turning her horse away, Haven dismounted. Blythe wasn't going to move. She would keep her gaze on the queen at all times for fear she would try something heroic. She'd have to be smart to slip past her guard.

Sighing, Haven handed her reins over to Blythe and trudged into the outer city.

While searching the wreckage for survivors, Haven and her guards dodged burning objects that fell from the sky. They moved from home to home, pulling out anyone they could find. Some had passed out from smoke inhalation, while others were trapped beneath debris.

They had saved nearly a dozen men and women when Haven found herself alone outside yet another house. She glanced at the door. How far could she get before Blythe came after her? Anticipation raced through her limbs. She'd have to find out.

Haven leapt down the street, racing as fast as her feet would carry her. Her boots slapped the cobblestone in time with her heart. Wind whipped in her ears, nearly drowning the shouts behind her. Only a few more blocks and she'd be at the gates. She could do this. She could save them.

The gates were wide open, their wood ablaze. Several wooden pillars had fallen by the entrance, but she could probably jump them. She would do anything to save even one of those crying voices.

A scream erupted from a nearby home. Haven skidded to a halt, nearly slipping onto her side. Her heart leapt. A small burning shape ran from the home. Haven dove forward and slapped the fire. The small shape beneath the cloak collapsed to the ground. Haven went down with it, hissing in pain as she patted the flames out. The orange slowly died out, giving her a moment to catch her breath. She stared at the charred cloak.

Were they dead?

A young boy groaned.

She sighed in relief. Thank the blue skies. Haven turned the boy over. He was maybe twelve, with brown hair and blazing green eyes. His face was streaked with tears and he shook with fear, but he was alive.

"Hush. Don't fret. You'll be fine now." Haven smiled, cradling her hands as they mended.

The boy stared at her fingers with wide eyes as her burned flesh mended itself. "Lady Queen!"

The rush of boots stopped at her back. Lareina kneeled by her side.

Haven shook her off and stood. "I'm fine. Help the boy."

Lareina nodded and kneeled next to the boy.

After a quick assessment, it appeared the boy only suffered from minor burns and bruises. He was dehydrated and coughed like mad, but he was otherwise fine. By the time her diagnosis was finished,

Haven's hands looked as if she'd never touched a thing in her life. No calluses. No scars. Only a small amount of redness remained. The boy continued to stare until she splayed her hands for him. He gasped.

"See? We're both fine." Haven grinned.

The boy continued to stare until another guard arrived to usher him away.

"Haven," Blythe hissed. "Please tell me you were not running toward those gates."

"I heard a scream," Haven lied.

"You saved that boy." Lareina beamed

"Of course I did. Now, we should carry on."

Blythe led them away from the burning gates. Over the next few hours, they saved a few more souls before they came close to Ithrendel's stone walls once more. Every time Haven neared the massive doors, the itch to run past those gates nearly overtook her. Unfortunately, it wouldn't be so easy to get away again under Blythe's suspicious and ever-vigilant gaze.

"*Help!*"

Haven's head whipped in the direction of the city gates.

"Help!" a ragged voice called again.

Haven froze.

"*Please!*" the man cried in agony. "Help me!"

"Do not go toward that voice, Haven," Blythe warned uselessly.

Haven stared at the open gates. Flames crackled over the wood. The hinges creaked under the force of the wind. They would fall soon.

"Help!" the voice called once more, strained and garbled by smoke.

"Haven." Blythe's voice rose an octave. She was supporting an elderly gentleman, leading him from his home. Her hands were full.

Lareina remained inside, and Malka helped Blythe.

Under the man's weight, there was no way they could stop her.

"Haven," Blythe repeated.

"Help! *Please!*" the voice dragged out.

Her heart leapt.

Haven ran. The rows of homes, the shouts of her friends, and the rough stone beneath her all disappeared as she flew across the ground and jumped through the fire.

Her boots slammed against solid ground, jarring her legs. She glanced back and forth, covering her mouth with her shirt. Thick smoke assaulted nostrils. Her eyes stung.

Keeping low to the ground, Haven called out. "Where are you?" She waited for an answer.

The desolate cobblestone street had once been home to dozens of merchants. Now, only charred remains were left.

"Blue skies, thank you! I'm here!"

Haven followed the voice to the left of the gates. Just inside the city walls, two stations for soldiers were completely ablaze. She sucked in a breath. She could do this. She just needed to have courage. Heat bathed her face as she approached the door.

"Stay clear of the door!" she shouted.

Haven lifted her foot and kicked the door. It creaked but didn't collapse the way she had hoped. Trying to remember her lessons on hand-to-hand combat, Haven reset her balance to put all of her weight behind the kick.

"I'm coming in!" She kicked again, once, twice, three times.

The third time was the charm. The door fell free.

Finally. Haven stepped over the door. Flames licked her boots. The large main room had many beams and pieces of roof scattered across it. From the back room came a cry of pain.

"Hurry!" the voice groaned.

Dodging between debris and fire, Haven crossed the room. A smaller space led to a staircase headed up to the second floor. It must have gone all the way up to the outpost on the wall.

At the bottom of the stairs, a man was caught with one leg through a step and the rest of his body bent forward at an awkward angle. Stuck beneath a burning beam from the ceiling, he could hardly look up.

The building moaned above them.

"You came," he gasped. His cheek pressed against the worn wood of the floor. A few inches of clear air hovered above the boards, just high enough for him to breathe freely.

"Of course," she said.

His leg had to be broken at the knee, or else such a position wouldn't be possible. How was she supposed to get him out of there? Fire danced across the broken beam, biting at the metal armor on his back. He must have been a soldier, probably the city guard from the night before.

"It came so suddenly." He tried to glance up, but she was sure all he saw were her shins.

Haven nodded. She needed to get the beam off of him. Gripping it with her hands, she tried to raise it.

"What are you doing?" he barked. "You'll burn your hands off before you've saved me!"

"No, I won't." Haven put all of her strength into moving the beam. It fell back some, rolling onto its other side, but it didn't clear his entire body. "What came suddenly? The fire?"

"You're mad!" he gasped, struggling for freedom. He bit down on his lip as the pain grew to be too much. He'd have a hard time getting that leg out unless she could get the beam off him. "Yes, the fire," he said. "It should have been impossible, but when I came for the shift change, the gates were open."

"They were open?" She paused.

"All the way. The only way that could happen was if someone left them open from the inside."

"A traitor?"

"Maybe," he coughed.

That wasn't good.

"Wait here." Haven dashed into the next room.

"No!" he cried. "Don't leave me!"

Haven paused in the outer room. She needed to find a sturdy enough plank of wood, preferably one that had yet to catch fire. She scanned the room. There.

A long plank was stuck between two fallen tables. It was only a few inches thick, but it'd have to do. Haven returned to the staircase. Her wounded hands had already healed by the time she returned.

"I'm not going to leave you," she whispered, propping the plank under the beam before she heaved.

"Blue skies, I thought I would die here."

Pushing as hard as she could, Haven tried to dislodge the beam. If this had happened a few months ago, this man would have been a goner. She had been weak and useless before, but now, she was strong. Using every ounce of her weight and strength, she pushed on the plank. After several shoves, the beam fell from his back.

Haven collapsed onto the floor in front of him. She caught her breath for a moment before pulling his arm over her shoulders. She stood, bringing him with her. Putting all of his weight on his good leg, the man winced before coughing as he inhaled smoke. Her lungs burned as she pulled him from the building and onto the street.

The weight of a horse leaned against her, nearly knocking her off-balance at every turn. She ground her teeth as they worked together to move across the street and back to the gates.

A large wooden beam as thick as her waist lay across their path. She needed a way across it. Flames pooled on either side of the gates. There was no other way out. They had to go over the beam. Haven steered to an area where the flames weren't as high.

"This is our best bet," she mumbled through her shirt. "Go quickly." After ripping her cloak from her back, Haven laid it over the fire.

The man staggered and limped as best he could, leaning against the beam and swinging his legs over. He'd just cleared the beam when helping hands pulled him to safety.

Her guards. Haven grinned.

"Haven!" The voices of her guards rose above the cracking of wood and fire.

Her head swam, and her eyes watered. Too much smoke. Haven stepped back to make the jump.

Crack.

Her heart leapt. She glanced up to the hollow area between the gates.

"Haven, jump!" Blythe called from the other side.

The huge gate doors creaked as the hinges finally gave way. Her eyes flashed wide as the door slowly fell to the ground below. Haven raced for the beam and leapt over the flames before running for her life.

She did not want to find out what being crushed felt like.

"Run!" someone screamed.

Her thighs burned as she pushed herself like she never had before. The snap of wood echoed as the second hinge broke and the door came toppling down.

She leapt free of the door moments before it crashed against the cobblestone.

Haven collapsed into the safety of her guards' arms. They pulled her farther from the gates, chastising her while simultaneously checking her for injuries. Once she was fine, as she always was, Blythe and Lareina lowered her to the ground beside the soldier she had saved. Lareina and another medically trained guard kneeled by his side, bracing his leg.

"You made it," the man coughed. Her paused, his eyebrows furrowing. After a moment, his mouth fell open and his eyes widened. "Lady Queen!" He inhaled audibly before collapsing into a coughing fit.

Haven laughed. "You don't need to call me that. We've been through a lot together." Her bones ached from the stress she had put them through, and the burning in her lungs had just started to subside. "Call me Haven."

"Lady Haven." He continued to stare at her with wide eyes. "I am humbled."

"What is your name?" she asked.

"Thrane, My Lady."

"A lovely name."

"Thank you, Lady Queen." He paused. "How have your hands healed so quickly?"

Her cheeks warmed. "Have you not heard the stories?"

"I have, but I never knew them to be true."

"Now, you know."

"They call you the queen who cannot be killed."

"An accurate a statement as any, Sir Thrane."

* * *

SEVERAL DAYS LATER, Haven returned to her kingdom with hundreds of wounded. The doctors in the city made room as much as they could, but soon, the ballroom and the hospitals were overflowing with Salander refugees. It was a predicament she immediately set her advisers on. Soon, there would be a secret meeting, and she had to be ready.

As Haven walked the halls in search of Emeril, Kadia's words echoed through her mind. She had said that she would set fire to Ithrendel, but she hadn't thought it would happen quite so literally. True to her word, Kadia had set the entire city ablaze in a night. Thousands had been killed.

That vile woman needed to be stopped.

Pausing outside Emeril's chambers, she knocked. A Salander guard opened the door.

"Lady Queen." He bowed and let her through.

"Haven." Emeril breathed a sigh of relief. He crossed from his bedchambers to the sitting room. "Thank the skies you're safe." Then he greeted her with an embrace.

Though she froze once again, it was only for a moment. Haven hugged him back, happy to be comforted after the past few days.

"If an arrow to the heart can't kill me, you really think a small blaze could?" she teased.

"What was I thinking?" He chuckled, but his heart wasn't in it.

In the bedchambers in the inner room, Emeril and Haven sat at his dying father's side. King Brae had lived a long life, which showed in the aged lines of his face. Her heart clenched. His chest rhythmically rose and fell beneath the silk sheets. He was fast asleep.

If the king were to open his eyes, would he have the same beautiful gaze as Emeril? Or was that a gift from his mother? She could no longer remember.

"How long has he been like this?" Haven asked.

King Brae's breaths came in wheezes. His skin was paler than snow, and it possessed a sickly gray tinge.

"Since before the attack." Emeril sighed.

Haven took a moment before answering the young prince. Her eyebrows furrowed. Something about that night bothered her, especially after she recounted the events in her mind. The guard she had saved, Thrane, had spoken of the gates being open from the inside that night. He said that the attack had come quickly, but how had the young prince and the king escaped unscathed?

"Emeril?"

"Yes?"

"How did you escape Ithrendel?"

Emeril paused. The kind of long pause that almost made her suspicious. "A note arrived not long before. We fled in the nick of time. If that letter hadn't arrived, we would both be dead."

"You received my letter in time?"

"Your letter?" Emeril raised an eyebrow. "We received no letter from you, Haven. The note delivered was addressed to me but held no seal or signature."

Strange. A secret note in the middle of the night, helping the king and his only heir to escape just before flames wrapped their castle and licked their pillows. Could this be Kadia's work? Though she had addressed and signed Haven's letter, could she have done something similar for Emeril?

Haven bit the inside of her cheek. Had Queen Kadia saved them for her?

She shivered.

"Are you all right?" Emeril asked.

"Yes," she said. "Just the thought of all those we couldn't save."

Emeril's lips flattened into a grim line. "Word has come from my remaining soldiers. The people of Salander have fled in all directions. Many seek refuge in the mountains."

"That is madness." Her fingers clenched into fists.

"I know, but there's nothing we can do. They flee out of fear because I could not protect them."

Haven placed her hand on his. "You did what you could."

Emeril shook his head and took his hand away. Haven stared at her empty fingers.

"I will go with you to Seaburn." Emeril met her worried gaze.

"You will?"

"What other option do we have?"

TEN

"*K*ing Alton?" Haven gasped.

The aged king sat at the head of the meeting table, slumped against the worn wood. Grief was plain on his face, as was the defeat they all felt. It had been weeks since his disappearance, yet somehow, he'd survived the attack on Ryulung.

"Yes, it is I." The king sighed.

"You're alive." Emeril's surprise mirrored her own.

"Yes."

"But how?"

Alton straightened. The others joined him at the table, taking their new seats. With their old meeting place now unusable, Evander had offered up another in the home of a recently abandoned farmer. The aged king mentioned that they had fled into the mountains, a fact that worried Haven even more.

Lantern light lit the plains of Alton's face. Pain lay in every crease. Alton had aged ten years in only a few weeks. The death of his children and his wife plagued him.

"The night of the attack on Ryulung, my family was killed." His voice broke. His fists shook on the table. "That evil witch killed them. My pregnant wife."

Haven gasped, her hand flying to her lips. Tears sprang to her eyes.

"I found them in our chambers. An assassin had been sent for me, but he killed them in my stead. I wouldn't have survived if my King's Guard hadn't dragged me from the castle." Alton stared at the table.

Silence descended upon the royals. It was one thing to have family killed, but a pregnant wife on top of that? She couldn't fathom what Alton must have been feeling. Being a monarch had never seemed so awful until this moment.

"Lord King." Haven reached forward, her hand on the table. "I am so sorry for your loss."

"There are no words to describe a loss such as this," Evander said.

Alton nodded but didn't look at either of them.

"We will avenge them."

They all turned toward the doors of the farmhouse. Corrin stood in the dining room entrance, outlined by the moonlight filtering in through the large windows. He swept inside, taking a seat beside King Alton. The older man glanced up at the young king, a glimmer of hope in his eyes.

"We must fight back. We must attack Cidra and kill Queen Kadia," Corrin continued.

Haven sat back, shaking her head. She understood Alton's loss, but this need for revenge would accomplish nothing. Though Alton seemed initially interested in the proposal, he was staring at the table again a moment later. He knew as well as they did that no amount of killing or vengeance would bring his family back. He was spent, and he no longer wished to rule, let alone be in this war. Alton would not stand with Corrin any more than the rest of them would.

"Don't be absurd, Corrin." Evander sighed. "We cannot attack Cidra when three kingdoms are in shambles."

"Two kingdoms, Evander," Corrin snapped. "Wakefin is recovering quickly."

"Fine." Evander met the young king's gaze. "But I will not lead my soldiers to slaughter."

Corrin blanked, disbelieving. "How can you say such a thing? What other option is there?"

"Seaburn," Haven spoke up. She didn't want the kings to escalate to blows. "We can go to Seaburn."

"Across the sea? Are you all mad?"

"It's not that far," Emeril said.

"We can make it easily with your ships," Evander added.

"Oh, I see!" Corrin laughed as he stood. The legs of his chair scraped along the floor. "You wish to use *my* ships for this absurd mission of yours?"

"You know it's a good plan. Better than attacking a well-armed enemy."

"Attacking while it is unexpected would give us the advantage!"

"We don't even know if Kadia is in her castle, Corrin."

Corrin reconsidered.

"Even so, if we could show her how it feels to lose her kingdom, surely she will back off from ours," the young king protested.

"Enough of this," Haven snapped. She rested her gaze on Alton.

He slumped farther and farther into his seat, his arms braced on the table. This king was no more ready for war than the rest of them.

"Your kingdom is not what it used to be, Corrin," she said. "Eris and Salander may never be the same. Those are *two* kingdoms in ruin. Our cities are overflowing with their refugees, and we barely have enough resources to keep them all alive, let alone take our people back to war. Many will not survive the winter if we try to attack Cidra. *We* may not even survive."

Corrin dropped back into his seat with a thud. "Why must the beautiful, young queen be the voice of reason?"

Haven blushed.

"You make it much more difficult to argue than Evander," Corrin said.

She fought the smile threatening to take over her face. That was the Corrin she had heard stories about: the confident, womanizing king. Maybe he wasn't so bloodthirsty after all.

"Then you will listen to our proposal?" Haven asked.

Corrin nodded, and Evander quickly launched into the explanation. Evander explained how they would quietly usher their people through the kingdoms, taking them to Wakefin's port. They would board the ships and ride across the sea to the Republic.

"And you all agree to this?" Corrin asked.

Haven and Emeril nodded.

"And you, King Alton?"

The elderly man shrugged and nodded as well.

"Then I suppose I can't go to war by myself."

"We only need to add one more part to our plan," Evander said.

All eyes fell on the proud king.

"We need a distraction if this plan is to work."

Haven agreed. "Yes. Kadia would surely notice if we moved thousands of our people across the kingdoms to Wakefin."

"Precisely," Evander said. "We need a large enough distraction to give us the time we need to move."

"And what do you suggest?" Corrin asked.

"Ironically, young king"—Evander chuckled—"I have to suggest war."

"You're serious?" Corrin snapped.

"Of course I am. I do not take war lightly."

"But isn't the point of fleeing to avoid war?" Emeril raised an eyebrow.

"Yes." Evander met the young prince's gaze. "But we don't need many to distract Kadia. We will stage a retaking of Eris. Then when she is busy on that front, we will also stage an attack on Cidra from Wakefin. This will provide a distraction on two fronts and give us the time we need to flee."

Haven nodded along as he spoke. "It would be a distraction big enough."

"It would, but what of the soldiers left behind?" Emeril asked.

"Boats will be left for them of course. When their commander says it is time to retreat, they shall. They will follow behind us," Evander explained.

"I will stay," Alton said.

"What?" Evander stared at the king.

"I will stay and lead my army."

"You can't be serious."

"I am quite serious, Evander." Alton stood. "I will lead my soldiers so that Kadia does not suspect a thing. We will retreat when the time comes, but I will lead the charge."

"Why?"

"I have nothing left to lose," he said.

"But we will need you in Seaburn," Haven protested.

"You will have enough kings. You don't need another." Alton stepped away from the table. "We will attack in two days' time. You should be ready to move at once."

With that, the once missing king fled the room in a hurry, leaving the others to stare after him.

"I suppose we leave in two days, then," Emeril said.

"I suppose we do," Evander agreed.

"We will be ready," Haven said. "We have to be."

The others agreed.

* * *

THE CLANG of swords echoed throughout the great courtyard.

"Not bad, Lady Queen," Blythe said.

"Thank you." Haven pushed Blythe's sword away.

Haven's final lesson on swordplay had just begun, and the rest of the women in attendance fought with vigor. Word of the evacuation had spread quickly throughout the city, causing some to stand up. Others decided that it was best to flee. People left for the mountains while others ransacked the food stores. Chaos had descended upon her fair city. Her people worried over the lack of food, the long journey ahead, the coming war, and their possible looming demise. But, after the initial upheaval had ceased, Haven had addressed her subjects and told them of the plan, reassuring them they would succeed and survive. This had calmed the rioters and restored some semblance of calm during their final hours.

Blythe struck back at the queen. Haven spun, snapping her sword out. Another clang reverberated down her sword and up her arm.

"Brilliant!" her guard praised.

Haven smiled and struck out again.

In the months leading up to her improvement, Haven never could have guessed she would be able to fight like this. Where once the metal blade had been difficult to hold, she could now wield it as an extension of herself. The weight didn't set her off-balance, and her body had grown strong and free. The familiar routines had become calming, a solace in such times. She would mourn the loss when they fled her castle.

Blythe moved quickly, swinging, spinning, and attempting to push Haven off her feet. Haven jumped back, swinging her own sword. This time, Blythe barely raised her sword in time to block the blow.

"You almost got me!"

They both laughed.

"Almost!" Haven pushed back and lunged forward.

They continued their dance until they both tired. Blythe still over-powered her and the queen lost, but even in defeat, she felt proud.

"This brings our final lesson to an end, ladies," Lareina called through the room. "May your sword guide you and your shield always protect you."

The group gave a small bow and dispersed. It was nearing dinner-time on their last day in Rythern. The women thanked the guards and shook hands before leaving for their homes, where they would ready provisions for the coming days.

"How are preparations coming?" Haven asked as Toma joined them.

Toma beamed at the four girls. "Very well, Lady Queen. Everything should be ready before dawn."

"Excellent."

It had been some time since things had gone quite so well. Haven tried not to worry about what could still go wrong as she left with her friends. They took the stairs to the third floor, where Haven stopped to stare out the large windows. From this high up, Haven could see the gardens, the courtyards, and the fountains throughout their inner walls. Beyond the castle lay the city, and farther beyond, the mountains. The sun was beginning to set, filling the sky with pink.

It was a truly magnificent sight, one Haven savored. It was the last time for a long while she would look at these familiar mountains, see the trees in the distance and the rivers beyond those.

As the sun drew closer to the horizon, the light began to fade. Haven sighed, turning back to her guards. They were all caught up in the masterpiece that was the outside world. Smiling, she cleared her throat to gather their attention. Three sets of eyes met hers.

"We should be going," she said.

Nodding, the little group stepped away. Only a few paces later did Haven realize Lareina hadn't joined them. She turned back. Soft light spilled through the window, casting the blond woman in a golden glow. Lareina squinted into the growing darkness.

"What are you doing, Lareina?" Haven laughed.

A moment passed with no response. Haven joined her friend at the window, unease settling in her stomach.

"What is it?" she asked.

Lareina started and glanced at her queen. then back outside. "I thought I saw something on the walls." She shook her head, dismissing it. "The shadows always move this time of night."

"Dusk does often trick the eye," Toma agreed.

Haven nodded, though she was the one to stay by the window this time. Peering through the glass, she looked for anything unusual about her castle walls. Small turrets rose at each corner. A few soldiers roamed the distant wall next to the gates.

The dim light of dusk spread out over her kingdom, and at first, that was all she saw. But, after a long moment had passed, something dark moved along the edge of the stone outer rim.

"The shadows move," Haven murmured to herself. A memory caught fire inside her mind.

"What was that, Lady Queen?" Toma asked.

"The shadows move," she repeated a bit louder. Her eyes widened. She remembered why this was a terrifying thought. "The shadows move!" Haven spun toward her guards. "Kadia is here. Sound the alarm!"

Understanding dawned on the small group. Blythe raced to the stairs and took them two at a time until she was out of sight. Her shouted orders echoed below.

Malka and Lareina surrounded her, ushering her down the hall. Toma followed, watching the windows as they went. Shifting darkness could only mean Kadia's army had finished with Salander. Her magic had already penetrated their walls, and only now did they notice. Only a few days had gone by since Salander had gone up in flames, and now, her own city could be sent into mayhem at given moment. What were they to do when the enemy was already upon them?

Flee or fight had never seemed a more difficult decision.

ELEVEN

Sitting on her windowsill, Haven kept her gaze glued to the shadows pouring over the castle walls and into the courtyard. As the dark mass fell, it leapt forward onto soldier after soldier, tearing through her warriors with ease.

Unable to think, Haven simply stared, her mind blank with shock. The horror of it all kept her from the quick words exchanged behind her. Only vague murmurs met her ears; their words were lost. Black continued through the courtyard. A young woman screamed and ran. Blood spilled through the streets. Soldier after soldier fell to the blade of a shadowy creature that could not possibly exist. Chaos filled Palmyra and she was locked inside her own castle. What could she possibly do against such madness?

"Haven! Haven!"

Haven glanced at Lareina. Was she speaking to her? She stared dumbfounded at her friend, not sure what Lareina was trying to tell her. Her mind was heavy with fog, her thoughts trickling like molasses. The young queen struggled to move through to her friend's voice.

"Haven, we must flee at once," Lareina said. "The secret passage will get you to safety."

Her personal guards stared expectantly at her, as if they wanted her to do something. Haven blinked and looked back out the window. Blood bathed the southern courtyard. Shadows continued to pour into her home, defiling the only safe place she had ever known.

"Haven, please." Lareina grabbed her shoulders and shook.

Haven looked back at Lareina, but images of blood flashed before her eyes. The last time she'd seen so much blood in the main court-yard was the day her mother had died at her feet. She hadn't been able to save her any more than she could save herself.

"We must go. Please snap out of it!"

"It's no use." Toma sighed. "She's panicking. Grab a travel outfit for the queen. She already has her sword. I have sent for our horses, though I fear they may never arrive."

Lareina dashed into Haven's dressing room.

A fist thudded against her chamber doors. The person did not wait to be let in. Instead, they dove inside with several others behind him. Her advisers filed into the room, followed by Blythe.

"Why are we not moving yet?" Blythe snapped. Her gaze flickered across the room, assessing it to make sure it hadn't been breached.

"Haven is in shock." Malka tilted her head toward the queen.

"In shock?" Blythe looked at Haven. She closed the space between them in a few bounds before bending to face the queen. Blythe slapped her across the face.

Haven blinked rapidly, raising a hand to her face. Her cheek stung and her mind slowly wobbled back to life.

"Get yourself together. Your people need you!"

Haven slowly nodded. She shook her head to clear it. Forgetting about the horror outside as well as the terror in her mind, she stood. "I-I'm sorry. I don't know what came over me."

Lareina returned with a satchel slung over her shoulder. "It's all right, Haven." She gently touched her elbow. "But we have to go *now*."

Nodding, Haven led the way to the secret passage deep within her chambers. Toma stayed at her side. Together, they ushered her advisers, her guards, and any others they came upon through the hidden door and out into the night.

As Toma had feared, their horses were nowhere to be found.

Racing through the trees, they made haste for the nearest village. Alarms rang in her precious capital city. A bell clanged loudly in the night.

"Keep moving!" Blythe urged.

The snap of a branch echoed through the trees. Blythe held a hand up to stop them. Haven froze in her tracks. They all remained quiet and low to the ground.

After waiting a full minute, Blythe finally motioned to the few guards surrounding them. Lareina and Malka remained at Haven's side, while Blythe and three armed guards moved through the brush. Slowly moving from the group, Haven peered through a hole between the trees. A bush rustled beside her and a man jumped forward, his battle cry alerting everyone within a one-mile radius.

Haven rolled back, his sword barely missing. She ripped her sword from its sheath in time to stop his next attack. The grunts of her comrades told her that a fight was raging around her. Lareina and Malka battled assailants of their own while the maids scattered into the trees, screaming in fright. Haven pushed back on her opponent's sword and sliced at his chest. The tip of her blade scraped his armor. She bounced back.

What had she learned about fighting someone with armor? She should stay on the defensive, for one. Haven moved into the familiar stance. She didn't have a shield. The young queen compensated. The weak points in most armor were at the neck and the joints as well as the waist. She'd have enough strength to thrust her sword through the armor if she could get the right angle and force behind the blow.

The man in dark armor advanced. His blade sliced through the air for her head. Haven ducked and spun away. Her speed was her advantage. Beginning her dance, Haven dodged blow after blow, using her sword to block when she could.

She jabbed at his vulnerable points, her blade just missing every time. The man was a good fighter, and he dodged her attacks with ease. His experience would be her undoing if she weren't careful.

Haven faked a blow to the chest. While he moved to block her attack, she spun, bringing her sword back. She ducked into his arm, getting behind him. She pulled back to thrust her sword through his spine. Before her blade could pierce his armor, pain sliced through her leg.

She gasped and bounced from reach. A second attacker emerged from the shadow of a tree. The first man spun around. Her moment was gone, and now, she was injured.

Covering the bleeding wound, Haven glanced between the soldiers. Her friends were busy, and she doubted that her advisers would join this fight. She had to hold these men off until Blythe returned with the other guards. The wound wasn't deep. It'd only take a few minutes to heal. If she pretended the wound was worse than it was, she could hold them off and surprise them when she'd mended.

Haven limped as she circled the two men. They followed, their swords at the ready and their eyes vacant. The second leapt forward. He might have been smaller in stature, but he was just as slow. After blocking his sword, Haven pushed back and ducked behind a tree.

Use your surroundings, she remembered Malka saying.

As an archer, Malka was much more privy to a hide-and-surprise tactic. Haven tried to recall her other advice as the first man embedded his sword in the tree where her head had once been.

Haven rolled from reach, putting weight on her leg to test it. The bleeding had nearly stopped. Another minute or two and she'd make her move. The second man swung at her again while the first pried his blade from the tree. The soldier extended his foot to trip her before slamming his shield into her chest.

That, she hadn't expected.

She crashed to the forest floor, the wind exploding from her lungs. Haven heaved in great lungfuls of air. White dots danced across her vision. No. She couldn't pass out now. Haven raised her sword as she climbed to her feet. She tested her leg again. Perfect.

As the man advanced to deliver the final blow, Haven braced her leg under her and pushed her sword up. Metal grinded in her ears as her sword pierced his arm and found flesh. Blood seeped down her blade as she shoved it deeper.

The man gasped and cried out. He fell back. Haven drew her sword from his body. Blood gushed after it.

Her stomach turned. Pride swelled in her chest, as did dismay. She had killed someone, even if it had been in defense of her own life. Only she couldn't be killed, and these men could.

Had this really been a fair fight?

The brush rustled beside her. Haven spun, raising her sword to defend herself. A blade clanged against hers. Haven stared as Blythe emerged sword first. She sighed in relief

"You took on two opponents?" Blythe couldn't hide her smile.

They both lowered their weapons.

"Well, I tried to." Haven shrugged.

"Very brave."

"It had to be done. Is everyone all right?"

Blythe glanced at the rest of the group. Bodies lay at their feet, all the Dagan enemy. Good. Her people were safe.

"Minor injuries only. Two of the maids have fled, but they couldn't have gone far."

Haven nodded. "Send two guards after them. The rest of us will move on. We will meet them at the village."

"Are you sure it's best to lessen our numbers, Lady Queen?" Blythe asked.

"We'll be fine as long as we don't separate again."

Blythe gave a stiff nod before sending two guards to pursue the girls. Haven prayed that they'd be found soon and not attract any more attention.

With little fuss, the group moved through the trees once more. Blythe pushed Haven to the middle of the group, even after her protests. At least it would give her guards more peace of mind.

A half hour passed before the roar of the river rose above the trees. At last. The village wasn't far now.

They descended a small slope to the last crop of trees outside the river. Haven squinted through the trees. Though the river was nowhere to be found, the dim light of torches broke through the surrounding darkness.

"Wait," she began. "Are there—"

Just as their small group hit the clearing, Blythe splayed her arms and pushed everyone back. Haven ducked behind a tree. In the meadow beyond the tree line, several black-clad soldiers stood in a protective formation. A dozen were spread in a loose ring, all along horses.

Dread crept inside her stomach.

Atop a gorgeous black mare sat a woman of unearthly beauty. Her platinum hair curled all the way down her spine. Even from Haven's spot in the trees, her strong features and striking sky-blue eyes were obvious. With lips as red as rubies and dressed in all black, she had to be Queen Kadia.

"That *witch*." Haven gripped the hilt of her sword.

Fire burned inside her chest. Never had she hated a person more in her life. This woman had killed not only her mother and her father, but her brothers as well. She was the reason her only living relative was hiding away in the mountains. She was the reason her city was being ransacked and her people destroyed. She was responsible for so many deaths, and there she was, just sitting on the outskirts of the city. She had wide smirk on her face—so wide that Haven wondered how hard it would be to cut off her lips. She would have been startled at such a dark thought if it hadn't been for the rage burning through her chest.

This had to end. Now.

Haven stepped from behind the tree. Before anyone could stop her, she had Malka's bow in her hands and an arrow notched.

"Haven, don't!" Lareina gasped.

Haven took aim and let the arrow fly.

Time seemed to slow as Haven watched it go. She hoped her aim was true. If she could avenge her family and all of Warshard, this would all be over.

The arrow missed.

Lodging itself in the ground just behind Kadia's horse, the arrow mocked her. Her eyes widened as Kadia's gaze fell on the young queen. The Evil Queen's eyes grew round—not in shock or terror, but with sick delight. Haven would have recoiled if she hadn't already been being pulled back.

"Lady Queen." Kadia's sultry voice slithered across her skin. The woman breathed her title out like ecstasy filling her flesh.

Fear gripped Haven's heart. What had she done?

Shouts echoed around her. Her guards tore her back so fast that she could do nothing but turn and follow. They raced through the trees, arrows lodging in the ground around them. Cries of pain ascended into the sky.

Haven tripped. Her heart snapped up into her throat. Blythe yanked her right back up. They did not stop. They couldn't. Haven was pushed and pulled, run to her ends as they headed west. The farther they went, the farther away the pounding footsteps behind them dropped off. They had escaped, but at what cost?

After what felt like hours had passed, they stopped in a small clearing with a shallow pond. It reminded her of the night Emeril had told her about his old lover. There was even a fallen tree to sit on.

"We'll rest for a few minutes." Blythe breathed heavily, still catching her breath. She was in full armor, which made the journey even more difficult for her.

Haven glanced around the small group. Each member of the group collapsed in the small clearing. It was far into the night, and they were all tired. Lareina and Malka washed their faces in the pond while Toma sat with one of the other advisers on the fallen log.

Her brow furrowed as she realized something. "We're missing one."

Blythe glanced from beneath her thick bangs. "One of your advisers was shot."

Her eyes widened. "What did you say?"

Blythe couldn't meet her eyes. "He's dead. It ended quickly."

Haven collapsed beside a tree at the edge of the group, staring at the moon's reflection in the pond. Her carelessness and her own bloodlust had killed one of her own, someone who had served her for years and hadn't deserved to die because of her recklessness.

She was once again reminded of the mortality of others. She could be quick in her own decisions, put herself in danger, but she could not put the lives of others at risk. They could die. She could not. Placing her face in her hands, she prayed for forgiveness. She hadn't meant to hurt anyone.

It occurred to her what a hypocrite she was. She had shamed Corrin and Alton for wanting blood and vengeance, while she had taken it upon herself to do the same. At least neither of those kings had gotten anyone killed. Hot tears burned down her cheeks, falling into her palms.

Clutching her fists, she prayed for a better tomorrow, for the end to this war, for the end of bloodshed, and for an age of peace.

A soft hand settled on her shoulder. Haven glanced up. She hadn't expected the blue eyes staring down at her.

"Corrin," she said.

A sad smile spread across his face. The young man sat beside her.

"I was sent word Palmyra needed help."

Haven wiped her eyes, but the tears kept coming. For a moment, she thought her mind had conjured him. She was surprised by her own naivety.

"We did." Haven took an unsteady breath. "We do."

"I'm glad I stayed in Calisa, then." Corrin offered an arm around her.

Never had she expected such gentleness from the king. He'd always seemed like an obnoxious man, but there he was, offering her kindness.

"Do you want to talk about it?" he asked as she relaxed into his shoulder.

"I killed a man," she whispered.

"I'm sure it was in battle. You were defending yourself."

"No, I killed one in battle. But..." she trailed off, taking a deep breath to compose herself. "It's my fault my adviser died. I saw Kadia and I...I couldn't control myself. I shot an arrow at her."

"Did you hit her?"

Haven shook her head.

"It wasn't your fault, you know."

Haven began to protest, but Corrin cut her off.

"You're young and reckless. You can't be hurt, but you don't remember it's not the same for everyone else."

Haven leaned back, staring at him with wide eyes. It was as if he'd read her very thoughts.

"Don't look so surprised. You're easy to read." Corrin squeezed her shoulder.

She settled against his chest, closing her eyes. She was so tired.

"We'll get you through this, Lady Queen. We'll all get through this."

Haven nodded and then found herself accepting the dark embrace of sleep.

TWELVE

The light of dawn peeked over the trees on the Calisan border the next day. With Corrin's entourage, the going was slow, but the protection was worth it. Haven chastised herself again and again for her recklessness while simultaneously recalling where she had fallen asleep late last night. On King Corrin's shoulder. Heat rushed to her cheeks every time. His words of assurance had been kind, but it all had seemed quite embarrassing by morning.

Keeping her distance from the young king, Haven rode alongside her guards. Another fortunate part of Corrin's arrival: he'd brought horses.

"Is something bothering you, Lady Queen?" Lareina asked from her left.

Haven shot a wide-eyed look at her before composing herself. "No, of course not."

An amused smile crept up Lareina's face. The guard hadn't badgered her about Corrin yet, meaning she still had that unpleasantness to look forward to.

"Are you sure?"

"Quite."

Lareina laughed, and once again, silence fell.

The Calisan valleys descended over the hill. Mountains rose on either side, towering up to the clouds, their peaks covered in snow. She'd never ventured into Calisa before. What were the people like? The land inside these valleys?

A man on horseback appeared on the road ahead, riding swiftly toward them. The group froze for a moment before the guards shifted into a protective formation, pushing Haven and Corrin's horses side by side. Haven refused to look at him, keeping her eyes trained on the approaching messenger.

"Stop!" one of Corrin's guards shouted. "State your business."

The man skidded to a halt, yanking on his reins. He caught his breath as he fiddled with his pockets. "I am here"—he breathed heavily —"to deliver a message from King Evander."

Haven steeled herself against exchanging a look with the Wakefin king. Her blood ran cold. What now?

"What is it?" Corrin pushed forward.

Reluctantly, she followed.

"Here." The man thrust a letter out, the Calisan seal unbroken.

Corrin took the letter and snapped the wax seal. Haven tapped her fingers on her thigh as she waited none too patiently. Corrin scanned the page. Warm morning light cast shadows across his angular jaw, which was darkened by stubble. He was more handsome by daylight than in the darkness of caves. Haven swallowed. She needed to get ahold of herself.

His brow furrowed, and his lips twisted into a frown. Dismay took his features over. "No." He glanced up at the messenger, back at the letter, and then at Haven.

"What is it?" A cold spike of fear brought her back to reality.

"Kadia."

"What has she done?"

"She's destroyed my fleet with her darkness." Corrin glanced away. His fist closed on the parchment. "Our way to Seaburn has been blocked. How could she have known of our plan?"

Haven couldn't say. All of their people would have known by now, but they wouldn't have told Kadia's men. Could there be a spy among them? She paused. It would have been fairly easy to find out about their plan if the evil queen had someone within their ranks. Her fingers tightened on her reins. She ushered her horse forward with the tap of her heels. The messenger met her gaze.

"You must hurry back to Evander with a message from us." Haven steeled herself in an attempt to appear confident as all eyes fell on her. "The distraction must continue. The first must begin in three days' time. We will continue to Seaburn without the ships."

"But how?" the man asked.

"We will take the path under the sea. It's the only way."

The man slowly nodded and pulled back on his reins, ready to take off again.

"Wait," Corrin said. "Give word to Evander to send for my people. They are to do the same. We will all meet at the tunnel. He must command my army into the second distraction and meet with us when he can."

The messenger nodded and took off, rocks kicking up beneath his horse's hooves as he disappeared through the trees.

"We must turn south." Corrin faced the others.

Haven agreed, and they turned their party toward Eris.

* * *

TWO DAYS WENT by as their large group traveled along the border of Salander. They moved south through Eris before turning east again, moving through the Southern Lands of Rythern. As they went, Haven and Corrin came upon many of their people as well as refugees from Eris. Their people had fled in all directions, but they gathered those determined to stay with their monarchs.

Before they'd even reached Salander, their party had grown from twenty to nearly a hundred seemingly overnight. These people had no desire to flee to the mountains, only to follow their rulers to safety. They trusted them, even if they had little supplies.

Haven had to stay strong for them. At night, she spoke with the children, and by day, she sat with the injured whenever they paused for a break. She distracted them from their pain as best she could, playing games, singing songs, and telling tales from long ago.

When night descended on the second day, Haven began scouring the camp for Mirabel. Their numbers were growing even still, which made it hard to keep track of the children. Many were orphaned, while others were simply lost. Haven assigned a nurse to keep track of and take care of the orphans, but she still had trouble locating just one.

"Looking for something?"

Haven turned and found Corrin watching her.

"Yes." She smoothed her shirt. "The nurse in charge of the orphan children. I'm looking for a girl."

"I haven't seen any of the nurses tonight, but maybe I can help you find her." Corrin stood from his log by a small fire.

Haven nodded, surprised he wasn't sitting with his guards or by his tent.

Haven continued through camp, trying to ignore her clammy hands and the knot tightening her chest. She couldn't help being embarrassed around someone so unfamiliar who had witnessed her in such a weak moment. She couldn't remember the last time she'd cried around someone she didn't know well. Had she been a little girl the last time? She could no longer remember.

"Who is this girl you're looking for?" Corrin asked.

They weaved through the crowds of people who sat around fires and tents in an attempt to warm themselves.

"She's one of your refugees, actually." Haven smiled. Mira's blond curls and stunning, blue eyes were hard to forget. "Her name is Mirabel."

"And you know her well?" He sounded surprised, but Haven wasn't sure what for.

"Not very well, but I've become fond of her." Haven glanced at the king. His gaze hadn't left her. Her cheeks flushed. "She's a beautiful child who lost her parents. I enjoy her company. She lifts the spirits of everyone around her."

"She sounds wonderful." Corrin smiled, his cheeks dimpling.

Haven quickly looked away. "She was—is!" Haven corrected. "I will find her."

"Of course you will."

They proceeded with their search, Corrin asking her questions about herself or her people every now and then. Haven had never been very good at small talk, and she grew awkward quickly, forgetting to ask him questions in return. The young king didn't seem to mind, nor did he run out of things to ask her. When the moon was high in the sky, he urged her to take a break. They weren't going to find the nurses tonight.

"Why don't you have a seat?" Corrin motioned to an empty log beside an unoccupied fire.

Haven nodded. They had a long journey ahead of them and plenty of time to find Mira. She folded her cloak beneath her as she sat.

"It is a beautiful night." Corrin joined her on the log.

Haven looked at the stars. "Yes, but a cold one."

Corrin laughed. Haven quirked an eyebrow.

"You think you'd be used to the cold, living in Rythern."

Heat rose to her face.

"Not that it's this chilly all the time, I'm sure."

It was Haven's turn to laugh. "Oh, it is. I've honestly just never noticed before."

Corrin looked at her in a way she wasn't familiar with. His eyes smoldered in the light of the fire, flickering flames reflecting across his irises. Everything about him was unfamiliar, and though she didn't sense anything dangerous about him, she couldn't help but be wary.

"You are a very strange woman." He sighed wistfully.

Her eyebrows cinched, and her mouth dropped open.

Corrin laughed. "Not in a bad sense, of course. You're just different from the girls I've known."

Feeling cheeky, Haven smiled. "Most of the girls you know also have large breasts and frequent the beds of many men." She paused. "Or so I hear."

Corrin laughed a very real, very true laugh. He hadn't expected such words from a queen's mouth. "You *might* be right."

Maybe it was the way he'd said it or the way he'd smiled after, but Haven wasn't so sure the rumors were true about the young king.

"Am I?"

Corrin raised an eyebrow. "Are you what?"

"Right."

He smiled and shook his head. "You're a smart girl, Lady Queen."

"Haven," she corrected. Then she froze.

It wasn't appropriate to have a man she barely knew call her by her first name. Even though she'd used his name before, it had been under different circumstances. Still, Haven found herself wishing he'd use her name. There was something different about the young king, something interesting she couldn't quite put her finger on. She wanted to know this man in a way she wasn't quite familiar with.

"Haven," Corrin said as if trying out her name for the first time. "A beautiful name for a beautiful girl."

"Well." Haven blushed. "Thank you." What was she supposed to say to that?

"Call me Corrin, likewise," he said. "I'd like it if we could be friends, Lady Queen."

Haven nodded and stood. "Yes, I would as well."

Corrin stood with her, and for a moment, they were much closer than she had meant to be.

"I should go," she blurted. "My ladies will worry if I don't rejoin them soon."

The young king nodded before bending and giving her a kiss on the forehead. "Goodnight, Lady Haven."

"Goodnight." Haven disappeared back into the safety of camp.

* * *

WHEN DAWN BROKE on the third day, Haven knew they must hurry.

The first distraction would begin soon. They needed to make as much ground as possible before Kadia had spotted them. With Salander, part of Eris, and a good portion of Dagan to cross yet, the distance was more daunting than expected.

They approached the river separating Rythern and Salander, the roar of the water drowning most conversation out. A whisper slowly rose through the crowd, hardly audible about the river.

Haven glanced at the people surrounding her. Something was happening at the front of the line. She dug her heels into the mare's sides, urging her to the front of the group.

She stilled. Her heart leapt. "Emeril!" Haven leapt from her horse, joining the prince and his guard.

"Haven!" Her friend enfolded her in his arms. He squeezed so tightly that she fear he might crush her.

"You're all right," she gasped.

No one had been sure who had escaped Palmyra in time. But there he was. Alive.

"And you." Emeril released her.

"What of your father? How many do you have with you?" she asked.

"Many more than I can count." Emeril chuckled. "And my father is alive but still as he was."

"That is good to hear." Haven paused. "Of the people. Not your father, of course."

"Of course," he agreed. "We have much to discuss, I hear."

"Yes, we do." Corrin dismounted beside them, his boots slamming against the wet grass. His obnoxious smile had returned, as had the cage around her heart. The smile helped her push thoughts of the previous night from her mind.

"King Corrin."

The men exchanged proper greetings before they moved from the crowd.

"I'm surprised to see you," Emeril said.

"I was in Calisa when I heard Rythern was under attack," Corrin explained. "We met with Haven and her party that night. Unfortunately, we were too late to help in Palmyra."

Haven blanched at the callous way he'd said her name. Emeril did as well.

"We did manage to gather a following as we made our way to you," Corrin continued, oblivious to what he'd said. "You have gathered many as well, I see."

Emeril cleared his throat and nodded. "Yes. Many of Rythern's people fled this way. We've assembled a few hundred I believe, maybe more."

"That's good news!" Haven sighed her relief. "Do you have a roster started yet? Who is taking care of the children? How are your supplies?" she asked, bombarding him with questions until Corrin's laughter interrupted her.

"Always the caring one," Corrin said.

Her chest tightened, and she glared at the young king. "Don't presume to know me, Lord King," she snapped. "Emeril, please show me to your nurses. I wish to speak with them at once."

Emeril nodded and led them away, his shoulders relaxing as they left Corrin behind to stare after them.

Normally, Haven wouldn't have reacted in such a way, but she could see what Corrin was doing. He was trying to make Emeril jealous. Why? She couldn't imagine, and she didn't want to, either.

After taking stock of what they had, Haven and Emeril agreed they were well supplied for the journey to Dagan. Under the sea was another story. Haven returned to her tent, taking a seat on the small cot at the back. Her guards joined her, along with Toma and Emeril.

"We will barely make the crossing, I fear," she said.

"We will make it," Emeril assured her.

"I hope so."

"Have you told him the plan?" Toma asked.

"I haven't," Haven said before quickly describing the coming distractions and the journey for the tunnel instead of across the sea.

Emeril froze upon hearing that Corrin's ships had been destroyed, and their present location suddenly made sense. The people had remained along the river for a few days, gathering supplies and readying themselves for the journey. Haven assured her friend that his actions were still warranted, but they had a much shorter distance to travel now.

"It's the only option, isn't it?" Emeril asked.

"Yes," Haven said.

"Then I suppose we should head out today. There is still plenty of light left."

Haven agreed, and together, they dispatched word throughout the colony. They would move through Salander to Eris within the hour.

THIRTEEN

The dense forests of Salander slowed the expedition. Many people dragged trolleys and carts filled with belongings, and the wheels constantly caught on the thick tree roots. Scouts constantly rode back and forth on horseback, telling the queen, the king, and the prince of the people they led as well as anything standing in their path. Many were urged to abandon their carts, but for the many who agreed, there was always an equal number in disagreement.

"Lady Queen, Lord King, Lord Prince." A scout hailed them as he trotted up to the group, breathing heavily. "There is fire in the woods."

"What else can go wrong?" Her heart sank.

"The forest has been set aflame. With no rain, the city still blazes and everything in its path has caught fire," the scout explained. "I'm not sure of its reach yet."

Emeril gaped, clearly dismayed by the news.

Corrin nodded. "Send more scouts, and find its path. We will continue in the meantime. Once its path is determined, we can easily avoid it."

"Let us pray that it doesn't lead us into the flat lands." Emeril groaned.

Haven stayed silent as the scouts took off. The fire was bad news, but she couldn't help but be impressed by how King Corrin had handled it. While Emeril had immediately launched into despair, the young king had stood firm and made not only a quick decision, but a smart one. It made her regret her earlier iciness toward him.

The day wore on, and the scouts returned. The royals were pleased to hear they could easily avoid the fire while remaining hidden in Salander's thick forests. While this was welcome news for the large group, they were still moving far too slowly. The injured and the sick lagged behind while the remaining trolleys fell to the back. Many stopped to help, but there wasn't enough time to constantly lift and readjust their wheels.

She worked her lip between her teeth. What would happen if they didn't get to the tunnel in time? The distractions would have been for nothing.

"Thank the blue skies above," Emeril said.

"Finally, some good news," Haven agreed.

Still, doubt clawed at her insides. They needed to hurry. With only a few days of war for distraction, they still had an entire kingdom to cross.

Corrin rode up beside her. "We aren't moving fast enough"

Haven made a mental note to ask the young king how he constantly read her mind. "You're right. We should have been well into Eris by now."

"The trolleys are slowing us down," Emeril pointed out.

"It isn't just them," Haven began. "It's the people as well."

"What do you propose?"

Haven glanced at the people around her. Mostly guards surrounded the royals, but beyond them were her people and those of Wakefin, Eris, and Salander. Many were tired, with deep-gray rings beneath their eyes. They trudged along as fast as they could, some stumbling over the tree roots.

A Rythern boy with brown hair and eyes, maybe twelve years old, limped by his mother's side. A crudely cut patch shielded his right eye. The woman pushed him as fast as she dared. Her limbs sagged, and her fingers shook.

Haven frowned. How unfair. They didn't have many horses in their troop, but it didn't seem right to continue to ride herself when she was perfectly capable of walking.

"That's it!" Haven leapt from her horse, stopping the guards around her.

"What is it?" Emeril asked.

Her guards muttered protests as she slipped between the horses, but she did not stop.

"Excuse me," Haven said as she approached the mother and child.

They both looked up and then quickly attempted to bow.

Haven waved them off. "Do not trouble yourselves." There was no need for such formalities around Haven. She bent beside the boy to assess the damage to his knee. Linen wrapped two thick sticks on either side of his leg. She couldn't tell how bad it was, but the cast had her imagining the worst. "What happened to your leg?"

The boy stammered, so the mother stepped in.

"Apologies, Lady Queen, I do not mean to slow the troop." Tears sprang to the woman's eyes. "His knee was shattered when he fell in our escape."

"And his eye?"

"One of those monsters." Angry tears slipped down her cheeks.

Her heart clenched. It was her duty to help them.

Haven stepped up to the boy's other side. Then she lifted his arm over her shoulder just as the mother did on his other side. "Please do not fret, and come with me."

The woman stammered out more apologies, but Haven simply led them between the guards and their horses. When they arrived at her empty saddle atop her gray mare, Haven motioned for Blythe's aid.

Blythe dismounted, understanding dawning on her.

"You will take my horse," Haven said. "You shouldn't be walking on that leg."

"No, no, My Lady," the woman said. "We couldn't."

"You can and will." Haven smiled. There would be no arguing with her today. "Please. I only wish to help ease your journey."

After a bit of prodding, the woman finally agreed with tearful thanks. Haven and Blythe helped the boy onto the horse before helping the mother up behind him.

Haven squeezed her hand and nodded goodbye. Before Haven had a chance to rejoin the others, all the guards and the royals among them were dismounting their horses. Haven blinked in surprise, as Corrin was the first to approach an elderly woman and help her onto his horse. Emeril was next, followed by her guards, her advisers, and the rest of the uninjured. Suddenly, guards were moving through the crowd to find the most in need, gently taking them back to their horses and helping them on.

Her heart swelled with pride.

Soon, every horse was ready to go and the troop continued at a much steadier pace.

By NIGHTFALL, they were in Eris. With spirits still high, fires blossomed around camp. Children ran about, and women sang. Haven sat by a particularly large flame, observing a few young girls as they held hands and danced.

Smiling and laughing, they clapped as they round the fire in a circle. Lareina sat by her side, and together, they immersed themselves in the night's festivities. No one knew what tomorrow would bring. No one knew how this journey would end. Her stomach rolled, which stole her smile. As much as she tried to stay in the moment, singing along to the familiar tune, her heart ached and her fingers twitched against her legs, anticipation eating away at her.

"You look like you're enjoying yourself."

Haven glanced up as Corrin sat on her other side. She didn't need to look at Lareina to know a smile had sprung to her face.

"I am." Her stomach knotted.

"Do you want to dance?"

Her eyes widened. "Dance?"

"Yes." Corrin laughed. "Have you never danced before?"

"Well, yes."

"She'd love to." Lareina leaned forward, gently pushing Haven from behind.

Haven glared over her shoulder at Lareina, but it was too late. Corrin had already taken her hand and pulled her to her feet.

"It's so nice of your friend to volunteer you." He grinned, towing her closer to the fire and the dancers.

"Yes, how kind of her." Her tone was flat. Her palms were sweating. Heat coursed through her limbs.

Corrin took her hands and twirled her by the light of the fire. The women watching cheered and the dancing girls giggled. The dancers encircled them, joining hands and in a circle. Her heart leapt, which pulled a laugh from her throat.

Their joy was contagious, pushing the bubbling anxiety away and replacing it with fluttering butterflies inside her belly. Corrin spun her away and back again. His fingers wrapped around her waist, her hips, and her hands as they twisted into different steps. More voices joined the singing, and a few small instruments joined the mix.

Haven laughed and sang, a fog of joy replacing her worries.

"It's nice to see you smile," Corrin said as he pulled her back into his arms. His hot breath brushed her hair from her cheeks.

She'd barely heard him before he twisted her away and back again. Laughter bubbled from her, and she caught his eyes.

"It's nice to enjoy myself for once." She twirled, and he caught her before she fell.

They both laughed and sprang back into the dance, the dancers screeching with delight.

"Haven!" a voice shouted through the song.

Though the music didn't stop and the dancers didn't pause, Corrin swung her back, their chests meeting. He froze mid-dance, her hand in his and one arm wrapped around her. Haven breathed heavily, her brow furrowing as she glanced around the fire. Lareina appeared between two of the dancers, who parted to let her through. Haven stepped out of Corrin's embrace.

"What is it?" Haven brushed her hair behind her ears while she caught her breath.

Lareina took her hand and pulled her from the crowd. Corrin followed.

"It's King Brae," she whispered. "He's dead."

Haven gasped, but Lareina shushed her. She pulled the two royals to a quiet area away from curious ears.

"He's gone," Lareina continued. "Emeril is a wreck. I'm sorry, but he needs you."

Haven nodded, all thoughts of song and dance fleeing her mind. "Take me to him." Forgetting her fun with Corrin—and the man entirely—Haven followed Lareina through camp. Corrin accompanied them to where the dead king lay.

"Prince Emeril, I'm sorry for your loss." Corrin hesitated outside Emeril's ring of guards.

Emeril nodded as he trudged past his soldiers. Haven joined him, and together, they walked between the trees, away from the bustle of camp.

"Emeril, I am so sorry," she said once the songs had faded behind them.

He sat against a tree, placing his face in his hands. Haven couldn't tell if he was crying or not, but she couldn't imagine how he wasn't. She'd been unable to contain herself after the death of her loved ones.

Emeril shook and trembled all over. Haven sat near him, recalling how Corrin had done this for her. She put her arm around the prince. Emeril stiffened for only a moment before leaning toward her.

"He's gone," he muttered into his hands.

"I know." Haven rubbed his shoulder to soothe him.

"My father is dead and I am not ready to be king."

Her heart clenched. "No one is ready to rule a kingdom, Emeril. You will do what's right by your people."

"How can I do what's right when I've already done so much wrong?" He pushed her away, leaving Haven sitting in the dirt alone. He stood and began pacing back and forth. What did that mean?

Tear stains streaked the cheeks of the prince—now king.

"What could you have done wrong, Emeril?" Haven asked.

"Everything!" He angrily gripped his hair.

"Emeril, you aren't even technically king yet." She stood. "You couldn't possibly have done *everything* wrong."

"But I have." He looked back at her. So many emotions swirled inside his blue-green eyes. Despair. Anxiety. Guilt.

She reached out to him and gently touched his arm. "But you haven't. Please be reasonable, Emeril. You will be a great king."

"I will be nothing!" he shouted. "As I am nothing to you!"

Haven stared at him, dumbfounded. "Nothing to me?" She couldn't help but laugh humorlessly. "Emeril, you're my friend. We've known each other since we were children. How could you say that you are nothing to me?"

"Because of him! You barely even know him and you're off dancing and talking in secret," Emeril growled. "He even called you by your first name. The absolute *nerve* of that man!"

"You're jealous?" Haven gasped. "Of Corrin?"

"I want you to be mine, Haven! Why can't you see that?"

Haven stared at Emeril with wide eyes. All of Emeril's talk of Nakta, heartbreak, and how they had once been thought to be married. Had it all been because he had feelings for her? They'd always been there for each other. Had she somehow led him to believe she was interested in him as more than a friend?

"I can't be, Emeril," she whispered. She couldn't look at him. Couldn't believe the words she was hearing.

"Why not?"

"I can't be with anyone."

"You can if you wish." Emeril stepped in front of her, tightly gripping her arms. He held her against the tree.

What was he doing? This wasn't the Emeril she knew. The bark dug into her back painfully. She was so surprised that she forgot to squirm away.

"You can be with me," he said. "You know you want to. We've never been simply friends, Haven."

"We *are* just friends." Her heart raced, pounding in her ears. "Emeril, you're hurting me."

"You cannot be hurt."

Haven met his eyes. She didn't recognize the man she'd always known. "I can be hurt. I cannot be killed, Emeril. Please, let me go."

Emeril shook his head, pushing closer. Haven struggled in his grip, realizing what he meant to do. His fingers tightened on her arms. Before she could stop him or slip away, he kissed her.

Her head spun, and her skin went cold. She tried to yell at him to stop, but he forced his mouth against hers again and again, his tongue slipping between her lips. Tears burned her eyes.

When he finally moved his face from hers, she was crying.

"What's wrong?" he asked, breathless.

"Please stop, Emeril. This isn't you," she whispered. "You're just upset. You don't know what you're doing. You know we can't be together. I don't want children. I don't want a husband. I don't want anyone to have this curse of immortality." Her voice trembled with every word. Tears ran down her cheeks.

"But it isn't a curse, Haven." Emeril pressed his body against hers. "Don't you see?"

Haven turned her face away.

He kissed her neck. "If only I could have given your gift to my father, then Salander wouldn't have burned."

"What?" Haven gasped. She twisted her wrists in an attempt to pull from his grasp.

"She said she would heal him if I just let her have my city. She said he would be all right, that I wouldn't have to be king." He left cold kisses down her neck.

Haven thought he might be crying too, but she refused to look at him. Every inch of her skin burned with discomfort.

"If only that *witch* had kept her word, then Father wouldn't be dead."

Emeril collapsed against her waist, his arms around her hips. He sobbed into her shirt, wet streaks falling onto the dark-red fabric.

Her racing heart stilled. The soreness in her wrists was already dissipating, as were her tears. She breathed deeply in an attempt to collect herself and decipher exactly what Emeril had just confessed.

Emeril had made a deal with someone to heal his father. In exchange for that, Emeril had let that person have Salander. Haven stifled a gasp. Her fingers turned to fists.

He'd made a deal with *Kadia* to heal his father.

In exchange, he'd opened the gates and let her burn Ithrendel to the ground. Haven froze, staring at the crying man before her. Her heart didn't soften at the sight of his boyishly mussed hair or his soft blue-green eyes. It only contracted in disgust. Nausea burned her throat.

How could he be so selfish?

Once his tears stopped and his sobs quieted, Emeril stilled. Haven pulled away, stepping far out of reach. Her skin burned. She felt violated in more ways than one.

Emeril glanced between his hands and Haven. Finally, he saw his mistake.

"Haven." His breath caught. Tears sprang to his eyes again. "I'm so sorry. I didn't mean to—"

"Emeril, enough."

"Please forgive me," he begged.

"Do not ever touch me again." Haven stared him in the eye.

"Haven." He stood.

She stepped away.

Emeril stilled. "Please don't be afraid of me."

"Goodbye, Emeril." Haven turned to take her leave.

"Haven." He didn't follow. "Please, Haven."

She didn't say a word, only continued through the trees and back to the safety of the fire and her guards. Never again would she be alone with Emeril.

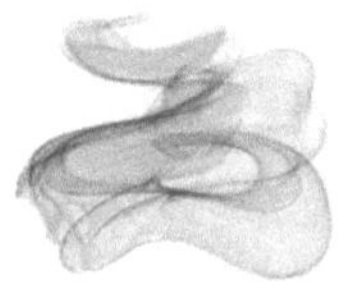

FORTEEN

"*E*meril is here to see you, Lady Queen." Blythe glanced back from the entrance of Haven's tent.

Haven stiffened. Her guards had badgered her all night long about what had transpired between the two, but Haven wasn't ready to discuss it with anyone, let alone her guards. If she told them, Emeril would be lucky to escape with his life.

"I don't wish to see him." Haven pushed her breakfast around on her plate.

She wouldn't tell them of the horrible things Emeril had done—not to save his kingship, but to save his life. He had once been her friend, and though he had ruined that in a few moments of sorrow, she didn't want him to lose his head.

Lareina exchanged a look with Blythe. "Did something happen last night?"

"I just don't want to see him," Haven said.

Blythe relayed the information to Emeril before returning into the tent. "What happened?" her guard asked gruffly, seating herself at the queen's side.

"Nothing," Haven said. "Do not concern yourselves. Only keep him away from me."

"Haven, if he's done something—"

"Nothing has happened!" She took a deep breath. "Just...keep him away. We aren't friends anymore. I don't want him near me."

Lareina laid her fingers on top of Haven's clenched fist. Slowly, she relaxed, and her guards let the matter go.

After finishing her breakfast, Haven stood. "We should get everyone moving."

Her guards agreed, and they all packed up.

WITH THE WORST of the road behind them, it wasn't long before Haven and the others reached the edge of Dagan. Once inside the Evil Queen's kingdom, there was only so much forest left to protect them. They used it discreetly. Haven had the scouts running at all times with updates from ahead. Once their position was solid and their people were left to rest, Haven and Corrin met at the head of the pack to discuss strategy.

It was assumed the first distraction had already been implemented. The attack on the Cidra was imminent, and they had to be ready to run.

"The people will not want to leave anything behind." Corrin sighed.

"They must. Trolleys will only slow us down," Haven said. "This has to be quick. The people must run as if their lives depend on it because they very well might."

Corrin met her gaze and nodded. They both understood what had to be done. They would address their people together. If the distraction came tonight as planned, they would make a run for it. Beforehand, they would let everyone know what to bring and what to leave behind. Speed was paramount if they were to succeed.

"We should address everyone soon, before they get too comfortable," Corrin said.

Haven agreed. They let their advisers know, and soon, the masses were gathered as close as possible to listen to their king and their queen.

"Good evening, everyone." Corrin went first.

Haven stood next to him, her cheeks warm under the gazes of so many. She'd never spoken to so many at once.

"Our escape is imminent." His gaze roamed the crowd. "The next distraction will come at any time, so we must be ready. The tunnel to safety is not far off."

Haven glanced through the trees. The black spires of Kadia's castle were visible over the horizon.

"I know it will be hard, but I must urge you to leave your belongings behind. They will only slow you down."

Before a protest could mount, Haven added, "Take only what you can carry. Provisions for the coming journey would be preferable if we are all to survive."

"We will get through this alive if we stick together and make haste. The sick and wounded will keep the horses to fly quickly over the land," Corrin continued.

Murmurs spread through the group before they could go on. Fear was kindling.

"Soldiers will lead the way in case anything is to come. Do not be frightened." Haven exchanged a look with Corrin before continuing. "While the distraction is underway, we will only have so much time. We won't be able to take the trolleys or carts any farther. Any of the cattle, sheep, birds, or otherwise you have brought should be left behind. I know this may be inconvenient to you, but these things will be returned to you one day. Right now, we need to escape with our lives. That is the priority."

Once a consensus had been reached, Corrin addressed the crowd once more. "We must be ready at a moment's notice. Once you are prepared, please rest, and we will let you know when it is time."

The crowd dispersed and everyone set about their duties. Word quickly trickled through the camp to those who had not been present or too far back to hear.

Before they knew it, dusk was upon them, and the masses were prepared, but the distraction had not yet come.

"What is taking so long?" Corrin muttered. He stared through the trees.

"I don't know," Haven said. The moon had risen not long ago, the stars appearing in the vast night sky.

They were silent for some time. Haven relaxed against the log at the edge of camp. She enjoyed the quiet of Corrin's company. At least she had someone to wait with. They sat together for some time before the silence was broken.

"How did things go with the prince last night? He seemed quite distressed." Corrin asked. He didn't remove his gaze from the horizon, even though the sky had darkened, leaving no trace left of day.

Haven froze and forced herself not to look at him. If he saw her eyes, would he read her again? She didn't want anyone knowing what Emeril had done. It would be treason to harm another Royal. If Emeril was lucky enough to escape alive, he would be exiled from Warshard forever. She couldn't wish that fate on anyone but Kadia.

"Fine," she said after a long pause. "He just needed a friend."

Ever the observant one, Corrin glanced at her. "You seem quite withdrawn from your friend today."

It was true; Haven had gone to all lengths to avoid Emeril. She had blatantly ignored him at times, and she'd even chosen to run when their eyes had met across camp. She wished Corrin hadn't noticed.

"Did something happen?" he asked.

"No," she said quickly. "He was just upset."

Corrin continued to stare at Haven while she avoided his gaze. In this case, she might have made him more suspicious with her lack of eye contact. Thankfully, the young king left it alone.

"I'm worried the distraction has failed," he said.

This time, Haven did look at him. "It couldn't have," she said, though she had been thinking the same thing.

"What if it did?"

They both sat in silence for a few moments.

"If it did, we need a new plan." Haven bit her lip.

Corrin nodded. "Yes, we do. But we can hardly spare the men for an attack of our own."

Haven agreed. "We can't attack them ourselves. We need to come up with something smart, something that would divert Kadia's attention completely."

"We should sleep on it," Corrin said.

"Until tomorrow, then." Haven stood.

"Goodnight, Lady Haven."

"Goodnight, Corrin."

* * *

WHEN THE SUN rose early the next day, there was still no sign of the distraction. Haven and Corrin met in the same spot to discuss a plan of action. This time, their advisers and Haven's guard attended.

Throughout the night, the idea of a new plan had plagued her. Something about Kadia twisted her stomach in knots every time she thought of her. Her skin crawled and chilled. The madness of the queen should be played on. After the letter Kadia had sent, her fascination with Haven had become obvious. A plan soon formed in her mind. But would her guards agree to it?

Haven had to hope Corrin would come up with something better. She doubted very much that her guards would let her plan come to fruition.

"Good morning, Lady Queen." Corrin nodded respectfully.

"Good morning, Lord King." Haven sat at their makeshift table, her advisers and her guards joining her and the king. It wasn't long ago that she'd sat around a table much like this during their secret meetings in the mountains. Only her friends were there this time and they were missing two kings and a prince.

"Is there any new information from the scouts?" Haven glanced at the king.

Corrin shook his head. "None."

Haven sighed.

"Have you thought of a plan?" he asked.

Haven worked her jaw back and forth while trying unsuccessfully not to squirm under the gazes of her friends. They knew her all too well.

"You were up awfully late, Lady Queen," Blythe said.

"Surely you've thought of something," Lareina agreed.

"I'd like to hear your thoughts first, King Corrin," Haven said.

"Unfortunately, my own plan comes in the form of a very brazen attack that is sure to get all involved killed." Corrin shrugged. "Which, of course, is not acceptable. In other words, I have no plan, My Lady."

Haven slumped. She had feared as much.

"I do have a plan," Haven admitted. "But you're not going to like it."

* * *

"WHY MUST your plans always risk your own life, Lady Queen?" Blythe asked.

Though Blythe was simply being dramatic, Haven's gut twisted. They both knew that her life would never truly be at risk, but there were things worse than death.

King Corrin, Prince Emeril, her guards, and several remaining Wakefin soldiers accompanied Haven into the open. Her plan was simple. They had to lure the queen outside her palace walls. To do so, they needed a ruse.

After their meeting, Haven dispatched a messenger with a letter for the queen. Lies about bartering for surrender were involved. She had to hope Kadia's madness led to over confidence. If Kadia sent an emissary instead of herself, the plan would be ruined.

While Haven and her little group distracted Kadia's watchful eye, the rest of their people would safely run to the tunnel and escape. The deception didn't need to last long, only long enough to get everyone clear.

Of course, her guards had rioted about the idea. It was only when a small army of guards hiding in the nearby trees was suggested that they agreed. Still, no one liked the plan. It could get any number of them maimed or killed if they weren't careful. If Kadia really did want

Haven that badly, she would surely come herself, but would she leave alone as well?

There was only one way to find out.

Taking a stand outside Cidra in the open plain, they waited. The great black city towered above, casting long shadows over the surrounding grassland.

Haven twisted her lip between her teeth. How had Kadia kept her people inside this entire time? Surely they wanted to get away from their terrible queen.

The main gates cracked, echoing in the clearing. The heavy iron fence drew upward into the stone wall.

Between the open doors, a small party road. Eight soldiers clad in black Dagan armor accompanied the blond-haired, blue-eyed Queen Kadia.

Haven stiffened. Her hands tightened on the reins. They waited in silence. Her anxiety rolled through her like waves. Each of her friends stared wide-eyed at the approaching group. Her fingers inched toward their weapons, and their nostrils flared. Was it possible they were more afraid than she?

The group slowed to a stop a few feet from them.

"How lovely of you all to come," Kadia purred. Her sickly sweet smile made Haven's skin crawl. "You wish to surrender?"

Corrin cleared his throat. "We wish to discuss terms."

"Terms?" Kadia threw her head back and laughed. "If you don't mind me saying, I don't think you have much to barter with." Her gaze fell on Haven, and her eyes widened.

Haven shivered.

"Lovely girl." Her voice was sweet like velvet and honey. "You've finally come to me. I told you we would soon meet." Kadia held her gloved hand out as if she expected Haven to come forward and take it.

Haven backed away. Fear gripped her heart like talons.

"Queen Kadia." Corrin cleared his throat again to draw her attention away.

Begrudgingly, Kadia turned to the young king. Her smile fell.

"We want our kingdoms back. What are your terms?"

"I already have your kingdoms. I won't give them back so easily." Kadia's gaze hardened. "But, if you and your people want to escape with your lives through the tunnel, be my guest. I will allow that."

Her heart leapt. Haven and Corrin exchanged a panicked glance. *She knew?*

"Why would you let us flee?" Emeril asked.

Kadia shrugged. "I do as I wish, and now, I have what I want. I will even be so gracious as to leave the rest of your people alone."

"That is good news." Emeril glanced back at the others.

Haven wasn't so sure. Kadia wouldn't let all of this happen without a price.

"You won't consider the return of our kingdoms? You won't consider peace?" Corrin's brow twitched up.

"I'll have peace when you're all gone, won't I?"

"It seems fair, Corrin." Emeril glared at the young king.

"What do you want?" Haven asked. She had had enough of this.

They needed to know what Kadia wanted and be done with it. If she wanted to let them go, then they needed to go. With the queen's gaze on her once more, Haven's stomach lurched.

She knew what the queen wanted.

"I want you, of course."

"What?" Emeril gasped.

"You can't be serious, Lady Kadia," Corrin growled.

"Of course I'm serious." Kadia laughed as she urged her mare toward Haven.

Haven's guards quickly circled her.

"All I want is Lady Haven. Then you may go. That is my only requirement, my only term, and the only thing I want. You will not change my mind. I have things to do, so come along, little queen."

"We won't let you take her," Blythe snapped. Her fingers closed on the hilt of her sword. She urged her stallion back.

Haven's horse chuffed and shook its mane as it was forced to back away.

"She isn't yours to take." Lareina withdrew her dagger.

"You're all so *adorable*." Kadia smiled. "You've already delivered her right to me. I'm not asking anyone's permission."

Kadia raised her hand over the ground beside her horse. Shadows swirled like dust from her gloved back. The darkness twisted and curled on itself like a living thing, growing more solid as it neared. The horses began to whiny and rear. Something about the shadowy fog felt as wrong to them as it did to the rest.

"Retreat!" Corrin shouted.

The group backed away, moving slowly in their panic to get to the trees. Haven's heart pounded in her ears as yanked on her reins in an attempt to turn around. Before they could move into formation, the darkness sprang forward in the form of soldiers.

Kadia laughed as her creatures attacked.

Haven's and Corrin's guards ripped their swords from their sheaths. Their blades clanged against those of the dark soldiers, the clearing filling with grunts and snaps as their soldiers leapt forward to protect them. Haven withdrew her own sword, her fingers clammy against the cold metal.

The darkness bit at the legs of her horse. The mare whinnied and reared. Her heart lurched into her throat as she nearly tumbled back. Haven held on to her reins in one hand while slicing at the black fog with the other.

Her mare reared again. The leather slipped between her fingers. Haven clung on, but her sword flew from her hand.

Lareina's mare nudged hers as it tried to escape. Each horse bumped into one another, trying to flee.

"Leave the horses!" Blythe called. "They're useless like this!"

Battle cries rose as the rest of their small army ran from the woods, swords drawn and shields up. Kadia's gaze whipped toward them. Her smile turned into a smirk. She flung her hand toward them. Her darkness became waves, washing over her people and knocking them onto their backs.

Haven leapt from her horse alongside the others. The stallions and the mares took off across the plains.

"So much fuss over one girl!" Kadia cackled.

Haven plucked her sword from the grass. A dark soldier swung for her head. Her heart raced as she ducked and rolled to the side. Lareina jumped in front of her, their swords colliding.

The soldier became not one, but two, and then three. Lareina took a step back. Haven dove forward to join her alongside Malka. She would not let these *things* hurt her friends.

"Get Haven back to the trees!" Blythe called from somewhere in the fray.

Shadow soldiers fought their soldiers, metal clanging on every side.

She couldn't leave them behind. She wouldn't.

Haven sliced through the beasts. Her knuckles whitened, and her teeth ground together. Her adviser dead in the forest flashed before her eyes. She wouldn't have her guards dead. She wouldn't risk them again.

She would fight for them, as they fought for her.

Her blade cut through shadow soldier after shadow soldier. They disappeared into black wisps, only for several others to leap forward. A growled ripped from between her teeth as she lunged and drove her sword through the belly of one. It burst into fog.

The soldiers in the trees joined them, but still, shadows overtook them.

"Every swing is futile!" Kadia taunted from somewhere behind the wall of darkness.

Haven plunged her sword into one's chest then ripped outward. Though her blade slipped through them with ease, another constantly stood in her path.

"We need to get away from her!" Haven shouted

"We will." Lareina cut the head off another.

A cry of pain cut through the grunts and clangs of metal. Haven whipped around as a shadow soldier tore its blade through Blythe's shoulder. Her heart plummeted.

"No!" Haven dove toward her.

A hand clamped around her wrist and yanked her off her feet. Her breath fled her lungs as she hit the ground. Haven gasped desperately for air as she clung to her sword. A dark soldier bent over her, his hands reaching for her shoulders. Haven swiped upward and rolled out of the way. She leapt to her feet, right into the arms of another.

"Haven!" Lareina cried. Her blond hair bobbed between the shadows.

"Lareina!" Haven struggled in the dark soldier's grip.

An arrow shot past her face. Dark wisps erupted. She was free.

"Malka!" Haven gasped. "Get Blythe out of here!"

Pain exploded through her gut. The tip of a blade protruded from her belly, covered in blood. Her blood.

Haven's eyebrows furrowed as darkness took her.

Grass swirled back into shape, tickling her cheek. Copper blossomed on her tongue. She spit blood from her mouth. Her ears rang, which added pressure inside her skull.

"Bring her to me!" Kadia yelled over the commotion.

Haven got her hands beneath her. A fight. She'd been in a fight. She needed to get up. She got her feet beneath her. Hands closed on her biceps, yanking her arms behind her. Shadows kept her on her feet and dragged her across the ground, away from the forest and her friends.

This wasn't good.

Her head swam as she raised her head to call for help. A long trail of blood lay in the grass behind her.

"Haven!" someone screamed.

The clang of swords and *shing* of metal grew hollow. Haven could see the fight for what it was now: futile. Just as Kadia had said. Her friends were overwhelmed. Soldiers lay dead on the ground. Blood soaked the plain.

Her heart rammed against her rib cage. It was useless. There was only one thing they could do.

"Run!" Her voice rang in her skull.

She desperately sought the gazes of her friends. She needed them to listen. Just this once.

"Run!" Haven caught Corrin's eyes. Then Lareina's, Emeril's. "Run!"

Haven could only watch as her friends retreated. Corrin grabbed

Lareina and pulled her from the shadow soldiers overwhelming their ranks. Lareina struggled, losing her daggers to the plain as she screamed.

Darkness crept across her vision. "Run," she murmured. It was the last thing she said before she blacked out.

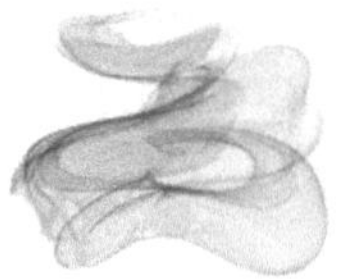

FIFTEEN

*H*aven awoke with a start. For a moment, she lay still, images of blood-soaked grass, bodies lying on the plain, and a sword ripping through her friend's shoulder flashing through her mind. Lareina's and Corrin's faces as they'd retreated flashed before her eyes. The young king had literally dragged her away.

A sword had ripped through her abdomen. Her hand flung to her side. The wound had long since healed. Haven sighed in relief. At least she could always count on whatever bizarre power she had to keep her going.

Beautiful morning light flooded the bronze ceiling. She started. Where was she?

Golden walls decorated with burgundy-and-bronze-wrapped pillars and adorned with jewels and large paintings of animals, places, and people she had never seen or could hardly imagine filled the space. She turned to look over her shoulder. A stained-glass window with equally strange images let daylight inside. Silks hung from the ceiling, along with a gorgeous chandelier.

If she hadn't known better, she'd have thought she was dead.

Haven shifted onto her elbows. Something tightened on her wrists, which did not quite allow her up. Her eyebrows furrowed.

Leather binds wrapped her wrists and her ankles, chaining her to a thick slab of wood several feet off the ground. She gasped.

Haven yanked on her restraints, her mind swirling and her heart racing. She pulled and twisted the shackles until her wrists ached and blood trickled onto the table.

No. This couldn't be happening.

Haven ground her teeth as she tore her arms in every direction. Pain stung her wrists and her ankles. After several long minutes had passed, she sighed and collapsed back onto the table. The ache in her wrists quickly faded.

It was useless. She wasn't going anywhere.

"*Finally*, you are awake!"

Haven stiffened. Kadia swept into the room, her regal, black silk gown wafting around her ankles. Her ash-blond hair shone in the golden morning light, and her blue eyes danced in a frightful way that had Haven cringing.

"Good morning, sleeping beauty." Kadia sat in the chair beside the table. Her warm fingers pressed against Haven's hand, drawing it to her cheek, where she nuzzled it. "Trying to get away already, I see."

Haven's stomach flipped.

"Why do you want to leave me? We've only just met." Kadia blinked large, almost childlike eyes at her. The way she smiled and looked, even her movements—they were all increasingly juvenile. "And your wound has already healed!" she gasped as she stood. She groped Haven's shirt with her long fingers, looking for some trace of a scar. She would find none.

"I need to go with my friends," Haven said. Her heart pounded in her ears. What else was she supposed to say to this woman? Her mind swirled, and her head ached. She couldn't think.

Kadia threw her hand down and growled. Her heels clacked as she paced the room. Haven took a deep breath. Her limbs relaxed now that the queen's touch had fled. Haven glanced after her. In the corner by the window was a lush bed of silks. A door at the far end of the room was slightly ajar, revealing a bathing room.

Haven glanced away. She needed a way out of there. She needed to get these restraints off and flee.

She froze. Next to the table was a small spread of metal instruments. Covering a metal sheet were knives of all shapes and sizes as well as different objects she had never seen.

Kadia stopped pacing. Her once wide, childlike gaze had grown hard and calculating. Her eyes darkened, and a smirk spread across her pale face. "You like them?" She tilted her head toward the cart of torture devices.

Haven gulped as Kadia slid her fingers along the metal edge. "What are you going to do with those?" Haven shivered.

"Many things, I'm sure." Kadia picked up a small knife that Haven thought might be a medical scalpel. "I want to know how you work, little queen."

Kadia eyed not her face, but her body.

Haven squirmed under her gaze. "Please, Lady Kadia, don't hurt me."

Kadia's grin only grew. Her fingers trailed from Haven's collarbone down to her hips and her thighs. Her touch sent goose bumps over her skin.

The mad queen stood straight again. "You can't be hurt." Kadia plunged the knife into Haven's thigh.

Pain exploded through her leg. Haven cried out, her scream echoing back to her. Blood gushed from the wound, spreading warmth over her leg.

"Hush now," Kadia purred. She placed her fingers over Haven's lips.

Haven moaned and whimpered in pain. Tears sprang to her eyes. She pulled against her restraints as Kadia continued to drag her hands over her body, poking her ribs, her stomach, and her legs with the knife. Her skin broke again and again, stinging with every touch.

"What's wrong?" Kadia smiled as she wiped the tears from Haven's face. "Why are you crying?"

"You're hurting me." Haven shifted her face away.

"But you can't be hurt, little queen." Kadia ripped the sleeve of her blouse open. She plucked a much larger knife from the table and drew it over the soft flesh of Haven's inner arm.

Haven gasped, bucking her head back against the slab. "Please stop," she cried.

Kadia climbed onto the slab, bracing one knee on Haven's hand to stop her from struggling. Her hand ached under the pressure. Gently, Kadia dragged the knife over Haven's skin. Haven gritted her teeth to keep from crying out.

"You fuss so much!" Kadia threw the bloody knife onto the tray. She sat back, straddling Haven's hips.

Warmth blossomed through Haven's arm as it healed. Haven sighed with relief.

"Astonishing."

The pain slowly subsided. Thank the blue skies.

"How do you work?" Kadia prodded Haven's arm where the wound had sealed. "I must know. What are you?"

"I don't know," Haven admitted. She'd always wondered herself. No one else in her family had this ability.

"You're incredible," Kadia murmured. "Do you heal from everything? Burns, cuts, bruises, sickness? Could you drown, suffocate?" She paused, staring at Haven with what she could only describe as madness. "If I cut off a limb, will it grow back?"

Panic lurched inside Haven's chest. Her struggle began again. "You mustn't, Kadia! Please! I can't be killed, but I can still be hurt!"

"Nonsense," Kadia huffed. "Bring it in!"

A tall man with a large, black pot stepped through the dark oak door. Heat poured in waves from the pot.

"Please, Kadia, don't!" Tears flew freely. "You can still hurt me!"

Kadia dismounted the slab and pulled a long prong from the hot coals. The end of the poker burned orange like fire.

"*Please!*" Haven begged.

Kadia yanked Haven's shirt up, exposing her midriff. "I want to see you heal again." Her eyes widened with glee.

Mad. She was absolutely *mad*. Haven closed her eyes as Kadia drew the poker near. Its heat brushed her skin until it seared her flesh. Haven couldn't keep herself from screaming this time.

"Stop! Please!"

Kadia laughed and paused as Haven healed. Then she did it again and again.

"Fascinating!" she cooed, absorbed in the act of defiling Haven's body. "I knew you'd be perfect. You're just like me: special in every way."

Haven's head lolled to the side like a rag doll. Tears spilled down Kadia's perfect skin from her widened eyes.

Haven screamed again as Kadia dragged the poker across her ribs. Then it lifted. She exhaled sharply. Relief. Pain pierced her chest as Kadia plunged it through her sternum.

Haven blacked out.

WHEN HAVEN CAME TO, Kadia had put away the poker and was obsessing over the healing wound in her chest. Haven started, the searing pain in her chest returning her to the waking world. She tried to move her wrists. The leather bit her skin. She sighed.

"Absolutely wonderful. You've almost completely healed."

Haven didn't need Kadia's update to know. She'd still be unconscious if she hadn't.

"My assassin said he shot you through the heart and you lived. I never believed him until now."

Haven's eyebrows furrowed. "*You* sent the assassin?"

"Of course. I suppose he was telling the truth, then, wasn't he." Kadia sighed. "Maybe I shouldn't have killed him. Oh well." She shrugged and covered Haven's bare chest.

If the assassin had been Kadia's doing, then Nikolai's death was on her hands as well. This monster needed to pay.

"You're a marvel, Haven." Kadia played with the red ends of Haven's otherwise brown hair. "There's just one more thing I want to try."

Haven groaned. Her entire body was drained from healing. Every ounce of her strength went into staying awake. She couldn't bear much more of this.

"Guards!" Kadia called.

Two entered. The two men's gazes were fogged, lifeless.

They removed the leather from her wrists and her ankles. Haven pulled her wrists away the second they were free. One of the men grabbed them, his hands impossibly strong. Hoisting her under her armpits, the men dragged her from the table and carried her toward the bathing room.

"Just one last little thing," Kadia purred as she slipped into the room before them.

Water poured into some kind of basin, echoing through the small, white marble room. Fear stabbed her heart. She'd nearly drowned once as a child. It was the first time her parents had thought something was different about her.

"Kadia, please don't!" She thrashed wildly with all of her remaining strength.

The men pinned her arms behind her back.

"I've drowned before. I will live! You don't have to do this!"

Kadia fixed her with a sweet smile as the guards pushed her to her knees on the cold marble floor. A large tub was in the center of the room. Water filled it.

"Of course I don't have to," Kadia said. "I don't have to do anything."

"Then *please* don't do *this*." Haven tried to catch her gaze and keep it to break through whatever insane haze this woman was in.

Kadia flicked her wrist at the tub. Fingers wrapped around her skull as she was shoved in face-first. Cold burned her cheeks. Her nose stung as water forced its way up her nostrils. Haven twisted her wrists, but nothing could escape their iron grasp.

Haven kicked her feet, but even as her boots collided with their legs, the men didn't move. Bubbles brushed her cheeks as her breath escaped her.

Her lungs ached, and her eyes watered. She needed air—*now*.

Haven pushed away from the tub with all of her might only to be forced in farther. Her cheek struck hard porcelain, and her gut dug into the edge of the tub.

Her chest burned. Slowly, her muscles lost their strength and the fight drained from her body.

Darkness crept in, and she was soon lost to it.

HAVEN GASPED as air flooded her throat before water spilled from her lungs. She coughed, her chest aching as she expelled water from her body while simultaneously sucking in air. Cold stone pressed against her cheek. Her wet hair obscured most of her vision. Shivers racked her body.

Why did this evil witch insist on testing her?

She glanced up, her fingers shaking as she brushed hair from her face.

Kadia gazed down at her, a crazed grin on her lips. "I wish I knew more about you."

Haven sagged against the floor. "I'll tell you anything you want if you stop hurting me."

Kadia perked up. "Really?"

Her childlike demeanor returned in her widened eyes. One moment, she was a little girl, and the next, a mad queen.

Haven nodded. "Yes."

"So you'll tell me anything? Anything at all?"

Haven's arms shook as she pushed herself onto her knees. Again, she nodded.

"We can be friends, then!" Kadia lunged forward, wrapping her arms around Haven's shoulders.

Haven froze as the queen yanked her to her feet.

"I knew you were special, beautiful, and quite intelligent, but I never imagined you'd be my friend too."

Haven's terror sent her heart racing. She blinked back the tears that burned to the surface. This is what Kadia truly wanted? A friend?

Was it possible she could convince the queen she was her friend? In time, maybe she could escape.

"We'll be the best of friends." Haven's lips twitched into the smallest of smiles.

Kadia squealed with delight, jumping up and pulling the knife from Haven's leg. Haven gasped, and her eyes watered.

"A friend! I'll have a friend!" Kadia laughed, throwing the knife away and dancing back into the bedroom. "I can't wait for us to share secrets, braid each other's hair, take long walks in the courtyards..." She rambled as she flew from her chambers, leaving Haven to her solitude.

Haven leaned back against the tub. Finally, it was over. But for how long? Could this be just the beginning? Curling up on the floor, Haven fought her tears back.

How had she ended up there? Her power had never seemed more of a curse. Her skin crawled as she recalled the stabs, the pokes, the prods, and the rod through her chest. She trembled. Though the pain was already gone, its ghost chilled her skin.

After pushing her dripping hair from her face, she peeled herself off the cold tiled floor and returned to the main chamber.

NOT LONG AFTER Kadia had fled, guards came in to take the instruments away. Haven refused to let them see her relief. Instead, she sat up in the soft silks of the bed. Perhaps she could appeal to one of these men's better natures.

"Hello," she said tentatively. "Why do you work for her? She only causes pain."

The man didn't even glance in her direction.

"Could you help me escape? Is there a way out?"

Nothing.

"Did you not hear what she was doing to me in here? *Please* help me." Desperation flooded her.

The man glanced up with vacant eyes. It was for barely a moment, but he stared right through her. He removed the table from the room. Haven sighed as they both left, closing the door.

Something was wrong with Kadia's people. The way they blindly obeyed wasn't normal. Collapsing back onto the bed, Haven buried her face in her hands. She hadn't known what she was getting herself into when she'd told the others to run. She hadn't known there would be so much pain, so much suffering. She shouldn't have told them to go. But, if she hadn't, they all might have died. She sighed.

She never wanted to be touched again—certainly not in the way Kadia had touched her. Haven shivered.

Haven didn't regret her decision to tell the others to leave. If they had stayed, they would have died because of her. She wasn't worth it.

Sitting up, Haven glanced around her prison. It was the nicest cage she could have imagined. Haven stood. She needed to act, to move, to forget. If she kept herself busy, she wouldn't think about her last few hours. She wouldn't think about the knives, the poker, the drowning.

Haven rushed across the room, searching for a way out. She started by checking the door. Locked. Haven checked the window. Locked. She inspected the glass. Several inches thick. There would be no breaking it.

She peered outside and started. She had to be on the third floor at least, just like her chambers in Rythern.

Haven shook her head and continued her search. She wasn't getting out of there by reminiscing about a home she might never see again. In the bathing room, Haven found the same thick glass and nothing she could use to pry any locks off.

She returned to the main room. An easel and a basket of paints were by one wall. Haven kneeled on the floor and dumped the basket's contents. She sifted through paints until a long, wooden brush stuck out from between the contents. Finally.

Haven returned everything but the brush to the basket. She returned to the bathing room, her heart hammering in her chest. If she had a weapon, she could at least defend herself.

Using the windowsill, she scraped the wooden handle back and forth. If she made it pointed enough, it'd be as deadly as any blade. At this point, anything would have been better than remaining unarmed and meek.

"You can survive anything," Haven whispered to herself. "You will survive this."

She repeated it to herself over and over until she believed it. She would survive, she would escape, and she would flee to the tunnel and follow her friends to Seaburn. She would do this. Kadia would not be the end of her. The people of Rythern needed their queen.

Haven would rise to the occasion.

THE SUN DROPPED below the horizon, casting shadows along the tiled floor of the bathing room. Her muscles ached, and her head swam with exhaustion. The brush was almost pointed enough to use. It would have to do for now.

After returning to her chambers, she hid the brush between the mattresses of the bed. Sleep drooped her eyelids and forced her to lie down. Silk sheets brushed her bare skin.

Don't let your guard down.

Haven blinked slowly. She had to stay awake in case Kadia returned. She had to be ready.

She settled against the down-filled pillow. She couldn't help it. After the trauma of the day, she needed a moment. Even a few minutes would be a blessing.

Haven let sleep take her.

"LITTLE QUEEN, you've gone to bed without supper!"

Haven jerked upward. She spun onto her back, her chest heaving. A lantern was at her bedside, casting eerie shadows of Kadia's haunting face. The queen sat on the edge of the bed, her fingers resting on the silk inches from her knee.

Haven shifted away. Her hands trembled as her fingers tightened on the sheet.

"You don't need to be afraid, my little queen." Kadia smiled. "We're friends now, remember?"

Haven nodded. She did remember that Kadia said that she wanted that. Kadia wanted a friend who was special like her. She might not have been like Kadia, but she had power Kadia didn't possess. If Haven wanted to get out of this, she'd have to play friend to this psycho.

"Yes, of course. Friends." Haven feigned a smile.

"I've come to bring you a gown and take you to dinner. You will be my honored guest." Kadia jumped up and rushed to the blank-eyed maids who carried in several gowns in varying styles and colors. "Pick any you like!"

Haven got out of bed, keeping as much distance between her and Kadia as she could. The maids paraded in a straight line, pausing to line the wall and demonstrate each style. Haven's eyebrows rose. She'd never seen anything like them. Silks and cottons adorned with jewels and crystals. Plunging necklines, short skirts, long skirts. They came in all shapes and sizes. Haven had worn something so lavish only a few times in her life. One had been not long ago at her coronation.

"I think you'd look stunning in red," Kadia cooed. She motioned a maid forward.

The long-skirted gown dipped low at the bosom. Its long sleeves and its corset bodice were the color of blood. Haven gulped.

"You should wear that one!"

"If you think so." Haven's smile twitched slightly. Her blood ran cold. She was utterly horrified by the dress. Wearing it would be like bathing in blood.

"Quickly, put it on!" Kadia clapped her hands.

Haven was quickly undressed and redressed by unfamiliar hands. Fingers poked and prodded at her skin, her hair, and her clothes. It was agony to have so many people touch her. Though they moved quickly and barely glanced at her bare skin, Haven fought back tears and the memories that followed.

She was not being violated, simply dressed. She had to remember that. Her face heated as they finished with her dress and moved on to her hair, braiding the long strands back from her cheeks while letting the rest flow freely over her shoulders. Once they had finished, Haven was ready to collapse.

"Absolutely gorgeous!" Kadia took Haven's hands.

It took every ounce of strength Haven had not to recoil.

"You may very well outshine me!" Kadia laughed as she pulled Haven out of the room.

In the flurry of motion, Haven took in as many halls and staircases as she could, trying to memorize the maze while simultaneously pushing awful memories from her mind. Hall after hall flew by, and then they were in the grand dining room.

Red silks were strung from the ceiling, and the red serpents tail of Kadia's family crest hung from banners on every dark stone wall. Too dizzy to take in much more of the room, Haven let Kadia lead her.

This first dinner would begin the charade Haven needed to play to survive this nightmare. She'd play nice, dress up and have dinner, but when the night ended, Haven would plot her escape. It was all she could do.

SIXTEEN

"Sit, sit!" Kadia insisted. She flicked her gloved fingers at the head of the table.

Haven glanced at the noblemen and women seated at the table. They all gazed forward, their eyes vacant. Silence rested in the dining room. Haven took her seat at the head of the table while Kadia circled to the opposite end. A tall, dark oak chair carved with swirling vines and flowers and upholstered in red velvet marked the queen's seat.

Kadia sat, her large skirts poofing up around her. She swatted them down as Haven shifted uncomfortably.

Porcelain plates—one small, one large—lay before her, with silverware at their sides. Three forks, two spoons, but no knives. Haven's brow twitched up. She would have liked the use of a knife.

"Servers, you may begin!" Kadia flicked her wrist, calling in a long line of servers dressed in white-and-black suits. They carried silver trays atop their hands and whisked in quickly to remove the tops and setting the first course before each of the Mad Queen's guests.

Round fish eyes stared up at her. Haven started. Steam rose from the fish, yet its head remained on her plate. The rest had been cooked and laid in strips behind it. An interesting presentation.

"Eat, everyone!"

At Kadia's command, the nobles scooped their forks from the table and went to work on the fish. No one spoke a word. No one glanced at one another. They simply ate.

Haven plucked her silver fork from beside her plate. It cooled her fingertips.

"It's awfully quiet in here, wouldn't you say, little queen?" Kadia tilted her head, her big eyes round and innocent.

"A little bit." Haven took a bite of the fish. It might as well have been water. She tasted nothing.

"Squire, call in the band! I'll have music while we eat." Kadia sipped from her goblet of wine.

A serpent twisted around the metal base. Haven glanced at her own goblet. The same serpent twisted around hers, its teeth bared in a snarl.

"Are you not enjoying the fish?"

Haven froze. She took another bite and smiled. "Yes, it's fine."

"Good." Kadia beamed as she downed the rest of her wine and then placed her goblet on the table. "I think we should have a dance after dinner, don't you think?"

Her blood ran cold. A dance? Haven glanced at the nobles. More people to touch her. More time for Kadia to poke and prod.

"I'm quite tired this evening." Haven's voice shook.

Kadia's smile fell. Her gaze darkened. "You won't dance with me?"

Haven's eyes widened. What could she say to get out of this? The last thing she wanted to do was incur Kadia's wrath.

Haven stuttered, unable to form any words. Her head spun.

Kadia stood, her fists slamming against the table. The wood shook, the silverware clattering against each other. "Little queen, I thought we were friends." Her innocent demeanor washed away like the tide. Her large eyes narrowed into slits.

"We-we are."

"Then why do you insist on *lying*?" Kadia backhanded her plate to the floor. It crashed against the marble, shattering into a thousand pieces.

Haven glanced at the nobles, the servers, and the band flooding in. No one paused in their activity.

"Lying?" she squeaked.

Kadia's ruby lips twisted into a snarl. "Yes, *lying*. You don't enjoy the fish. You don't enjoy my company. You don't want to dance with me. *What* have I done to deserve this?"

Her fingers shook on her lap. What could she say? What could she do? If she didn't calm Kadia's beast quickly, blue skies only knew what she might do.

"I'm sorry." Haven swallowed the lump forming in her throat. "I don't know what I was thinking."

"You *weren't*." Kadia rolled her eyes.

"Of course I'd love to dance with you. I'm s-sorry." Haven offered a small smile.

Kadia raised an eyebrow. She looked the young queen up and down. Her eyes burned into Haven's skin. After a long moment of hesitation, Kadia smiled. Her lips twisted, and her hardened gaze softened.

"Apology accepted." Kadia returned to her seat.

A server promptly shuffled forward to refill Kadia's goblet and replace her meal. Kadia waved him off.

"I'm not hungry anymore. Let's dance now."

The nobles froze. Their cutlery clattered onto their plates as they stood. Haven glanced between them as the small band at the far end of the hall began to play. The melody rose into the high ceilings, soft and rhythmic.

"All right." Haven stood along with the Mad Queen.

Kadia stepped around the long table and held her hand out.

Haven gulped. Her fingers shook as she joined Kadia, who took her hand and led her to the open space beside the banquet table. The nobles joined in pairs, waltzing around the space, careful to avoid the queen and her guest.

"Did you dance often in Rythern?" Kadia placed her hands on Haven's shoulders, lacing her fingers behind her neck.

Their hips brushed as Haven placed her hands on Kadia's waist. The Mad Queen ushered her onto the dance floor, where they spun to the band's melody.

"No, I didn't." Her skin burned beneath Kadia's gaze.

"I'll have to teach you how to dance properly, then." Kadia stepped back and took her hand, placing the other on her back. She pulled her closer.

Haven's stomach flipped, recoiling from Kadia's touch. She placed her empty hand on Kadia's shoulder as if Kadia were the man leading their dance. The Mad Queen stepped forward, and Haven stepped back.

Kadia led her across the floor, their heels clicking as one. "See? You can dance after all with the right direction." She smiled.

Haven simply nodded. Her head spun with each turn, and her stomach soured. What would Kadia do if she were to pull away to vomit? Would she sentence her back to her chambers? Torture her again? Or something worse?

She young queen swallowed and clenched her stomach muscles. She couldn't retch. Not now.

"We'll have so many nights like this, little queen. I can hardly wait." Kadia sighed blissfully as she spun Haven in a circle.

Haven only smiled for fear more than words might tumble from her lips.

"I'm so sure Daddy will be pleased with you. He's going to love you, just as I do."

"Your father?"

Kadia halted their waltz but didn't let her go. "I'll tell you more of Daddy later. This is our night."

Her stomach lurched once more, but she nodded. Kadia continued their dance, sweeping her across the floor in every direction. Her mind continued to fog. She bit down on her lip for fear she might pass out.

But maybe she should. Maybe she should embrace the darkness. It had to be better than this night.

Haven took a deep breath. No. She couldn't pass out. Not now. She'd endure whatever Kadia threw at her until she could make her escape.

* * *

"Little queen, good morning!" Kadia beamed as she stood to greet the young queen.

Haven had been called to breakfast in the courtyard gardens the following day. She'd attempted to memorize the way, but the guards had taken her through a confusing route, which had left her dizzy by the time they'd reached the beautiful garden. A stone path weaved through flowers in all shapes and sizes until it reached a small tableau surrounded by roses.

She froze. Red like blood. She knew the flower all too well. They'd been present at two scenes: her assassin on a pike and Nikolai's decapitated head. Haven swallowed the lump in her throat. So the roses had been Kadia's signature.

Kadia stood beside a small, black marble table and chairs beside a stream beneath a lattice pergola. A full breakfast spread covered the small table.

"How did you sleep?" Kadia asked as she motioned for Haven to sit.

Haven obliged, her stomach rumbling as she sat. After her dinner with the Mad Queen, she'd hardly eaten a thing. "Well. Thank you," she lied. Haven had barely slept at all. Nightmares had plagued her when she had.

Kadia spooned eggs onto her plate before plucking perfectly juicy strawberries from a silver platter. Once Kadia sat back, Haven snatched some breakfast of her own. She wasn't worried about poison and wasn't sure if she should be. If she couldn't die, could poison affect her? She hoped not.

"I'm glad to hear it." Kadia smiled. "Do you like the gardens?"

Carefully picking at her food, Haven tried not to think about how close Kadia was. The insane queen was a touchy woman, and Haven didn't want to have more physical contact than necessary.

"Yes."

"They are quite beautiful," Kadia continued. "I enjoy spending time amongst my roses. We will have to take a walk later."

"Of course," Haven mumbled. The sweet taste of strawberry blossomed on her tongue.

"It is quite lovely here in the summer. I wish you could have been here before this dreadful fall began. Every flower was in bloom, and the aroma through the castle was incredible." Kadia sighed, leaning her cheek against her hand. "Summer is my favorite time of year. Wouldn't you agree it is the best of seasons?"

"Yes."

"Are you enjoying your breakfast? I had the chef make it especially for you. The bread was baked fresh this morning! Do you eat a lot of bread in Rythern? What is the climate like this time of year? Cold, I imagine, beside the mountains. How do you keep warm through the winter?"

On and on, Kadia asked her simple questions, and usually, she answered them herself.

Haven replied now and then when Kadia paused, but she seemed quite content to prattle on by herself. Before she knew it, Haven finished her meal and her tea, while Kadia had barely begun. She tried to busy herself with looking at the flowers while Kadia commented on her own city. But then she missed a question.

"I'm sorry. What was that?" Haven glanced back at the queen.

"I know the flowers can be distracting. They are quite beautiful." Kadia's fingertips brushed the roses closest to her. "But I asked you what your parents were like. I know they've died, which is why you became queen, but did you know them well? Did you have siblings? Brothers? Sisters? I've always wanted a little sister."

Haven blanched. Her eyes widened in dismay. It had been some time since she'd spoken of her family, and the last person she wanted to speak with about them was Kadia. She was the reason they were dead. If Kadia hadn't started this war, maybe her parents and her siblings still would have been alive.

"They were fine," she said, her tone clipped.

"They were *fine*?" Kadia laughed. "I'm sure there's plenty for you to say. I never knew my parents like I'm sure you knew yours."

"They were... great parents." Her eyes burned. "I miss them." Her fingers clenched in her lap. Haven wanted to say that it was all Kadia's fault. She wanted to jump up and scream and rip the hair from her obnoxiously pretty head. But she didn't.

Kadia's expression melted, her eyebrows turning up and her eyes widening, which gave her the appearance of a worried mother. She reached across the table to hold Haven's hand.

Unthinking, Haven recoiled. "They were great rulers. Everyone looked up to them. My mother sang to me, and my father taught me how to ride a horse like a man." She hurried to speak, hoping Kadia wouldn't notice how quickly she'd pulled away. "The people loved them and my brothers. They were both older than I am. And very smart, but quite hotheaded. I only have my younger sister left, but she disappeared when the city was attacked," Haven lied. "She is feared dead." She would not let her only remaining blood be hunted by this woman. Astrid was safe in the mountains, or so she hoped.

"A younger sister?" Kadia gasped, her gaze turning from that sweet, innocent child to the predator she was. A sick curiosity filled her. "Is she like you?"

"No. None of my family was."

Kadia nodded, but her fascination remained. Haven swallowed hard. She wished she had never mentioned Astrid.

"They're all dead?"

Haven nodded.

"How sad. My *sad* little queen."

Haven sat back, putting as much distance between her and the queen as possible. The way Kadia spoke made her want to jump up and run. If she even thought she could get out of the gardens, she would have leapt up right then.

"It is sad," she agreed.

"Do you miss them?"

"Of course."

"I miss my daddy sometimes too." Kadia sighed, returning to innocence. "I never knew my mother, but Daddy gave me so many things, such great gifts."

"Great gifts?" Haven raised an eyebrow.

"How else would I have abilities like these?" Kadia laughed. "My daddy gave me every single one. He always called me his favorite daughter. He said I would do great things and conquer any lands I wished. He'll return to me someday and take me back. I'm sure of it."

Haven's eyebrows furrowed. What did she mean? "Take you where?"

"Izenfir, of course, to see the Spyre. He promised to show me if I was a good girl." She giggled. "Or bad, in this case."

Haven had never heard of a land called Izenfir, and she had no idea what the Spyre could possibly be. Was this a land over the sea? Or possibly beyond the mountains? She had no idea where Kadia had come from. Kadia had come into power when Haven was only a child, and she'd only heard stories since. It was rumored that Kadia had never been the next in succession, that she was from a noble family and seized power when the last king died. Could this be true, or was Kadia really from far away? Her white-blond hair certainly marked her as foreign.

"So you do have siblings?" Haven asked.

"No, no." Kadia sighed. "Half-siblings, but they don't matter. They'll never measure up to me. *You* on the other hand..." She leaned forward. "You come quite close. You can be my sister *and* my friend if you wish, Lady Haven."

Haven tried to smile. "Of course. We would be the best of siblings."

"Just having me would replace every one of your family members." Kadia beamed.

Her gut twisted. She nodded, trying not to let the horror swelling inside show on her face. How could this woman think she could replace her family? Anger burned inside her chest so fast that she had to take a deep breath to calm down.

"Anyway, I'm sure Daddy would like you. Maybe he'll take you with me."

"I'd like that," Haven said.

Kadia glanced at Haven's plate and frowned. "You're done eating."

Haven nodded.

"Good. I wanted to apologize once you were finished. My actions were unforgivable yesterday, though it *was* before we were friends. I don't hurt my friends unless they make me angry." She smiled. "You haven't made me mad though. I was just so curious about you, Haven. I want to know how you work, but I shouldn't hurt my sister in the process."

That, Haven could agree with. "It's all right," she lied. "It doesn't hurt anymore."

"Excellent!" Kadia jumped up. "If you're in good condition, then I want to walk with you." She pulled Haven up and linked arms with her.

Haven's breath caught in her throat, and she tried to stay calm. She held on to her queasy stomach.

"You absolutely *must* see the view from the edge of the courtyard. These are my highest gardens and you can see just over the walls! We'll have to come back at sunset later for you to see the colors over the horizon. It's as if everything turns to blood! You can't even imagine it. You *must* see it!"

Haven would rather not, but she smiled and nodded, letting the queen lead them while she tried to hold her breakfast down.

Kadia spoke at great lengths as they walked, occasionally stopping to adjust her hold on Haven, switching to holding her hand or brushing her hair back. Every touch sent her head spinning, but she continued to force a smile to her face. Once they'd reached the edge of the courtyard, they stopped. Half the kingdom spread out below the castle, along with the ocean and the entirety of Cidra. Waves lapped at the distant shore. Gulls flew overhead.

It was a beautiful view. She would have preferred to see it after they'd taken down Cidra—and Kadia along with it.

"It is breathtaking," Haven said.

"Isn't it?" Kadia sighed. "This is my favorite view. It's where I do most of my thinking."

"What do you think about?"

"My dreams, the kingdoms, the world. I want it all. Every inch of soil will be mine." Kadia basked in the sun.

Haven's jaw dropped. She wanted *everything*?

"I bore *so* easily. With everything at my fingertips, I know I can't be lonely. Maybe you can rule with me one day. I will be queen of the world, and you can be my princess, even if we aren't truly related."

Haven stilled. Kadia wanted so much, and with her power, Haven wasn't sure they could stop her from taking it. But they had to try.

"That would be lovely."

"It would, wouldn't it?" Kadia ushered her to a bench, where they both sat. "Maybe you can even help me find a king to rule at my side."

"A king?"

"Yes. A husband," Kadia said. "I've always wanted one."

Haven cringed. She couldn't imagine anyone wanting to marry this witch. "That would be nice."

"Do you see a husband in your future, little queen?" Kadia smiled. "I know you fancy the young Prince Emeril."

Once, that might have been true and she would have blushed and pretended not to care for him. Now, the thought of him sent her skin crawling. "I do not fancy the young prince." Her fingers became fists.

Kadia raised an eyebrow. "Did something happen?"

"No, nothing."

Kadia took Haven's hand and leaned her head against hers. The touch was meant to be comforting, and it almost was. "You don't have to lie to me, little queen," she said. "You can tell me anything. We're friends now."

Haven denied it.

"If he hurt you—"

"He didn't."

"Then is it his betrayal that hurts you?"

Haven glanced at the queen.

"It is." Kadia smiled slightly. "That was my fault. I'm sorry, sister."

"It's okay," Haven murmured. Kadia might have been partly to blame, but Emeril had made the decision on his own. "He chose his path, and I will choose mine."

"And you'll choose it without him?"

"Yes."

"Is there anyone else?" she asked.

"I will never marry, Kadia. I won't pass this on to anyone else. I won't have my children cursed for the rest of their lives. My immortality will end with me and me alone."

"But it would be such a shame to waste your gift. You could have it continue for generations. I'd love to have little nieces and nephews running around my castle." Kadia grinned, her eyes shining as she stared off at the sea.

Cold terror filled Haven's chest. "This isn't a safe place for children."

If Kadia went a step further and forced a husband on her so she might have children, Haven would truly have to find a way to kill herself before she could accomplish that.

"If you're constantly taking other kingdoms, I can't very well stay with you in your travels *and* bear children."

Kadia laughed. "Well, if it were for you, I could take a break from conquering the known world!"

"I would not have that." Haven waved her hand. "I could not ask such things of you."

"I will just have to rule the world much faster, then! So we can both settle down and have our babies. Oh, that would be so wonderful, Haven! We should get pregnant together!" Kadia clutched Haven's hand again.

Haven couldn't imagine a worse fate. "Maybe someday."

"Someday," Kadia agreed.

If Kadia wanted to force children on her, perhaps it wasn't she who should die. The closer the women became, the more open Kadia would become with the young queen. Only then could Haven strike. She would kill Queen Kadia and rid the kingdoms of their misery.

SEVENTEEN

$\mathcal{H}$aven heaved a sigh as she sat at her windowsill. She was worried she might go mad if she had to spend one more day in this castle.

The distant ocean called to her. The sandy shore wasn't far, a few dozen yards from the castle. The strange little building concealing her tunnel to freedom was inches from the highest tide.

She tapped her fingers impatiently against her thigh. Several days in Cidra were driving her mad. Kadia had paraded her around to dinners, lunches, and even a beautiful ball. Her moods varied and were sometimes explosive, but she hadn't hurt the young queen again —she'd flown off in a rage.

Every time Haven spoke with the guards, the maids, or the noblemen, they were quiet, with distant eyes. She tried to awaken them, even went so far as to slap a nobleman, but they remained trapped in whatever spell Kadia had them under.

How long would it take Haven to fall under Kadia's spell too? Would she be trapped there, a zombie in her own personal hell?

She brushed her fingertips on the cool glass. Her heart ached with longing. The tunnel could be her salvation. She had to make it there. If she couldn't kill herself or the queen, she had to run.

That morning, when Kadia came to join her, a thought occurred to her.

"Kadia?" Haven inched as far back on the sill as she could.

Kadia sat at the other end, gazing at her with big doe eyes.

"You've conquered the six kingdoms now, haven't you?"

"Why of course, little queen. I did that for you." Kadia smiled and leaned forward, placing her hand on Haven's knee.

Haven smiled and gently slid her leg away. "Where do you aim for next?"

Kadia scooted closer, her eyes sparkling with delight. "If you *promise* to keep it a secret, I can tell you, sister."

"I promise," she said.

"I will attack Seaburn."

Haven gaped. She had feared as much. If Haven didn't escape in time to warn them, Kadia would attack the Republic over the sea and her friends would all die for nothing.

"Why do you choose Seaburn?" Her voice quaked.

"Because I can't very well go over the mountains." Kadia laughed. "Well, I could, but I don't want to bother Daddy. I want Seaburn. It's warm and beautiful. I dream of their golden palace and sandstone cities. Once we take it, I imagine we'll stay for some time. It would be a wonderful place to raise children."

"It sounds wonderful." Haven smiled.

"It is, little queen. You will enjoy it, I'm sure! But, first, we need to reconstruct my fleet for the journey." Kadia paused. "There may be someone waiting for us in Seaburn. Perhaps another sister. I can't be sure yet, but we shall see."

Haven quirked an eyebrow. "Who?"

"I don't know yet. I only know her face." The Mad Queen sighed longingly. "We'll find her. Don't you worry, my sister." The queen perked up. "I can show you her face!"

"How?"

Without another word, Kadia ran from the room. Haven waited in silence. How was it possible she knew this girl and her face but not her name? The Mad Queen grew more confusing by the day.

Several minutes later, Kadia returned, a large grin on her face. "Behold!" She danced inside, motioning to the women who trailed in behind her.

Haven stood, unable to believe her eyes.

Girl after girl of every shape and size filed in. She'd never seen women such as these, with skin as white as snow or as dark as night. Some were all too familiar. At least a dozen were from each kingdom of Warshard. The others were unfamiliar. Magnificent images were painted across their naked bodies.

Paintings of lands she had never seen or could hardly imagine were drawn all over their skin in vivid colors, swirling from their necks down to their knees. Some had amazing creatures on their skin, similar to the ones in the paintings on Haven's walls. Others had people, places, and things drawn across them. Each told a story, though none of them went together. When Haven's gaze settled on a young girl from Rythern, she gasped. Haven's face was painted on her stomach. Fire surrounded her like a rising phoenix.

"She is how I knew of you." Kadia clasped her hands together.

Haven gawked at her own image, her amber eyes bright like stars and her red hair enveloping her form in flames. She had never thought herself beautiful until this moment. Dragging her gaze from her own image, she took in the other paintings, trying to make sense of them all. She paused at the painting of a young girl, maybe eight years old.

This had to be their other sister. The curly, golden hair and startling blue eyes reminded her of Mirabel. There was something about those eyes Haven couldn't quite put her finger on, but they were somehow magical. Haven glanced up at the face of the woman with the painting. She had black hair, skin, and eyes. Haven had no idea where this woman was from.

"You see her now?" Kadia asked. "She may be our third sister. I cannot wait to meet her."

Understanding bloomed inside her. "You're from Seaburn." Haven tried to catch the eyes of the foreign woman.

Her gaze was as vacant as the rest of the castle occupants. Haven sagged as if defeated by this. She wished that these beautiful women with their gorgeous paintings would somehow be her salvation.

"She is! Smart little queen, aren't you?" Kadia clapped her hands together.

All the women stepped back against the wall, standing stiff and staring straight ahead. They remained in a perfect line.

"I can't wait to see what your future holds," Kadia said.

"My future?" Haven glanced at Kadia. Cold rushed over her skin.

"Yes. What do you think these paintings are for?" Kadia laughed, gazing at Haven as if *she* were the crazy one. "I see the future in the skin of my subjects. Of course, not just anyone will do. You should be honored, young Haven."

Haven took a step back. "You don't mean..."

"Yes. You will be my next subject. I will paint the future on your skin, as I have done with these beautiful ladies." Kadia snapped her fingers.

In came three men. One was carrying a basket of paints and brushes, while the other two advanced on Haven.

"Wait. Kadia, what are you doing?" Her shoulders slammed against the wall. Why hadn't she brought her brush weapon with her?

"I just told you, silly girl."

The two men grabbed Haven, their fingers painfully squeezing her biceps as they dragged her into the middle of the room. Haven struggled in their grip, pulling until she slammed her heel against one of their knees. Haven slipped free. She raced for the door.

She was caught before she could reach it.

The taller of the two pushed her onto the floor.

"Kadia, *please*! I don't need to know my future."

"But I want to know it. You should be nicer to your sister." Kadia readied her paints while the two men pulled Haven onto her back.

One pinned her hands above her head while the other ripped her clothes from her body. Haven cried out and thrashed violently, kicking the man in the face. He continued, unfazed.

"Stop!" Haven commanded. "Stop it!"

"Haven." Kadia sighed. "Shut up, will you?"

Haven glared at the woman and continued to try to pull away. Tears sprang to her eyes. She hated their hands on her and, worse, their hands stripping her naked.

Cold stone pressed against her back. Their hands fled, leaving her completely nude and at Kadia's mercy.

"Please, don't."

"Be silent!" Kadia leaned over her.

"No!" Haven twisted her wrists until she freed a hand.

"Knock her out."

"Kadia, no!"

Everything went black.

WHEN HAVEN CAME TO, everything was a blur. It took her a moment to focus, the haze lying heavily on her brain. A dull ache formed and left as quickly as it had come. When her vision cleared and sense had returned, she startled. Haven gasped as she glanced down. At first, she couldn't bear to watch. She turned her face and buried it against her arm, trying to think of better places than this. The cold swipe of a brush and liquid passed over her flesh, tickling her skin.

As the minutes ticked by, her curiosity took over. She peeked up at the Mad Queen. The same vacancy the others had was in her eyes. All expression had left her face, and her blue eyes shone dull gray.

As the brushes continued to glide across her skin, an image took shape. Black and red were the dominant colors, but from this angle, she could hardly see what it was Kadia was drawing.

"Kadia," Haven whispered. "What is it?"

Kadia didn't say a word. Haven was sure she hadn't heard her. All of her focus was on her painting, almost as if she were in a trance. Did Kadia know what she was painting? Her brushes flew forward and back, side to side, swirling, moving in straight lines. Yellows, oranges, whites, blues, and grays—she added them all. Haven took a deep breath and lay back. She could wait this out. She didn't have another choice.

Sometime later, Kadia sat back with a pleased sigh. Haven glanced up as Kadia stretched and rolled her shoulders and her head back. A blissful smile replaced her vacant expression, and her eyes were closed. She seemed completely at peace—until her blue eyes opened to see her masterpiece.

Kadia's face to contorted in fury before she screeched.

"You little brat!" Kadia grabbed Haven's thighs, digging her nails in. "You terrible little thing! How could you do this to me?" she screamed. Kadia rose, shouting obscenities into the air. "How *dare* you!"

Haven's eyes widened. Kadia grabbed whatever she could find, throwing things around the room, upsetting tables, and kicking chairs. When she returned to Haven, her anger sparked anew.

"You have—you *will* betray me!"

"But I would never—"

"Spare me your lies, you insufferable worm. Your treachery has already been made known." Kadia motioned the men away from Haven. "If you will betray your own sister, then I no longer care what you want. If you will not behave like a proper princess, then you will stay in this room until I am satisfied that you will not hurt your own."

Haven backed away, trapping herself against the end of her bed.

Kadia advanced, violently motioning toward her. "If you're going to betray me, I will at least get something from you."

Haven didn't understand what the queen meant until she caught her reflection in the full-body mirror near the door. Even from across the room, with Kadia partially blocking her, she saw it.

Cidra up in flames.

Whether it was a metaphor for Haven Fyre bringing the castle down or literal fire itself, she understood Kadia's rage. Haven smiled. She now knew she could do this. She could escape there or stay and still bring Kadia down. The mad queen had predicted it herself.

"Cidra will burn." Haven's fists clenched.

"Cidra will remain whole as long as I live. Your betrayal will only hurt you, *Lady Queen*," she mocked. "If you will betray me, then I have no use for you." Kadia turned to an adviser, who entered the room in a hurry. "Fetch the sons of the nobles. If our young Haven will betray me, then I will make use of her before she is disposed of. She will bear me a child as a replacement."

Haven's joy over Cidra's fall suddenly faltered. "Kadia." Her eyes widened. "I don't wish to marry. I don't want children!"

"Whether you like it or not, you will have a child for me." Kadia's cold glare was indifferent. She turned back to her adviser. "Bring them to me, and I will choose one suitable to be with the little queen. If she won't have him, then he'll rape her until she becomes pregnant."

Kadia motioned her painted women from the room and fled after them. The door slammed behind her.

Haven's legs collapsed beneath her, dumping her onto the edge of the bed. Cold bathed her limbs and pulled goose bumps to her skin. She couldn't be serious. She wouldn't do something like this. Even for the Insane Queen, this was *mad*.

She sat in shock for several minutes before putting her clothes back on. Now that she was alone, she fled to the corner of her room and sat on silk bedding. She couldn't imagine an act crueler than rape. She could barely believe that anyone would ever wish it on another.

LOST IN HER OWN THOUGHTS, Haven barely noticed when the door opened again. Several hours had passed, and her limbs ached from remaining in the same position. Someone's legs meandered into the corner of her vision. Haven started and pinned herself to the wall. This was the worst vantage point she could have imagined.

A tall, handsome, vacant-eyed lord stared down at her. He towered at least a foot above her. His mussed, brown hair and cold, blue eyes gave him a boyish charm.

"I am Lord Merick." He looked right through her.

"Stay away from me." Haven narrowed her eyes.

"If you do not comply, I have my orders."

Haven's heart pounded in her ears. Panic welled inside her chest, threatening to overwhelm her. She had to stay calm, but her mind raced.

"You will stay away from me. Do not touch me! That is my order as Queen of Rythern."

The man crawled in front of her onto the bed.

"I command you to stop! You will not touch me!" Haven shouted.

He grabbed her ankle and yanked her to the middle of the bed. He pinned her down with his body. His lips pressed against her neck. Every touch sent another splinter of panic through her mind. She cried out and tried to move her arms, but he pinned them down. She kicked her legs up, but he squashed them under his weight.

"Stop!" she screamed. "Please! Don't do this!" She couldn't believe this was happening. She'd trained so hard to protect herself and there she was, useless again. The last thing she ever wanted was to get pregnant, to be raped and bear a child from such an atrocity.

Every touch, every grab, and every pull at her body brought more tears to her eyes.

"Please, stop this," she begged. Haven twisted her wrists in his grasp.

He sat up, straddling her hips. Gazing over her body like she was a piece of meat, he bent and ripped her shirt open. Buttons flew in every direction. While her arms were free, she slammed them against his stomach and squirmed violently onto her stomach, closer to the edge of the bed. He groped her and kissed her bare back. Haven's fingers wrapped around the silk sheets, her nails scraping the fabric as she pulled herself to the edge of the bed.

"Please, stop," she whispered.

"I have my orders," he mumbled against her skin.

Haven blinked away the tears blurring her vision. She had to get away; she had to make him stop touching her. Every part of her trembled. She felt violated, dirty, and wrong. He pulled at the waist of her trousers.

"No!" she cried. "Do not touch me!"

"I have my orders." He yanked again.

"Stop!" she screamed. Haven pulled forward again. Her hand met air. His metal belt buckle jingled. Her whole body froze.

His belt tore free and thumped against the bed. While he was distracted, she searched beneath the mattress.

"I have my orders," he said.

Haven's fingers wrapped around her makeshift weapon. *Finally!*

The man flipped her onto her back. Haven screamed a battle cry as she slammed the point against his throat. Blood surged from the wound, dousing her in red. He gurgled and fell to her right.

Haven squirmed out from under him and collapsed onto the floor. Her breath came in sharp gasps as she tried to regain her wits. She shivered over and over while pulling herself along the floor to the opposite wall. Tears dripped down her cheeks and onto her chest, leaving long track marks over her blood-drenched skin.

Haven cried into her hands for some time before the shivering stopped and she gradually returned to her own mind. Taking deep breaths, Haven pulled her clothes back on. Every piece of her felt wrong.

"You can survive anything," she murmured to herself, recalling the words she'd used after Kadia had tortured her with knives. "You will survive this." She repeated it over and over until she could move.

She stood. There was only one way out of this. After moving over to the dead body in her bed, she yanked the paintbrush from his neck. She wiped some of the blood from her hands and proceeded to the door. She knocked quietly.

"Hello?" Her voice shook. "I need your help in here."

Haven hid behind the door. A moment passed before the door clicked open. A guard stepped in.

"Lady Queen?" he asked.

Haven leapt, driving the wood into his neck just like she had to the other. Blood sprayed the wall before he clutched the wound with his fingers. Haven slammed her boot into his back. He landed face-first. After pulling his sword from its sheath, Haven drove the blade through his back.

"You can survive anything." Haven repeated. "You will survive this."

She continued her mantra while she fled the room. Her bare feet slapped against the smooth stone as she swiftly made her way through the halls, trying to remember the way to the stairs.

"Queen Haven has escaped!" The words echoed throughout the castle.

Haven skidded to a stop and glanced back the way she'd come. This was it. She had to get out—now.

She glanced back and forth down the hall. She turned and ran. The quickest way out of the castle was before her. A long hall ended with a stained-glass window. Two feral cats circled each other in the glass, their orange fur brilliant in the evening sun. Haven raced toward the cats, her heart ramming against her ribs. Beyond the glass were the plains, the sand, and the sea.

Shouts rose behind her. "Stop!"

"You can survive anything. You will survive this." She covered her face.

Haven dove through the glass.

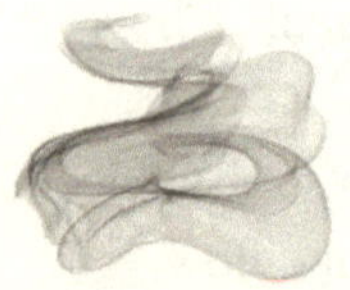

EIGHTEEN

You can survive anything. You will survive this.

Those words echoed through her mind as Haven awoke in agony.

Crying out, Haven turned onto her side. Her legs were broken, and at least one of her arms was out of place. Glass pierced her body every which way. She screamed, turning onto her back again. She breathed heavily, the haze clearing from her mind.

Voices echoed overhead. She had to move. Haven sat up, gritting her teeth as she pulled a piece of orange glass from her shoulder. She reset her arm. Hissing in pain, Haven struggled to remain conscious. She repeated her mantra aloud, pulling her legs in front of her. The bone protruded from her left thigh. She pushed it back into place. Blackness danced at the edge of her vision. She pulled a piece of glass from her other leg and twisted her bone back into place.

For a moment, she embraced the black, lying in the grass in complete pain. Shouts from the castle woke her. Haven sat up and pulled a large shard from her stomach. She cried out time after time, pulling the glass from her arms as she rose. She had to get moving. There was no telling how much time she had already wasted.

"Get to the tunnel," she murmured. "Just get to the tunnel."

Exhaustion washed over her. Her head spun as she stood. Haven limped up the small rise and onto the plains. With her constant movement, it was difficult to pull the glass from her body, but at least her legs improved as she went. Before she was halfway to the beach, she was running, ignoring the sting of pain as she pumped her arms.

"Get to the tunnel. You can *do this*!" she shouted into the wind.

As she yanked another piece of glass from her arm, the small dark wood building atop the sand came into sight. She silently cheered, a grin spreading over her face.

A scream rose from the castle. Haven faulted mid-step, but she caught herself before she crashed to the ground. She turned. Kadia stood in the window from which she'd leapt. Her screams carried on the wind.

"Haven!" Kadia was furious. "If you leave now, I will find and kill everyone you love!"

Haven paused as darkness spilled from the window. She didn't have time to stay and listen to idle threats. If those shadows got to her, she'd wish she were dead. Turning back to the sea, Haven ran as fast as her legs would carry her.

"Haven!" Kadia's voice grew distant.

Her eyebrows furrowed as her name carried from ahead. The doors of the small building opened, and out poured her three guard girls. Tears sprang to her eyes. Her adrenaline pushed her over the plains and onto the path in the sand.

"Haven!"

Lareina, Malka, and Blythe raced toward her. Behind them emerged Prince Emeril, King Corrin, and several soldiers from Rythern, Wakefin, and Salander.

The young queen almost collapsed in relief right there, but she had to keep going in order for them all to escape.

"Haven, watch out!" Blythe yelled.

Haven turned as a shadow massed behind her. It grabbed her by the ankle and threw her into the air. Her breath exploded from her lungs as she sailed through the sky for a few moments.

Her shoulder cracked against the earth as she landed. Her head spun, but her grip on the sword didn't waver.

A dark soldier appeared above her, driving his blade down.

Haven snapped her blade up. Their blades clanged together. Haven pushed him away and rolled back to her feet. Several soldiers surrounded her, as well as her friends. Rage pulsed inside her chest like a hurricane. Haven lunged into battle, letting her adrenaline fuel her as she swiped, slashed, and drove her blade through the darkness.

Her guards fought alongside her. Relief swelled inside her chest. Familiar movements guided her hands. She protected her friends as best she could, especially Blythe, who was wielding her sword with her left hand. The soldiers, the king, the prince, and her ladies destroyed man after man, but still, the darkness amassed before them.

"It's no use!" Malka called, shooting arrows from the building's door.

"We have to retreat!" Blythe called back.

Haven had to agree, but she kept swiping. Anger like none other consumed her. Fire burned her belly. She was angry with Kadia for so much. The torture she'd put her through, every stab, every burn, every poke and prod. The rape she'd nearly been subjected to, and the continuous outpouring of psychological pain. Haven fought until she could barely breathe, could barely swing. She would not let a single one of those things touch her.

An arm wrapped around her waist, pulling her back. Haven nearly screamed, whipping around. Corrin's worried gaze met hers. She lowered her blade.

"Do not touch me," she begged, her eyes wide. Haven blinked tears back. Heat fled her body, leaving her cold and shaking. "Do not touch me." Her blade clattered to the ground.

"It's okay." Corrin reached for her again.

Haven recoiled.

"Very well. I won't touch you, but you need to come with me."

After a moment, Haven nodded.

"Follow me." Corrin led her into the building.

Malka moved to the side, shooting arrow after arrow into the fray. "Let's go!" she shouted.

Everyone flooded into the small room. Shadows slammed against the doorway as if hitting a barrier. Haven's eyebrows furrowed.

Blythe shoved the door closed, leaving them all in darkness. A torch was lit. Thuds assaulted the door, but nothing burst through.

Corrin led them down a staircase that circled the passage walls. The stairs turned so swiftly that she grew dizzy within a few minutes.

"Careful. You'll eventually get used to it." Corrin flashed a smile over his shoulder.

Haven took deep breaths, trying to calm her racing heart. Her emotions pulled her in every direction. Joy over seeing everyone alive. Relief at having escaped Kadia's grasp. Pain from everything that had happened. Sadness at having rejected Corrin. Anger over the things Kadia had done, and above all else, panic at having to feel all of those things at once.

Hours passed as they descended deep into the earth, down the never-ending spiral. Her body sagged, and her mind grew hazy. Her heels slipped beneath her several times. She caught herself on the wall. The farther they went, the clumsier she became.

"We're almost there," Emeril said from up ahead.

Haven remained quiet, as did most of the others. Minutes later, they hit ground. Her guards ushered her into a small camp they had set up. A fire was lit. It warmed her tired bones. Haven slid down the wall on the far side of the small camp, sitting heavily on the ground. Her whole body ached.

"Haven, we're so glad you're okay." Lareina kneeled beside her and reached to hug her.

Haven recoiled and held her hands out defensively. "Please don't touch me!"

Worry creased Lareina's brow as she sat back. "We wouldn't hurt you, Haven."

Haven just shook her head and hugged her knees to her chest. She knew they wouldn't hurt her. It wasn't that. Her skin still crawled at the thought of anyone's hands on her.

Shadows from the fire danced along the walls. She shivered. It was cold that far in the earth. She hadn't noticed it so much while they'd been moving, but now that they had stopped, the cold wall on her back might as well have been a slab of ice.

"Get the queen a blanket," Lareina told a guard nearby.

The man nodded and disappeared farther into the tunnel.

"What happened in there? It's been weeks."

Haven shook her head. She didn't want to talk about it, only forget. If she thought about it, she might break down. She didn't want that happening in front of everyone.

"Why did you all stay?" she asked through chattering teeth.

"As if we were going to leave you behind," Blythe scoffed. She leaned against the wall. Though she appeared nonchalant, worry creased her brow.

"You should have."

"Haven, you're covered in blood," Emeril gasped. He stood at the other side of the small fire, his gaze glued to her clothes.

Haven glanced down and froze. Her tattered clothes bore not only her own blood, but that of the two men she'd killed in her escape. They hadn't known better; they'd been under a spell. But, in her desperation, Haven had seen no other way. Shame filled her.

"It's not all mine." Haven ran a hand through her hair. Her fingers stuck in a braid Kadia had made. Her heart clenched. She quickly pulled it out, her fingers trembling violently as she did.

"Not all?" Lareina asked, reaching for her queen again.

Haven stilled. "Do not touch me." She shook her head, shifting away from Lareina. "Do *not* touch me."

"Okay." Lareina backed off. "It isn't all your blood? But some is?"

Haven nodded. She prodded her hair in search of more braids.

"Did they hurt you in there?"

Haven nodded slowly as she worked another braid from her hair.

"What happened?"

Haven shook her head. "I don't want to talk about it."

"But we can't help you if you don't tell us what happened," she insisted. "We're all here for you, Haven. We're your friends."

Haven buried her head against her knees. She couldn't talk about it. She wouldn't. A moment later, someone gently laid a blanket around her shoulders. She pulled it tight around her, willing the shaking in her bones to stop.

"You should move closer to the fire," Malka urged gently. She stood against the wall by the tunnel entrance.

Haven obliged. As she sat back down, holding her hands out near the flame, her legs shook. It was a welcome relief when the shivers stopped. Warmth soothed her aching bones and numbed her brain. Her eyelids drooped. She was so tired.

"You should change." Lareina stood and took the satchel she'd carried since they'd left Rythern from Malka. "We still have your riding clothes. They'd be warmer than what you're wearing."

It took a bit of coaxing, but eventually, Haven complied and took the satchel. The girls held the blanket up for her to change behind while her male soldiers and the royals turned away.

Haven stepped behind it, cold embracing her bare arms. She shivered. Only a few more moments and she'd be warm again. She pulled her shirt up. Dark paint peeked below. Haven froze. She'd nearly forgotten that it was there. Dark swirls of black and red climbed her stomach.

"Wait." Haven turned to the others.

Lareina and Malka glanced at one another, then lowered the blanket at her behest.

"Look," Haven said.

The men slowly turned. Haven held her shirt up, exposing the painting of Cidra engulfed in flames.

They all gasped.

"What is that?" Blythe asked.

"The future." Haven glanced up at the others.

"Cidra's demise," Corrin said.

"The Mad Queen predicted it herself."

NINETEEN

"Haven, may I speak with you?"

Haven had just settled into her cot when Emeril approached. Ever vigilant, Blythe stepped forward, her hand on the hilt of her sword.

"I'm tired, Emeril." She sighed, sitting up.

"I know," he said. "You've been through a lot, but I just wanted to speak with you privately for a moment."

Haven shook her head. "I told you that will never happen again."

Emeril paused. They'd all seen the rags of Haven's clothes, the cuts in the fabric, the marks that had clearly come from wounds inflicted and not from the blood of others. Haven had insisted they be burned and forgotten. Emeril was the only one not ready to let it go.

"I know," he said. "But I want you to know I'm sorry. What I did was unforgivable. But, if you ever find it in your heart to speak with me again, I'll be here for you. I'm sorry for what you had to go through alone. We're all here for you now."

Her guards shifted uncomfortably. In this regard, they agreed.

"Thank you for your apology," Haven said. "Please leave me be."

Emeril nodded and said his farewell before leaving to go farther down the tunnel. Before they'd made camp, they'd put some distance between them and the staircase. Cold earth surrounded them on all sides. Her shivers returned.

Sleep drifted at the edge of her mind, heavy, but still, she remained awake. Haven lay back and waited. Several minutes passed and she continued to wait, but sleep did not come.

"Haven?" Lareina asked through the dark. "Are you awake?"

Haven sighed. "Yes."

"When you're ready, we're here for you," she said.

"I know."

"All of us are. We'll protect you no matter what the cost may be."

The notion stung her heart. Though Haven wanted to protect her guards more than anything, that protection had come with a price: her blood and bits of her innocence. If she hadn't been so eager to protect everyone, would she have ended up in Kadia's castle? Most likely.

"And I will protect you all," Haven whispered. "To my very end."

Lareina's breath caught. Haven turned toward her friend. She hoped she wasn't crying. She couldn't handle her friend crying for her.

"Lareina, are you all right?"

"Yes."

"Then what is it?"

Lareina swallowed audibly. "We almost lost you. I know it. Those tears in your clothes." She sniffed. "Someone did that to you. That on top of the painting and I can't imagine what else." She paused to take a breath "We weren't there for you when you needed us. We should have stormed that castle and taken you ourselves."

Her lips twisted ruefully. "That would have been madness on par with the Evil Queen's."

Lareina laughed through her tears. "You're probably right."

"You should sleep," Haven said. "We'll have a long day ahead of us."

"All right," she said. "Goodnight, Haven."

"Goodnight, Lareina."

* * *

HAVEN AWOKE several times that night. Once, she was shouting, and another, she nearly leapt from her bed. Her guards hushed her back to sleep, but after the third try, Haven remained wide awake. As she stared at the ceiling, flashes of paintings, stabbings, and a man on top of her flew through her mind. Would she ever sleep well again after Kadia's castle?

She sighed and rose from her bed before pulling on the jacket Malka had given her. She fastened it tightly, the fur hood tickling her cheeks and her neck. It smelled of pines and reminded her of home.

Stepping quietly through the cavern, Haven followed the dim light to the fire around the bend. Corrin was sitting on a long rock protruding from the earth. He leaned forward, his back to her. Her heart clenched. Did she want company?

As if sensing her presence, Corrin turned.

"Lady Queen." He smiled and motioned for her to join him.

Haven hesitated.

"I don't bite." He laughed, but his heart wasn't behind it.

Haven joined him, sitting as far away from him as she possibly could on their little rock bench. "You can't sleep?"

"My mind is too preoccupied for sleep." He sighed. "More nightmares?"

Heat rose to her cheeks, and her stomach twisted. She had hoped no one besides her guards had heard her screaming. "Yes," she admitted. "What occupies your mind tonight?"

"Many things."

"Maybe, if you discuss them, you'll be able to sleep," she suggested.

"Maybe, if you talk about what happened to you, your nightmares will go away." Corrin gave her a sly smile.

Haven couldn't help the smile pulling at her lips. "If you tell me what's on your mind, maybe I'll share what plagues my sleep," she said, unsure if she'd actually be able to deliver on her promise.

Corrin nodded and straightened in his seat. "That seems fair," he said. It took him a moment to continue.

Haven had a feeling he could be dismissing some of his worries and picking which ones he wanted to share.

"Most of my thoughts are about you, Lady Haven."

She flushed.

"When they took you, I realized something about myself. I've spent a lot of time mourning the loss of one woman, so much so that I fear I might let a great one pass me by. I don't know you well, Haven, but I truly want to." He glanced at Haven. Her eyes widened. "Watching Kadia take you away was the hardest thing I've ever done. I regretted it the moment we were in the trees. I should have fought longer and harder for you. I should have protected you. You never should have gone to that castle."

"It's not your fault, Corrin." She avoided his intense gaze.

"It is and isn't. More should have been done, but sometimes, these things are unavoidable. I've barely slept while you were gone. Which is why I'm surprised to still be awake now. I thought having you back would help me rest."

"I don't think my being back is helping anyone," Haven said.

Corrin reached for her hand. Haven recoiled before she could stop herself. She stood and stepped away.

"Don't touch me."

They stared at each other for a long moment.

"I-I'm sorry," she said.

"No, I'm sorry. I shouldn't have." Corrin returned his hands to his lap.

"It's not you—" Haven struggled to find the words while forcing back the water building in her eyes. "I just don't want to be touched. I can't be—not for a while, at least."

Understanding dawned on his handsome face. "Okay. I promise I won't until you're ready."

After a few moments, Haven returned to her seat, clenching her fists to stop her hands from shaking. "Thank you," she said. "So, what did you realize about yourself?"

Corrin smiled. "I realized that I want much but only need a little. I make bad decisions, and I let my feelings or fears get in the way of what's right. I want to be more like you. I…" He paused. "I want to be with you, Haven."

Her heart leapt. She hadn't expected this confession, yet it warmed the ice layering her heart. He let his words sit with her for some time. What could she say to such honesty?

"I don't think I can be with anyone, Corrin. Not now, and maybe not ever."

If Corrin was hurt, he didn't show it. "I understand. But I'm counting on that maybe. You're worth waiting for, Haven."

"Am I?"

"You're much more special than you realize."

It was simply his choice of words that rattled her. Kadia's voice flowed back to her in waves. *Special,* she'd called her. More times than she could possibly count. Haven was her special little girl, her sister, her little queen. Haven shivered, forgetting all about their conversation.

Seeming to sense the change in mood—and maybe even her drifting mind—Corrin turned to her. "What did she do to you in there, Haven? You haven't been the same since you returned."

It was true. But how much could she explain to the young king? How Kadia had stabbed her, burned her, drowned her, and tortured her? How she'd pretended to be Kadia's friend while slowly losing her mind? How Kadia had stripped her bare, knocked her unconscious, and proceeded to paint her naked body? Or how, in the end, when Kadia had seen what Haven truly wanted, she'd sent a man to rape her until she was with child? Haven slowly hugged herself, rocking back and forth, staring into the fire. Orange licked the air, colors dancing with the shadows. She shook her head.

"Haven?" Corrin asked.

The stab to the thigh, the burning poker pulled across her skin, the water rushing down her throat, the men pinning her down and ripping her clothes from her body—all because she was *special.*

"Haven?" Corrin repeated. The young king reached for her again.

Haven fell to the floor to get away, curling into a tight ball. "Don't touch me," she whispered over and over again. "Stop. Please, don't." She remembered that weight on top of her, the cold kisses left down her neck. She shivered violently. "Don't touch me." The way he'd groped her, touched her body in such indecent ways. "Please stop."

It was as if she were there again, feeling it all happen. What if it had gone further? What if he'd truly been able to fulfill his orders? How long would she have been defiled until Kadia was happy? Days, weeks, months? How long would it have taken her to get her pregnant? Haven couldn't bear the thought of bringing a child into that life, let alone leaving her son or daughter in Kadia's clutches.

"Haven!" Corrin shouted.

Haven gasped as if rising from cold water. "Corrin!" She almost reached out for him, but the fear slicing through her mind stopped her.

"Haven, it's me. It's just me." He moved closer as if he wanted to touch her, console her, but he remained at a safe distance. She appreciated that. "You're okay. You're not there anymore. You're with your friends."

Haven slowly nodded, understanding coming back to her. She wasn't in Kadia's castle, she hadn't been raped, and she couldn't be tortured anymore. "I'm okay. I'm here. I've survived it."

"Yes. Yes, you have." Corrin's eyebrows furrowed over sad eyes.

Haven concentrated on her breathing. In and out. Steady. Her gaze wandered around the cave. The images fled her mind as she took in the dark stone, the fire, and Corrin's handsome, sculpted face turned with worry.

"I'm here. I'm safe. I'm with you." Her legs fell from her embrace. "I'm safe."

"What's going on?" Blythe appeared around the bend.

"Haven's just had a bit of an episode." Corrin stood.

Blythe came to the queen's side, but Corrin quickly motioned for her not to touch the queen.

Haven rose, wiping the tears she hadn't been aware of from her face. "I'm okay."

"You should get back to bed." Blythe exchanged a look with Corrin.

He nodded. "That is probably for the best."

Nodding, Haven let Blythe lead her back to bed, where she quickly fell into a dreamless sleep.

TWENTY

$\mathcal{U}$nderground, it was impossible to tell the time of day. When the supposed morning came, Haven woke to gentle words from her friend. She was happy Lareina had bent to wake her, speaking to her softly instead of poking or nudging her. She smiled at her friend and rose. In the dim light, the small group readied for departure. They had a long journey ahead of them. Haven wanted to put as much distance between them and Kadia as possible.

The tunnel was cut from the earth, dark rocks surrounding them on all sides. The only light came from their torches until the terrain began to change.

They proceeded with caution as one of the Wakefin guards led them onto new terrain. The tunnel opened up into a huge cavern with soft sounds of its own: cawing in the distance and water dropping from the trees. A dim light came from an unknown source. The group emerged into a jungle. Its thick leaves and its tall trees towered above them. Vines hung on all sides, and ferns constantly blocked their path. But it was warm there. Humid, even. It was a welcome change to the freezing cold of the rock tunnels.

"What is this place?" Blythe whispered.

"It's beautiful," Haven said.

A loud buzz came from the trees. A winged bug flew between the leaves, diving over their heads. Haven and Blythe ducked as it flew into the trees on the other side of their path.

"What was that?" Lareina glanced between them with wide eyes.

"I have no idea." Blythe scratched the back of her head.

"Let's keep going." Corrin motioned them ahead.

They continued forward, avoiding the small reptiles scuttling past and the birds hovering nearby. The lush trees were nothing like she'd seen before in the six kingdoms. Compared to this forest, Rythern was boring, barren of life. With every step they took, they spotted a new plant or animal. Part of her wanted to remain in this jungle. She could investigate how it remained there under the sea. It didn't make sense; she was utterly mystified by it.

After hours of hiking, there was still no end to the jungle. Malka observed from the ridge above, an arrow at the ready. Though most of them had grown relaxed in this new territory, Malka had become wary.

It had to be at least high noon when Malka motioned for them to stop. "There's something following us."

Haven barely caught her words. She glanced around, her bliss over new findings shattered. What replaced it was a familiar rising panic. Could Kadia have followed them down there? Or maybe her dark soldiers? Had she sent another assassin after them, or was it just the forest playing tricks on Malka?

"What is it?" Corrin asked.

"I'm not sure, but it's not human," she replied.

Their soldiers moved to the outer edge of the group, pushing the royals within. They drew their swords, their peace only a memory as they continued in worried silence. If it wasn't human, it could be the dark soldiers, but she had to pray that it wasn't. As they went, Haven kept one eye on her archer and the other on the trees.

Malka moved almost soundlessly across the terrain, dropping in and out of sight on the ledge above. Vines brushed her shoulders under a thick canopy of trees. Malka disappeared from sight as between the wide leaves. Brush shifted all around them.

"Blythe, get down!" Malka yelled.

Haven whipped around in her friend's direction, ripping her sword from its sheath. A huge orange cat at least twice the length of her body leapt from the trees. It was something familiar yet a creature she'd never seen in the flesh. Haven pushed Blythe out of its path.

The cat's body collided with her shoulders, slamming her into the ground. Huge teeth snarled inches from her face. Yellow eyes glared into her own. Haven held the creature back with her sword across both of her palms. She pushed up on its neck to keep its large fangs from snapping at her face.

"Haven!" Blythe called.

The cat yowled and leapt away. Blood dripped over the leaves as it fled.

"Are you all right?" Blythe bent to help her up.

Haven glanced at her hand and shook her head. She pulled herself up, dusting the dirt from her back. "I'm fine."

"What were you doing, then? Why did you push me out of the way?"

Haven slammed her sword back into its sheath. "You know very well why I did it."

"You can't be risking your life like that!"

"I don't risk my life when I do *things like that!* You do!" Haven snapped.

She didn't understand why, but anger blossomed inside her. She'd never been an angry person, and she hardly ever raised her voice. This sudden burning inside her was startling and violent.

Haven tried to snuff it out; she didn't like the feeling one bit. "I'm sorry, but my life won't be risked when I jump into situations like that. I could be hurt, yes, but I won't be killed. You can be. I won't let you risk your lives for me when I can do something about it. Everyone here should know that." She looked them each in the eye. "Do not protect me if it means your life over mine."

Without awaiting a response, Haven pushed through the brush.

Once the others regained their wits, they caught up and fell into formation. Another archer joined Malka on the ridge, and they were much more vigilant.

"Yellow eyes in the trees!" Malka called.

"Two behind!" the other archer confirmed. "At least one ahead."

When the next attack came, the group leapt into battle. The beasts prowled from the ferns lining the path. Haven tore her blade free.

Haven stood with her guard ladies as another cat leapt from between the trees. Its large body knocked Blythe off her feet. Haven drove her sword through its side. The cat snarled and leapt at her next. Haven ducked as a dagger flew for its shoulder. Haven stood and found Lareina watching her back.

"Thank you," she said.

"Any time." Lareina smiled.

Haven and Blythe fought the beast off while the others dealt with the threat from the rear.

"Another from above!" Malka called.

Arrows zipped overhead. While Blythe handled the wounded beast, Haven turned in time for another to slam into her chest. Air exploded from her lungs. She gasped for breath. The beast snapped at her shoulder, its teeth ripping through her jacket and down to her flesh.

Haven cried out, trying to get her sword beneath the beast. With its large weight on top of her, she could hardly move. Memories of that man, Lord Merick, on top of her flooded her mind. Her eyes widened as she struggled violently, even as the claws of the beast dug into her arms. She thrashed with the beast was killed on top of her, and then she was pulled out from beneath it. Hyperventilating, Haven twisted onto her stomach.

"It's all right, Haven," Lareina whispered. "You're all right."

Haven reeled back from her touch, leaning back against the wall below the ridge. She took several deep breaths while the others gathered around in a protective formation.

"You're hurt." Corrin stepped up beside her.

"I'm fine," she snapped.

"You don't look fine." Emeril joined them.

"It's not the beast." Her fingers shook. She wasn't in Kadia's castle. She was safe with her friends.

"Then what is it?" Blythe lowered her blade. Blood spattered her armor, but it was clearly not her own.

"Nothing." Haven leaned away from the wall. "Let's just keep going."

They all exchanged glances with one another. It took a moment, but they all seemed to understand what had happened and why Haven didn't want to speak of it. They let it go and fell back into line.

Moving through the jungle, they fell into a routine. Malka and the other archer above called out every oncoming assault while simultaneously shooting the ones far away and leading them through the brush to the other side of the forest. It was slow going, but after a few more attacks, they left with only minor injuries.

"There's a tunnel up ahead," Malka called down.

Haven had never been more relieved to hear those words. Though the jungle had been beautiful and filled with wonder at first, she'd grown tired of the constant attacks. She yearned for the quiet of the cold, dark stone tunnel they'd left behind.

They made it to the tunnel without further delay. It was wider this time, and they could easily walk in a row of four or five if they wished. They remained in their solid formation, keeping the royals near the center for the most safety. Malka and the archer fell in behind them, keeping their bows ready as they watched the rear. A different soldier from Salander led just as cautiously as the last. They moved slowly through the tunnel, the growls and the yowls of the beasts they'd left behind echoing. When the sounds finally vanished, they could all finally breathe easy.

"It seems we're through the worst of it." Lareina sighed. "I thought that jungle would never end."

"Neither did I," Haven agreed.

The chatter of the guards replaced their worried silence. Haven sheathed her sword. The hum of conversation grew distant.

Something up ahead shined against the darkness. They'd been

walking for some time through the dark, and with only the dim torches, it was hard to tell what lay ahead. The farther they went, the brighter the light grew. So it wasn't a trick of the eye. At the end of the tunnel, a pink glow emanated.

"What is that?" Corrin asked as if echoing her thoughts.

"I don't know," Haven said.

"We should proceed carefully," Blythe said.

The *shing* of swords being pulled from their sheaths replaced the chatter. Haven did the same. After the jungle, there was no telling what they were about to walk into.

As the pink light grew brighter, the end of the tunnel became obvious. Soon, they emerged onto a glass ledge.

The stark contrast between the dark of the tunnel and the sudden light was unbelievable—even more so than the jungle. A room of mirrors filled with glass and water stood before them. A pink glow shone from some areas, while a soft-blue aura emanated from others. Ripples moved through the water. It was almost impossible to see the path with their reflections glaring back at them.

"Where are we?" Haven asked no one in particular.

No one answered. They all stared with wide eyes and open mouths. There seemed to be no way to pass, yet they had to get through somehow.

"There." Malka pointed for the far wall.

Haven followed the direction in which she pointed. At first, Haven couldn't tell what she was looking at. It just looked like more of the same. She narrowed her eyes. A glass ledge led up to a small tunnel. She couldn't tell how far away it was, but it was their best bet.

"Lead the way," Haven said.

Malka nodded and proceeded across the glass without a word. Many areas were narrow, and the glass appeared thin. They continued single file and stepped lightly in case the glass broke.

After nearly an hour, Malka held her head up. They all stopped.

"We need to go through the water," she said. "There's no ledge to lead us over there."

Haven nodded, but a sinking feeling settled inside her. The murky water might have been pretty in pastel colors, but who was to say what lay in wait.

"Let's go then." Haven stepped into the warm water, wading slowly until she reached her waist. She held her sword above her head and tried not to enjoy herself too much as she slipped in to her collarbone. Something hard and sturdy enough to walk on laid beneath her feet. At least they needn't swim.

Malka led in silence. After their encounter in the jungle, they were all on high alert. They needed to be ready if any creatures came barreling out of nowhere. But, when a half hour lapsed and nothing had come, the group relaxed.

"This is actually rather pleasant," one of the guards laughed behind them.

Haven smiled.

"It's nice to finally take a bath!" Lareina agreed.

"I wonder if they have warm water like this in Seaburn," another said.

"If it's as warm as they say, I'm sure the surrounding seas are like lava!"

They all laughed.

"What was that?" One of the Wakefin guards stopped, gazing through the water. "I felt something move by my leg—I swear it."

They all froze and looked back, their laughter dying out.

"Are you sure it's not just your sheath?" His fellow soldier laughed beside him.

The first soldier motioned to his sheathed sword over his shoulder. Both men blinked at each other then looked to their king for direction.

"We should keep moving," Corrin said.

Haven nodded, and Malka led the way. Several minutes passed before they stopped again.

"I felt something too," Emeril said.

"So did I," another soldier chimed in.

Haven and Corrin exchanged a look. They were about to continue when a loud splash echoed through the cavern. The sound reverberated throughout, echoing over and over again. Haven turned. Lareina was gone.

"Lareina!" she cried, searching through the clouded water.

"Stay back, Lady Queen." Blythe stepped forward.

They both looked through the water, moving farther and farther from the group.

"What was that?" Haven spun toward the group.

Malka was staring at the water nearby. Ripples moved from the spot at which she gazed.

"What is it, Malka?"

"I saw something." The archer glanced up, worry clouding her green gaze.

Panic sent her heart racing. She couldn't lose one of her guards. Not now.

Red blossomed in the water around them.

Haven gasped. "Lareina?" she cried. "Lareina!"

The water broke several feet away and the blue-eyed blonde rose from the depth. Haven went to her, but Blythe was closer. She held Lareina above water while the blonde spluttered and spit the water from her lungs.

"Creatures," Lareina said between ragged gasps. "There are creatures in the water. It wrapped around my leg and pulled me under. We must make haste."

Haven returned to the rest of the group. They were peering into the water with nervous gazes.

"Let's go, Malka." Haven looked to the front of the group.

Malka was gone.

"Malka?" Blythe's voice rose an octave. "Malka, where are you?"

It was the first time Haven had ever heard Blythe's voice break. The strong woman handed Lareina off to another Rythern guard then moved to the last place Malka had been seen. Haven joined her, as did Corrin and the Wakefin soldiers.

"Find her," Haven commanded. "We must find her."

Blythe stared at the water in panic, trying to see through its murky depths to her beloved.

Haven waded through the water, moving off ahead in her search. "Wait, Blythe I think—"

Something wrapped around her boot. Haven gasped before she was pulled under water.

TWENTY-ONE

$\mathcal{H}$aven inhaled water time and time again as the creature dragged her beneath the surface. Her lungs filled, and her throat burned. She coughed again and again, bubbles flying from her mouth and her nose.

The current picked up around her, which made it difficult to thrash against its grip. Haven clawed at the water. If she didn't break the surface, she'd drown down there.

The grip on her leg tightened as she kicked out. It spun through the water, flinging her in every direction. Her head spun, and blackness crept across her vision.

Her limbs weakened, slowly shutting down. She struggled valiantly with the last of her strength, reaching to grab the tentacle gripping her boot. Though she'd lost her sword, a dagger Lareina had given her was hidden in her boot. If only she could reach it in time.

Thrashing against the current and the pull, Haven finally locked her fingers around the dagger. She tore it out as her fingers squeezed around the slimy tentacle wrapping her boot.

Her chest ached as she drove her blade down with the last of her strength.

Something like a screech echoed through the water. The warmth of darkness embraced her.

Gasping, Haven coughed and spluttered water from her lungs. Someone put pressure to her chest until she came back to life. Her entire body was heavy, leaden against the glass surface of the path.

Water droplets clung to her eyelashes, blurring her vision. She blinked them away, her mind slowly catching up with the present.

She started. The creature. Haven sat up, glancing around for the beast.

"Haven, can you hear me?"

Her eyebrows furrowed. Her ears must have been full of water.

"Haven, it's Corrin. You almost drowned."

Understanding dawned on her. She rested back on her elbows. So she'd survived it. Whatever the monster had been, she hoped she'd done some damage. Her throat ached from coughing and her lungs labored to bring her fresh air, but otherwise, she felt fine.

"Malka?" Haven said. "Is she okay?"

"See for yourself." Corrin nodded over her shoulder.

Blythe cradled the shivering Malka a few feet away. She strong woman spoke softly, tears leaving tracks down her cheeks. It was the first time Haven had ever seen the woman cry.

"Did everyone make it?" she asked.

Corrin fell silent and sat back, propping his arm on his knee. "No. Two of the guards were lost. One from Rythern, another from Salander."

Haven slowly nodded, a cold pit settling inside her stomach. This journey was taking a lot more out of them than she had expected. She couldn't begin to imagine how many had been lost when the rest of their people had come through.

"We should get going," Corrin said.

Haven nodded. "Everyone needs rest, but we can't stay here."

Corrin agreed. After a few minutes of rest, they gathered the remaining members of their flock and climbed the glass slope into the next tunnel.

* * *

WEEKS PASSED before they saw the end of the tunnel to Seaburn. Time lost all meaning, and the group only rested when they could. When sunlight finally shone down the tunnel ahead, the group found new energy to climb the spiral staircase to the world above.

Relief flooded Haven's bones as she collapsed in the sand. She smiled and laughed. Most fell onto the beach, while others rolled in the sand. Finally, they'd gotten through. Finally, they were safe.

"We made it." Haven closed her eyes against the brightness of the sun. She tilted her face to the sky to bask in its warmth.

Being in the dark so long had taken its toll on everyone. Finally being in the sun was a joy like no other.

"Finally," Corrin agreed. He sat beside her on the sand.

"Can we just stay in the sun forever?" She sighed blissfully.

"In our dreams, we can."

They both laughed.

"Then I never want to wake up," Haven said.

They sat together for some time, enjoying the last of the afternoon sun. It was the perfect time to emerge from their dark hole in the earth. Haven had meant it when she'd said that she wanted to stay on the beaches of Seaburn forever. All of her problems drifted away there. Her panic fled, as did the memories of Kadia's castle. For a while, she could forget who she was. She wasn't Queen Haven of Rythern; she was just a girl lying in the sand with a boy. She could only imagine a life so simple and wonderful.

"Company approaches," Blythe said.

She flashed her eyes open only to be blinded by the sun. Sitting up, Haven rubbed her eyes and readjusted to the light.

Haven and Corrin both rose, joining Blythe and the gathering guards. Her heart pounded in her ears. Could this be more trouble on its way?

A small group of men atop beautiful while horses emerged over the sand dunes, a carriage at their backs. They were wearing incredibly detailed white-and-gold uniforms, and all shared a similar dark complexion. They stopped several feet away. Only two dismounted and approached them.

"Greetings," the first said. His accent slurred the word. "I have to assume you are the long-awaited party from the six kingdoms." He smiled, crossing his hands politely in front of him. He bowed, as did the other man.

Her heart settled. Thank the blue skies. She wasn't sure she could have dealt with another battle right now.

"Good day." Corrin stepped forward. " I am King Corrin of Wakefin."

"A pleasure." They both bowed again.

"This is Queen Haven of Rythern and Prince Emeril of Salander."

Again, they exchanged polite greetings and bows.

"We have to assume, if you've heard of us, that our people have arrived safely."

"As safe as can be through that tunnel," the second man said.

"We know all too well," Emeril said.

"Please come with us and we will accompany you to the palace."

"Thank you," Corrin said.

The two men led them back to the group of white horses. Soon, they were far from the beautiful sand beach and Haven's serenity, moving into the city where Haven hoped to find her people safe at last.

THE JOURNEY to the palace was almost as dizzying as the one through the tunnel. With all the beautiful sights, it was hard to keep her jaw up. They passed through the sandstone streets to the golden palace in the distance. Haven had heard mention of it from the others, but she had never imagined that it would literally have golden turrets.

The landscape and the weather were made all the more beautiful by the people. Men, women, and children ran through the crowds at the edge of their carriage. Everyone bowed and smiled as they passed. The people were all well kept and dressed in the finest silks and jewels. Haven felt grungy and unattractive in comparison. Though their accents were thick and their words sometimes unfamiliar, Haven was mesmerized by it all.

The closer they came to the palace, the more her awe grew. The palace was atop a hill at the rear of the city. It split into three parts. The middle building was the largest, with a huge golden dome and a spire atop it. A huge courtyard spread out before it, lined with lush gardens and tall trees with leaves only at the top of their trunks. The other two sides were diagonal to the middle piece with smaller but still sizable gold turrets and courtyards of their own.

The carriage rocked to a halt. She hardly noticed as she gaped at the palace.

"This place is incredible." Haven hopped out alongside Corrin.

The others dismounted behind them.

"It's certainly unique," he agreed.

Haven gazed all around as the Seaburn men led them through the courtyards and up through the golden palace doors. Fine details and designs were carved into the surrounding stone, wrapping the pillars like fabric.

"Well met, lords and ladies of Warshard!" A booming laugh filled the entryway.

Haven glanced up at the large marble staircase that led to the second floor. A large black man in blue-and-gold-trimmed robes descended.

"That is how you foreigners say it, is it not?" He grinned, his white teeth dazzling in the warm light filtering through the two-story windows.

"Yes, it is quite accurate." Corrin nodded and introduced them all.

"King Corrin, Queen Haven, and Prince Emeril. We welcome you to the Republic of Seaburn!" The man beamed. "I am council member

Vasily. You may call me Vas. Make yourselves at home." Vas motioned them inside.

Leading them up the grand staircase, he went on and on about the palace, the amenities, and where their people were set up.

Haven listened and let herself be led. She was too distracted by her surroundings to pay much attention to where she was going. Eventually, they stopped in a small indoor courtyard with a stone fountain and beautiful gardens decorating a sitting area. Archways around it shielded any passersby from rain. Or at least Haven assumed that was their use. Vas stopped before one of the arches, motioning to the courtyard. Lining the walls under the arches were doors.

"These will be your rooms." He smiled. "I hope they are up to your standards." Vas bowed slightly. "I hope to see you all at dinner tonight." He flashed one last smile before he took his leave.

As if appearing from nowhere, several young girls flitted through the group, each leading the royals and their respective guards to their rooms.

Haven said her goodbyes to the others and followed the young girl. Her heart clenched with anticipation. There was nothing she wished for more than a bath and a good night's sleep in a real bed.

The tawny-skinned girl opened the door and motioned Haven and her three guard girls inside. The two remaining Rythern guards stood watch at the door.

Haven gasped as she entered. Sandstone walls had gold inlets and large windows carved from stone. Silks were draped from the ceiling and around the bed. Mirrors decorated the walls alongside gorgeous paintings and tapestries. Haven stepped farther inside.

The windows looked out onto the city and the sea beyond. Waves sparkled in the distance. Heavy curtains hung across the room to separate the sitting room from the bedroom. A plush bed of furs and silks called her name. Her shoulders sagged with relief. If it hadn't been for her grungy skin and dirty clothes, she'd have collapsed right then and there.

"The bed beckons, but I must take a bath." Haven sighed.

The girl leading the way brought Haven to a bathing room off the bedchambers. "I will send in ladies to assist you," she said, her accent so thick that Haven paused a moment to take in what she said.

Haven froze. "No, no! That won't be necessary! I have my own ladies."

The girl glanced at her ragged group of guards. Her brow quirked slightly, but she bowed, respecting the queen's wishes. "Garments will be sent in shortly. Choose any you like. They are a gift."

Haven thanked her, and the girl left.

"How old do you think she was?" Lareina asked.

They all looked at each other.

"I'm not sure," Blythe admitted.

"She couldn't be more than thirteen or fourteen, could she?" Haven puzzled it over while they adjourned to the bathing room.

"That seems awfully young," Lareina said.

They all had to agree.

"Haven, you must wake up."

Haven groaned and rolled onto her side.

"It's time for dinner with the council."

She recognized Lareina's voice, but still, she buried her face in the pillows.

"Aren't you hungry?"

Haven's stomach answered for her.

"That answers that." Malka chuckled by the window.

"Fine." Haven sighed. "I'm getting up." She rose from the sheets, her body protesting all the while. She'd only had a few hours of sleep, and considering their trials in the tunnels, her body was calling for more. Healing constantly took a lot out of her.

In the bathing room, Haven gazed into the mirror. Her hair was slightly tousled, but aside from that, she still appeared fresh from her bath. She'd spent nearly an hour soaking in the tub and scrubbing the grime off herself. Her ladies had done the same, and they were all feeling refreshed from the experience.

Brushing her hair out, Haven watched her amber eyes. There was something different about them. The last time she'd really looked at herself in the mirror was before her coronation. That seemed like eons ago. She looked much more attentive, even to herself. Her eyes weren't a young girl's anymore. They belonged to someone who had experienced too much yet seen too little of the world. She barely recognized herself.

"The clothes have arrived!" Lareina called from the other room. "Blue skies, they are beautiful!"

Haven smiled as she joined her guards. The three surrounded the dresses carefully laid out on the bed. Lareina was right. The dresses were all made in a similar fashion, but in different styles and varying pale colors. Some were gold, while others were white, pale yellow, pale blue—all equally beautiful and refined. They were stunning. Haven had never seen material woven quite like it, let alone embroidery as complicated.

"How on earth do they expect me to choose?" Her brow furrowed.

"What about this one?" Malka pointed to a light-blue one.

"Malka, blue does not go well with Haven's hair!" Lareina chastised.

"Sorry." Malka smiled and stepped back, raising her hands in mock surrender. "I'll leave it to you." She slid away.

Lareina took over, holding each dress up to Haven before she decided on her favorite. "This one! It will look wonderful with your skin tone."

Haven complied with her friend's wishes and slipped the gown on.

"Haven, you look incredible!" Lareina beamed at Haven like a proud mother.

At the closest full-body mirror, Haven gaped at her own image. The gold dress clung to her curves and lapped at her heels like water. Jewels were weaved through the entire dress, sparkling in the evening light.

It was incredibly lavish, and Haven couldn't take her eyes off it. The style fit her body closely until her hips, where the skirt dropped down and flowed around her feet. The top was snug around her arms and her torso, the neckline dipping down between her breasts. She'd never worn anything so revealing in her life.

"Do all women in Seaburn dress like this?" she asked.

They all shrugged.

No one really knew, but they'd soon find out.

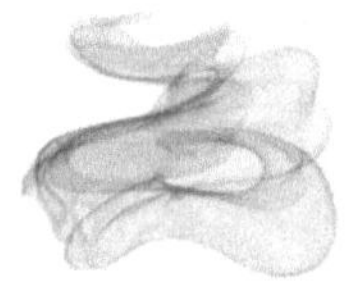

TWENTY-TWO

aven arrived at the grand dining hall feeling rather overdressed. Nerves flickered through her shifting stomach. Lareina had continued to dress her in matching jewels and shoes before tentatively fixing her hair. Part of it stayed pinned to her head in fancy swirls and rings with jewels throughout, while the rest flowed in waves over her shoulders. She had to resist pulling at the tight pins as she entered the massive hall.

It was similar to her ballroom in it was two stories high, with windows in the top half. That's where the similarities ended. The room was circular, with sandstone walls, marble floors, and a gold ceiling.

Haven had a hard time not gawking at the magnificent sight.

"Presenting Queen Haven Fyre of Rythern, from the realm of the six kingdoms of Warshard."

Haven glanced at the squire next to the door. Heat flooded her cheeks as everyone in the room stood. Her guards quickly lined the walls along with the others. She only wished she could do the same and blend in.

A long banquet table spread out at the center of the room, while a smaller table sat about a dais. The council members surrounded it. Corrin and Emeril were sitting side by side near the head of the dining table, across from Evander. Haven gasped as she rushed over to greet the king.

"King Evander, you're here." She shouldn't have been that surprised. It had been part of their plan for him to follow.

Haven beckoned the rest of the guests to sit as she took her seat beside the Calisan king.

Corrin and Emeril stared at her from across the table.

"You are a marvel, Lady Queen." Evander smiled.

While silence over her appearance had filled the room, the muttering of idle chatter resumed.

"Thank you, Lord King," Haven said.

"Not only did you survive Kadia and the journey under the sea, but you look as if you never endured any of it at all." He chuckled.

Haven's grin faltered. She might have endured it, but she hadn't escaped without scars of her own. "They call it the gift of long life."

Several chuckled around her. Haven glanced at who she assumed to be noblemen in their fine collared suits. The four foreign royals had the attention of half the table. Haven's lips twitched into a nervous smile. She felt like an animal on display, but she tried not to fidget too much in her seat.

"A gift indeed," Evander agreed.

"That dress suits you."

Haven's gaze fell on Corrin, who smiled sheepishly. "Thank you." She flushed, unable to meet his gaze. "Lareina picked it out."

"She has good taste."

"She knows me well."

Servers appeared by their shoulders, bringing plates of food and goblets of wine. They silently watched their trained movements. When they had all been served, Haven turned back to Evander, partly to avoid the stares of Corrin and Emeril.

"Tell me: what news is there?" Haven asked. "What have we missed?"

"Quite a lot, my dear." Evander laughed.

She was glad to see him in good spirits again. Their last meeting had been anything but good.

"Our people have settled in well. They stay throughout the city and its bordering towns. Some even remain here in the castle." He smiled. "The council has done much for our kingdoms."

Haven sighed in relief. Thank the blue skies. "How did you arrive in Seaburn? What of Toma?"

"Toma is fine. He is in the outskirts of the city, leading the organization of your people. As for the rest, that's a story in itself, Lady Queen." His eyebrows rose dramatically. "After the first attack went awry, the second was delayed. Kadia took care of Alton's men so fast that we could barely recover quickly enough to attack at all. When we did, it was long past when we had discussed. During the attack, your friends came and told us what had happened. We left Cidra alone and continued through the tunnel ourselves. We lost a few good men in the expedition, but we emerged in Seaburn not long after the rest of your people."

"And what of King Alton?" Haven asked.

Evander's smile faltered, and his gaze fell to the table. Her heart plummeted to her stomach. Haven had feared as much.

"All of his men were destroyed. Including the king himself."

"Blue skies, embrace him."

The other monarchs muttered the same.

"What else has happened?"

Silence met her question. Her eyebrows furrowed. She repeated herself. Worry turned her stomach into knots.

Evander exchanged a look with Corrin, who sighed.

"They will not grant our request," Corrin said.

Haven gasped. "*What?*"

"The council denies our request for soldiers," Evander clarified. "They will not assist in our war."

"But we need their help! We have nowhere else to turn!" Her voice rose with her panic. Her heart thundered against her ribs, threatening to break free and take off.

Evander raised his eyebrows to signify he knew she was about to react badly.

She took a deep breath to calm herself. "What are we to do if we can't use their soldiers?"

"I don't know, Lady Queen," Evander admitted. "But at least we're all safe for the time being."

"Yes, *for the time being*," Haven snapped. "How long will that last? A day, a week, a month? Maybe a year if we're lucky? How long do you think it will be before Kadia comes for Seaburn?"

The room fell silent with her escalating tone. All gazes rested on the young queen. Heat rose to her cheeks. Even the council members up on their dais looked at her.

Haven stood, her mind made up.

"You deny our request?" She approached the council.

Vas stood and bowed slightly. "We regret to inform you that, yes, we deny the request of the six kingdoms."

Haven narrowed her eyes. "If you will not lend your soldiers, will you take gold, jewels, silks? Will you let us barter for them?"

Vas exchanged a look with the council. He frowned. "We do not need your coin, Lady Queen, or the coin of anyone. The Republic of Seaburn is wealthy enough as is. We simply do not wish to send our soldiers on a suicide mission."

"Suicide mission?" Haven snapped. "What's suicide is staying here and doing nothing!"

"This isn't our war, Lady Queen," another council member spoke.

"But it will be."

The council members froze. Vas's eyebrows rose with shock. Finally, they were listening.

"What are you saying?" Vas asked.

"I'm saying that I've heard it from the Evil Queen herself. Kadia will come for Seaburn next. This isn't just our war anymore. Kadia's ambitions extend far beyond our realm. She wants everything—the entirety of the world, if she can." Her fists clenched. The rings she was wearing bit into her hands. "When I was taken prisoner by that evil witch, she held me in confidence. She told me of her plans and, in her insanity, informed me that Seaburn would be her next target. As soon as her ships are repaired, she *will* come. She wants your climate, your gold, and your armies. She wants your Republic, and if we don't stop her, she *will* take it."

Hushed voices filled the room.

Vas held his hand up to silence them. "We will take your words under advisement. If what you say is true, Seaburn may be in danger." He paused. "We will hold a meeting shortly and return with our decision."

Her shoulders sagged with relief.

"Please enjoy your meals."

The people paused their murmuring, waiting as Vas took his seat and Haven returned to hers. She sat carefully and crossed her hands in her lap. She couldn't believe she'd just done that. Never had she spoken in such a manner—in front of so many people nonetheless.

"Thank you."

Haven met Evander's gaze. "For what?"

"For possibly saving our kingdoms," he said.

Haven smiled. "I did what I had to."

ONCE THE MEAL was finished and the people had dispersed, Haven headed toward the great hall doors. Her guards fell in step just in time for someone to approach from behind. She felt his presence before she heard her name.

"Lady Queen."

Haven turned and found Corrin pursuing her in a lovely suit of brown, beige and gold. "King Corrin," she greeted.

Corrin fell into step beside her.

"That outfit suits you."

"I prefer my Wakefin wear." He smiled, and together, they continued down the hall. "You're much braver than people give you credit for."

Haven laughed. "Because I stood before Seaburn's council?"

"Yes."

"I'm sure you would have done the same," she insisted.

"Not in the manner you did." He grinned.

"And what manner is that?"

"So brash and brazen with your words. If your tongue had been any sharper, you would have cut them."

Haven considered swatting him. Instead, she rolled her eyes. "I spoke the truth in the only way I assumed they would listen."

"I like the way you speak." Corrin laughed. "Your people have a very honest queen."

"Haven."

They turned and found Emeril trailing behind them. Haven froze. Again, he would try to speak to her?

"Emeril." Her good mood ripped free of her chest.

"I know you don't want to speak with me, but"—he paused, looking pointedly at Corrin—"may I have a moment?"

Haven shifted. "I suppose. I will see you later, Corrin."

The young king nodded, a concerned glance sliding between the two of them before he took his leave. Haven's guards remained close.

"Blythe, you don't need to do that."

The woman quickly removed her hand from her sword. She made no apologies. Emeril stepped up beside her, and they continued their walk, veering into a lush courtyard.

"What is it, Emeril?"

The prince didn't speak at first. Instead, he simply walked with her. Her stomach twisted with confusion. His presence was so famil-iar. They'd been friends for so long that it seemed hard to believe that it had all been torn away by one act. She shook her head. Though he'd assaulted her in his grief, the prince had not meant to hurt her.

"I know I've apologized already. But it still doesn't feel like enough," he began. "I should never have done that to you." Emeril risked a glance at her guards. "I shouldn't have touched you that way. I should have stopped when you asked it. I honestly do not know what came over me. I was so caught up in my grief, and I wanted you there so badly. I shouldn't have let my feelings cloud my judgment. I'm sorry for everything, Haven. I miss you. We were once such good friends, and I'm so angry with myself for destroying that friendship."

Haven bit the inside of her cheek. Her heart raced. She had to fight to replace the moments he spoke of with the moments she cherished. They'd played in the castle courtyard as children. They'd woven crowns from thorns and practiced skipping rocks. They had been friends for years, and maybe almost lovers once. Though she didn't see him that way anymore, she did miss the friend she had once known.

"I forgive you, Emeril." If her time with Kadia had taught her anything, it was that evil people did evil things, and Emeril wasn't a bad person. He hadn't meant to hurt her.

Emeril froze mid-step and looked at her with big eyes. "You do? You mean it?"

Haven nodded. Emeril's fingers splayed as he struggled with wanting to push forward and hug her. She was glad he restrained himself.

"I accept your apology. Maybe we'll be friends again someday."

"Thank you, Haven." His fingers closed. "Thank you so much. You don't know what this means to me."

Haven smiled. "I must warn you though. It may take some time to stabilize our friendship. If you're willing to be patient with me, I think we can get along again."

Emeril nodded vigorously. "Of course. Take all the time you need. Thank you, Haven."

"You're welcome." Haven cleared her throat. "Now, I wish to return to bed. We've come a long way."

"Of course. Goodnight, Haven."

"Goodnight, friend." Haven couldn't help but return Emeril's smile. It was nice to see her old friend happy again. She hoped that things would work out, just as they had once before.

TWENTY-THREE

"The morning light here is like none other." Haven sighed. She'd taken to the courtyards the next morning, perusing the palace with her guards and Corrin. She basked in the sun, the flowers, the blue skies, and the general beauty of Seaburn.

Never in her wildest dreams had Haven pictured such a place. Rythern was cold and stark in comparison.

"It is wonderful," Corrin agreed. "The sea is endless from this height."

Haven peered at the blue water washing along the horizon. Where the palace was at the top of a hill, the city fell away beneath it, giving way to seas for miles.

"It is," she agreed.

They walked beneath an overhang and into a long hall with giant windows facing the ocean. It was a well-planned design, she had to admit.

"It's like we're still outside," she said.

Corrin stopped, and together, they leaned against the stone railing, taking the view in from the comfort of indoors. The heat was wonderful, but if they stayed in it too long, she feared she might faint. Still, she craved the wonderful views and the spectacular landscape.

"I could stay here forever." Haven leaned her cheek on her hand.

"You would like Wakefin." Corrin smiled.

"Is it like this?"

"Not as beautiful, but quite warm in comparison to Rythern." His grin turned sly. "We have beautiful views from the harbors while still getting to see the mountains in the north. It's a nice mix."

Haven nodded. If she stayed in Seaburn, she would miss her mountains. It had been a long time since she'd seen Wakefin; maybe she would get to visit once they returned home. "I'd like to see it someday."

Corrin glanced at her, hope lighting his eyes. Haven clamped her lips shut. He assumed far too much, but for the moment, she let him. The surprised delight on his face made him appear younger somehow.

"You should visit when this is all over," he said. "I could take you on a tour of the castle, the cities, the kingdom, and the ports. You'd love it."

Haven laughed. "I'm sure I would."

Corrin leaned forward, placing his hand on hers, his fingers brushing her wrist. Only a moment passed before they both pulled apart, Corrin realizing his mistake and Haven cringing from the touch.

"I'm sorry." His eyes widened.

Goose bumps rose over her flesh, and she stared at her hand in horror. She tried not to remember the feeling of men holding her wrists down or the way she'd had to grip the makeshift weapon and stab two men to death.

"Haven, I'm sorry. Please say something."

Haven slowly nodded, taking a deep breath. She held her hand to her chest and stepped away. "It's all right," she said. "It's not your fault. Please don't blame yourself."

His eyebrows cinched over swirling, blue eyes. She'd hurt him and sent away the delight she'd basked in moments ago.

A loud cough interrupted them. Haven turned and found Vas standing nearby.

"Vas," they both said.

"Good morning." Corrin bowed.

So did the council member. "Well met, Lord King, Lady Queen," he greeted respectfully.

"Well met," they repeated.

"I have someone I'd like you to meet," Vas said.

A young girl of maybe twelve, with hair as golden as the sun and eyes deep like the oceans, was behind him. Haven blanched, her lips parting in a silent gasp. She knew this girl.

"Well met," Corrin said.

Behind the girl was another man, who towered above even Vas.

Haven and the girl stared at each other. She'd seen this doe-eyed, beautiful little girl before, though she had been younger in the painting. The girl was luminescent. Was she even real? She was the girl on Kadia's painted women, the girl to be their third sister.

"Hello," the girl said sheepishly.

Corrin and Vas glanced between the two.

"This is Nina," Vas continued carefully. "Nina has had a large impact on the new council and how Seaburn has been recently formed. She's a very smart young girl." Vas smiled. "And this is her father, Lieutenant Drakkone. He's one of the few Seaburn-born warriors in our army."

"Greetings," Drakkone said, the timbre of his voice deep and his accent thick. He had the look of the people of Seaburn, while Nina could have been from Wakefin. It was hard to believe they were related.

"Good day," Corrin said.

"I know you," Haven said.

All eyes fell on her.

"Well, that's quite impossible—" Vas began, but he was cut off.

"How?" Drakkone asked. He shifted as if he might step in front of Nina.

"I believe she does, father." Nina stepped forward, interest flashing through her large eyes.

"How could you know her, Haven?" Corrin asked, as confused as the others.

"You were much younger in your picture," Haven said.

Understanding bloomed in Nina's eyes. "You've been through a lot, Lady Haven, haven't you?"

Haven nodded.

"Vas has told me some things. I want to help you if you'll let me. I can see into your past, your present, your feelings, and especially traumatic events. If you let me, I can help you with that."

Haven began to nod again. "How can you do that?"

"How can you heal from any injury?" Nina smiled. "I will have to touch you, but only long enough to see it all."

Haven shook her head.

"It will not be for long, Haven. It will help you."

Her eyebrows furrowed. If she allowed this girl to touch her and it did help, it would be worth it. But, if it didn't, she might have another anxiety episode. Haven finally nodded. It would be worth it if this stopped it all.

"All right."

Nina smiled, and they stepped into the middle of the hall together. Corrin and Drakkone hovered behind their respective women, watching to see what was about to unfold. Nina held her hands out.

Haven's fingers twitched as they inched forward until she placed her hands in Nina's.

Darkness encased her vision. Then Haven wasn't in the halls of Seaburn anymore. She was in many places. Her castle in Rythern flashed before her eyes—tall, dark stone walls and burgundy banners. She smiled as she fought in her sword-fighting lessons.

Then she was singing in the ballroom, her voice rising into the rafters. Then the courtyard. A man was stuck through with a pike. A rose lay in his severed jaw. Nikolai's head was on the meeting table, his eyes gouged out. Then she was up against a tree, Emeril pinning her down and kissing her while she wept.

A dark castle with shadows swirling from its base came next. She was fighting for her life in front of Cidra. A sword pierced her back. A scream ripped through the silence of her visions. Was that her?

Tears slipped down her cheeks as she awoke in Kadia's castle.

Bindings pinned her to a slab of wood. A dagger pierced her leg. Two screams. A poker burned across her stomach. More cries of pain. A knife over her arm. Then water gushed down her throat, which made her choke again and again. Tears flowed freely.

Then it was over. Or so she thought.

Haven walked the courtyards of Cidra with Kadia, who constantly touched and poked at her. A moan sounded. She appeared in that room again. Men held her down and stripped her naked. Kadia hovered over her and painted her bare skin. When it was over, she screamed and threatened Haven with rape. The images fast-forwarded.

She sat in the corner, staring absently at something. All of a sudden, a man was there. He pulled her onto the bed and began to kiss and grope at her body, rip her clothes off, and defile her innocence. Haven stabbed him and then another. Blood dripped from her hands and her clothes. Another scream tore loose as Haven threw herself from a window. Darkness greeted her. When she awoke, gasping for air, she spit out the water drowning her. Loud coughing replaced the gasps.

No, those sounds weren't her. Then where were they coming from?

Finally, Haven was standing in warm sand and gazing at a beautiful city. She sighed in relief. The darkness fled.

Haven and Nina collapsed to the ground. Tears spilled down their faces as they held each other. Haven shivered violently while Nina struggled to breathe. Her whole body ached, and her mind raced. She stared wide-eyed at the ground, trying to sift through her thoughts and put herself back in the present.

Corrin and Drakkone rushed forward as the girls fell. Their boots hovered at the edge of her vision. They shifted uncomfortably.

"I'm so sorry, Haven," Nina whispered against Haven's hair. "I'm so sorry."

Haven's voice was stuck in her throat, so she nodded and let two girl hold her. Nina was small, but her arms wrapped around Haven's torso.

"I'm sorry you had to go through any of that. I feel your pain like it is my own." Nina sniffed. "I'll carry it with me. You don't have to be alone."

The haze slowly pulled from Haven's mind, as did the ache in her bones.

"You can accept and get past this. Don't let Kadia win. You're not with her anymore. You're in Seaburn. Heavens, I'm so sorry." Nina stroked her hair.

Haven closed her eyes, willing the tears and the shaking to stop. When she felt she had returned to her own body, she took a deep breath. She froze. Nina's touch didn't bother her. In fact, the comfort was welcome. Haven leaned against the blonde, hugging her back. If Nina had seen and felt all of that as she had, she understood where the screams, the gasps, and the cries had come from. Nina hadn't known pain like Haven did. Haven had gotten used to it as she'd healed time and time again. Nina was so young and had probably never been hurt that gravely in her life.

"You shouldn't have done that if you knew you'd feel it," Haven said. "It's too much pain for someone so young."

"It's okay." Nina squeezed her shoulders. "You needed it."

Haven nodded. Nina let her go as she scooted back. Heat flooded Haven's cheeks. No one had paused to watch the scene. Thank the blue skies. She was embarrassed enough with Corrin, Vas, and Drakkone hovering.

"We should go outside and get some fresh air," Nina said.

Haven agreed, and they slowly stood. When Corrin reached to help her up, she didn't recoil or cringe away. His fingers closed around her elbow. No flashes of her past accompanied the touch. Though she wasn't completely comfortable, his touch no longer terri-fied her. Corrin couldn't stop himself from grinning from ear to ear as he seemed to realize this.

"You're okay?" Drakkone asked. His eyebrows cinched, the concern of a father all over his face. He brushed his daughter's hair back and held her tight.

"I'm fine, Daddy," she whispered.

"Good." He patted her hair as she let go.

"I should be going," Vas said awkwardly from the edge of their group.

The rest of them nodded and said goodbye before adjourning back to the courtyards.

The sun warmed Haven's cheeks. She sighed, happy to have the sun chase her demons away. They sat beside a small fountain deep within the greenery of the courtyard. Stone benches surrounded it. The spot was private enough that they need not worry about anyone listening in.

"You like the gardens?" Nina asked.

"Very much." Haven smiled. She wiped the tears from her face, happy to find her nose clearing.

"I love being outside within them. They're very calming," Nina said.

"They are," Haven agreed.

"What is your realm like?" Nina asked.

"Different. Not quite as beautiful as yours."

"Tell me about it."

Haven and Corrin were happy to discuss their home, stories and descriptions coming easily. It had been some time since they'd been in their respective kingdoms, but the memories were fresh and vivid. Corrin became more animated as he spoke of Wakefin while Haven laughed at how ridiculous some of his details were. The rivers flowing through his kingdom were *not* in the thousands, though he'd certainly have them believe it.

"You remind me much of my mother," Nina said once they had finished.

Drakkone froze. His dark gaze swirled with sadness. Haven recognized that look. He truly loved her. She couldn't imagine such a loss.

"What was she like?" Haven asked.

"Strong, beautiful, and very protective." Nina sighed. "She was like you in that way. She always protected me, even at great costs to herself."

"She died protecting you?"

Nina nodded.

"Blue skies embrace her," Haven said.

Nina thanked her and reached forward to hold her hand.

Haven tentatively complied. "She sounds like an amazing woman."

"And much like you," Corrin agreed.

Haven smiled and shot him a look. He replied with a grin of his own.

"If only she had the same ability as you, Lady Queen." Drakkone sighed.

"Mother was happy, Daddy." Nina let Haven's hand go so she could take her father's. "She got what she wanted in the end. She's looking down on us, I'm sure."

Drakkone nodded, but he didn't say anything further.

"I'm sorry for your loss," Corrin said. "Was it some time ago?"

"Yes, quite a while now." Nina squeezed her father's hand. "Her name was Breen. She went through a lot like you have, Haven. But it made her stronger. Everything that happened made my mother stronger. She was the fiercest warrior in Seaburn."

"She always will be," Drakkone agreed.

"I hope to be like her one day, then." Haven smiled. "Breen sounds like an exceptional woman."

"She was," Drakkone said.

"She still is." Nina leaned against her father. "She'll always be great."

TWENTY-FOUR

Several agonizing days passed before the monarchs of Warshard gathered in the council room. They had finally reached a consensus.

Haven stood with the kings and the prince, holding on to Corrin's hand tighter than she needed to. A lot rode on this one decision. If the council chose to come with them, fight Kadia, take their kingdoms back, and depose the Evil Queen, all would someday be returned to normal. At least she hoped. If they refused, it was only a matter of time before Haven and her friends would be forced to flee again. Kadia would come for them. She'd destroy Seaburn, and Haven would be the only one left standing.

"Thank you for coming." Vas stood behind a long, pale wooden table with carvings through the twisted legs.

Nina and Drakkone joined them, sitting nearby. Haven met the young girl's gaze across the court. She smiled and nodded at Haven. That simple look held more comfort than she thought possible. Her shoulders sagged with relief.

"We've reached our decision on the matter of lending troops to the six kingdoms."

They all held their breath in anticipation.

"We will not lend you our soldiers."

Haven's mouth fell open as the rest of the council stood.

"We will not lend you them because we wish to lead the charge. We will, of course, have you accompany us on our ships and join in battle. We would like your help in the attack and will form a plan with you. But, if this is to be Seaburn's war, a lot rides on this final battle." Vas paused, looking to each of them in turn. "We will leave in two weeks' time. The council hopes this is an acceptable alternative."

"This is marvelous!" Evander said.

Her heart swelled. Haven and Corrin embraced. His warm arms folded around her, chasing her demons away. Emeril and Evander shook hands beside them. Each Royal thanked the council members, bowing respectfully before them. They all smiled from ear to ear as Vas addressed them again.

"You shouldn't thank us," he began. "It was because of Nina that our decision changed. We hold her opinion in high regard, and after her encounter with the young queen, our decision was unanimous."

"Nina." Haven glanced at her young friend.

The girl rose and came to Haven, taking her hands. "Your intentions are so pure, Lady Haven." Nina smiled. "We will help you in any way we can. Kadia must be stopped, and I think I can help."

"But how?" she asked.

"My abilities go beyond seeing into the minds of others and calming them with my presence." Nina squeezed her fingers. "I can change and control the mind as well."

Haven gasped. "That sort of power could be dangerous."

"It would be in the hands of another." Nina's lips pressed into a grim line. "Many believed it would be too much, but I've proven otherwise time and time again. If I can get to Kadia myself, I can stop her and her power. I'm sure of it."

"But that could get you killed." Haven's voice rose an octave. Her stomach twisted with concern. The urge to protect her was overwhelming. "Can you even wield a sword? Or fight at all?"

"I've never needed to with my powers. Do not worry yourself. I will have many to protect me if I should need it."

"And I will be among them," Haven said.

"Lady Queen," Corrin cautioned her.

Haven shook her head. "I will be among them, Nina. I will not let you face Kadia alone." Though the thought of seeing Kadia in the flesh again sent goose bumps over her skin and fear needling at her chest, she stood firm.

Nina slowly nodded and smiled. "You are a wonder, Lady Queen," she said.

* * *

AFTER RECEIVING THE GOOD NEWS, the royals proclaimed a celebration that night. But, until night came, the young royals would accompany Drakkone and Nina into town for a tour of the city.

Buildings carved from sandstone, markets full of people, silks, beads, and mouth-watering fruit seemed to be around every corner. High towers loomed in the distance, music soothed the ear on every street, and smiling faces constantly crossed their path. Everything was beautiful, from the architecture to the people of the Republic. Haven took it all in with thinly veiled awe. Her gaze darted from the port in the distance to the gold pillars nearby and back again. Drakkone, Nina, and a few of their Seaburn guards pointed out many of the well-known landmarks in the area: the bazars, the temples, and more. They told stories while leading them through public and private areas, into courtyards, and out in the streets.

Dusk fell as they reached their final destination. The crown jewel of Seaburn was its army, which provided extensive training to its soldier. The Academy was known far and wide.

"The Academy is almost as large as the palace." Blythe gawked at the huge structure.

The pillars towered like sentinels, thick and tall, rising as high as Haven's castle walls to hold up the roof of the Academy. Beyond the rows of columns, the sandstone building shimmered in the afternoon light. Stained-glass windows filled with depictions of different battles or kings lined the front of the structure.

They stood in the main courtyard as soldiers ran to and fro. Crossing the courtyard barely gave her enough time to take it all in before the great wooden doors opened and they were ushered inside.

"Welcome to the Academy." Drakkone smiled widely.

It was the first time she'd seen a smile on the man's face, and the look suited him. Not many people from Seaburn joined the military, but when they did, they rose high in rank.

The farther they delved into the building, the more people they passed, each with a different look than she'd come to know of the people of Seaburn. Soldiers marched by in two lines. The droning of Drakkone's voice fell into the background as he went on about a particular statue or another.

Her footsteps slowed as she fell behind. The squad formation passed her. Not one pair of eyes darted to hers. Each man and woman held a stern face and stared straight ahead, intent on their task. Wherever they were going, they appeared to be fine soldiers. But they definitely were not native to Seaburn. With tawny skin, smaller eyes, and flat noses, these people weren't Seaburn-born—she could say that with certainty.

How could these people fight for Seaburn if they weren't even from the Republic? They were taken from the Southern Lands, lands they called savage. But some couldn't be older than sixteen. She froze. She knew so little of this place. The voices of her friends echoed in her ears.

They wouldn't tell Haven how the soldiers were broken because they had known that it would hurt her, and if she knew, she might not be able to use them to get her home back.

Haven clutched her arms. A chill sent a shiver down her spine. It was time to head back to the palace. She'd let the others finish the tour.

She hoped her presence wouldn't be missed, but she couldn't stand to be there anymore and look at these faces so completely devoid of emotion. Something awful was going on there; she could feel it.

Moving through the halls, Haven tried to make her way out. In the maze that was the academy, she weaved through endless halls and up and down steps, every passage appearing like the next.

"What have I done?" She sighed.

Then Haven burst through another door. This had to be the way back to the main hall. She'd been going in circles for far too long.

Soft moans drifted down the dimly lit stone hall. Haven stopped in her tracks. She was not meant to be there.

Haven shifted from foot to foot. What was this place? She lifted her dress from the floor and proceeded quietly, her curiosity getting the best of her. The gold of her gown shimmered in the soft, orange glow, which cast dapples of light across the sandstone walls. Though she'd felt safe in Seaburn up until now, she'd never been so glad to have a sword at her hip.

The stone floor was rough there, as were the walls. Instead of the polished slabs she'd grown accustomed to, these uneven rocks were held together by peeling plaster. Torches lined the walls, as did cells dug into the earth on opposite side. Most were empty, but every now and then, she passed a wooden door. Moans emanated from within. The windows on each door were too high for her to see through.

The farther she went, the wider the hall grew. The walls became dirty, almost thick with grime. How could they keep people down there like this?

"Stop!" a woman screamed up ahead.

Haven froze. The woman's accent was so thick that she had a difficult time making the word out, but that scream had her running. Her heart raced as she tore her sword from its sheath. The muffled grunts and shuffling of a struggle met her ears.

Something thudded against a wooden wall, one after the other. A cell door was ajar. Another scream pierced the quiet.

Haven dove through the entrance of the cell. A man clad in Seaburn armor was standing over a tawny-skinned girl of maybe sixteen. Her eyes were wild, widened with fear. He tore at her clothes with fervor.

Images of hands gripping her wrists and pinning her down flashed through her mind. Those same hands moved over her body in indecent ways, and cold lips kissed down her bare neck. Her cries echoed in her ears as she tried to get him off, but they weren't her cries this time—they were this poor girl's.

Haven held the tip of her sword to the back of the man's neck, her whole body trembling with rage. He froze.

"You will release her this moment," Haven commanded. Her hands shook as the anger built, her knuckles white on the hilt of her sword.

"Yes, of course." The man released the woman, who shuffled to the back of her cell, her dark, messy hair shielding her from the world. "No need to be rash."

"I want to see your hands." Haven glanced at the sword on his hip.

"You aren't too steady with that blade."

Haven blanched, staring at the back of the man's dark head. She took a breath to calm the shaking her of fists. "I don't need steady hands to cut your head from your shoulders."

The man chuckled. Haven stilled. Did he find this funny?

He laughed as if she wouldn't kill him. "You're a brave little girl, aren't you? Just like this one." His words slurred, sickly sweet.

"Put your hands up and shut your mouth." Haven took a step back to allow him space to stand.

He pulled his sword from his sheath faster than she could blink. The man rounded on her, slashing his sword outward. Haven leapt back in time for the tip of his blade to only cut a clean line across her cheek. She hissed at the sting and instinctively reached to wipe the blood from her face. The pain disappeared before the man stepped from the cell.

His sly smile twisted into a frown, and his eyebrows furrowed. "The immortal queen." His eyes widened.

Haven swiped at him. He backed into the cell door. It banged against the wall and he lost his balance. She took her advantage and pushed her sword through his shoulder. The man howled in pain and kicked out. He slammed his boot against her ribs, sending her flying back into a stone pillar.

Her breath whooshed from her lungs. She gasped for breath as he regained his footing and attacked. Haven blocked, their swords clanging together, before she twisted out of the way of his next assault, moving into the open portion of the small room.

The woman in her cage screeched her battle cry like an animal as she lunged onto the man's back, clawing at his face with her nails. The man cried out and dropped his sword. Blood blossomed in the long scratches across his cheeks. He took her hands and threw her from his back.

"You savage brat!" he growled.

Haven slammed her foot into his stomach. He fell back with a thud, air exploding from his lungs. Haven leapt forward and drove her sword through his chest.

"You're the savage," Haven hissed through clenched teeth. She jerked the sword as deep as it would go. She watched the light leave his eyes before she moved.

With the chaos having past, Haven crouched beside the limp body, catching her breath. Her adrenaline slowly faded, which calmed her racing heart. With calm, her sense of mind returned.

Looking at the young savage girl, Haven stood and offered her hand. "You're safe now."

Large, brown eyes met hers and welled with tears. The girl put her face in her hands, her shoulders shaking with sobs. Haven slid to the floor beside her and wrapped her arms around the small girl. She didn't say a word. She didn't tell her it would be okay. She didn't lie, only sat there with her and let her feel the safe touch of a comrade in arms.

If this was how women were broken in these cages, Haven could not accept the aid of Seaburn. These women were raped into obedience before becoming soldiers. Her heart clenched, a fire kindling inside her chest. She would kill every last man who stood in her way to free these girls.

"Haven!"

The young queen looked up. Corrin's voice echoed off the walls, and her little friend stiffened.

"It's okay." Haven rubbed her shoulder. "It's just my friends looking for me."

The girl glanced up with wide eyes. "The immortal queen." The same awed look the other man had given her reflected in this girl's face. "You saved me."

"The immortal queen?" Haven asked. "Is that what they call me?"

"That's what everyone in Seaburn calls you," she said. "And it's true. There's no cut on your face."

Haven felt her cheek. "I heal quickly."

"Haven?" Her guard girls and the rest of their friends tore down the long hallway before halting at the scene before them.

"What happened?" Lareina gasped, coming to her friend while Blythe and Malka secured the hallway.

Corrin, Nina, and Drakkone piled in after them. Both Seaburn residents froze.

Haven narrowed her eyes. "You should have told me."

Nina shook her head. "Haven, you don't understand."

"That man was going to rape her." Haven squeezed the girl tight. "Is that how Seaburn does things? Is that how it has evolved? You call the southerners savage, but there is no act more savage than this."

Drakkone stood stock-still while Nina's face softened.

She tried taking a step closer. "Lady Haven, please listen."

"We cannot accept the help of such a foul country." She didn't want to hear any excuses or lies. She wouldn't allow this to go on, and she certainly wouldn't use these people in their war. "You dress this place up like it's a beautiful modern paradise, but it's only to hide the dark belly of the beast. I'm taking these people out of here, and I dare someone to try to stop me." Haven rose to her feet, bringing the young girl with her.

"We can't let you do that," Drakkone said.

"Haven, please let us speak." Nina shot her father a look.

The people of Warshard seemed shocked into silence, staring at one another in horror, but they moved to rally behind Queen Haven, ready to come to her aid.

"What will you tell me, Nina?" Haven snapped. "Nothing you can say will change what's happening down here."

"This is not how it is supposed to be." Drakkone sighed. "This isn't how the people down here are supposed to be treated, but it has been happening for so long that the men think it's normal now."

"This is in no way *normal*."

"I know." Drakkone met her gaze. "But we're working to change that, and we have been for a long time. It used to be worse, Lady Queen. Trust me."

"I've been working with the council on this from the beginning, Haven," Nina added. "We're working on a treaty with the Southern Lands. We will stop taking their people and doing this to them. I promise."

"I can't just go on your promises." Water slowly filled her eyes. Though Haven stood with her arms around the young warrior, she couldn't be sure who was holding up whom.

"*Please*, Haven." Nina gently touched her elbow.

Haven stilled as Nina flooded her consciousness. She could see her own thoughts and memories, but Nina's were present as well, filling her with assurance. Nina showed her images of treaties in the works, young soldiers brought to the council, and the other many steps already taken. Haven stepped away in a haze. Corrin held her up this time.

"Are you all right?" he asked.

"Yes." Haven blinked the images away. "You will fix this?"

"I promise I will," Nina said.

"I'm still taking these people from here."

Nina nodded. "I knew you wouldn't leave without them." She smiled and motioned a Seaburn guard forward. "Get the keys and release everyone. We're taking them upstairs."

The man didn't protest, only slipped off to do his duty.

"Thank you," the young girl whispered beside her.

Nina smiled again. That dazzling look seemed to capture people in the depths of her ocean-blue eyes. "My mother was like you once. She needed my father to save her. It's about time we did the same for the rest of you."

TWENTY-FIVE

"What is the meaning of this?"

Vas's deep voice boomed through the lobby of the academy. It reverberated off the three-story-high columns and echoed deep within the Academy.

Once the group of southerners had been gathered, Haven and the others had ushered them through the halls into the main corridor. They were all quite skittish, glancing around as if the council might jump out at any moment and drag them kicking and screaming back to their cages. They had done their best to soothe them until they'd reached the main hallways. If possible, they were more terrified there than in their cells. Haven finally understood why when they reached the lobby.

Word must have reached the council, as Vas and a group of soldiers were blocking the main doors. While the foreigners stopped in their tracks, Haven advanced on Vas. Her heart pounded in her ears, and adrenaline poured through her like waves.

Anger flared to life inside her chest, its flames licking the mental wounds that might never heal. Vas was just like Kadia in a way. He had taken these people from their families, captured them, and tortured them into submission. Anyone like Kadia deserved to die.

Her sword was out of its sheath before she could think beyond her fury – the tip held to the councilman's throat.

"What is the meaning of *this*?" she hissed his question back. "What is the meaning of barbarically *dragging* these people from their homes only to torture and rape them into submission—all for the sake of your army?" Haven nearly screamed the words, her knuckles white on the hilt of her sword. Her whole body shook.

The *shing* of swords filled the silence left by her words.

Many points were directed at her, while fewer pointed away. Haven didn't flinch, only held Vas's wide-eyed gaze. They could stick her with their swords all they wanted and she would survive. Haven had never acted so recklessly since the day she'd rushed into the burning Salander capital. It was a relief to feel in control of her reck-lessness, to know that, even if she was acting rashly, *she* was the one acting and no one could stop her.

"It is a traditional practice," he said. His eyes widened like orbs. He was terrified of her. Sweat beaded on his forehead, and his hands shook. He had been such a poised man, and there he was, literally quaking in her presence.

"An ancient one, you mean." Haven narrowed her eyes. "A cruel, ancient practice. I'm taking these people from this place. They will come with me, go home, or stay here, but they will do it of their own free will."

Vas began to shake his head.

Haven pressed her blade in harder. The cold burn of metal bit her skin. She barely noticed. "It wasn't a request. Tell your guards to back away now or I will kill you."

Vas turned his gaze outward, panic rising. "Y-You can't—"

"I can do anything. You call me the Immortal Queen, isn't that right?" Haven paused, knowing that her question didn't need an answer. "I could show you just how accurate a title that is. It would only take a moment. I can push this sword through your throat and your guard will push his through mine. The only difference is I will wake and you will not."

Her words must have driven home, because it only took a moment for Vas to cry his command out.

"Step back! Drop your swords! Do as she says!" His voice rose. It took a moment, but his men did as he'd asked. "You just want to take this group with you? That's all?"

Haven paused, lowering her sword slightly. "I want you to free anyone who wants to leave, whether they be part of your military or not."

"That could completely ruin our plans to save *your* kingdoms!" Vas gasped.

"You will do as I ask. If they wish to follow you of their own volition, then let them. But anyone who wants to leave will be granted total and utter freedom as of this moment." Haven raised her sword again. "Or I *will* kill you. It's your choice."

She could hear herself being unreasonable, being cruel, just as this man had been to these people. But she couldn't stop. Someone had to protect them.

Vas glanced back and forth at the guards, who now seemed to be paying much less attention to their council member and more attention to what Haven was saying. They mumbled back and forth to each other in a foreign tongue. Their muscles relaxed, and their battle stances dropped.

Vas made his mind up. "They can go free. But whatever happens next will be your fault, Immortal Queen."

Haven sheathed her sword and stepped back. She would accept responsibility for whatever future came for them. She never could have lived with herself knowing that these people had suffered so they could garner an army. She turned to the people surrounding her.

At least twenty men and women had been freed from their cages in the chambers below, but many more were standing behind her now. Seaburn guards flowed from every direction, poking their heads in from hallways and peering over the balconies above. Her words had gathered a much larger crowd than expected. It was Haven's turn to gulp.

"You are free." Haven glanced around at all the unfamiliar faces, unable to hide her relief or her smile. The flames of her rage flowed away like the tide, leaving her limbs tingling with something akin to anticipation. "You can go wherever and be whatever you want. It's your choice. Stay if you will, return home if you want, or come across the sea to Warshard. You will be as welcome there as you will be here—and you *will* be free."

Silence greeted her. Many sets of stunned eyes stared back. It was the young girl Haven had saved in the dungeon who broke the silence.

"I, Aura of the Southern Delica tribe, pledge myself to you, Immortal Queen." She dropped to one knee, her head down.

Haven blinked in surprise at Aura, whose mangled, black hair fell to the floor around her bent head. She had never seen someone pledge themselves to anyone, and she certainly hadn't expected it of such a young woman.

"Are you sure?" Haven hesitated. She wouldn't want anyone to be forced into her service, whether it was because they felt some debt was owed or not. "You are free. You owe me nothing, Aura."

"I'm sure." Aura paused. Her accent was thick, but when she spoke again, Haven knew that it had taken her a moment to find the words of the six kingdoms. "My Lady Queen."

Haven stepped forward, unable to hide her smile. Before she could speak again, several men and women behind her dropped to one knee, echoing Aura's statement. Soon, the entire group she'd saved from the dungeons was bowing before her. She was lost in a whirlwind of names and tribes she could neither recognize nor remember. Her heart swelled as she locked gazes with her guards. Then Nina, Drakkone, and finally Corrin. They all smiled, pride radiating from their gazes.

She turned back to her new subjects. "Rise." She cleared her throat. "I'd be honored to have you."

* * *

IN THE DAYS that followed the savage proclamation to Warshard's cause, much changed in Seaburn. Many of the so-called savages returned to the Southern Lands to aid their people, while just as many stayed to fight for the six kingdoms.

At first, Haven had feared that no one would remain to help save her home, but as the days passed and their journey grew near, more men and women came to her, pledging their allegiance to the six kingdoms and the Immortal Queen. Haven was grateful to each of them, overwhelmed by it all, and unable to express how truly in awe these gestures made her—not just for their aid, but for the happiness their freedom had brought them. She would treasure every smile and every face for the rest of her days.

The evening before their departure, Haven wandered the lit gardens facing the sea beyond the city. Corrin stayed near, watching her from a bench as she moved calmly through the flowers, her fingers brushing their silky petals. Her bare feet sank in the soil, her dress dragging in the dirt behind her. It had been a long time since she felt so at ease. In a way, setting the others free had returned her to life. The touch of others didn't make her flinch like it once had. The proximity of men in general didn't seem to bother her anymore. Whatever Nina had done to her mind had truly worked. She hoped that her scarred memory would one day only be a thread in her mind, one she could release if need be but would never touch for fear the entire garment might unravel.

Haven stopped at the edge of the gardens where the ground fell away to the city. The surrounding rocks were smooth, worn by water, but she couldn't imagine the tide having ever been so high. The moon hovered over the horizon, setting the sea aglow. Stars danced across the skyline. Haven wished she could fly up and join them. Seaburn would be a true sight to behold from so high in the sky. From so high, would the stars be envious of the city's bountiful beauty, or would they be content in their own vast empire?

"What are you thinking?"

Haven turned as Corrin laid his hand on her back. He smiled the handsome, sweet smile she'd come to know.

"I was thinking about what it'd be like to be a star," she confessed, returning her gaze to the black sky above.

Corrin chuckled. "Not about the upcoming battles or your new army who's pledged their allegiance to you?" He grinned and followed her gaze. "The Immortal Queen thinks about being a star. Now, that's a new one, Lady Queen."

Haven laughed with him. It did seem silly when he put it like that. "That's the first time you've called me that."

"What? Lady Queen?"

"No." She gave him a look.

Corrin grinned, revealing a perfect set of teeth. He knew all too well what she meant. "The Immortal Queen? Isn't that your new title?" He raised an eyebrow. "You don't like it?"

Haven paused. At first, it had felt like a daunting title—something she couldn't live up to. Then it had felt like a title for a bad queen, like Kadia. The Queen of Dagan had been called many things throughout time: the Insane Queen, the Evil Queen, the Mad Queen. Was the Immortal Queen the same? Was it a title she'd been given out of fear or hatred?

She shook her head. Her title was nothing like the names given to Kadia. The Immortal Queen was a title she would embrace. It was strong like her. It had taken her a long time to accept it, but she was strong. Haven had stood up for herself, her people, and, in the end, what she believed in. Only good had come of her title, so Haven would be whatever queen her people needed. If they needed their Immortal Queen, that's who she would be.

"I do now." Haven smiled.

"Haven, may I ask you something?"

She met his gaze. "Of course."

"What will you do when this is all over?" He shifted from foot to foot. "The war, I mean. What will you do once it's over and we're left to pick up the pieces of our kingdoms?"

Haven paused. She hadn't thought much about it yet. She had to assume she would go back to being a regular queen. She'd do what her people needed, forging a new kingdom with the help of her new friends. Her eyebrows furrowed. Is that the sort of answer the young king sought?

"I'll return to my people. Be queen, I suppose. I'll do my best to restore my kingdom and help the others as well, of course."

His face fell, and he nodded. Was he disappointed by her answer? Corrin's hand dropped from her back. He stepped away.

"Did I say something wrong?" she asked.

"No. No, of course not." He avoided her gaze, and suddenly, she understood.

Her heart leapt. "Do you mean what will *we* do?"

What would he expect of her? Her stomach clenched. Flashes of Emeril pinning her to a tree leapt to her conscious mind and she had to fight to keep still. If she rejected another man, would he be unable to control himself? But Corrin wasn't a boy; he was a man, a king—and a good one at that. She took a breath. She had to stay sure in her belief Corrin wouldn't hurt her if her fears were realized.

Corrin finally met her gaze with big, hopeful eyes. "Yes." He took her hand and brought her back to the path.

They sat together on a stone bench, hidden from any wandering eyes in a ring of ferns.

"Haven, I have something quite serious to ask you, and I need you to know that I don't want to pressure you in any way, but..." He trailed off.

Haven stared wide-eyed at him. She knew with utter certainty what he would ask of her. It was almost worse than being pinned to a tree. Her whole body froze, along with her mind.

"Haven, will you marry me?"

Haven stared in shock while Corrin stared hopefully back at her. Silence crept between them. Before she could straighten her thoughts, she stood, words unprepared falling from her lips.

"I can't, Corrin. You know I can't." Her voice caught in her throat, and her heart beat wildly in her chest. "I am a queen, a queen of Rythern. I can't be the queen of Wakefin too. I can't choose between my people and you." She stepped away, her eyes burning and mind swirling. A bubble of panic rose in her chest, pressing against her lungs as if trying to suffocate her. "I can't love and lose you when you grow old. I can't bear the thought of you dying in battle, of illness—" Her voice broke.

Corrin stood, taking her hands. "You won't, Haven. You won't lose me."

"But I will!" she cried. "Everyone dies, Corrin, but I don't know if I ever will." Tears escaped her eyes, leaving tracks over her olive skin. "You could die tomorrow or today. You could die in battle in several weeks' time or of the plague years from now. But if I let myself marry you, love you—" She shook her head and ripped her hands from his. "No. No, I can't." The bubble in her chest swelled in size. Though she had plenty of escape routes, she felt trapped. "I can't. I won't. I can't give you children, an heir. I can't give you my hand, and I won't give you my heart."

Before Corrin could answer, Haven ran.

The look of utter heartbreak on his face was enough. She couldn't stand to see him like that for one more moment. Picking her skirts up, she tore through the flowers and across the path. Behind her, Corrin called her name. She didn't turn back, didn't pause to listen.

Haven disappeared from the courtyard, leaving nothing but her heart behind her.

TWENTY-SIX

"*D*oes my cruelty know no bounds, Nina?"

Haven sat beside her young friend. The light of the moon shone through the glass back of the ship, which swayed below. It was their first night at sea, and the previous night's events lay heavily on her conscience. Not only had she rejected a wonderful man, who was fond of her enough to ask for her hand, but she had quite literally run away from him. Instead of trying to explain herself or reason with him, she'd picked her skirts up and disappeared.

Haven sighed, leaning her forehead against the cool glass. The women were alone in her cabin. The room was quite spacious compared to the others she'd seen. Even the Seaburn ships were quite lavish. Even with a large bed and curtains of silk, she had enough space for this cushioned seat at the window.

White-capped waves rolled by outside, splashing against the ships behind theirs.

"What are you talking about, Haven?" Lareina huffed, plopping herself on the bed. "You haven't a cruel bone in your body."

Nina met the young queen's gaze. Haven's friends had scoffed at her foolishness, but she knew that Nina would hear her out. Though she was young, she was possibly the wisest person Haven had ever met. Had Nina's mother been that way? Her father seemed quite sage and intelligent but more of a soldier than an intellectual. From what Haven had heard of the warrior Breen, she sounded more like Drakkone than her daughter. Maybe Nina's brilliance was all her own. Her power might be as unique as Haven's.

"Did Corrin ask you?"

Haven nodded to Nina's question. She refused to meet any but Nina's gaze. She didn't want their excitement or their judgment.

"And what did you say?"

"It's not what I said, but what I did." Her mind swirled. "Much more should have been said."

Nina nodded and smiled. "What are you afraid of, Lady Haven? Love or loss? Or are you just afraid to live?"

Haven couldn't quite explain it. It had been a long time since a current of emotions swirled had inside her breast like this. She felt like she was drowning until a thought came to her. Though she couldn't properly explain how she felt with words, Nina didn't need words to understand. Haven offered Nina her hand.

"Are you sure?" Nina asked.

"Yes. But please don't hurt yourself like last time."

"Keep only Corrin in mind and I won't go further." Nina took Haven's hand.

Everything went black. When the world swirled back into shape, Haven was crying in the woods. It was the first time she'd met the real Corrin. He put his arm around her and let her cry. Then she was in meetings and her castle. Several scenes flashed by before the war drove Haven from her home.

She walked with the young king through the hordes of people. They talked for hours every day. Warmth blossomed through her limbs, catching her in a sea of feelings she hadn't been aware of.

She knew what it was now but couldn't bring herself to admit it. When darkness embraced her again, she reawakened in a dim cave. It was night, but she couldn't sleep. She sat with Corrin, but she was afraid of him. No, not *of* him, but something that had happened to her. The thought was gently pushed away.

Gardens rested beneath her feet. Corrin stood with her then brought her to sit. He asked her to marry him, to be the queen of two kingdoms. She panicked. Words gushed from her mouth unbidden. Moments later, she ran.

With a gasp, Haven opened her eyes. Nina's lovely gem-blue eyes stared back at her. Nina smiled and patted the back of her hand before releasing her.

A hurricane swelled and ebbed inside her. She shook her head, taking deep breaths to clear the fog. Nina looked utterly unfazed. The creak of the ship filled the silence of her cabin.

"Haven, you've spent so much time worrying. You've worried for your kingdom, for the others. You've saved the southerners and yourself from an evil tyrant. Anyone can see from the fire in your eyes that you've experienced much. You're alive because of your power, and it has served you well." Nina paused. "I can't imagine how hard it is to be you. I know how afraid you are to love because you don't want to lose it again. You don't want to be the last one left alive, I know that. You're alive, Haven, but when are you going to start living?"

Haven's brow furrowed as she let Nina's words sink in.

"People will always die, but you can't live your life as if you're the only one who won't. You'll live a long and sad life, Haven. Love is the best feeling in the world, and I know you feel it for King Corrin."

Her cheeks flushed. Again, Haven avoided the gazes of her friends.

"And he loves you too. If you let yourself, you can be happy. You don't have to be afraid. It's better to experience love and loss than to never have at all."

Tears stung the backs of her eyes. She tried to fight them back, but it was impossible to keep them from spilling over. Lareina settled in behind her, gently wrapping an arm around her shoulders. Haven turned and rested her face against Lareina's worn jacket. She was tired of crying, tired of losing people, and, most of all, tired of being afraid.

"I do love him," Haven whispered.

Lareina stroked her hair. "I know you do. But it's not us you need to tell."

"But how can I?" Haven stifled a sob. "What if he dies? What if I get pregnant? How can I be the queen of two kingdoms?"

"Now, you're just making excuses," Blythe said.

They all smiled. Haven's tears stopped, and she sat up.

"Those are only possibilities." Nina smiled and took her hand.

No flash of darkness or images in her mind grabbed her. This time, there was only a wash of confidence and serenity.

"If you live your life worried about the what-ifs, you're going to live a very desolate life. If you get pregnant, it'll be the happiest day of your life. If Corrin dies, you will live on knowing that your love was real and that, one day, you will join him."

"You'll figure out the rest." Lareina squeezed her other hand.

"Thank you." Haven smiled. "All of you."

"We should all get some rest." Lareina stood.

"Of course."

"I'll see you in the morning." Nina left her side, but the feeling of calm stayed with her.

"Goodnight, Nina."

"Goodnight, Lady Queen."

* * *

WHETHER IT WAS the clash of swords, the shouts from the crew, or the crashing waves that woke her, Haven couldn't be sure. Staring at the wooden ceiling, Haven tried to catch and hold the snippets of her dreams that so quickly fled. Something about home resonated in her bones, but that's all she could remember.

With a sigh, Haven listened to the waves for what seemed like a long time. The noise was so steady, so rhythmic, that she almost fell back asleep. That is until she remembered she *had* heard the clashing of swords.

Haven sat up, reaching for her sheath. The blade was propped up at her bedside. She grabbed it just as Blythe's snoring stopped and she rolled to her feet.

"What is it?" Blythe asked, clearly unaware she'd slept through her guard duty.

"There are clashing swords outside."

This woke her other guard ladies. They all leapt to their feet. Lareina and Malka pulled their boots on and strapped their weapons on. Again, the *shing* of metal sounded outside, muted somewhere down the hall, maybe even out on the deck. Wordlessly, her guards fell into a familiar formation, slowly proceeding out the door and down the hall. Haven dressed quickly and strapped her sword to her belt.

She followed her soldiers to the main deck, where Aura and Drakkone were fighting wildly. Aura's curved blades slashed again and again at Drakkone, moving in arcs around her body, a true extension of herself. While Aura was on the offensive, Drakkone easily dodged or blocked her attacks. He moved calmly, as if this were a regular drill he'd done a thousand times. Aura, on the other hand, breathed heavily and moved savagely in purpose.

"What is happening?" Haven gasped.

Her words must have distracted them both, because Drakkone almost forgot to duck while Aura barely retracted her swing in time to avoid cutting the large man's head off.

"Lady Queen!" Aura echoed the gasp of her queen. She quickly sheathed her sword and bowed.

"Practice." Nina bounced down from the observation deck above. "Aura wanted to run some drills, and Father volunteered."

"Oh." Haven blinked, dropping her hand from the hilt of her sword.

"You thought they were fighting each other?"

"Well, I didn't know what to think." A smile began to creep up her cheeks. An idea sprang to mind at the sight of their two friends. She'd never seen a fighting style like Aura's, and clearly Drakkone knew how to handle it. Somehow, he deployed both techniques simultaneously—Seaburn's and the Savage Lands's. "You have a very interesting technique."

"Thank you," Aura and Drakkone said in unison.

Haven smiled. "I want to learn."

"Learn what, Lady Queen?" Drakkone raised an eyebrow.

"To fight like the two of you. No one in the six kingdoms fight like this. Your technique could be invaluable against Kadia's army," Haven explained. "Teach me."

"Lady Queen, I assure you, you will not need to fight in the upcoming battle," Aura said, seeming aghast that she would even suggest such a thing. "We will fight for you and destroy your enemies."

Haven laughed. "Aura, you've seen my ability. There is simply no need to protect me. I will be fighting with the rest of you. I could not ask you to fight for me while I sit back and watch." Haven smiled. "So please teach me how to fight like you and your people." Her gaze fell on Nina's father. "And, Drakkone, please teach me how to counter and fight like you as well."

Drakkone and Aura exchanged a look. Then they turned back to the young queen.

"It would be my honor," he said.

It was high noon by the time the deck has been cleared enough to practice on. In the meantime, Aura scoured the ship, informing every soldier she could find of what was about to happen. At the same time, Drakkone found curved swords for Haven and Nina to practice with. It had come as a unanimous decision that, if Nina was going to take on Kadia, she needed to know how to defend herself. The young girl had been skeptical at first—nervous, even—but as Haven had reminded Nina of her experiences, determination settled in Nina's gaze.

While Blythe and Drakkone took Nina through the basics, Aura handed Haven a curved blade. They faced each other on the deck. The only way to assess her abilities was to show them. Her stomach twisted. Haven had agreed, but suddenly, she felt unsure. Not for her safety, but for her ability to learn. The surrounding crowd didn't help.

"Whenever you're ready, Lady Queen," Aura slurred with her thick accent.

"Ready."

Aura came at her without mercy. Swinging quickly, Aura arced and flashed through the air, her blades spinning in rapid succession. Much to Haven's surprise, her training kicked in.

Haven swung her sword up, their blades clanging loudly together. She pushed back. The curved blade was new to her, but it wasn't completely unlike her own straight sword. The curve gave her faster movements while simultaneously being heavier. Directionally, she wasn't used to the blade and found that her movements were off when she tried to block. The curved blade did not suit her Warshard fighting style. It wasn't long before she faltered and nearly became a victim of Aura's twin blades.

"You are a good fighter, Lady Queen." Aura smiled, both surprised and pleased. "You have much potential to be a fine warrior."

"Then teach me to fight like you." Haven breathed heavily. Though her energy remained high, her adrenaline flared like fire in her veins. "Teach me to be a warrior."

"You know you're nothing like the council of Seaburn." Aura lowered her swords and relaxed.

Haven mimicked her, disappointed their fight was already over. "Of course not," she said, trying not to picture all the gruesome wrong doings this girl must have experienced at their hands.

"You want to fight while they sit in their temple and rot in their lavish clothes. They ask us to go to war while they sit back and wait for the spoils we bring. You're not like that, are you?"

Haven shook her head. "No one in Warshard is like that."

"And do you take people into your armies against their will?"

"Of course not. All of our men and women are volunteers. They are well paid and respected."

"Respect," Aura murmured, looking her in the eye. "I respect you, Lady Haven. I can't say the same for our former masters."

"You will never have a master again as long as I have a say in it, Aura." Haven reached for her.

Instead of taking her hand, Aura held her forearm. Haven returned the hold, assuming it was some sort of southern handshake.

"You are a queen worth fighting for."

"Thank you, Aura." Haven released her arm, and they stepped back from each other. "You're a brave woman."

"I have to be to fight the Immortal Queen."

Haven laughed. "I suppose you do."

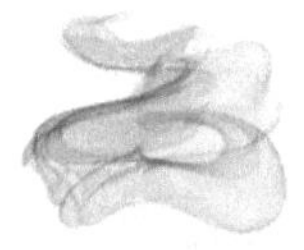

TWENTY-SEVEN

More than a week had passed, and their training continued.

"Lady Haven, you need to use the curve of your blades," Drakkone would tell her.

"Defend with your swords like you would a shield," Aura would chime in.

"If you want to fight like a southerner, you need to use your emotions, Haven," Nina added while on a break.

Time and time again, they threw new information at her. They taught her how to block, how to press on, and how to swing both blades together in rapid succession. The lot of it was exhausting, but every swing exhilarated her. A crowd always gathered to watch her fight, whether it be against Drakkone, Aura, or one of the other southerners. They all drove her on and on, not allowing her a moment's rest. It made her limbs weak and her body sore by nightfall, but in the end, her weeks of training were worth it. More than ever, she was ready to face Kadia, even if her teachers hardly thought her prepared.

"I am using my emotions," Haven said between blocking one of Drakkone's blows and simultaneously stabbing forward at his abdomen.

The large man easily turned away while knocking one of her swords aside and swinging at her in a wide arc. Haven hopped back to avoid the blow but lost her grip on her sword.

"Lady Haven, you aren't using your instincts." He sighed, pausing their fight for another lesson.

Nina scurried over to Haven's fallen sword and handed it back to her.

"Thank you," Haven said. "What am I doing wrong?"

"You aren't angry."

"Yes, I am," she argued.

"No, you are not."

"Lady Haven." Aura stepped forward. "The way we fight in the tribes, we use our feelings. We put our soul into every blow."

"You need to use your emotions to focus your strength. Until you do, you won't be embracing our way of fighting," Drakkone said. "I know you have a lot of anger in you, Haven. Use it."

Haven sighed, raising her swords again. Drakkone did the same.

Again, they launched into it. Drakkone came at her much like Aura, his movements controlled, powerful, and somewhat savage. The difference, she had begun to realize, was this emotional way of fighting they were all trying to make her learn.

While Aura fought in a rage, using her emotions heavily to her advantage, spitting and hissing like a snake, Drakkone was much more controlled. Only the dark look in his eyes told her of the beast hiding behind his mask of composure.

Haven tried to be angry. She tried to think of Kadia, of the former slaves of Seaburn, anything to make her skill improve. It was a difficult task when she also had to concentrate on blocking and dodging. Drakkone and Aura were fast and precise. Their way of fighting was completely unlike that of the six kingdoms. Even after a week, she had a hard time thinking about anything but stopping their barrage of attacks.

"You aren't angry," Drakkone said while he aimed another swing at her torso.

Haven dodged at the last minute and stabbed back at his side. Drakkone blocked and spun before using his left sword to attack.

"I'm trying," she spat, ducking low and cutting her blade up toward him.

"You shouldn't need to try so hard. Just feel it. Think about what has happened to you." Drakkone swatted her blade with his own, turning from her attack and bringing his blade down on her.

Haven rolled away just in time, springing to her feet only a moment before his sword struck her. "I can't think when you move so quickly," she hissed, blocking his blade with her own.

"Then let me help you." Drakkone pushed back, forcing her to the edge of the crowd, which parted around them. Drakkone leapt, bringing his sword down on something wooden just as Haven moved from reach. "Think of what that woman has done to you. Think about Kadia."

Haven swung at Drakkone. "I am."

He blocked and swung back. "Think about all she's done."

"I am!" Haven growled, dodging and slicing back with more aggression this time.

Drakkone's sword met hers before he spun and swung again. Haven jumped onto a nearby ledge, and her heart pounded wildly as she leapt at him. Drakkone dodged easily.

"Think about what she's done to your kingdoms, to your family." Drakkone still came at her.

As Haven's blood pressure increased, she fought back harder. Images of her mother beaten and bloody at her feet sprang to mind.

"She's the reason your parents are dead, isn't she? Your brothers too?"

"She's the reason for all of this," Haven hissed.

"You can't see your sister, your only remaining blood, because of her. Isn't that right?"

"Yes." Haven's sword collided with Drakkone's and she pushed hard against it.

"That's right, and how does that make you feel?"

Haven narrowed her eyes and twisted from their locked swords, driving her blade at his abdomen. Drakkone once again dodged, much to her growing frustration.

"It makes you angry, doesn't it? Not only has she ruined your family, but she's the reason you came to Seaburn. She's the reason your kingdoms are lying in ruin."

Haven spun and their swords crashed together. Her pounding heart filled her ears. Drakkone pushed her blade away.

"Kadia is the reason you have to fight this hard. Without her influence, you wouldn't need to fight to stop it from ever happening again."

Haven stepped back from Drakkone's next hit and plunged her sword at his shoulder. Just when she thought she'd land a hit, Drakkone turned and swatted one of her swords from her hand. It clanged to the ground. Using his weight, he pushed the young queen into the mast of the ship. Her breath rushed from her lungs. She glared into his dark eyes, baring her teeth. A tingle of adrenaline rushed through her limbs. Her palms started to sweat. A torrent built inside her chest.

"If that all wasn't enough, don't you remember what she did to you?"

Haven's breath caught in her throat. She tried not to let the fear come to the surface. She tried not to think about that room, those knives, that water slowly drowning her. Most of all, she tried not to remember that look of sick fascination on Kadia's face as she'd tortured her.

"Of course I remember." Haven locked eyes with him.

Drakkone leaned back, which gave Haven the chance to put her leg between them and kick him away. He flew back, his arms swinging to catch himself. Haven took a moment to collect herself and grab her fallen sword. It was probably a foolish move, because she'd barely picked it up when she was rolling away to dodge Drakkone's blade again.

"If you remember, then fight like you do!"

Haven swiped at him, but Drakkone blocked her shot. "I am!" she shouted, frustration boiling inside her.

"You aren't. I need you to remember, Haven." Drakkone slammed the side of her sword with his own, nearly ripping it away again. He pushed on and drove the other blade at her stomach.

Reacting quickly, Haven moved just out of reach and pulled her swords back. But Drakkone wouldn't give her time to collect herself again; he came at her in a flurry of blades.

"What did she do to you?" he snapped.

All of her concentration went into blocking, dodging, and returning his hits.

"She ruined your family, your kingdoms, and then she took you from your friends. She took you and kept you in that room. She strapped you to a table and tortured you."

Haven nearly blanched and let one of his blades through her barricade. She blocked just in time and angrily struck back at him. Nina had to have told him.

"Be quiet," Haven hissed.

She didn't want to hear this. She couldn't.

"She tortured you, Haven. She stuck you with knives, stabbed you, cut you, burned you, and even threatened to cut off your limbs," Drakkone continued.

Haven swung harder, pushing him back as she went on the offensive. "Shut *up!*" Something deep and primal burned inside her.

"When that wasn't enough to satisfy her, she let her men drag you across the floor and drown you just to see if you would live through it."

Haven drove her sword at him again and again. She wanted to scream at him; she wanted to hurt him; she wanted to make him stop.

"Not only did she physically torture you, but she kept you in that castle for weeks. She threatened you, your people, your friends, and then stripped you naked and knocked you out. She used her powers to predict her own demise."

Drakkone pushed back, but Haven's fury was burning too high. All thought fled her. She wasn't thinking about his safety anymore, and she definitely wasn't thinking of her own.

"*Shut up!*" she screamed at him.

"If all that wasn't enough, the worst of it was when she sent that man to impregnate you. She didn't want you anymore, just your power. She wanted a child of her own. *Your* child to fill the void you would leave. She sent him to rape you, and finally, you had to fight back."

Haven had had enough.

Pushing back harder than she had yet, she swung time and time again, pushing her opponent off-balance. She spun hard in a way Aura had shown her and slammed her boot into his chest. Drakkone toppled to the ground as she let out a battle cry and lunged. After dropping one of her swords, she took the remaining in both of her hands and leapt on top of him.

"*Haven!*" someone screamed.

She froze. It brought her out of her rage just in time. Instead of driving her sword through his body, she slammed it into the deck, inches from his ear. Chest heaving and limbs covered in sweat, Haven stared with wide eyes at Drakkone. His expression mirrored her own.

What had she just done? She'd never been so angry in her life. If someone hadn't interrupted, she might have just killed this man. Cold fear splintered her heart like knives. Her whole body shook. She released her sword. It clanged against the deck as she sat back.

Haven held her hands to her mouth, disbelief flooding through her in waves. Drakkone had aired her story to everyone. Every last moment. Everyone knew what had gone on in Kadia's castle, and what was worse, it had brought out an uncontrolled rage. If she could hone this strength, this power her anger gave her, she could truly be dangerous.

"I'm sorry," she whispered, shakily coming to her feet.

Those around her finally came to life. A hand gently touched her elbow, but she ripped her arm away.

"I'm sorry." Haven turned from her opponent and the crowd. Only then did she catch Corrin's eye.

He was standing at the stairs by the hall to her chambers. Haven dropped her gaze and hurried past, trying to forget the look of shock all around her.

"LADY HAVEN?" A soft knock on the door echoed.

Upon returning to her chambers, Haven had locked her door and buried herself in the soft silk bedding. At first, it had been comforting, but as reality had slowly crept in, Haven had realized she couldn't hide from herself any more than she could hide from her friends.

"Yes?" She sighed.

"May we come in?"

Haven recognized the voice of her personal guard as well as the soft whispers of the others beyond the door. "If you must."

There was a short pause, more whispers, and then a click as the door unlocked. Her three guard girls piled inside and carefully shut the door behind them. For the first time, they hesitated. They had known only bits and pieces of her ordeal, but because they had been present for the fight, they were finally privy to exactly what had happened in Kadia's castle. Not only that, but in the telling of it, she had nearly killed one of their friends in a practice fight.

Haven wasn't sure what she thought of herself anymore, let alone what these girls thought of their queen.

Lareina sat next to her on the sheets. A storm brewed in the woman's eyes. She sat in silence for a moment before she leaned forward and tightly wrapped Haven in her arms. Before Haven could speak, two other sets of arms surrounded her, and suddenly, she found it hard to breathe. The young queen smiled and held fast to her friends. Even though she felt herself a monster, they still comforted her.

"We didn't know it was that bad," Blythe whispered against her hair.

Haven blinked the forming tears back. They all sat back and looked at one another. "We don't need to talk about it."

"But do you want to?" Lareina took her hand. "You've been holding on to this alone for so long."

"You can talk to us about anything." Malka settled in by the backboard.

"I know." Haven looked at each of them in turn. "But I'm not ready to get into the details yet."

"We're here when you're ready." Lareina smiled.

"I know you are." Haven paused. "I think there's something I need to do."

Her guards exchanged a look with each other.

"We'll come with you," Lareina said.

"It's not a bring-your-guards-along kind of thing." Haven chuckled.

"It doesn't have to do with Corrin, does it?" Malka raised a knowing eyebrow.

Haven bit her lip and shrugged.

"Are you certain?" Blythe asked.

"You don't have to talk to him yet. Especially after what's happened." Lareina squeezed her fingers.

"But, if I don't now, I might never get the chance." Haven sighed. "Tonight is the last night before we reach Dagan."

Her guards froze. In the drama of the past few hours, they'd all forgotten why Drakkone had pushed her so hard. This was the last night before the final battle against Kadia. In the morning, they would draw up the final plans with Vas and his generals. By noon, the plans would be fully underway and they would be at war once again. It was now or never.

"I have to go." Haven rose from the sheets.

"Good luck." Lareina smiled.

"Thank you."

Tomorrow, Corrin could be dead. Tomorrow, they all could be dead. If she didn't do this now, she might regret it for the rest of her life. Haven said her goodbyes and left into the night.

WHEN HAVEN FINALLY FOUND CORRIN, she had a hard time approaching him. Not because she was scared or because she wasn't prepared. She knew what she wanted to say, but in the light of dusk, she had never seen a man more beautiful than he. It felt as if this were the first time she was truly seeing him.

Corrin was leaning against the edge of the ship, his arms casually resting on the rails. He watched the light of the sun die beyond the horizon and the stars begin to wink in the darkening sky. The soft light lit his blue eyes like diamonds. The color danced around him in such a way that she could hardly believe he was real. The light immensely complemented his tanned skin as well as the soft blond of his hair. Though he was handsome in ways she couldn't fully explain, it was his kind heart that had drawn her to him in the first place. When she had been afraid and crying, he'd come to her, helped her. He'd been her friend when she'd needed one most, and he'd stayed with her even when it had seemed like everything would end in ruin. He believed in her plan to go across the sea, and in the end, he still wanted to marry her. Haven had never met a man like him.

She must have been staring for some time, because when she finally broke from her reverie, Corrin was staring back. His gaze was guarded but curious.

"Haven?" He raised an eyebrow.

Her heart leapt. She paused for only a moment longer. She ran to close the gap between them. After leaping into his arms, she kissed him. It was the first time she'd kissed anyone, and it was much nicer than she'd imagined. Once Corrin's surprise wore off, he pulled her close and wrapped his arms around her, kissing her back.

All of her fears and worries melted away. She didn't think about the coming war or her embarrassment in training. She only thought about this and what she wanted. When she finally pulled back, it was only slightly. They both breathed heavily and stared at each other.

"Yes," she said.

Corrin blinked at her. "What?"

"Yes." A smile pulled at her lips.

"Yes?" His eyes widened. Corrin finally realized what she was saying. A smile like none other lit his face. He pulled her back into his arms, twirling her around and kissing her again. When he finally set her down, he didn't let her take a step back. "I love you."

"I love you, Corrin."

"I want to spend the rest of my life with you if you'll have me."

"Promise me you won't die tomorrow. Promise me you'll live a long life."

"I promise."

Haven embraced him. "I want to live forever with you, but you can't die on me."

"I won't. I promise."

For what seemed like a long time, they held each other tightly, unwilling to let go. Even as all light faded from the sky and they were left under the light of the stars, they stayed. This could be the last night they'd have together if he didn't live up to his promise.

Fear crept back in. She met his gaze. He'd promised her he would live. She had to trust that promise and pray that he would be able to keep it.

Haven leaned up and kissed him one last time. "I love you."

"I love you, Haven."

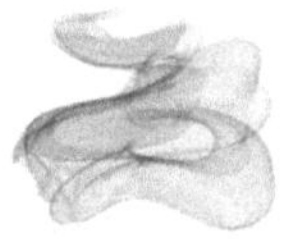

TWENTY-EIGHT

"Warshard is in sight!"

The shout quieted everyone on the ship. All gazes drew ahead and locked on the coastline. To the left of the ship, the great trees of Wakefin rose in the distant morning fog. To the right, an abandoned fishing village dotted the open land. Somewhere in the distance rose the turrets of a dark castle.

Kadia's castle.

Swallowing audibly, Haven stepped up beside her guards, Aura, and their two Seaburn friends. Their team was small, aided by only a couple dozen soldiers. It would be a challenge to gain entrance to Dagan's capital, Cidra, but Haven was confident they would reach the castle in one piece.

As she turned from the front of the ship, her hair whipped and danced in the wind. She was suddenly glad for the braids tightly locking one side of her hair to her head. If it hadn't been for them, she'd have had a lot more hair in her mouth. Pacing to the rear of the ship, she thought over the plans that had been finalized in the dark predawn light.

Early that morning, Haven had met with the captains, the generals, and the council of Seaburn to finalize their plan of attack. Their plan was simple, though it eerily reminded her of the retaking of Wakefin, which had lost them many. While the majority of the fleet would head directly for Cidra and lay siege to Kadia's castle, Haven and her group would infiltrate Cidra from the north. Their plan was to get Nina in the same room with Kadia. Her ability would negate Kadia's powers and stop any assault Dagan could muster. Once Nina did her duty, Haven's team would subdue Kadia and the kingdoms would be saved. The plan was contingent on many small things working in their favor, but they had no other choice.

Glancing back at the coast, Haven raised her voice for the captain to redirect their vessel. "We will head south to the abandoned village." She glanced toward the upper deck to make sure her message had been well received.

A swift nod told her that it was.

It wasn't long before their ship reached the docks, where they disembarked to slip through the deserted streets. The fog hung low to the earth, the sun barely on the horizon. If they moved quickly, they would make it to Cidra under the cover of mist. Haven called them into formation, and everyone kept alert. With the siege beginning anytime, Haven set their pace at a brisk jog, slowing to stop behind a building every now and then to peer out into the forthcoming open space.

Small villages dotted the land around the capital city; though she couldn't see them, she knew they were there. They had studied the map well that morning.

At the edge of the small fishing village, the group gathered in a crouch behind a large boat beached on the shore. One of the soldiers drew the map and they planned a route as direct as possible to the city.

While the group planned, Haven drew back, watching the mist. Aside from their whispers, it was dead silent on the moor. A shiver ran down her spine.

She couldn't help imagining the worst: dark soldiers leaping from behind buildings and dropping from above, Kadia walking through the fog and decimating them all, leaving their plan a failure. Haven shook her head to rid the thoughts and turned back to her group. Nina met her gaze. Though the air was frosty, sweat coated Nina's brow. Anxiety flickered through her eyes, and she chewed her lip nervously. Haven reached a hand for Nina, and the small, blond girl moved closer her.

"Don't be scared," Haven whispered. "Our plan is solid. Everything will work out."

Nina nodded, squeezing her fingers. Haven squeezed back to offer her comfort. Though Haven wasn't sure if anything would work out, she had to hope. For herself, the six kingdoms, and her friends. If their plan failed, they could all be dead by nightfall.

Before either of them could say another word, the soldiers stood and motioned for everyone to move out. Haven gave Nina one last reassuring smile before they parted and began the trek to Cidra.

THE SMALL PLATOON had nearly reached the black city when the first cannons fired from the bay. They froze in the dark alley between two stone houses. Goose bumps rose on her skin, and Haven turned toward the sea. Though she couldn't see through the mist, the battle had begun. Nerves prickled inside her chest for her soldiers, the other kings, Corrin, and all on board those fighting vessels.

"We must make haste," Haven snapped, turning her attention to the street before them.

All remained eerily quiet. Without waiting for an answer, she shimmied out between the soldiers beside her and took off at a sprint, dodging between buildings for hiding places. The faster they reached Cidra castle, the faster they'd rid the world of Kadia.

Her stealth was unnecessary, as not a single person peeked from their homes, not a single guard patrolled the streets, and not even a stray cat moved across their path. It all seemed too easy.

"Lady Queen, *please* stop. We need to be careful," Blythe hissed behind her.

Haven hadn't realized yet that she'd been traveling several yards in front of everyone. She paused to let the group catch up. Though they were still hidden in lingering fog, Haven shifted, uncomfortable in the looming shadow of the castle. Several more feet and they would pass through the open gates of Cidra.

"Sorry. I got carried away." Haven tried not to let her gaze linger too long on the gates. They were open, and that could mean one of two things. Either Kadia was expecting them or things had gotten much further out of hand in this city than they'd come to realize.

The booming of cannons reverberated over the damp, empty street.

"Let's go." Blythe nodded and led the way.

As they passed through the gates, the sounds of war drew near. Shouts sounded faintly in the distance, booms echoed, and cracks shot through the black stone ahead. Even though all of this came clearly through the fog, the city remained silent.

"Where are the civilians?" one of the soldiers asked another.

"The city is deserted," another added.

"Silence," Drakkone snapped.

The soldiers shut their mouths. Haven raised an eyebrow. If Drakkone was a lieutenant in his home country, why he would want to leave Seaburn and be part of this war? Wouldn't he have rather stayed in his home country to keep Nina safe? Haven assumed that it would have been the latter, yet there he was.

"It may be quiet, but that doesn't mean no one is around." Blythe drew everyone's attention, glancing side to side to make sure they were indeed listening. "I want complete silence until we reach the castle. Only speak if *completely* necessary. We're too close for there not to be a trap set. I want every single one of you on alert." Her gaze rested on Haven a moment before turning to two of the younger soldiers. "The two of you."

They straightened under Blythe's gaze.

"Scout ahead and report back."

They nodded and disappeared.

"The rest of you." Blythe faced them. "We will gather in a protective formation around Queen Haven and Lady Nina."

"Lady?" Nina squeaked.

Haven smiled. "If you decide to stay in the six kingdoms long, you will surely be dubbed a Lady."

Nina blinked at her in wide-eyed confusion. If they had been in any other situation, she might have laughed, but her whole body tensed in the dissipating fog. They were too close to Kadia for humor.

"Let's go." This time, Drakkone led the way, side by side with Blythe.

They nodded in some sort of silent agreement before the group formed a protective ring around the two women. Malka and Lareina stood closely on either side of them, with Aura guarding their backs. Haven sighed at their overprotective stances. She tried to assure herself that this was to protect Nina and not her, but she knew better.

Haven kept pace with her comrades as they made their way through the winding streets and the twisting alleys. The closer they came, the louder the cannons and the shouting grew. The dark castle reared its ugly head, and they set about searching for a servants' entrance.

"You two, search that way," Blythe commanded. "And you search along that side." She pointed and ordered while Haven glanced toward the sea.

Was Corrin all right? Their goodbye had been too brief, and though he had once again promised her that he would be fine, she feared his death. Her heart ached to know her future. If only her power could stretch to future sight like Kadia's. Though her toes curled at the thought, she still wished it.

"We found an open entrance to the kitchens," said the two soldiers who rejoined the group in a hurry. The castle put them all on edge.

"Excellent. Fetch Genry and follow us. We'll wait for you there," Blythe said.

"Understood." The soldiers disappeared around the bend, where the third had gone.

When had Blythe found the time to memorize all the names of her soldiers? She shook her head. Before she could ask, her guards whisked her downhill and silently ushered everyone into a regal-sized kitchen. One fit only for a malevolent queen.

"It's too quiet in here," Lareina said. She paced the room on silent feet, investigating for any signs of a trap or danger lurking.

Malka joined her, mirroring her position on the opposite side of the kitchen. Her bow drawn, Malka hitched a single arrow. Haven and Lareina weren't the only ones concerned about the silence of the castle.

A boom shot through the building and the entire kitchen shook, rattling glassware and dishes, sending a stack of plates crashing to the floor, which was startlingly loud in the hollow space. Her heart leapt. Everyone held his or her breath in anticipation.

Haven winced and kept her hand on the hilt of one of her swords. If any guards had heard that in the halls, they might have been tempted to investigate, even if the cannon fire had been the source of the disruption.

Malka moved to the door and pressed her ear to it. She must have been thinking the same thing. Malka leapt back, and Haven jumped to attention, drawing her curved blade. Three armed guards with vacant eyes and withdrawn expressions charged through the door.

Haven hesitated. She vaguely remembered the glassy eyes of the guards when she had been held captive there. They had the same look her own guards had had after her assassin had been found on the pike.

One of the Seaburn soldiers leapt over the table and took the first enemy down. Malka shot the second with an arrow through the heart, and Lareina let loose a dagger into the forehead of the last. All three collapsed in a heap.

"Move the bodies back. Quickly!" Blythe ordered.

So they were moved. Something clicked for Haven then, but what, she couldn't quite put into words. Those sightless eyes and vacant streets meant something. Where were the people? Why did the guards follow Kadia so absolutely?

Before she could voice her concerns, Lareina ushered her through the kitchen, over the bodies, into a small cafeteria, and out into a long corridor. Tapestries of grisly creatures hung from the walls where no light shone through darkened windows. The hall stretched endlessly, pockmarked by many doors.

Whispered voices reached her ears from a larger room up ahead. She hadn't the time to silence anyone behind her. A Dagan guard in black armor stepped into view ahead of them. He froze. *Blue skies.* The guard turned and ran. Shouts echoed through the castle.

Kadia knew they were there.

TWENTY-NINE

*D*agan guards piled into the hall faster than they could be dispatched. So far, they were human, so Haven didn't have much time to dwell on the lack of shadow soldiers. Blade after blade met hers as her platoon launched into battle. Her heart raced as each side fought for space in the long corridor. Though the hall was fairly wide, it was difficult to gain ground while her soldiers continued to push ahead in their attempt to protect her.

"Protect *Nina*," she ordered one man who broke in front of her, blocking a sword she had already seen coming.

The soldier glanced at her blazing, amber eyes and pushed his opponent back before obeying her and disappearing into the throng of people at her back. Haven dove forward once he was out of the way, spinning with her twin curved swords and cutting through a new opponent. He fell easily under her new blades, his sword clanging to the ground.

Before Haven could turn to the next enemy, a crack split the air. Her eyebrows furrowed. The castle didn't shake. A cannon didn't boom. The noise had come from outside.

Her heart fell. She needed to see outside *now*. Fighting wildly, Haven pushed her way through the crowd, dodging, blocking, and cutting until she reached a large window. The fog had cleared and the sun shone in the blue sky, lighting every piece of the devastation below.

An impossibly huge, black serpent wrapped around three of their ships, curling around their masts and bodies before snapping them like twigs. Kadia. She was doing this. The dark form curled and coiled around the wreckage, seeking further prey.

Something inside her chest snapped. She couldn't peel her gaze from the carnage: the broken, battered bodies lying in the water, the pieces of ships slowly sinking. Her heart lurched, and her whole body went numb.

What if Corrin was in that mess?

Her fingers curled tightly around her swords, her knuckles white. This was all because of Kadia. That evil woman had gone one step too far. Every stab, every poke, every prod—that had been one thing. She'd done it to get her people safely away from Kadia. But hurting her people, her friends, and her love? That was something else altogether. She had to find Kadia—now.

She needn't bring Nina to stop her power; Haven would kill her for this.

Turning back to the guards racing down the stairs, Haven swung her two swords in her hands before charging at them. A battle cry ripped from her throat. Ducking low, Haven slid between two guards, using her momentum to propel herself as she sliced through their stomachs and their torsos. When she came back up, she spun, one sword cutting through the next one's shoulder to his collarbone.

When she turned again, she ripped her sword free of the wound and threw her blade. It arced several times before piercing the chest of a man several feet away. He'd been charging, a battle cry of his own echoing through the stairwell.

Haven let every piece of anger ripple inside her until she wasn't seeing guards anymore—she was seeing Kadia again and again and again.

Her fingers trembled as she cut through this Kadia and that, cutting their heads off, kicking them in their chests, slicing through them with her twin blades, stabbing through their midriffs.

Before she knew it, a pile of bodies lay at her feet, and she breathed heavily. Blood dripped from her blades, joining the rest of the pooling red.

Haven looked up. A huge foyer led to a two-story staircase. At the base of the twisting set of stairs were two small daises with shallow bowls of fire to light the large room.

Flames lapped the air. Her nostrils flared. Haven stalked toward them. Pushing one with her hands, she toppled it onto the ground. The fire didn't catch immediately, but when she kicked the second over, the ceiling-high curtains burst into flames.

Her fists tightened. Kadia had painted her own demise on Haven's body. Cidra castle would be devoured by an inferno of her own making.

"Haven!" Lareina's gasp echoed behind her before soft hands turned her to face her friend. "What have you done?"

Haven glanced over Lareina's shoulder. Her friends collecting in the entryway, the soldiers spreading out to secure the area. When she looked back into Lareina's eyes, they were wide with something akin to panic. It was a strange expression, and at first, it seemed misplaced until the glow of fire began to warm Lareina's cheeks.

"Kadia predicted I would be her demise, that I would burn her castle to the ground." Haven stepped away from Lareina. "I will turn it to *ash.*"

Lareina glanced back at the group. They slowly moved toward her like she was some sort of caged animal. All stopped several feet away —all except for Aura.

Aura held her fist to her chest. "Your orders, Lady Queen?"

Normally, her loyalty would have struck Haven. Even her friends were staring at her and, for the first time, questioning her actions. While they judged her, this new part of her flock stepped forward, believing in her. Haven smiled, something soft finally breaking through her anger. Or at least it did until she had another look at the flames burning their way to the rafters.

"We must evacuate Cidra. All of you head into the city and evacuate as many as you can." Haven paused. "Check the servants' quarters in the castle as well, but do not endanger yourselves." For the first time, she ordered the soldiers to do her bidding.

They stilled, and she wasn't sure they would comply, but after a moment, they nodded and sprang into action.

"Blythe, go. Lead them."

Blythe wouldn't go so easily. "You can't be serious."

"I am very serious, Blythe." Haven arched an eyebrow. "Take Lareina and Malka as well. Take them and *go*." She put as much emphasis into the one word as she could. She didn't want her friends there. She didn't want them to see her heart. She wouldn't see them hurt, and frankly, she didn't need them for this last part.

"Haven," Lareina gasped. "We're not leaving you."

"Fire is spreading and anyone left inside will be killed," Malka said, stepping up to join them.

"I want you to leave. I don't need you for this," Haven said, hoping they wouldn't take offense. She didn't want them guessing, let alone see, her murderous intent. "I have Drakkone and Aura to back me up and Nina to dispatch Kadia. I won't see any of you die unnecessarily."

"But, Haven—"

"I will *not* argue this," Haven snapped. "You will leave *now*."

The women exchanged looks. For a moment, Haven thought they were going to dig their heels in and stay, but after a brief pause, Blythe stepped back.

"As you wish, *Lady Queen*." The formal title stung, but Haven knew she'd won.

While Malka joined Blythe in their retreat alongside the soldiers, Lareina sagged in defeat. Haven wished she could talk the look of hurt off her face, but there wasn't time. Cidra was burning and they needed to find Kadia as soon as possible.

"If anything happens to me, I love you all," Haven said. "And tell my sister I love her too, and be with her if she becomes Queen. She'll need your help."

Tears welled in Lareina's eyes, and she shook her head. "You can't ask that of me, Haven. You can't."

"Please, Lareina." Haven stepped forward and took her hands.

Lareina shook her head and pulled away. "We'll take care of your sister, but you'd better come back from this." She fixed Haven with as stern a look as she could conjure.

Wordlessly, Haven nodded. Lareina sighed and joined the others. Once they were out of earshot, Haven turned to those left.

"Let's find that evil witch."

THIRTY

earing through the castle, Haven worked with her team of four to navigate the halls, avoiding the building inferno as much as possible. While they searched, they hacked away at anyone who came near, Aura often stepping in before she could react.

Aura fought with the prowess of a wild cat, attacking quickly but always with precision. She had just defeated a pair of two in no more than three strikes when a cackle echoed through the hall.

Haven's blood ran cold.

The group had spent nearly a half hour searching the first two levels, but they were on the third floor now. There was no sign of Kadia and her dwindling numbers of soldiers. The ground grew hot, and smoke wafted through the air. They all carried forth with calm determination, following their friend and queen even though it could possibly be to their deaths.

The cackle sounded again, and they all halted. Kadia.

She tightened her fingers around the hilts of her blades. They continued forward. The voice had been so close that she had no trouble figuring out which door it had come from.

The hall, the door, and the room beyond were all too familiar. The stained-glass window at the end of the hall had been shattered, right where Haven had leapt through it.

Haven took a deep breath. This was it. She slammed her boot against the door. It flew inward, cracking off the wall.

The gorgeous platinum-blonde spun toward them, her red gown swishing and her blue eyes blazing. Haven threw one of her swords at the woman's chest.

A smirk pulled at Kadia's lips as she raised a hand. A black soldier appeared to take the blow before dissipating in black wisps. Haven's sword clattered uselessly to the ground. Several more rose from the remains, their dark bodies blocking her path to the Insane Queen.

"Little Haven, so nice to see you again," Kadia purred, one hand on her hip while the other twisted at her side, controlling her powers in some manner Haven couldn't see.

"I can't say the same."

Her friends stepped up behind her: Aura to her left, Drakkone to her right, and Nina peeking out from behind her father.

Kadia's hand stopped moving, and her eyes widened. "My sister, you've come!" She nearly rushed forward before her gaze skipped up to the face guarding the little blond girl. She barely noted Drakkone before flattening her skirts and smiling at Nina. "So nice of you to bring her to me, little queen. Maybe I will forgive you after all."

The look of sick interest in her eyes reminded Haven all too well of the weeks she'd spent trapped in this room. The same furnishing and dressing—even the same bed cover remained, bloodstain and all.

"I very much doubt that." Haven stepped forward, her sword raised. "I didn't bring her *for* you, I brought her to *stop* you."

With great disdain, Kadia slid her gaze from Nina and fixed it on Haven. One moment, her eyes were nothing but malice, and in the next, they flickered in amusement. The crazy woman tilted her head back and let out a boisterous laugh, the sound filling the silence of the room.

"Stop *me*?" she said once her laughter had died out. "How in Solipher's name are you going to stop *me*?"

Soliper? Haven had never heard the name, though anything this woman said could have been dismissed as insane ramblings.

Haven inched closer while Kadia was distracted. She wouldn't be able to get much closer without dark soldiers attacking her, and with darkness dripping between Kadia's fingers, the shadows could attack at any moment.

"Yes, stop you," Haven said. "You've caused enough grief for the six kingdoms. Surrender to us and we won't have to use Nina or kill you."

"Use little Nina girl against me? You must be *dreaming*, Haven." Kadia rolled her eyes. "As for killing me, you'd only be delaying the inevitable. Why don't you lay your toy down and come beg for your sister's forgiveness?"

Kadia's smirk returned, and with a twitch of her hand, a dark sword pointed at Haven's throat. The blade hovered a good foot from her flesh, but the threat was clear.

Haven stepped back. "I would never beg you for anything. If you want a fight, so be it."

Aura jumped ahead. Two shadow soldiers appeared from the dark mist at Kadia's feet. Aura clashed with the soldier closest to Haven. She sliced through its black flesh and it disappeared into black smoke.

Drakkone dove for the next at the same time Haven leapt for another dark figure. Hacking at dark skin, the three of them made it through wave after wave of soldiers until Haven broke free and grabbed Kadia by the arm.

Startled, Kadia sent a blast of darkness into her chest, which flung Haven into Aura and sent both of them sprawling across the floor.

At last, Kadia had been distracted. Nina stepped forward and cornered the queen, pinning her to the wall with a dagger to her throat.

By the time Aura and Haven leapt to their feet, the room had grown still. The dark soldiers halted mid-motion, their images shaking with transparency. Both women joined Drakkone and Nina, who glanced at the others to make sure they were okay.

"It's over, Kadia," Haven said, her fingers twitching on the hilt of her sword. More than anything, she wanted to forgo formalities and drive her sword through the woman's chest, but something told her not to. Nina had this under control, and she wanted to see what the young girl could do.

"It'll never be over," Kadia hissed. Her former beauty twisted into a venomous snarl, and her perfect nails scraped the wall.

"Whenever you're ready, Nina." Haven took over holding her sword to Kadia's throat while Nina sheathed her dagger and closed her eyes before placing her small hands on the sides of Kadia's head.

For a moment, nothing happened.

The crackling of embers was the only sound in the castle. It reminded Haven that they didn't have much time for this. Haven looked at Drakkone, who stared intently at Nina.

Her eyebrows furrowed. Haven turned to Nina. The young girl's normally calm façade had washed away, replaced with raised eyebrows and a gaping mouth. Sheer terror. Tears spilled down Nina's face as she began to shake violently.

"Nina!" Haven gasped. "Nina, are you all right?"

She didn't answer.

Then a scream ripped from Nina's throat. Drakkone lunged forward, grabbing Nina's shoulders and pulling her back just as the screaming stopped.

Nina's eyes flew open, and her whole body froze. Haven had never seen that look on another person's face before. There was something more than pure terror conveyed in that look, something dark and disbelieving. Before anyone could ask what was wrong, Nina's lips moved silently.

"There are more of you?"

What?

Nina reeled back, clinging to Haven's arms. A wave of nausea rolled through her, and darkness flashed before her eyes. She didn't see anything specific before she was back in the present, staring into Nina's frightened eyes, terror coursing through every inch of her.

"We have to stop them. We have to find it!" Nina whine. "Izenfir! The Spyre! We've got to destroy it!"

Before Haven could digest what Nina had said, a sob broke

through Nina's chest and she collapsed into her father's arms. Haven and Aura stared at each other for a long moment before their gazes returned to Kadia, who blinked slowly as she emerged from the memory-induced fog Nina had brought on.

With Nina incapacitated, it was her turn to step up.

Raising her blade she readied herself to plunge it into Kadia's heart.

A loud crack reverberated through the room. The ground quaked and shifted beneath their feet. Haven turned to her friends.

"Aura, get them out of here!" Haven said.

Aura looked back at her, and for a moment, Haven thought she might argue. Something in her eyes must have told her not to, because she nodded.

"I understand," Aura said, and Haven really thought she did. This was her battle, and she was going to finish it once and for all.

Ushering the others from the room, Aura gave her queen one last look. Then she disappeared into the smoke-filled hall.

Haven turned back to Kadia as the ground settled. She gave her a once-over before lowering her sword. She crossed the room, Kadia's gaze burrowing a hole into her back. Haven slammed the remains of the door shut and dragged a decorative table in front it before turning back to Kadia. Haven picked her second sword up and put her back to the door.

One last battle. She took a deep breath.

Kadia's ocean-blue eyes met her amber ones. She must have understood what Haven meant to do, because a devious smile worked its way across her face. She must not have thought Haven capable, as she looked far too presumptuous. While Haven readied her battle stance, her swords at her sides, Kadia drew her darkness, letting it swirl from her fingertips to the floor. Haven stepped away from the wall to face her opponent.

"You will not leave here alive." Kadia smirked.

"If I don't, neither will you," Haven said.

"We will see about that."

"I've set your precious castle on fire, Kadia."

Kadia's eyes widened as if she'd been too busy this entire time to smell the smoke wafting in.

"If you didn't already know, I've won."

"My castle?" Kadia stared blankly at Haven.

"Yes. Just like your vision." It was Haven's turn to smirk.

Kadia stared with wide eyes. Her nostrils flared. She smelled the smoke. Her face contorted in pure rage. "You will *burn* for this!" she screamed.

"If I burn, you burn with me. Only *one* of us may survive this."

Kadia screeched, lunging at her like an angry lioness, her fingers poised like claws, darkness whipping all around her. Haven dodged, raising her swords to cut through the blackness. Her twin blades ripped through, twisting it and throwing it away. Their battle turned into a dance of darkness and swords. While Kadia didn't lack in combat skills, she was certainly not as trained as the soldiers Haven had practiced with. Still, shadows came and came in waves. A tendril whipped out and slapped at her heels, nearly pulling Haven off-balance.

Haven adjusted her footing, hopping away from the black flicking across the floor.

"Die, won't you!" Kadia threw a hand at Haven. Darkness coiled in her palm and launched through the air.

Haven rolled out of the way and leapt to her feet. She lunged again, trying to catch Kadia off guard. A wall of black flew up in her way. She stopped mid-lunge to cut through it. By the time it turned to wisps on the floor, Kadia had attacked again, this time using dark swords of her own. Haven knocked one blade away in time, but the other grazed her side, leaving a long slice above her hip.

Gasping in pain, Haven danced away. Kadia pressed her advantage, swiping furiously at Haven, who blocked, dodged, and parried until she could get out of her corner. A few shallow cuts sliced across her arms. Haven hardly took notice.

While they fought on, smoke continued to poor into the room. Now, more than ever, Haven was sure she wouldn't be getting out of this room. Her lungs burned each time she ducked.

"You're insane," Kadia coughed. "You've trapped us. There's no escaping this room."

"A fitting end for you." Haven pushed Kadia's swords back and dove forward.

Kadia twisted in time to avoid a stab to the chest, but not fast enough. Haven's sword sliced into her back. A scream of rage ripped from the Evil Queen's throat.

Kadia spun and leapt at her. It was a foolish move. She left her chest open, completely unprotected. While Haven aimed her sword and pushed forward, pain exploded through her back.

A curved, black spike protruded from the center of her chest. Blood pooled in the wound and dripped down her body. She glanced up in time to watch Kadia's eyes widen as she landed on Haven's blade.

The darkness in her chest disappeared, and Kadia collapsed to her knees.

Pain coursed through her chest.

Kadia's lifeless body collapsed to the ground, her eyes staring vacantly at the smoke clouding the ceiling. Haven dropped a few feet away, black dots dancing across her vision. She would pass out, but she was ready. She would let the darkness take her.

Her mission was complete; she had saved Warshard, her friends, and the last remnants of her family. She'd even avenged her own time in Kadia's castle.

Haven had no regrets if she were to die there. She'd finally confessed her love for a man she couldn't do without. She'd said goodbye to those who mattered, and she'd rescued the six kingdoms from a lifetime of devastation. With or without her, they would be rekindled.

With or without her, her grace would live on.

EPILOGUE

*S*everal days had passed since the fall of Cidra, and its ashes still smoldered.

The war had been won, and though this should have been a time to rejoice, it wasn't. Aura sat in a loose circle of the remaining group dedicated to the Immortal Queen. In the days that followed their final battle, they'd gathered and sat vigil through night and day. Haven's three guards had were sitting the closest to her, comforting each other when they weren't looking off in penitent silence.

King Corrin and Prince Emeril sat nearby too, though they clearly tried to avoid each other. What had happened between the two? Were they both lovers of the Queen, facing this knowledge for the first time? Somehow, Aura doubted it. Though she'd only known Haven for a short time, the queen's love for Corrin seemed genuine.

The last of their small group talked quietly at the edge of the circle. Drakkone whispered what looked to be assurance while Nina nodded in vague understanding.

Ever since Nina had come screaming from Kadia's mind, the little girl hadn't been the same. She had withdrawn into herself. Her eyes occasionally darted to and fro as if she were expecting some demon to appear from nowhere.

While Aura watched on, she listened to the short conversations taking place. What was next? She was in a new place, without friends, family, or her queen. She could travel and explore this new territory or perhaps pledge herself to Haven's sister, such as the young queen had wished upon her guards.

Aura sighed, turning her gaze to Haven's previous guards. Blythe and Malka leaned against each other, quietly staring at the dirt, while Lareina watched the remains of Kadia's castle. She paused. Lareina's eyebrows furrowed. She wasn't staring off in thought. She had seen something.

Following her gaze, Aura tried to guess what it could be. It was hard to tell in the smoke rising from the smoldering city, but Aura thought she might have seen movement.

After slowly rising, Aura joined Lareina, who remained transfixed.

"What do you see?" Aura asked, again trying to lock on to whatever target Lareina had her sights on.

Lareina said nothing. Her eyes widened a fraction and she stood, forcing Aura to step back. She began to murmur something.

"What?" Aura leaned closer.

"Haven," Lareina whispered, and then she was running.

Aura blanched, staring after her. Haven? How could she have seen Haven? Surely the young woman was dead. But, when Aura looked again, she finally saw what Lareina had seen.

"Haven!" she called to the others, and suddenly, she was running too. Before she knew it, more feet pounded after her, and then the pack was upon her.

* * *

BLACK CRUMBLED AROUND HER. Blurry shapes moved, dropping from the wreckage. A faint sensation of consciousness came upon her, and she realized she was walking. Ash crumbled under foot. How had she gotten there? Where was she? Everything blurred gray, and it smelled awful. She wrinkled her nose.

Unsure what to look for, Haven stepped over broken glass, crumbled stone, and singed wood. Had there been a light? Was that what she was trying to find? She couldn't quite remember. Gradually, the numbness heavy on her skin fled. Haven gasped and held her arms to her body. Her skin burned, and her entire body ached like it never had before. She didn't look at herself, but she must have been hurt more than she ever had been before. How could she possibly be alive? But why did she think she should be dead?

After what seemed like hours of aimless wandering, light broke through the smoke. She squinted into it. The sky. A faint smile pulled at her lips, and she tried to blink away the blurriness in her eyes as well as in her mind. Everything was clouded over, and though most of her pain had begun to subside, she couldn't quite escape the wool over her eyes.

Sighing, Haven followed the light until something soft tickled her feet. She wiggled her toes. Grass. She looked around in a daze.

Where was she? How had she gotten there?

All thoughts escaped her until shouting approached.

"Haven!" they called.

Joy filled this one word so much so that Haven found herself happy to hear it. She didn't know why, didn't know what it was, but she took a step toward it. And then one of the shouting things collided with her and wrapped her in its frantic arms, their voices soothing and their questions desperate.

Haven blinked at them all, filled with confusion, but there was also a faint realization that she was safe with whoever these people were.

More arms encircled her, more questions, more exclamations, and more love. Overwhelmed, Haven hugged them back, clinging to the people in front of her and burying her face. Haven closed her eyes and breathed.

Then she remembered.

"Lareina," she whispered. Her arms tightened around her best friend. Haven looked up, tears in her eyes.

Lareina's sky-blue eyes shone as clear as day. Raw and puffy, they spilled more tears.

Her friends surrounded her: Aura, Blythe, Malka, Nina, Drakkone, and even Emeril. Finally, her gaze landed on Corrin. Her heart leapt into her throat, and she threw herself into his arms, desperately clinging to him while he gently held her and whispered consoling words in her ear.

After a long while, Haven peeled herself away from him, but not before he could drape his long, navy jacket over her shoulders. Haven pulled it close. A cool breeze brushed her bare skin. She hadn't realized she was naked.

"Thank you," she said.

Several embraces later, Haven let the group lead her from the desolate castle to sit in the soft grass.

"We're so glad you're well," Lareina whispered, tears still spilling from her eyes.

"I can't believe you're alive," Blythe agreed.

"I can't believe it, either." Haven smiled sheepishly.

Her final thoughts returned to her. She'd made her peace in that castle before the lights had gone out and she'd been swallowed by the dark.

"What happened in there?" Aura's eyebrows furrowed.

"I killed her," Haven said. "I killed Kadia. She won't hurt any of you anymore."

Corrin gently rubbed her shoulder. "You were the one who we were worried would get hurt again."

Haven leaned her head against his shoulder and smiled.

"What happened to your hair?" Nina blinked at her with wide eyes.

Something dark swirled in the depths of Nina's eyes. What had happened in her absence?

"My hair?" Haven reached for her head, expecting to find herself bald, her hair singed from her scalp. Her usual thick hair lie atop her head. Though very dry and in need of a wash, it fell to her shoulders.

She glanced at the others. They stared at her hair with wide eyes. Haven pulled the ends of her hair forward. It was shorter than she remembered, but what really struck her was the color.

Haven gasped, astonished by the fiery-red hair that ran the entire length of the strands. She prodded upward until her fingers were on top of her head. "Is it all red?" she asked, and they nodded.

"It looks like fire," Aura commented.

"It's beautiful." Corrin smiled.

Haven squeezed his hand. She couldn't imagine the state she was in. Soot clung to her skin from the ashen remains of the fallen castle. She couldn't imagine that someone still found her beautiful.

Haven tried her best not to smile like a fool.

"Fire for the Lady Fyre."

Haven and her group of friends turned their gazes to the newcomers.

"King Evander." Haven smiled and rose. "It's nice to see you again."

Evander's smile didn't falter, even as he quickly assessed her well-being. "It's good to see you alive. We all feared the worst."

"It's hard to kill an immortal queen, I hear." She grinned.

"So I hear." Evander chuckled. "I don't mean to interrupt your reunion, but I imagine you want to get washed up and get some rest. I was going to ask about the journey home, though I can't imagine you'd want to—"

"Yes, I want to go home." Haven sighed, realizing how relieved she felt at the thought. "I want to see Rythern again."

Evander smiled. "Then we leave shortly. We have plenty of room for all of you." He paused, his gaze lingering on Nina and Drakkone. "Assuming you're all staying and not returning to Seaburn."

"We'll stay for a time." Drakkone nodded.

"Excellent! Let's get you all on your way, then."

Haven nodded, and Evander led the others away. She couldn't help but pause, sticking to the back of the group. She rested her gaze on the burning rubble of Cidra castle. Smoke rose from the remaining bits of her former prison. Seeing the castle razed to the ground left her with a finality to this chapter in her life. The chapter of pain, suffering, and hardship had hopefully come to an end, while a new one was beginning, one of love and fixing the things that were broken.

Sighing, Haven smiled, turning and finding Corrin watching her.

Before she could ask what was wrong, he pulled her back into his arms and kissed her. Haven relaxed into the pleasant sensation as she wrapped her own arms around him. When they parted, Corrin searched her face for something.

"Are you really okay?" he asked.

"Is it really over?" She arched an eyebrow.

"Yes."

"Then I'm really okay." Haven smiled.

"You promise?"

"I promise."

THE END

SAVAGES

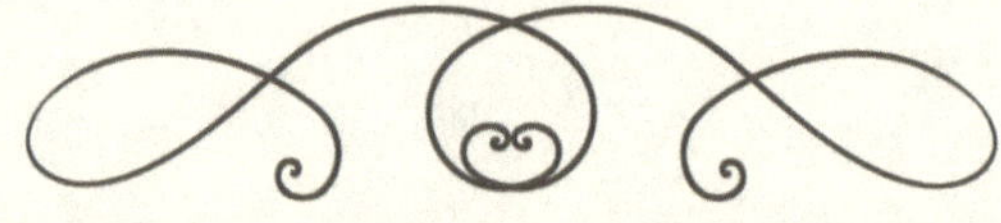

KATHERINE BOGLE

PREVIEW

ONE

The sun beat against her face, lending fire to her veins. A smirk pulled at the corners of her full lips and sweat beaded on her forehead. Hot sand pushed between her toes, unable to burn her calloused feet. Breen stared down her opponent on the opposite end of the ring while the surrounding Delica tribe howled for the fight to begin. Their savage song strengthened her bones and told of her victory.

Breen never lost.

"Are you ready to lose, my betrothed?" Lukerin grinned, stretching the tawny skin of his cheeks. He danced from foot to foot, his weight sinking into the sand.

Breen's brow furrowed. Lukerin knew very well that their betrothal wasn't solidified. Though her father, Chief Ruin, urged the young man to stay and win her hand, her heart belonged to no one but her tribe.

"I never lose." Her fingers itched at her sides. Her heart raced. As long as she was patient, Lukerin would lunge first. He always did.

Lukerin shook his head. His gaze wandered between her feet and her hands, most likely watching for the tightening of her muscles. He tried to guess her movements time and time again, but he had yet to learn she never leapt the same way twice—not with him. The only man to ever best her in a wrestling match; she would keep her guard up at all times and wait for his hasty steps.

"I've taken you down before, Breen." "Hardly."

Sand brushed over his feet as he inched closer. She kept her eyes on his, and his movements in her peripheral. *Don't move*, she urged herself. Like a wild jungle cat, as long as she kept still, Lukerin would grow tired of waiting.

"I suppose I'll have to show you again."

Breen smiled, her lips quirking to one side. She said nothing.

Lukerin's grin slowly twisted into a frown, and his brows cinched. There. His impatience betrayed him.

Her opponent lunged across the sand, sending thin grains into the air. Breen leapt from his path, her thick black braids tapping her shoulders and breasts. Lukerin spun, reaching for her wrist. She pulled away, dancing easily from his reach.

"You've got to be faster than that," she taunted.

He leapt again, his movements quick, but uncontrolled.

Breen stepped away once again, but this time, Lukerin spun and slipped his foot behind her calf. Her breath rushed from her lungs as her feet flew from under her. She caught herself on his leather vest, using all of her strength to flip him over her head. Sand assaulted her limbs as she rolled over Lukerin, bringing him onto his back beneath her. Her hands held him down.

"Good try." She flashed her teeth.

Lukerin growled and flipped her over. His rough hands tossed her like a sack of rice. Hot sand burned her bare arms. She leapt to her feet.

Her not-quite-betrothed waited opposite her. The howling tribe called for more. Their cries lent strength to her limbs, and a grin to her face. Her brothers and sisters, the fellow tribesmen, though not related by blood, encircled the sand ring. A line of dark brown rocks marked the borders.

"Is that all you have?" Lukerin raised his brow.

Breen shrugged. "Why don't you come and see?"

He took the bait. Leaping through the sand, he grabbed her forearm and twisted; giving her the momentum she needed to fling herself around his torso. Her worn leather tunic pressed against his back as she held her forearm to his throat, gripping her wrist with her opposite hand to keep him immobile. She pressed hard, bringing him to his knees.

"You should have learned by now, Lukerin," she breathed next to his ear, her voice husky and sharp.

His fingers clawed at her forearm, but she held too tightly. He'd never get the grip he needed to pull her off. Breen took a few deep breaths to still her heart. Any moment, she'd win. Lukerin would tap out, and the fight would be hers.

With a loud grunt Lukerin dove forward, swinging her over his head. Her eyes widened and a yelp pulled from her throat before she could stop it. She flew over his arched back, losing her grip. Her back hit the sand. Air exploded from her lungs.

Lukerin sat back, gasping in air.

Blue sky and a blazing sun shone overhead, stealing the color from her sight. She blinked white dots from her vision and leapt to her feet, dusting sand from her shoulders.

The weight of a wild horse collided with her chest, flinging her feet from beneath her. Breen instinctively latched on to Lukerin's arm and swung up and over so that her legs wrapped around his neck and she pulled him to ground.

Sand burned her bare skin, but she held on tight, squeezing his neck between her thighs while she pulled his arm back, stretching it at an awkward angle. Lukerin cried out. Though his muscles bulged with the effort to rip her legs away, again, she held too tightly.

"Give up," she hissed. Her arms strained with the effort to hold his heaving arm in her grasp. If she couldn't tame his arm, she'd lose her hold.

"Never," he choked.

"Breen!"

They both froze. The savage cries of her tribesmen died as her mother, Kianne, stepped between two of her larger brothers.

Delicate dark brown braids weaved in patterns secured the hair from her face, while thick waves drowned her shoulders and bosom. She smiled, her hooded gaze warm as she motioned to Breen. Thin golden bands upon her fingers glinted in the afternoon sun.

"Enough with the wrestling," her mother chided. "It's time for the young ones' lessons."

Breen heaved a sigh and slowly released Lukerin. He gasped for breath and rolled onto his stomach, coughing into the sand. She stood, hands on her wide hips as she met her mother's dark gaze.

"Mother, I'd nearly received Lukerin's surrender." She stepped across the ring to join her beautiful mother, clad in a dark blue gown, woven with gold stitching and leather belts.

"Nearly." Kianne smiled.

Breen frowned. "Lead the way."

Her mother dipped her narrow chin, the opposite of Breen's square one, and entered the maze of tents.

The tribesmen clapped her on the back, and sung her praises as she passed them by. Though she hadn't *officially* won, it was clear who the winner would be. She grinned, and thanked them, weaving through the few dozen men and women until she crossed the sand between the white tents.

Children younger than five ran between the homes, chasing chickens and swiping wooden swords at one another. Their laughter rose on the hot breeze. They grinned and ducked around Breen and her mother, waving as the small troupe disappeared behind a gnarled bush.

"You really are your father's daughter." Kianne glanced over her shoulder, mischief in her eyes. "He always prefers to fight than teach."

Breen smiled. "I'm sorry I didn't inherit your gift of lessons, Mother."

Kianne shook her head. "I'm not. But you could go easy on your betrothed."

Her joy seeped from her chest. Not this again. "*Mother*."

She laughed and waved her ringed fingers. "I know, I know. *He's not your betrothed, simply an observer*." Kianne recited the message Breen had given her parents time and time again.

Though she liked Lukerin and enjoyed his company and their wrestling matches, she couldn't see a life with him. She couldn't imagine being a wife to anyone, let alone mothering children yet. She'd gladly strengthen the numbers of the Southern Delica Tribe one day, but at sixteen, she wasn't ready for either of the things expected of her.

"Exactly." Breen nodded. "I can't imagine Father would be all right with me marrying someone I could best in battle."

Kianne laughed, her voice high like a bird's. "He wouldn't."

The large white tent of her mother's *Lesson Hut*, as she called it, rose above the sand, glaring in the sun. Breen narrowed her eyes against the white.

"What shall I teach today?" she asked.

"Your Father insists on more swordsmanship." Kianne's shoulders slouched, as if disappointed. She much preferred educating the children on the ways of the tribes, from the plants of the desert, to the wild horses that roamed the distant hills. None of these things kept the interest of babes, but she insisted on teaching them nonetheless.

"Perfect." Breen grinned.

Her mother narrowed her eyes, most likely sensing a conspiracy. Chief Ruin knew Breen's passion to train the young ones in battle, and often spoke on her behalf. The folds of the tent entrance parted and a thin girl of maybe six slipped outside. She glanced back and forth before spotting Breen and Kianne. The girl froze, her eyes flying wide. Aura. She hadn't been doing well in their battle training, preferring to focus on taming wild horses and identifying the desert fauna she could use to survive. Her large innocent eyes met Breen's, and her throat bobbed as she swallowed.

She was trying to flee before Breen's arrival.

"Aura." Breen inclined a brow. "Where are you off to?"

"Um…" Her eyes darted around the camp, searching for an answer.

"Get back inside." Breen motioned her in. Aura sighed before she spun back for the shadows of the interior.

"She's been doing well in all my classes." Kianne paused by the tent flap.

"Of course she is. Her thumbs are as green as yours." Breen grinned and her mother laughed.

"She'll get better with a sword, I'm sure."

Breen said her goodbyes and slipped inside.

Her whole body cooled in the shadows as she stepped from the hot sand and blazing sun into the tent. Though she preferred the freedom of the outdoors, she had to admit getting away from the sun during the day was a welcome relief.

"Good afternoon." Breen waved at the dozen children inside. Ranging from six to twelve, the young ones sat in a half-circle at the center of the tent, legs crossed, and dark eyes eager. All but Aura's.

Breen stepped from the entry and into the main area, rough cloth beneath her bare feet. Furs and tanned pelts lined the walls. Leather flasks hung from a dark brown lattice fashioned from jungle trees.

The Lesson Hut wasn't the most lavish of tents, but it served its purpose.

"Afternoon, Breen," they echoed back.

Opposite her small class, Breen placed her hands on her hips and smiled at the group. "We've gotten through the basics of holding a weapon and blocking. Most of you have done well and will move on to spar in pairs. This will help get you used to anticipating your opponent's moves."

While most of the children grinned beneath their heads of dark hair, Aura's lips turned into a frown, and her brows furrowed. Breen met her gaze briefly and nodded. She'd teach Aura separately to help her understand the importance of sword skills.

In the past, most children didn't start learning how to fight until at least eight years old. Their young years were for play, curiosity and exploration. But with Seaburn's glutinous Emperor ravaging the

Savage Lands for soldiers, they hadn't a choice but to train children younger and younger.

Their tribe needed protection against the Empire raids. Seaburn soldiers took the young warriors, such as herself, and her brethren. If they were one day taken, the younger generations would need to step into their place.

"Grab your swords. Be mindful and pretend you wield iron or steel." Breen raised her brows and met the children's gazes. She wanted them to take this seriously. Though right now it was all a game to them, one day it wouldn't be. "Watch your footing, guard your face, chest, and abdomen. Remember, those are the killing blows. A cut to your arm or leg will only slow you down."

Each of them leapt to their feet, racing the short distance from the main floor to the edge of the tent where a wooden rack held small carved swords in varying sizes. Though the wood wouldn't cut them like a real sword, it could still hurt enough to make them think twice about each block and hit.

Once her students paired up, Breen took Aura aside. She plucked a long, curved wooden sword of her own from a nearby rack, and handed a shorter blade to Aura, who twisted her lip nervously between her teeth.

"It'll be all right." Breen smiled. She hadn't always been good with a blade either. Although daughter of the chief, Breen had struggled for many months to learn the most basic of steps. She'd started around the same time as Aura, and could see herself in the young girl's round eyes.

Aura nodded.

They stepped near the entrance of the tent, while the other pairs took up the center. Clashing wood, and tiny grunts filled the space, while Breen focused on the small girl before her.

"Hold your hilt tightly, but not with such force your knuckles go white." Breen demonstrated, her blade a mere extension of herself. "Your sword is part of you, an extension of your arm. Treat it as such, and you'll move effortlessly."

She dipped her narrow chin, avoiding Breen's gaze. Her brows furrowed as Aura adjusted her grip and parted her feet on the sand, holding her wooden blade straight from her body.

"Relax your elbow, like this." Breen shook her arm, relaxing her elbow. Her blade crossed a foot from her chest.

"All right." Her tiny fingers twisted around the hilt and she relaxed her arm.

"Good!" Breen smiled. She could get this. Breen was sure of it. "Now that your sword blocks your chest, you can easily move to block an attack aimed for your abdomen." Breen slowly thrust her sword forward as if she were going to stab Aura's chest.

Most likely sensing her intention, Aura shifted the wooden blade to slap Breen's off course.

Breen grinned. "Excellent! See, I knew you could do it."

Aura's cheeks flushed, and she lowered her blade. "It's still a bit heavy."

"I know. Usually you wouldn't start training for another year or two. But you know how deep the Seaburn soldiers have come. They've been sighted near the Northern Tribe across the river. I only want you to be ready in case a day comes where I'm not around to teach you. Someone needs to protect the horses you're so fond of."

Aura's brows furrowed and her eyes grew wide. She knew as well as the rest of them, and somehow seemed to understand better than the other children. Once her surprise faded, determination set her gaze. "What next?" she asked.

Breen held her sword aloft, and so did Aura.

"Protect your head." Breen swiped her sword for Aura's braids. The small wooden sword shot up to block her attack. "Now your stomach." She twisted and thrust her blade out. Aura jumped back from reach. "As good a tactic as any."

"Thank you."

"Would you like to try swinging at me?" Breen stepped back into her ready stance.

Aura's brows shot up, and she glanced from the other children swinging wildly at one another, back at Breen, who waited patiently.

"I'm not sure I can do it."

"You can. Pretend I'm one of the Seaburn maggots." They both smiled. "Pretend you're not only fighting me for the honor of your clan, but for survival. Protect your kin from me. Protect your mother."

Aura's lips pressed into a thin line. Her father had been taken two years ago by Seaburn's army. He'd ventured too far into the jungle blocking the Savage Lands from Seaburn's great Empire. When he emerged north of the forest, he'd been captured. Aura's mother had barely escaped alive.

Breen held up her sword as Aura's fingers tightened around the hilt. The fire of the gods flashed through her dark gaze. It was that fire that gave Breen hope. Aura would one day be great, do great things, fight great battles; her determination and strong will would aid her in this. This mock battle was only the beginning. Someday Aura would mirror her warrior father's skill in battle.

Aura swung. Though her footing was awkward and she simply hit Breen's sword, there was determination in her gaze. "Again," Breen said.

The small wooden sword sliced through the air. Breen blocked the blow for her chest. Aura lunged, thrusting her sword at Breen's gut. Breen parried, sending the small blade flying from her hands.

Aura's gaze flew wide, and she breathed hard.

"Very good." Breen grinned. "Again."

The small braids at Aura's cheeks shook as she nodded. She plucked her sword from the ground, and stepped opposite to Breen, raising her blade in the ready stance she'd been taught.

The beating of horse hooves over sand made her freeze. Breen's brows furrowed as she looked at the edge of the tent, in the direction of the river running to the east. No hunting party had come or gone from the tribe today. No sentries stormed the land, or watched the southern hills.

Then who could it be?

Breen lowered her sword, as did Aura. Her small prodigy followed her gaze.

"What is it?" Aura asked.

Her jaw set and her fingers tightened around the hilt of her blade. "Trouble."

Breen sprung into motion, placing her wooden sword back on its mount before flying to the door. She peeled the flap of the tent back.

The ground rumbled, and war cries split the hot desert. Her breath caught in her throat. "All of you stay here." Breen glared over her shoulder, silencing the protests of the older students. "Do not leave this tent, no matter what you hear."

Wide eyes followed her as she fled the Lesson Hut.

Breen ran across the hot sand as cries of panic rose all around her. Her brethren ran through the tents toward the commotion, curved swords drawn, and scowls gracing their faces. She dove between tents until she reached the largest of the bunch—that of the Chief. She pushed the flaps aside and embraced the cool shadows. Sunlight poured through the opening as she raced between lavish fur rugs, and ornate tapestries her mother had woven.

She found her quarters beyond the main room, the space broken by wooden dividers and jungle cat furs. Breen grabbed her boots from the floor and yanked on the dark leather. She laced them to her calves before tearing her long burgundy sheath from her bedside. Glass jars of candle wax toppled to the floor in her haste.

Her heart raced. Whoever was here—be they raiders, foreign tribesmen, or worse—she had to protect her people. The faces of her students flashed before her eyes. What if one of them wandered from the tent to see what was going on?

They weren't ready. They wouldn't be for some time.

Breen fled the chief's tent, fear and anticipation quickening her movements. She joined her brothers and sisters, sword in hand, boots crushing sand.

Several mothers ushered their children by, pushing them inside their tents, and ripping daggers from the leather sheathes at their hips.

The tribe was united in this. United against anything that dare threaten their home, their family, or their way of life. Gritting her teeth, Breen leapt over the sand to the edge of the Delica tribe's camp. Steel glinting in the harsh sunlight, she froze atop the slope.

The river stretched to her left, heading east to the sea. On their side of the canal, unheard of before this day, dozens of horses stormed across the open sand. Soldiers clad in metal armor with the gold seal of the Emperor at their hearts, rode the beasts. With swords in their fists, and the flag of Seaburn whipping in the wind, the enemy had finally arrived.

Seaburn had come for them.

ABOUT THE AUTHOR

Katherine Bogle's debut young adult novel, Haven, came second in the World's Best Story contest 2015. She currently resides in Saint John, New Brunswick with her partner in crime, and plethora of cats.

Follow Katherine for all the latest updates:
katherinebogle.com
TheHavenSeries@outlook.com

facebook.com/AuthorKatherineBogle

twitter.com/KattyB3

instagram.com/katherinebogle

goodreads.com/katherinebogle

The Emperor's reapers are coming.

There's nothing Breen can do to stop it.

After her village is attacked, Breen is taken from her home to Seaburn Academy, where southern savages are broken and chained into a life of service. Through the beatings and the torture, Drakkone, one of the few soldiers against the mistreatment, brings solace to her days and gives her hope for the future.

When one night of unexpected passion turns into a problem bigger than either of them could have imagined, Breen and Drakkone must risk capture and flee the city or death might be a blessing compared to eternal imprisonment.

The world is made of monsters.

Adni might be one of them.

After the Evil Queen Kadia razed Warshard, leaving thousands homeless or dead, many of Salander's people fled to the Cinder Mountains, east of the six kingdoms, seeking refuge.

Adni, the daughter of a treasure hunter, has always despised her father's bizarre occupation and loathes every family trip in search of riches. Always desperate for more, her father shoves her off a waterfall to retrieve treasure at the bottom of a lake. Instead, Adni is swept up in a violent underwater current, only to be rescued by Julian, a mysterious woman with a flirtatious smile.

Desperate to flee the oppression of her family and the mountains, Adni escapes with Julian to Salander in search of her real father – who might just be a worse monster than the man she left behind.

Join Haven and her siblings on four unique adventures in a time when war ravaged the six kingdoms...

HAVEN has always hated royal gatherings, and jumps at the chance to sneak away for a race through town on horseback. But when the young princess is injured, her ancestry is brought into question.

Much is expected of the heir to the Rythern throne, but when **LUCIAN** is forced to leave the warfront by his father, his reluctant agreement comes at a price.

The battle for Helms Keep has disastrous consequences for **MARCEL**. Soon he finds himself fighting both enemy forces and his own memories.

ASTRID is sent to the family summer home in the Cinder Mountains for her own safety. Only she doesn't expect the knee-high snow and frigid temperatures. With only her guards to protect her, Astrid must dig deeper than she ever thought herself capable of in order to survive.

www.ingramcontent.com/pod-product-compliance
Lightning Source LLC
Chambersburg PA
CBHW051640180726
48284CB00006B/1804